TOUCHED BY FIRE

Moriah looked up at the muscled giant who stood before her. Was this really White Shadow?

"This is my domain," he growled. "Put down that rifle."

"You put yours down first," Moriah said.

He lowered his rifle, then looked her up and down. "Lady, you've got a lot to learn about these mountains."

"I'll manage," she proclaimed.

"Better men than you have tried and failed," he contended. He stepped closer to her and she could feel the heat of his body.

"I'm . . . not a man," she reminded him.

"I can see that well enough." His sensuous gaze slid down her arresting curves and he stepped closer still. "What's your name, tigress?" he murmured, his voice ragged with desire.

Before she could answer, Moriah felt his lips on hers.

His kiss was demanding, impetuous, like a flame feeding on the wind, billowing out of control. Moriah gasped for breath, but he had stripped it from her lungs, leaving her hanging in sweet hypnotic limbo . . .

FEEL THE FIRE IN CAROL FINCH'S ROMANCES!

BELOVED BETRAYAL (2346, $3.95)

Sabrina Spencer donned a gray wig and veiled hat before blackmailing rugged Ridge Tanner into guiding her to Fort Canby. But the costume soon became her prison—the beauty had fallen head over heels in love!

LOVE'S HIDDEN TREASURE (2980, $4.50)

Shandra d'Evereux felt her heart throb beneath the stolen map she'd hidden in her bodice when Nolan Elliot swept her out onto the veranda. It was hard to concentrate on her mission with that wily rogue around!

MONTANA MOONFIRE (3263, $4.95)

Just as debutante Victoria Flemming-Cassidy was about to marry an oh-so-suitable mate, the towering preacher, Dru Sullivan flung her over his shoulder and headed West! Suddenly, Tori realized she had been given the best present for a bride: a night of passion with a real man!

THUNDER'S TENDER TOUCH (2809, $4.50)

Refined Piper Malone needed bounty-hunter, Vince Logan to recover her swindled inheritance. She thought she could coolly dismiss him after he did the job, but she never counted on the hot flood of desire she felt whenever he was near!

Available wherever paperbacks are sold, or order direct from the Publisher. Send cover price plus 50¢ per copy for mailing and handling to Zebra Books, Dept. 3465, 475 Park Avenue South, New York, N.Y. 10016. Residents of New York, New Jersey and Pennsylvania must include sales tax. DO NOT SEND CASH.

Intresting Reading
L

CAROL FINCH

WILD MOUNTAIN HONEY

ZEBRA BOOKS
KENSINGTON PUBLISHING CORP.

This book is dedicated to my husband Ed
for all his encouragement, assistance, and support.
Thanks for doing the maps!
And to our children
Christie, Jill and Kurt.
With much love . . .

ZEBRA BOOKS

are published by

Kensington Publishing Corp.
475 Park Avenue South
New York, NY 10016

First printing: August, 1991

Printed in the United States of America

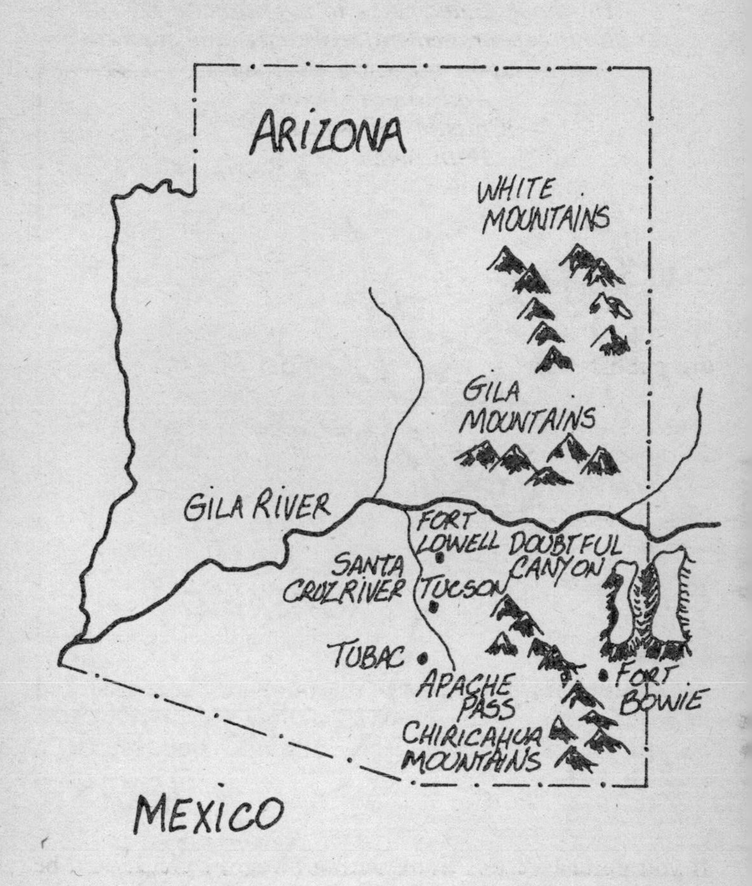
ARIZONA
WHITE MOUNTAINS
GILA MOUNTAINS
GILA RIVER
FORT LOWELL
DOUBTFUL CANYON
SANTA CRUZ RIVER
TUCSON
TUBAC
APACHE PASS
FORT BOWIE
CHIRICAHUA MOUNTAINS
MEXICO

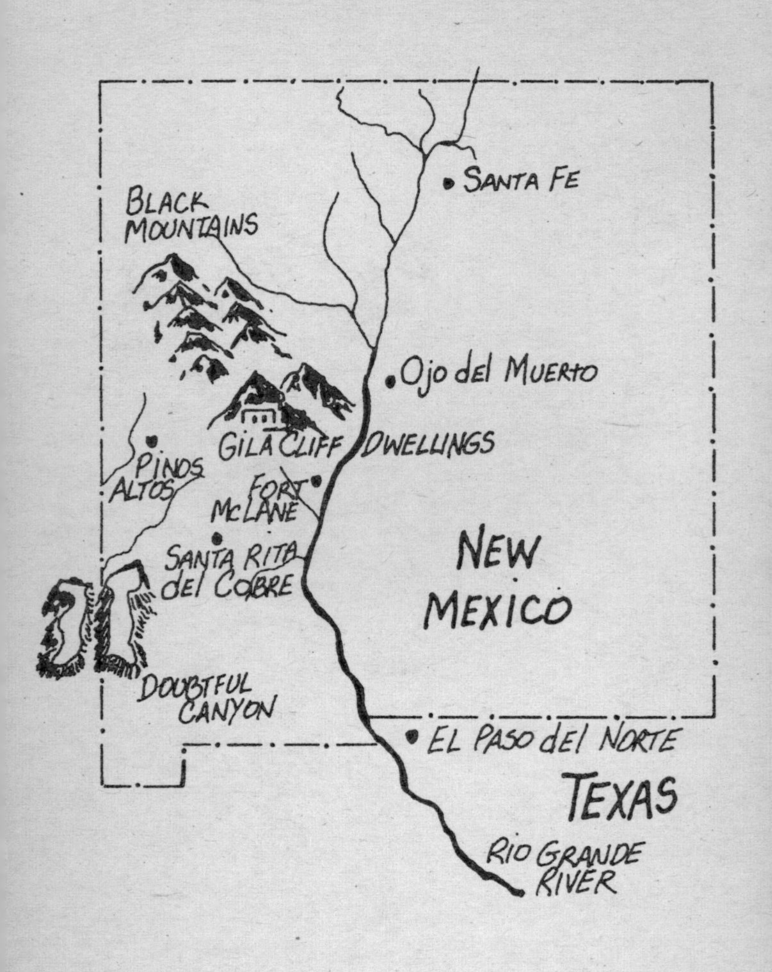

SANTA FE
BLACK MOUNTAINS
Ojo del Muerto
GILA CLIFF DWELLINGS
PINOS ALTOS
FORT McLANE
SANTA RITA del COBRE
NEW MEXICO
DOUBTFUL CANYON
EL PASO del NORTE
TEXAS
RIO GRANDE RIVER

Part I

Chapter 1

New Mexico Territory
1865

"My God, I've never seen such desolate land," Ruby Thatcher muttered sourly. "We've been traveling for days and we're still in Nowhere, New Mexico!"

Moriah Laverty gazed across the wide-open spaces, seeing the sun's fiery splendor splashing across the desert and casting deep-purple shadows on the eastern slopes of the buttes and mesas to the north. She was awed by the solemn grandeur of New Mexico rather than repulsed by it.

For the past several weeks the wagon train in which Moriah traveled had followed the Butterfield Trail through Texas, veering from the trodden path to view Palo Duro Canyon, which cut a wide, spectacular gash through the flat Texas plains. Moriah had marveled at all the changes in scenery as they trekked westward. She even saw the stark beauty in these arid plains.

She supposed there would always be those people, like Ruby, who would insist that this sprawling land wasn't fit for man or beast, but Moriah found something wild, challenging, yet very beautiful in this rugged country. It drew her gaze and held it fast, perhaps because of the feeling of hers that she was much like this untamed land. It was lonely, misunderstood, and forsaken, just as she was . . .

"I swear, not even a rattlesnake could make a living in this land God gave to the devil and refused to take back." Ruby glanced with distaste around her. "Even Satan has abandoned this horrid place!"

Ruby Thatcher's strident voice jolted Moriah from her thoughts. She glanced around the bulky form of Vance Thatcher, her stepfather, who was clutching the reins of the mules that clopped ahead of their wagon, and peered at Ruby's sour face. One glance at the Thatchers left Moriah wondering what she had done to deserve such a miserable fate.

No one had promised her that life would be a bed of roses, but she hadn't expected it to be a pit of thorns, either! Destiny had definitely frowned on her. After spending so much time with the Thatchers, Moriah had difficulty keeping her spirits from scraping rock bottom. It had been so long since Moriah had felt anything except chilling tolerance for her companions that she barely remembered how it felt to love and laugh and enjoy life. The only two people she remembered loving were dead and gone and she was left to endure the Thatchers—her pathetic excuse for a family.

Moriah was a far cry from the carefree little girl who had frolicked across her parents' ranch near Austin, Texas, a decade earlier. That life had crumbled when the horse her father was riding had stumbled during a high-speed chase at roundup. Michael Laverty had been thrown and crushed by his favorite steed. After that, Moriah couldn't remember seeing her mother smile again. And why Marianne Laverty had married Vance Thatcher was beyond Moriah. At least it had been at the time, Moriah amended as she listened to Ruby, the second Mrs. Vance Thatcher, grouse and complain about the heat and dust stirred up by the procession of covered wagons that ventured toward California.

Now that Moriah was older and wiser, she understood her mother's desperation. Marianne had firmly believed she needed a man to manage the ranch and she mourned Michael's death. To compensate for the desperation and loneliness, Marianne had consented to marry Vance Thatcher, who had worked on the ranch and mooned over her for years. But it had been a mistake. Vance was dull and lazy. He couldn't think for himself and he relied on the advice and direction of others. In short, he was easy prey for the devious, cunning individuals—like Ruby—who attempted to take advantage of him.

Moriah mopped the perspiration from her brow and tuned out Ruby's incessant whining. Lord, that woman got on her nerves faster than anyone alive!

When Moriah's mother died unexpectedly five years earlier, Ruby had employed her every wile to marry Vance, who had become Moriah's guardian. Now Moriah was not only plagued with a dense stepfather but had also inherited a shrewd, calculating stepmother who had sold the family farm, packed Moriah up—her intention to move them all off to the promised land in California. All Moriah had in remembrance of her carefree childhood was the dainty gold locket her mother had given her.

Even though Moriah had loudly protested moving and selling her inherited property she had not reached the age of twenty-one so she was unable to assume control of her own finances. Ruby—former calico queen from Austin—had known that, of course, and used it to her advantage, insisting on selling the property before Moriah came of age. By her financial maneuverings Ruby had been able to gather sufficient cash for the trip west.

"Sweet mercy, aren't we ever going to stop to rest?" Ruby muttered as she dabbed at the perspiration that dribbled from the roots of her hair and bubbled on her caked makeup. "My derriere has become flat after so many hours on this wagon seat."

"It won't be much longer, honey," Vance cooed at the wilting beauty who wore her age like miles on a road map. "The wagon master assured me we would stop at the Mimbres River for the night. It can't be much farther."

"Well, I should hope not!" Ruby sniffed disgustedly and then flicked at the renegade strands of blond-turning-to-silver hair that slipped from the bun coiled on top of her head like a spring. "The heat and dust are unbearable."

Ruby's hazel eyes darted to Moriah, who seemed to be faring much better, considering the uncomfortable conditions inherent to travel in the Conestoga wagon. Moriah looked none the worse for wear. She possessed youth and rare natural beauty. Ruby greatly envied her stepdaughter and she sorely detested the competition.

Moriah, with her stunning coloring, soft curves, refined features, and elegant bone structure, was a dazzling beauty. Although Moriah herself considered her appearance the curse of her life, Ruby would have given her eye teeth if Mother Nature had blessed her with this blue-eyed girl's comeliness. The chit was a constant reminder of Ruby's fading beauty and youth. Even when Ruby sought to downplay

Moriah's shapely figure with unflattering garb, the girl still reminded her of a princess from a fairy tale.

Ruby's own figure had fallen prey to the pull of gravity. She felt twice her age when men's admiring gazes flicked past her to feast on her stepdaughter's golden-blond hair and curvaceous figure. Ruby saw herself as a withering rose beside this fresh desert flower. God, how she resented Moriah! She even stayed up nights devising ways to detract from the girl's alluring assets. But nothing worked. Moriah was bewitching no matter what she wore. It was infuriating!

"I rather like the wide-open spaces," Moriah commented, just to get Ruby's goat.

It had become a favorite pastime of hers to needle her stepmother. If Ruby declared the sun rose in the east, Moriah contradicted her, just for sport and spite. Moriah usually wound up paying for her insolence because her stepmother prodded Vance into punishing his impudent ward. He was too simple-minded to realize that Ruby was a witch, and he always defended his wife, while Ruby continuously fed his male pride for her devious purpose of keeping him at her beck and call.

"You *would* like such a desolate place as this," Ruby sniped, flinging the young beauty a nasty smile. "It fits your temperament—hot and testy."

Moriah's fists clenched in the folds of her tattered calico blue gown. She itched to sink her fingers into the layers of makeup caking Ruby's leathery face. But what she really wanted to do was throw a few things—starting with Ruby and ending with Vance! Unfortunately, the only relief for frustrations came in the exchange of verbal blows with her stepmother. When Moriah opened her mouth to hurl a suitably insulting rejoinder, Vance gouged her in the ribs—a favorite reprisal of his.

"Mind your tongue before it runs away with itself," he scolded Moriah. "We'll all be in a better frame of mind when we freshen up at the river."

While the two women glared poison arrows at each other, Vance focused on the cloud of dust that heralded the arrival of unidentified travelers. When the procession drew nearer, the wagons circled around one another in case of trouble, but the sight of the flag flying above the column of cavalrymen put the members of the wagon train at ease.

Like a cautious hen settling on her nest, Ruby hugged her heavy skirts about her. She had sewn the money she and Vance had obtained from the sale of the farm into her petticoats, and she trusted absolutely no one with the cash. It was her intent to travel to California without losing one cent of the precious money she had wrested from Moriah's possession.

While Ruby guarded the fortune like a dragon, Moriah and Vance clambered down from their perch to join the other travelers who congregated around the dragoons. Moriah's crystal-blue eyes lifted to survey the one-armed commander of the regiment. She took one look at the army officer and disliked him on sight.

Lieutenant Colonel Lyle Burkhart was a sour-faced man with flaming red hair and a temper and disposition to match. His cold green eyes narrowed on the group of travelers who stared questioningly at him. As his gaze skimmed over the curious congregation, one face in particular caught his attention—that of Moriah Laverty. Although Lyle had devoted his life to exterminating every renegade Apache who crossed his path, he also had a penchant for hard liquor and pretty women.

Momentarily distracted, Lyle's gaze devoured the pert blonde with her enchanting face and arresting figure. It had been a long time since he'd had a white woman. The stunning sight of Moriah drove home that point and ignited lusty fires in his blood. Nothing would have suited him better than to lead the dazzling beauty away from the wagon train long enough to ease the gnawing hunger she so easily aroused in him . . .

"Are we to expect some sort of trouble?" the wagon master prompted, moving directly in front of Lyle's line of vision.

Lyle scowled, his thin lips practically disappearing beneath his scraggly red mustache. "There's always trouble in Apache country," he snorted derisively. "The mountains are crawling with those sneaky savages. They'll creep up to carry off anything that isn't nailed down, because that's what Indians do best—sneak up on people. If you don't remain alert, those heathens will be on you before you know it."

Lyle's shrill voice carried in the breeze, taking his words to Ruby Thatcher who protectively clutched her skirts around her and glanced every which way at once. The thought of losing the money she had stitched to her petticoats unnerved her.

"If I were you, I'd keep a close watch on the womenfolk," Lyle warned. "The Apaches delight in taking women and children captives."

Moriah blanched when Lyle shifted position so that his probing stare focused on her again. Somehow she doubted the Apaches could be any worse than this miserable excuse of an army officer. Lyle Burkhart had a cruel, sinister look about him. And the fact that he was eyeing her with lusty speculation soured her stomach. Moriah would prefer to take her chances with the Apaches any day, and when this rotund commander referred to Apaches as savages, she rather thought the pot was calling the kettle black.

When Lyle noticed Moriah staring back at him, he broke into a roguish smile. When he tipped his hat to her, Moriah gagged. She had little use for men in general and even less for this thick-necked commander with his carrot-red hair and wolfish leer.

The men Moriah had known in the past left her wondering why females had been forced to endure the plague of the male of the species. She supposed it was the Lord's way of making women earn their wings when they reached the pearly gates. Moriah had no doubt that there was a hell on earth through which women had to pass. She herself was the prime example of that, surrounded as she was by the Thatchers and the passel of men who would not leave her alone.

Ruby's spiteful method of countering Moriah's contrariness was to never allow courteous, well-respected bachelors to court the girl—only degenerates and miscreants who saw women solely as objects of pleasure. Moriah honestly wondered if she would know how to react to a well-mannered, considerate man, or if there *was* even such a creature on this planet. Thanks to Ruby, Moriah had a distorted view of the male of the species, and by the age of twenty had become a dreadful cynic on the subject. In Moriah's opinion, men were no more than a swarm of pesky insects and she avoided contact with them at all possible costs.

"And let's not forget the legendary White Shadow," John Grimes, Lyle's second in command, piped up.

A murmur rippled through the congregation of travelers like a wave cresting on an ocean, egging the cavalryman on. "He's the renegade who has eluded Commander Burkhart for over a year. He warns the savages away when we try to strike," Grimes continued. "The Apaches believe White Shadow was sent by the Great Spirit to rout the Americans from their stomping ground."

Moriah was reasonably certain the young officer had been out in the sun too long and that the overexposure had distorted his thinking. White Shadow? No doubt this imaginary champion of the Apaches was only the Army's convenient excuse to explain why they didn't meet with success during their campaigns against the Indians.

"I wouldn't wander too far from camp at night," Lyle advised the group of travelers with a scowl. "You might wind up dead—"

"Or have your favorite steed stolen." Captain Grimes added another two cents' worth. "Commander Burkhart lost his prize mount just last week. He was afraid to tie his white stallion in the picket line with the rest of the army mounts because the Apaches often sneak up to steal our horses. When the commander tethered the steed twenty feet away, it was the only one that wound up missing. Our guards didn't hear anything that alerted them to unwanted visitors in camp, but the next morning the steed was gone and the arrow with white feathers lay in the horse's place. And last month—"

"That's enough, Grimes!" Lyle snapped gruffly. "There is no need to glorify the ridiculous legend even more than it already has been."

Captain Grimes couldn't clamp down on his runaway tongue. "White Shadow is supposedly the avenging renegade who vowed to repay Burkhart after—"

"I said that was enough!" Lyle snarled, his harsh

tone striking a chord of finality. "That ridiculous legend is only the Apache's attempt to harass the cavalry and you know it." His green eyes hardened like chips of stone. "White Shadow is only a man, and a worthless one at that. When I catch up with that no-account varmint he will receive a punishment that is long overdue."

The captain glanced away after the reprimand. Silence hung over the parched ground like a dust cloud.

After a moment, Lyle straightened himself in the saddle as if it were his throne. "My men and I will accompany you to the river for your protection," he offered. "Although we are hunting renegade Apaches, we will detour to ensure you make camp safely."

Moriah wasn't particularly overwhelmed by Burkhart's offer. The probing stares he kept assaulting on her person made her frown in wary consternation. If he thought for one minute that she would show her gratitude for escorting the wagon train to the river with some sort of physical display, he had another think coming! She had never given men the time of day and she wasn't about to start now, especially with the likes of him. Lyle Burkhart looked dangerous to her, and the less association with him the better. Unfortunately, Moriah wasn't allowed a say in the matter . . .

By the time the cavalcade of wagons stopped to make camp beside the Mimbres River, Moriah had a throbbing headache brought on by her spiteful stepmother and an overdose of Lyle Burkhart. The stocky lieutenant colonel had ridden beside the Thatchers' wagon, boasting of his skill in hunting down and disposing of those Apaches who refused to confine themselves to the reservation at Bosque Redondo. Moriah wasn't the least bit impressed by his cruel methods of dealing with renegades. To hear Lyle talk, the Apaches were doomed to extinction. She wasn't sure if the "menace" to which Lyle constantly referred was the red or white man. But after giving the matter some consideration, she decided that the Anglos had been encroaching on Indian land for too many years already and whatever harassment the white men suffered, they probably deserved. Moriah could identify with the Apaches' plight; after all, she'd had her farm stolen away from her by Ruby's devious scheme!

The feel of a man's hand curling around her elbow like a winding snake provoked Moriah to jerk away. Her head snapped up to see Lyle staring at her like a hungry barracuda, and repulsion washed over her like a tidal wave.

"I thought you might enjoy strolling along the river with me," he remarked as he steered her away from camp. "Exercise is just what you need after a long day's ride."

How dare he presume to tell her what she needed! What she really needed, if he wanted to know, was for him to evaporate into a puff of smoke! "I *need* to assist with our evening meal," she said brusquely as she wormed her arm from his stubby fingers.

"You run along and enjoy yourself, honey," Ruby cooed in a syrupy tone that would have drowned a stack of pancakes.

Moriah compressed her lips to prevent hurling a degrading remark at her pretentious stepmother. The only reason Ruby was encouraging Moriah to keep company with the annoying commander was because she knew it was the last place her stepdaughter wanted to be.

Every step of their stroll was pure drudgery for Moriah. Being a hopeless cynic, Moriah knew Lyle would eventually pause to make his amorous advances. Men were like that. They never awaited an invitation. They saw women as a challenge and conquest, a prize to be used and then discarded.

And sure enough, Lyle halted to wrap his arm around her and hauled her up against him. His mouth came roughly down on hers, plundering her lips with hungry impatience. But Moriah was ready and waiting. She had found herself in similar predicaments with lusty men on more occasions than she cared to count. She didn't give a flying fig if Lyle Burkhart could provide protection for the wagon train. She wasn't selling herself to this bird-legged, pot-bellied scoundrel or any other man!

Moriah gave Lyle exactly what he deserved for taking liberties with her—a well-aimed knee in the private part of his anatomy. When he doubled over and groaned in pain, she gave him a sound slap on his cheek for good measure.

Lyle's true personality exploded with Moriah's physical attack upon his person. A menacing snarl swallowed his homely features and his right hand doubled into a fist, as if he meant to knock her flat to the ground. Moriah artfully dodged the blow and leaped out of his reach.

"You feisty little bitch!" he sneered viciously.

Wasn't that just like a man to put the blame on a woman when *he* was the one at fault? "This isn't *strolling* along the river; it's *mauling,*" she spumed. "If I had wanted your attention I would have asked for it, and I most certainly did *not* do that!"

Furiously, Lyle lunged. He wasn't quick enough to capture Moriah, but he did manage to slap her across the cheek, causing her to stumble backward.

Before he could cover her tempting body with his own, she snatched up a log to use as an improvised weapon and brandished it in his face.

"You touch me again and I'll make you wish you hadn't, so help me I will," she hissed venomously.

Rage boiled through Lyle's blood. If he and this minx had been a greater distance from the wagon train he would have taken her just to exert his male superiority. But as it was, Moriah was too much woman for a one-armed man to handle. Her shouts of alarm would bring the entire camp to her rescue and he would be accused of God only knew what. At present, his command was under investigation and he could not risk an incident that might besmirch his already questionable record.

Swearing fluently, Lyle wheeled around in the direction he had come. The last rays of sunshine splattered across the desert, bathing the world in glorious colors of crimson, orange, and gold, but Lyle was seeing nothing but red as he stormed back to camp. He was determined to be out of shouting distance when Moriah returned to spout her inevitable accusations about his attempt to molest her.

Lyle spitefully wished some renegade would sneak up to whisk that sassy bitch away. He would delight in hunting her and her captor down and scalping both of them! Being captured by the Apaches would surely break this vixen's spirit, he told himself. Then Moriah would plead with him to seduce her if he would only take her back to civilization! After being raped by savages, Moriah would welcome a white man's amorous advances for sure and she would be glad to do whatever he demanded of her!

The instant Ruby saw the commander stomping

toward his horse, she knew he had been rejected, the same as all of Moriah's suitors. Ruby scurried toward her husband with devilish thoughts dancing in her head. For months now, Ruby had awaited the perfect opportunity to dispose of Moriah. Now was the perfect time. They were miles away from home and no one in Texas would be the wiser if Moriah vanished. With the threat of savages roaming the area, the Apaches would take the blame for Moriah's disappearance. That feisty chit would be out from underfoot permanently and the inheritance money that was stitched to Ruby's undergarments would be hers forever!

"Now's the time," Ruby murmured as she tugged on Vance's shirtsleeve and gestured toward the river.

Vance glanced cautiously around him while he unhooked the team of mules from the wagon. Ruby had unfolded her plan to him soon after she had sold the ranch. He had nothing personal against Moriah, but she did cause constant conflict between him and Ruby. There had even been times when Vance had considered teaching Moriah the finer pleasures of life himself. But Ruby was insanely jealous of the young beauty and Vance feared he would bring his wife's wrath down on himself if he dared to seduce his tempting stepdaughter.

Ruby had thoroughly convinced Vance that he would be a pauper again if he didn't dispose of Moriah before she could claim her inheritance. The moment she came of age she would take the money and leave both her stepparents out in the cold without a cent. That was Ruby's assessment of the situation and since she did the thinking for both of them, Vance agreed that it was either him or Moriah.

Resolutely, Vance drew himself up and inched away from camp while the other members of the train clustered around Commander Burkhart, urging him to spend the night. With the perfect distraction provided him, Vance clomped off to locate Moriah.

A wicked smile pursed Ruby's lips as she watched Vance disappear into the crisscrossed shadows and canopy of trees that lined the river. At long last she would have her revenge on that girl. Very soon, Moriah Laverty would be nothing more than an unpleasant memory and her inheritance would be firmly planted in Ruby's hands.

Chuckling devilishly to herself, Ruby scuttled over to insist that the cavalry remain with the wagon train. But in truth, she didn't care whether they stayed the night or not. Her sole purpose was to distract the entire group while Vance did her dirty work for her.

Ah, what a clever woman she was, Ruby congratulated herself. She had set her sights on Vance and had easily manipulated him. By granting him sexual favors she had acquired his affection and loyalty. Now she was in the midst of her plan to dispose of Moriah and claim the money for herself. Sometimes her cunning amazed even herself! Ruby had committed the perfect crime and Vance was taking all the risks. And if she succeeded—and she was certain she would—she could discard Vance when she was settled in California. She could find herself another man who could give her the exciting life she deserved!

Moriah wandered along the river that wove across the flat plains like a silver thread. Still fuming, she peered at the moon-splattered mountains to the north. She tried to force herself to concentrate on the majestic beauty of her surroundings instead of the infuriating incident with Lyle Burkhart, but it was difficult since the encounter reminded her of so many other unpleasant episodes in her past.

Criminey, why did men have to be so pushy and overbearing? They behaved as if they were granting women some great privilege by being mauled by them. Hardly! And curse their black souls, men had the audacity to become offended when women protested being used to satisfy their animal lust. Lyle was another distasteful example of what a woman could expect from the male of the species. Lord, men had more shortcomings than they knew what to do with!

Moriah wanted nothing more to do with men, and especially not Lyle Burkhart! His touch made her cringe in revulsion. In all her twenty years Moriah had never gone willingly into a man's arms and she was beginning to wonder if she ever would. Not one of them had yet to appeal to her. The men Ruby forced on Moriah always pounced on her to steal a kiss or grope at her. Moriah detested being manhandled. She was certain there wasn't a man on the planet who would treat a woman with the respect and courtesy she deserved . . .

The crackling of twigs brought Moriah's head up to see Vance clopping toward her. He had always reminded her of a horse with that tuft of brown hair that lay over his head like a forelock and his bulging brown eyes—not to mention his huge teeth and his whinny of a laugh. His clomping gait further emphasized the comparison. The man had never been able to sneak up on anyone or anything in his life, and Moriah was sure that was the reason Vance was such an unsuccessful hunter. If she had been forced to depend on him for food she would have starved long ago.

As Vance lumbered toward her, calling her name,

Moriah's temper rose steadily. Vance was supposed to be her guardian, but he was never around when she needed him to chase off one of the overzealous suitors Ruby tried to foist off on her. Being in a snit already, Moriah lashed out at Vance, partially blaming him for the incident with Burkhart.

"I'm getting tired of having men thrust at me," she spewed at Vance. "Ruby never respects my right to reject those I have no interest in and you have never—"

To Moriah's utter disbelief and disgust, Vance assaulted her with a slobbery kiss. Instant revulsion channeled through every fiber of her being. Moriah reacted the way she always did when the octopus arms of men engulfed her. She kicked Vance where he was most vulnerable. But even when he buckled over to protect his privates from another blow that would render him useless to women forevermore, he managed to restrain Moriah from fleeing.

Like a wild creature in captivity, Moriah fought for release. She spewed out curses when his hands clamped over her breasts and slid down her belly. Moriah was sickened by the two maulings so close to each other and astonished that one of them had come from Vance! Her guardian, of all people!

In the past, she had caught Vance staring at her, but Ruby's blatant jealousy had apparently prevented him from doing what he was contemplating. Tonight he seemed hell-bent on appeasing his lusts.

The sound of cloth ripping about her neck caused Moriah to shriek indignantly. But she was caught completely off guard when Vance's fingers clamped around her neck. Moriah was struck by the terrifying realization that Vance intended to kill her! Frantic, she fought back with every ounce of strength she could muster, but Vance blocked her second attempt to kick him in the groin.

Before Moriah could hurl herself away, Vance yanked a rope from his pocket and bound her hands together. Moriah gasped for breath when his hands again went to her throat and she was no longer able to fight back. Left with no other recourse, she made the decision to pretend to choke to death. With a gurgle and a breathless groan, she sank limply into Vance's arms.

When Moriah's eyes fluttered shut, Vance was certain he had succeeded in his mission. Lifting the lifeless weight, Vance carried Moriah to the riverbank and deposited her beside a fallen log. Hurriedly, he secured her hands to a second rope that he bound around the log that would carry her body downriver and far away from the wagon-train search party that would inevitably be sent to locate her.

After he had set her adrift, Vance took the fabric he had purposely ripped from the collar of Moriah's gown and the ribbon he had yanked from her hair and draped them on a scrubby bush. Following Ruby's instructions to the letter, Vance danced around in a circle to leave the impression that Moriah had struggled with her captors. While his ward floated down river, Vance scurried back to camp to pretend nothing out of the ordinary had happened.

A triumphant smile hovered on his mouth as he joined the congregation to watch the cavalry patrol trot away. Ruby was going to be proud of him. He had accomplished his mission and Moriah was out of the way forever. Her inheritance now belonged to the Thatchers.

When Ruby spied her husband and his triumphant expression, a satisfied grin crossed her lips. At long last that persnickety chit was out of Ruby's life. She would work up a few crocodile tears for appearance' sake, of course, but Ruby wouldn't truly lament losing Moriah. Her youthful spirit and arresting good looks had been a tormenting reminder that Ruby wasn't aging gracefully. Although she would never see forty again, Ruby intended to go down fighting, doing all within her power to preserve what was left of her diminishing beauty. The expense that had once been begrudgingly spent on Moriah would now be utilized to enhance Ruby's appearance.

When one of the young men in the wagon train ambled over to inquire about Moriah, Ruby gnashed her teeth. She should have known the men would notice her disappearance. The girl had always attracted men like metal to a magnet. Ruby had hoped it would be at least an hour before anyone questioned Moriah's absence, but there was naught else to do now but pretend concern for her missing ward.

Four men volunteered to look for Moriah, and Ruby walked on pins and needles, fretting over whether the body would be recovered. Vance had better not have fouled up her plans, damn him! She flashed her husband a mutinous glance. If he had botched up her clever scheme, Moriah could return to accuse her stepparents of murder! Blast it, she probably should have seen to the matter herself, Ruby fumed.

To Ruby's relief, the foursome returned thirty minutes later with the ripped fabric from Moriah's gown and the ribbon Vance had planted beside the river. Calling upon her theatrical bent, Ruby wailed in grief. Even when two of the men offered to chase down the cavalry and inform them that Moriah had been stolen by Apaches, Ruby didn't fret. She knew the wagon train would be long gone, even if the body were discovered somewhere downstream. But the Apaches would still take the blame for the incident, Ruby assured herself confidently. Moriah was gone for good and Ruby couldn't have been happier, even if she was crying her eyes out. And these were tears of joy and relief, certainly not sorrow!

Chapter 2

After swallowing what seemed like half the water in the Mimbres River, Moriah sputtered and coughed to catch her breath. The log to which she had been strapped kept rolling over, dragging her beneath the surface. She swore she would drown before she managed to worm her hands free from the soggy ropes. And she probably would have if the log hadn't lodged in the bend of the river.

Looking and feeling like a drowned rat, Moriah dug her feet into the riverbank before the log swerved back into the flow of the channel. Frantically, she worked her hands until they bled, determined to wriggle free. By the time she escaped from the rope Vance had tied around the log, her arms felt as limp as cooked noodles.

With her hands still bound in front of her, but free of the log that drifted back into the middle of the river, Moriah floundered up the slippery bank.

There was no doubt in her mind that Ruby was responsible for the attempt on her life. Ruby had twice as many brains as Vance. That wasn't much of a compliment, though, because Vance had none to speak of. He had become conditioned to doing

Ruby's bidding. It was apparent that the aging witch wanted Moriah out of the way so she could have sole control of the money gained from the sale of the Laverty farm.

After the ordeals of the past two hours, Moriah didn't care if she ever laid eyes on another human being ever again. And men! Moriah silently seethed. Lyle Burkhart and Vance Thatcher were examples of what nuisances and threats men were to women. Moriah swore, there and then, to hate all men forever and to curse Ruby Thatcher until her last dying breath. Someday, somehow, she was going to pay that bitch back for the trouble and anguish she had caused Moriah these last five years.

Perhaps it would have been safer for Moriah to scuttle back to the wagon train and accuse Ruby of the vile crime. But she was too bitter to confront Ruby and Vance or even Lyle. Knowing Ruby, she would accuse Moriah of being hysterical and dreaming up wild stories. And Lyle Burkhart, of course, would chime in with Ruby to save face.

No one would believe me, Moriah reminded herself as she aimed herself north, following the river. When others were around Ruby pretended to dote over her ward. It had always been obvious to Moriah that Ruby was a two-faced harridan who played every situation to her advantage. Ruby and Moriah had tolerated each other out of necessity. No one in the wagon train would have believed the extent of Ruby's hatred for the girl and that she had plotted to kill her ward. Ruby would spout her innocence and she would be believed.

Left with no alternative, Moriah propelled herself toward the mountains that loomed in the moonlight, not caring if she stumbled upon renegade Apaches. They couldn't possibly treat her more cruelly than Ruby, Vance, and Lyle had. Sometimes Moriah was left to wonder if life was even worth living. Thus far, hers had been nothing short of misery. If she knew what was good for her she would probably head for higher ground and live out her days as a recluse in the mountains. It would beat the heck out of tolerating the type of people she had been forced to endure these past few years.

When Moriah made her decision to go to the mountains she was as cynical as one woman could possibly be. She had resolved to hate men everywhere and to avoid civilization whenever possible. Maybe in the future she would long for companionship, but not now. Now she would learn to survive by her wits or perish!

Relying upon the river to guide her north, and berries to satisfy her hunger, Moriah trekked ever closer to the mountains. By the end of the second day, she reached Santa Rita del Cobre. The town was located at the entrance of the Black Range. The community was low enough in elevation to be free of the heavy snows that blanketed the mountains in the winter and yet high enough to spare its inhabitants the blistering heat that parched the desert plains and the dust storms that hampered travel in the early spring.

The bustling town of more than two hundred people was comprised mostly of miners who trailed into the mountains each day to dig for copper and silver and gold. The triangular presidio, with its towers looming at each corner of the four-feet-thick walls, testified that it had once belonged to Mexico. The town consisted of adobe buildings that had been refurbished when American troops had employed the village as a garrison.

The old presidio, plaza, and the more than fifty buildings that now lined the streets gave the town a comfortable, prosperous appearance. But Moriah, having decided to become a hermit, skirted the community, comprised mostly of men, to scavenger what she could from what appeared to be an abandoned shack just to the north of town.

The part of the country through which Moriah had trekked was characterized by independent mountain ranges that stretched twenty to fifty miles before they untangled onto the Colorado Plateau. Some of the distant peaks were high enough to remain snow-capped year round. Many of them were cloaked with thick forests and deep chasms into which Moriah intended to vanish at the first sign of trouble.

This was where she belonged. Moriah decided as she discreetly darted through the crisscrossed shadows cast by the trees. She was a nomad, searching for peace and tranquility. If she could scratch out enough gold to purchase supplies she would be content for the time being. And if she ever forgave the human race, she might come down from the mountains to associate with her own kind. She would dress as a man and keep her identity a secret. . . .

"Well, what have we got here?"

So much for keeping her identify a secret, Moriah thought in disgust.

Clyde Finnegan blinked in confusion at the mysterious silhouette that hovered above him on the hill. The sun hung just behind the shapely nymph, partially blinding him and leaving him with the distinct impression that the vision before him possessed supernatural qualities. The aureole of gold that encircled her head stunned him. The fascinating color of her long hair against the backdrop of a spectacular sunset on the looming mountains gave his unidentified visitor a mystical appearance. Clyde swore he must be seeing things. The fact that he had imbibed a good deal of whiskey since he returned from digging in the mountains left him wondering if he could trust his blurred eyes.

Moriah flinched when the man in a floppy-brimmed hat and tattered homespun clothes ambled around the corner of the shack that she had assumed to be abandoned, in which she had hoped to rest and confiscate supplies.

When Clyde approached, a lusty smile spread over his lips. His reddened eyes ran the full length of Moriah's voluptuous figure. Beneath the fringe of her thick lashes was a pair of luminous blue eyes that sparkled in the intense sunlight. Lord, he had never seen such a lovely vision! Her hair was the exact same color as the gold he sought in the mountains near Santa Rita and Piños Altos. Her exquisite tanned features caught and held his admiring gaze.

Damn, he would give anything to get his hands on this delicious treat! Most of the women in Santa Rita were married to miners or were calico queens who had more male attention than they knew what to do with. They demanded an exorbitant price for their feminine charms, and Clyde's luck with mining barely allowed him to purchase food and drink. Clyde had been forced to curb his male appetite to feed his growling belly and he had been a long time without a woman.

He didn't have the foggiest notion where this golden-haired angel had come from, but he wasn't anxious to see her leave . . . And if the other love-starved bachelors in the community got a look at her, Clyde knew he would have to fend off his friends with his shotgun.

Warily, Moriah watched the pint-size little man, whose smile seemed to reveal a few missing teeth, wobble toward her. His whiskered face stretched into a wide grin and Moriah realized he had a *lot* of missing teeth, not just a few.

"Come on inside, honey, and I'll fetch you something to eat," Clyde offered with a decisive Irish accent.

Moriah didn't trust him for a minute. He had that look about him—the kind she had seen plastered on one too many male face. But she was desperate and she needed some kind of weapon and supplies to sustain her in the mountains. Ruby still had Moriah's inheritance stitched in her petticoats, curse her evil soul, and Moriah had nothing.

"You are very kind, sir," she murmured, even though she was certain he was anything but!

Moriah would never again trust a man. What *she* wanted from this scraggly prospector who was down on his luck and what *he* wanted from her were two entirely different matters!

"My name is Clyde Finnegan," he introduced as he pulled out a chair at the table. His dark eyes discreetly darted toward his cot, picturing himself on it with this gorgeous angel who had materialized out of nowhere to bedazzle him. "What's your name, honey?"

Moriah intercepted his glance at the bed, determined that would be the last place she wound up. And if he called her "honey" one more time she was going to sting him like a bee!

"Moriah," she replied, monitoring his every move with wary trepidation.

"Moriah . . ." Clyde rolled the name over his numb tongue and then expelled an audible sigh. "Lordy, that's about the prettiest name I ever did hear. It's like the whispering of the wind in the mountains. . . ."

The only wind around here was the hot air Clyde was blowing down her neck, she thought cynically. How many times had men blandished her with compliments in hopes of gaining sexual favors? Too many to list, she mused, disgruntled. Impatiently, she waited for another line of flattery, knowing it would come. Men always fawned over women when they wanted something from them.

"I don't know how you got here, angel, but I welcome the company." Clyde rattled on as he poured whiskey into two cups. His blurry gaze feasted on Moriah's shapely figure as he ambled back to the table to plop down in the chair across from her. "It isn't often the menfolk around here get a look at a lady as lovely as yourself." A wide grin split his stubbled face and his eyelid dropped into a sluggish wink. "You came here straight from heaven, I'd guess."

Of course she did, Moriah silently smirked. She had tucked her wings beneath her tattered gown and shoved her halo into her pocket before she fluttered down to this isolated cabin in the foothills.

"Straight down from heaven," she assured him with an impish grin that made her blue eyes twinkle in the waning light.

"I suppose you came to counter White Shadow's curse against the cavalry," Clyde surmised. He paused to take in Moriah's bewitching beauty and then gulped his liquor.

That was the second time Moriah had heard White Shadow mentioned. These miners seemed to be a superstitious sort, she decided. Clyde was referring to avenging spirits and descending angels. Perhaps if she lived too long in the seclusion of these mountains she was destined to become as nutty as he was!

"You are a clever one, Clyde," she remarked before taking a cautious sip of the whiskey. "I intend to see to this White Shadow business—" Her breath caught in her throat as fire burned her tongue. She sputtered at the fierce taste and wheezed to catch her breath.

Clyde's grin disappeared and he sighed disappointedly. "I was afraid you weren't real when I first got a look at you. I guess that means you won't be staying for long." Damn, how he wished he hadn't drunk so much liquor in the course of the afternoon. If his visit with this cherub was destined to be brief he would have preferred to commit every second to memory. But he had gotten himself soused and he couldn't think or see straight.

"If you would be so kind as to point me toward White Shadow," Moriah requested, amused by the comical expressions that chased across Clyde's wrinkled face, "I'll see if I can put an end to the curse he has placed on the Army."

His arm lifted to gesture at the mountains at large. "White Shadow is everywhere," he declared with great conviction. "Nobody finds him; he finds *them*. One minute he is looming on the ridge above you and then he vanishes into thin air. He's always out there somewhere. Some folks think he wants vengeance against the Army and others swear he's protecting the legendary gold mine that lies somewhere in these mountains."

"Pegleg's Mine? The Lost Dutchman?" Moriah managed to inquire without a ridiculing smirk that would betray the fact that she was amusing herself at Clyde's expense.

Clyde gave his shaggy brown head a contradictory shake. "Apache gold," he informed her in a convincing tone. "White Shadow probably doesn't want white men to find the mine for fear people will swarm to these mountains like they did during the California gold rush. He runs interference for the renegade Apaches that are wanted by the Army and he protects the gold from intruders who prowl his domain.

"No one is sure if he is flesh or spirit," Clyde continued. "According to reports, White Shadow clashed with the Army during an Indian parley at Ojo del Muerto. After what turned out to be slaughter on both sides, he is wanted for murder and conspiracy. Whether the man is alive or dead after living for more than a year in these treacherous mountains, nobody knows for sure. Some say he died up there and that his ghost haunts the ridges and chasms. Others say he takes his revenge against Commander Burkhart and lives only to strike at him. But it's my opinion that Burkhart deserves all the bad luck that comes his way. He's a little too shifty-eyed and sneaky for my tastes."

Even though Moriah was certain Clyde's superstitious mind had conjured up the myth, she was fascinated by the story and she shared his low opinion of Burkhart. For a moment she let her guard down. Clyde had very little else going for him, but he could weave an intriguing tale of adventure and the challenging quest for gold.

Clyde settled back in his chair, preoccupied momentarily with spinning his tale. "For more than a century, the Apache's have been at war with Mexico. The Mexicans offered one hundred pesos for male scalps, fifty for women, and twenty-five for Apache children."

Moriah cringed at the barbaric practice of scalp hunting.

"The Apaches hate the Mexicans for their cruelty,

and when the Americans came they tried to make peace and also joined forces with them during the revolution to win Texas. Most of the trouble with the Apaches and Americans started about four years ago. Mangas Coloradas, chief of the Mimbres Apache, tried to make peace with the miners and let us wander around his mountains. But more of us came and he wanted us to move on. Mangas came to town to speak with some of us, offering to show us the places where there was an abundance of gold."

Clyde chuckled quietly and he sadly shook his head. "But the chief didn't understand the white man's greed. He shared the legend of Eagle Valley with several of the miners, but they figured the chief was trying to set a trap to kill them. The chief couldn't understand why the miners were skeptical after he took so many of them into his confidence. All he wanted, I suppose, was to get us to leave Santa Rita because his tribe liked to set up camp by the river and the whites had invaded his territory. But white men lust after gold. If they strike it rich, they tell *no one* for fear their claim will be stolen."

The drunken prospector paused to guzzle his whiskey and then continued. "But being an angel, you probably already know what happened."

"Refresh my memory," Moriah requested sweetly. "We angels have a great deal on our minds, with all the goings-on around the planet."

Clyde snickered at her witty rejoinder and then sobered as much as he could, considering he was soused up to his eyebrows. "Well, the more suspicious prospectors tied Mangas Coloradas to a tree and beat him with bullwhips for trying to deceive them. When they cut him loose, Mangas swore vengeance on all miners. That wasn't a good thing since he was the leader of several Apache clans in southwest New Mexico, father-in-law to Cochise, and close friend of Geronimo.

"After the incident, we found several of the miners who were involved in the beating propped by their campfires with their heads bent down, looking as if they never knew what hit them. And I've come upon some men who were buried neck-deep in anthills. Some of the miners who had turned to scalp hunting and selling out to the Mexicans found *themselves* scalped. If you ask me, they should have stuck to searching for the rich vein of gold in these mountains."

"Has anyone ever seen the legendary Apache gold?" Moriah couldn't help but ask.

Clyde nodded affirmatively. "A white man not only saw it, but the miners were given the Apache riddle that supposedly plots the location of the mine, though no one has ever been able to figure out the hidden meanings or locate the mysterious valley in the mountains."

He paused for a moment to mentally rehearse the verse and then recited it for Moriah's benefit.

"Beyond the moons of winter skies
The eagle of the valley flies—
Until all battles have been won.
The heart on fire forever lies
Hot beneath Old Man Mountain's eyes,
At the lost temple of the sun.

Apache gold—the white man's prize—
Bleeds in the tears the Old Man cries—
Until the Spirit rain is done."

While Moriah was memorizing the lines in case she ever happened onto the Valley of the Eagle, Clyde rattled on. "Dr. Thorne, a physician in the area, once treated Mangas Coloradas's wounds after his battle with Mexicans. To repay the doctor, Mangas blindfolded Thorne and led him into a remote chasm where he was allowed to pick up all the gold he could carry. But since the whites had treated Mangas Coloradas so cruelly, the Apache no longer granted them amnesty. Nowadays most Americans have fallen into the same category as the Apaches' lifelong enemies—the Mexicans."

The old miner sighed heavily before sipping his brew. Pushing himself from his chair, he wobbled over to fetch a mild liqueur for Moriah. "Relations between the cavalry and miners, versus the Apaches, grew worse when Mangas came alone to confer with the miners in hopes of calling a truce two years ago. Some of the miners took Mangas hostage for their own protection against the Indians. Then they handed him over to the Army who murdered him and tried to cover up the incident by declaring that the chief had attempted to escape.

"Not long after that, Burkhart asked a white man who was blood brother to the Apache to lead his regiment to Ojo del Muerto and act as an interpreter so the Army and Apache could patch up relations. But for some reason, battle broke out and several Apaches and dragoons were killed. Seriously wounded though White Shadow seems to have been, he and the Apaches retreated into the mountains and the Army issued a warrant for his arrest. Now, according to the legend, White Shadow has placed a curse on Burkhart and swears revenge. Nobody but White Shadow, Burkhart, and a few soldiers who no longer ride with the Army really know what happened. But knowing Burkhart like I do, I wouldn't be surprised if he wasn't part of the problem."

Moriah was saddened by the grim tale. If the Apaches were using the ghost of White Shadow as a curse and had sworn revenge on the Army and every white settler, it wouldn't be unfounded. The treatment of Mangas Coloradas was abhorrent. Moriah knew it was easy to become bitter and mistrusting when one was betrayed by those he dared to call friend. Moriah was living proof of a bitterness that extended past her particular enemies into generalities. Because of her dealings with the Thatchers, Lyle Burkhart, and the other overzealous men in her past, she had become wary and suspicious of everyone with whom she came in contact. Even Clyde Finnegan, who seemed harmless enough, could not be trusted, and Moriah promptly reminded herself of that fact.

"I cannot say I blame the Apaches or White Shadow for retaliating," Moriah commented before taking a small sip of the liqueur.

"Those of us who know Burkhart and heard his side of the story—the twisted one he conjured up for the benefit of the military brass—don't, either. It sounded a little fishy to me," Clyde mumbled skeptically. "And in case you really are an angel, keep in mind that I have no beef with the Apaches. Live and let live I always say. All I want is the small space where this cabin sets and the chance to scratch out a little gold. I'm willing to share my space with the Indians without giving them trouble."

His dark eyes slid over Moriah's tantalizing figure and he smiled rakishly. "Of course, if I were wishing, I'd also like a wife who looked exactly like you, angel."

"We angels can't marry," she insisted, studying him like a cautious doe monitoring a hunter's approach. "It is not allowed."

"Well, maybe we could just fool around then . . ."

Moriah might have liked the crusty old miner if he hadn't allowed his male urges to overwhelm him. He was harmless while he was spinning yarns, but when he reminded himself that he was a man and she a woman, the fragile bond of friendship shattered. Moriah was suddenly the quarry, and she had already had enough manhandling to last her a lifetime!

The moment Clyde lunged at her, Moriah vaulted out of her chair and latched on to the rifle that was propped against the door. She wheeled around just as Clyde's arms clamped around her waist. A dull thud clanked against Clyde's skull when the butt of his own rifle made painful contact. Clyde pitched forward and sprawled on the dirt floor in an unconscious heap.

Criminey! When would men ever learn that a woman would announce when she was interested in accepting amorous affection?

Inhaling a frustrated breath, Moriah scanned the one-room shack in search of supplies that would sustain her for the next few weeks. She figured Clyde owed her that much after trying to steal a kiss and whatever else he thought he could get away with. Moriah had noticed where the miner kept his supply of dried pemmican and beef jerky, and she stepped over his limp body to snatch up the knapsack. Taking the barest essentials for cooking, the long-bladed knife that was tucked in his belt, and the rifle, Moriah started toward the door.

She paused on a mischievous thought. Setting her supplies aside, she ambled back to the bed to snatch up the white sheet and the pillow. Locating the worn edge of the pillow, she dug inside to grab a handful of feathers. All the better that they were white, she mused impishly.

After scattering a few feathers around Clyde, she replaced the pillow on the cot. Let the superstitious old goat think he truly had been visiting with an angel during his drunken stupor and that he had knocked a few feathers loose from her wings. That should give him a few more tales to relate to his friends. And it wouldn't hurt her one iota if the miners in the area believed there was an angel on the mountain. They might just be as leery of her as they were of the legendary White Shadow who prowled the Black Mountains.

When Moriah had struggled outside with her supplies, the bray of Clyde's mule caught her attention. Impulsively, she threw her gear over the sway-back creature and led him away as the sun sank behind the craggy precipices, bathing the vista in molten gold and deep purple shadows. If she ever came across the Apache treasure, she made a mental note to leave a few nuggets for Clyde Finnegan, to repay him for stealing his mule and his skillet. The sheet she would keep. After all, an angel needed a white robe, didn't she? And if her get-up frightened off miners and Apaches, so much the better.

By the time Moriah ascended into the rugged mountains, she wished she had also swiped Clyde's jacket. The cool night air sent goose bumps cruising down her skin. Twisting the sheet around her like a toga, Moriah attempted to ward off the chill while she kept walking toward higher elevations.

A pensive smile curved on her lips as she followed the narrow trail that seemed to wind forever into the lofty peaks. It was little wonder the Apaches journeyed along these obscure paths. They could travel unobserved for hundreds of miles, weaving through the winding canyons that were guarded by eerie rock formations that appeared to be carved by immortal hands. And it was also easy to understand why the miners became suspicious when they trekked through the forests to follow the labyrinth of ridges and chasms. There was something intriguing and mysterious about these Black Mountains that were supposedly haunted by White Shadow.

Moriah told herself the legend of White Shadow was nothing but a myth that made a good story to relate while the miners were sitting in the taverns sipping their whiskey. And yet, when she was ambling along the pebbled path spotlighted as it was by moonlight . . .

Hesitantly, she glanced over her shoulder. She had the unshakable feeling she was being watched when she paused to rest for the night. A shadow here and there seemed to materialize and then vanish into nothingness. The faintest sound of pebbles crunching beneath a moccasined foot reached her ears and she gulped over the lump in her throat. But each time she scanned her surroundings, she was met only with silence and moonshadows.

"If that's you, White Shadow, go haunt someone else," Moriah finally exclaimed to the darkness at large. "I'm too tired tonight for a fight. I will be able to confront you better in the morning."

Having said her piece, Moriah plunked down on her thin pallet and curled herself into the sheet as if it were her cocoon. When she had wormed about and settled herself comfortably, the soft cry of a distant owl rippled in the wind. Wide, luminous eyes surveyed the night, unable to determine from which direction the sound had come. But one thing she did remember from her lengthy conversation with Clyde

Finnegan was that the Apache ghosts occasionally took the form of owls and that the presence of an owl suggested evil spirits were lurking nearby.

Don't let yourself fall prey to those silly superstitions, Moriah scolded herself. But for a precautionary measure, she reached over to pull the rifle to her side. Of course, she didn't know how to use or load the damned thing, but if there was an unwanted visitor prowling the shadows, he wouldn't know that. Moriah cursed Vance Thatcher for never teaching her how to handle a rifle. The big baboon probably didn't even know how himself, she thought resentfully. Vance had been a miserable guardian and provider. He had done nothing to enrich her life. He had done all the taking, none of the giving, had taught her nothing except the treachery and betrayal of life.

"Curse you, Vance Thatcher," she muttered disdainfully. "And you, too, Ruby!"

Again the hoot of the owl shattered the silence and Moriah winced apprehensively. Well, if she were to die in her sleep, like some of the unsuspecting miners in the area, she would have had the satisfaction of cursing her stepparents soundly before being transported to a higher sphere. And that was what they deserved, damn them. They had tried to kill her to gain control of her inheritance and they had very nearly succeeded!

From the darkness, footsteps approached the sleeping form that was curled up in the sheet. As soundless as the flutter of a butterfly's wings, the shadowed silhouette circled the young woman who resembled a mummy encased in her sheet. He paused momentarily to admire the mass of thick curly hair that sparkled in the moonlight like a river of shimmering gold.

After surveying the saddlebags that were strapped to the mule, the nocturnal prowler carried all but one of them over to the sleeping beauty who was oblivious to the fact that she had a midnight visitor. Reaching into the pouch that lay diagonally across his chest, the noiseless apparition carefully slid the white-quilled arrow into Moriah's limp hand.

With catlike tread, the specter moved back to the mule to place several gold nuggets in the saddlebag and then led the animal back in the direction it had come. Casting one last glance at the sleeping form, the specter evaporated into the slanting shadows that were cast by the jutting mountain peaks.

Chapter 3

Peter Gibson rapped on Clyde's door and waited an impatient moment. When no one answered, Peter lumbered inside and stopped dead in his tracks. A shaft of moonbeams spilled through the window to outline Clyde's form sprawled on the floor.

Frantically, Peter checked for wounds and found the knot on the side of his friend's head. "For God's sake, what happened?" Pete bleated, shaking Clyde awake.

Clyde groaned miserably and as he tossed his head to get his bearings, feathers fluttered all around him. "Well, I'll be damned . . ." he gasped as he peered at the swirling feathers.

"Are you all right?" Pete demanded to know.

Blinking, Clyde glanced back at the empty table. The two cups he swore had been sitting there while he conversed with Moriah were nowhere to be seen. His dazed gaze riveted on the chair that Moriah had replaced just as she had found it.

"Clyde, damnit, answer me!" Pete insisted. "What's the matter with you?"

"I was visited by an angel," Clyde said with great conviction. "You should have seen her, Pete. Prettier than a picture she was. With hair like gold nuggets and eyes as clear and blue as the morning sky."

Pete didn't say anything. He was thunderstruck. He knew Clyde had been drinking heavily that afternoon because Pete was the one with whom the old miner had been drinking heavily! They had both been soused and had gone to their respective cabins to sleep off the effects of the liquor.

"She drifted down the mountainside on sunbeams and floated in here. Her name was Moriah and her voice was like the whisper of the wind." Clyde lifted a feather and twirled it in his fingers to lend credence to his story. "And when I tried to touch her—" A muddled frown knitted his graying brow when he suddenly saw all the color drain from Peter's face. "What's the matter with *me?* What's the matter with *you? I* was the one who saw the angel!"

Peter had wilted onto the floor and was sucking air in great gulps. "A messenger from the cavalry rode into Santa Rita this evening to warn us that the Apaches had murdered a white woman from a passing wagon train," he reported bleakly. "The courier said her name was Moriah and that her eyes were azure blue and her hair was pure gold . . ."

And that's how the legend of the Angel of the Wind came to be. Pete and Clyde hotfooted it to Santa Rita del Cobre to offer their description of the dazzling cherub who had appeared in Clyde's cabin. By the time Clyde, who could spin one whale of a tale, added a few embellishments for dramatic effect, the story of the angel's ascent into the mountains to confront the legendary White Shadow had spread all the way to Piños Altos mining camp to the northeast.

The way Clyde perceived the incident, the angel had been hovering near the mountains after she had been murdered by Apaches and had gone to confront

White Shadow in his domain. Clyde even brought along a few feathers that he had plucked from the angel's wings before she sent down a lightning bolt to strike him. By the time he awoke she had floated up into the mountains.

When Clyde returned to his cabin, full of whiskey, his mule met him on the path. And to Clyde's amazement, there were five gold nuggets stashed in the saddlebag that hadn't been there the day before.

Clyde had another astonishing tale to relate to the miners who were skeptical of his story. Being of Irish descent, Clyde was always babbling about gnomes, fairies, leprechauns, and such. But when he returned the following evening to flash the gold nuggets for one and all to see, no one contested his tale. In fact, Clyde suddenly became something of a hero in Santa Rita del Cobre. After all, it wasn't every day that a man was granted a visit from an angel with sky-blue eyes and hair spun from threads of gold!

With a weary groan, Moriah levered up on her elbow just as the sun peeked over the towering peaks above her. Long tangled lashes fluttered up to study the purple slopes that were dotted with trees and vegetation. A curious frown puckered her brow when she realized the mule she had stolen from Clyde wasn't where she had hobbled him. . . .

A startled gasp came from deep in her throat when she absently moved her hand and found she was clutching an unfamiliar object. When she identified the object as the white-quilled arrow that matched the description given by Captain Grimes four days earlier, Moriah dropped it as if she had been holding live coals. The tip of the white-pine shaft was chiseled from a gold nugget and the arrow was adorned with white feathers.

Moriah stared at the arrow and then spared a cautious glance in every direction. But there was nothing except moccasin prints. Her heart slammed against her ribs, threatening to stick there.

Lifting a shaky hand, Moriah shoved the long golden tresses away from her face and sat up cross-legged on her pallet. For certain, someone had crept up on her during the night, and that someone was obviously trying to frighten her away and discourage her by absconding with the mule she had stolen from Clyde.

However, Moriah didn't scare easily. After all, she had been mauled three times in less than a week and had survived an attempt on her life. What could be worse than that? It was for certain she wasn't going to turn tail and fly down the mountain.

The whole point of her coming here in the first place was to avoid civilization in general and men in particular. And if she happened to stumble onto the Apache gold, she would return one day to make Ruby and Vance pay penance for what they had done to her. But now she had to satisfy her desire to be alone with her thoughts and evaluate her life in her own private haven in the mountains.

After delivering that inspiring sermon to herself, Moriah unfolded herself from her sheet and took a sip of water from the canteen. But again she was stung by the unnerving sensation that she was being watched. When she turned though, there was nothing behind her except a few trickling pebbles that had tumbled down from the ridge above her.

Throughout the day, Moriah was hounded by the feeling that someone was not only watching her but also trailing her as she traveled northwest through the maze of canyons and buttes. A few pebbles danced down the path in front of her and Moriah lost the last of her patience. With hands on hips and feet askance, she glared at the towering ledge.

"Show yourself, coward," she challenged. The canyon walls flung back her words and sent them echoing across the valley below. "I'm tired of your cat-and-mouse games."

The challenge went unanswered as her voice evaporated in the wind. Grumbling to herself, Moriah snatched up the discarded rifle and trudged onward, pausing only to rest when she swore she couldn't stir another step without collapsing. By dusk she was exhausted, unused as she was to such long, rigorous hikes in the thin mountain air.

And sure enough, when she roused the next morning at dawn, another white arrow lay beside her and moccasin tracks led to the rim of the canyon which dropped off a hundred feet below.

"I have had just about enough of your pranks, phantom," she burst out as she snapped the arrow into two pieces and hurled it against a nearby boulder. "White Shadow is a yellow-bellied coward. He cannot even face a woman for fear he will be defeated on his own stomping ground."

There. Let this man or wraith, or whatever he was, chew on that insult and see how he liked it!

Moriah didn't know what possessed her to stoop to name calling. Her temper had been sorely put upon the past week and her stomach was grumbling about the steady diet of water, pemmican, and beef jerky. But she suddenly wished she hadn't been so snide when the mysterious phantom suddenly leaped down from the cliff like a pouncing cougar.

A shocked squawk erupted from her lips as she staggered back and fumbled to swing the rifle barrel toward her foe.

She found a similar shotgun staring back at her.

Moriah, who had never been particularly impressed by a man, was unwillingly awed by the brawny, bare-chested giant who loomed behind his Winchester rifle. Thick wavy hair that gleamed blue-black in the sunlight capped the man's head and framed his bronzed features. A beaded headband held the thick mane away from his face and piercing golden-brown eyes stared back at her. Chiseled features that appeared half savage and half civilized were carved in the ruggedly handsome face. Crinkles fanned out from unnerving eyes that glittered dangerously in the light. His gaze probed into hers, probably searching for her weaknesses so he could prey on them, she thought.

Scars from bullet holes riddled his left shoulder and ribs, detracting only slightly from the hair-matted chest that was as broad as a bull's. Taut lines bracketed his full, sensuous lips. Whipcord muscles rippled down his arms and shoulders as he steadied himself on the ledge above her. Buckskin breeches and moccasins clung to his powerful thighs and calves, assuring Moriah that this . . . man . . . was all rock-hard muscle and tigerish agility.

Moriah swallowed her tongue. If there was a legendary ape-man who inhabited the jungles, then there was also a wolf-man who prowled the mountains of Indian country.

Her marveling gaze flooded over bare granite shoulders and muscular arms that were also banded in Indian fashion. Again her eyes wandered over the dark furring of hair that spread over the wide expanse of his chest before her attention drifted to the doe-hide breeches that fit the masculine contours of his legs like a second skin. Knee-high moccasins that were fastened with silver conchos and decorated with leather strips and colorful beads dangled beside his calves.

A coward? Had she really said that? She had called this mass of masculinity a yellow-bellied coward? Damn, she should have bobbed her runaway tongue! Before her stood about six feet four inches and at least two hundred twenty pounds of rippling muscle and lightning-quick reflexes. The man was thirtyish or thereabouts, and the cool disapproval in his expression indicated that he did not take kindly to either her degrading comment or her presence. And the only coward around here, it seemed, was Moriah herself. Oh, how she wished she *was* the wind so she could flit over the rim of the canyon and glide away to safety.

Devlin Granger stared the wide-eyed young woman down for a full two minutes before his eyes began to wander over her curvaceous figure. When he first saw this stunning minx traipsing around the mountain path as if she belonged here—which she most certainly did not—demons of curiosity had hounded him. The last thing Devlin wanted in his favorite haunt was a female who could get herself into trouble without even trying. He had subtly attempted to frighten her away, but he had failed miserably. This spitfire was far more determined and persistent than he had expected! None of his scare tactics had worked worth a damn. But he had no intention of allowing this chit, gorgeous though she was, to share his territory . . .

His thoughts trailed off when his roving eyes feasted on the glorious sight of this daring beauty at closer range and in the revealing sunlight. Before him stood about five feet two inches of unparalleled beauty and strong will. Her luminous blue eyes dominated her pixielike face, and soft heart-shaped lips were pursed in a wary frown. A mop of tangled curls cascaded over her shoulders to the trim indentation of her waist. Her hair was pure gold. And if her elegant features and shiny mane of hair weren't enough to turn a man's head, she had a figure that would have stopped an Apache war party dead in its tracks. The torn bodice of her gown displayed the generous swell of bosom, leaving Devlin to speculate on how she would look if she were standing before him stark-bone naked.

When those eyes, like golden talons, raked over Moriah in an expression she had seen too often on a man's face, she jerked up her head and elevated a proud chin. "If it's rape you have in mind, you'll have a fight on your hands, I promise you that," she hissed venomously. "I'll blow the private parts of your anatomy to smithereens before you can lay a hand on me." Damn, if only she knew how to use this cursed rifle, she could make good her threat! She wasn't even sure if it was loaded. The way her luck had been running of late, it probably wasn't.

Devlin's face became an indecipherable mask that revealed none of his thoughts. Still, he made no move to blow her to kingdom come or to vanish as quickly as he appeared.

"Rape never crossed my mind," he replied in a rich baritone voice that was all too pleasing to Moriah's ear.

Was this really White Shadow? Although he appeared half savage, his command of the English language suggested that he was more than an uncivilized heathen. And if he was a white man, why was he dressed like a renegade Indian and following her like her own shadow?

"You are either incredibly brave or unbelievably stupid," Devlin insulted with a blank expression.

"I don't recall asking for your opinion," she

hurled at him, still clinging to her rifle and staring at the glittering barrel of his weapon that was still trained on her heaving chest.

"What do you want here, lady?" he demanded gruffly.

"To be left alone," she responded without hesitation.

"I don't want you here," he said with an air of deadly menace.

"I don't want you here, either," Moriah snapped back at him. Who did he think he was, the sole owner of these mountains?

"This is my domain," he growled, casting her the evil eye.

Moriah didn't knuckle under his intimidating glower. "I don't see any posters indicating you own the whole blessed territory," she sassed him.

"Possession is nine-tenths of the law," Devlin sneered, but Moriah still didn't cower; rather her determination increased in direct proportion to his resistance.

"Then I'll stay on the tenth you don't own," she offered with feigned generosity. "You keep out of my way and I'll gladly stay out of yours."

They had reached an impasse. Devlin didn't have the faintest notion what this feisty she-male was doing all alone in the mountains but she seemed determined to put down roots here. In all his thirty years, he had never run across a female who was as bold and daring as this one. No amount of ridicule or intimidation seemed to faze her. He could almost feel the animosity emanating from her snapping blue eyes, though he wasn't certain what had provoked her instant dislike of him.

In Devlin's estimation, it wasn't even a matter of whether they liked each other at first sight or not. It was a matter of principle. This was his stomping ground and he didn't want to share it. This lovely but sassy vixen had to go.

"If you intend to shoot me where I stand, be done with it," Moriah burst out after a moment. "If not, kindly say so. I'm growing tired of this futile stalemate."

"Put down your rifle," he demanded brusquely.

"You put yours down first," she ordered when he didn't pull the trigger.

Slowly, Devlin lowered the barrel of his weapon and Moriah did likewise. But Devlin snapped his rifle back into firing position the instant Moriah let her guard down. A devilish smile pursed his lips when Moriah blinked in confusion. For over a year, Devlin hadn't cracked a smile because he'd had nothing to smile about. But this saucy sprite amused him, intrigued him, challenged him.

Glistening blue eyes focused on the barrel of his rifle. Moriah was starkly aware that this looming giant now had a vulnerable target. There was no fear in Moriah's gaze, only curiosity that demanded to know her fate.

"Never give anyone the benefit of the doubt, lady," Devlin advised. "Trust will betray you."

With that, Devlin spun on his heels and gestured for Moriah to accompany him up the steep slope. When she didn't immediately follow, he glanced back to find *her* rifle aimed at *his* spine.

"You should heed your own advice," Moriah insisted with an elfin grin that made her eyes sparkle like sapphires. "I could easily take possession of your nine-tenths, White Shadow—and then you truly would be a phantom."

The second smile in over a year crossed his tanned face like a lazy cloud sliding across the sky. Devlin crouched on the huge boulder, reminding Moriah of a graceful jungle cat in repose. For a long moment he appraised the pert beauty who seemed long on gumption and short on sense. She didn't appear to be suited for life in the mountains, but she had defied them, and him as well.

The instant his spellbinding golden eyes roamed over her as if he were carefully scrutinizing a portrait, Moriah became defensive. She did not appreciate being undressed by masculine gazes.

"I thought you said you weren't interested in rape," she reminded him with a dubious frown.

Devlin couldn't help himself. Another smile burst free—a wide, reckless smile that softened his craggy features. "For a woman who claims disinterest in being ravished, you certainly speak of it often enough. I wonder if it is feminine curiosity that causes the subject to prey so heavily on your mind."

Moriah flinched after being slapped with another insult. How dare this big ape suggest she was inviting him to molest her. She wanted nothing of the kind!

"I need and want nothing from any man," she protested, letting loose her explosive temper. "I came up here to avoid all men because they are lurid, domineering, disgusting creatures. All I want is to be left alone to lead my own life in solitude!"

Devlin looked her up and down. "Lady, you've got a helluva lot to learn about these mountains," he smirked, amused by her fiery temper and the jut of her delicate chin.

"I'll manage," she proclaimed confidently.

"Better men than you have tried and failed," he contended.

"I'm not a man," she reminded him.

"I can see that well enough," he grunted as his gaze

slid down her arresting curves and swells, wishing he wasn't quite so affected by her.

Moriah inhaled an annoyed breath. If this renegade didn't stop gawking and ridiculing her, she would pull the trigger to determine if the confounded rifle was loaded. Hopefully the answer would be yes and White Shadow would become a legend of the past!

"I wouldn't if I were you," Devlin warned.

Moriah blinked like a disturbed owl. This man . . . or whatever he was . . . had read her thoughts! Was she so transparent?

"It's a gift," he responded to her silent question. "Sometimes, but not always, I can tell what someone is going to say before they say it, just by reading their faces."

A mutinous glare puckered her exquisite features. "Can you read these thoughts, oh great sage and soothsayer?"

Devlin's hearty peal of laughter clamored through the canyon. "Proper ladies shouldn't think such vile thoughts," he commented.

"I said nothing," Moriah corrected him airily.

"Perhaps not, but you were thinking them. It's the same thing," he parried. When her gaze instinctively wandered over his muscular torso he cocked a taunting brow. "You're wondering if I would be a gentleman or a savage in bed. Don't fret, tigress. I don't even sleep in one." His golden eyes twinkled in amusement when a crimson-red blush flooded up from the base of her throat, saturated her cheeks, and stained the roots of her blond hair.

Moriah was so flustered that her mouth dropped open and she had to slam it shut. Even her thoughts weren't private when this mysterious wolf-man was prowling about!

With an impressive display of masculine grace, Devlin got up from the boulder and pivoted. "You have no need to fear for your virtues, vixen," he blandly assured her. "I haven't had a woman for more than a year."

As he picked his way along the winding path, Moriah stared after him. She was dumbfounded by his parting remark and hypnotized by the sensual rhythm of his movements. Over a year? She didn't know it was possible for the male of the species to survive for more than a month without a woman!

"Why not?" she heard herself asking him.

Devlin missed a step and very nearly fell off his rock. He turned slightly to survey the bewitching face. "There are some things more important than appeasing male urges," he told her in a tone that rattled with bitterness. "I have forsaken all else to repay a long-standing debt. Until justice is served and I am cleared of the false charges against me, I have but one objective in life."

Involuntarily, Moriah dropped the barrel of her rifle and followed in White Shadow's wake. Silently she pondered their conversation. She was far from figuring out what this muscular giant meant by that remark because Clyde hadn't gone into detail about the incident that had made White Shadow a fugitive from justice. But her contempt for this man that myths were apparently made of dimmed slightly. He had warned her to trust no one and that was an opinion she was fully in accord with after being betrayed by the closest thing to family she had. Moriah fought down her unreasonable and ill-founded attraction to this powerfully built stranger who leaped around the mountain passes like a goat, and she trailed obediently after him. It was odd, but it seemed the natural thing to do.

They walked in silence for an hour before Moriah spied the inviting spring that gurgled from the rocks in the side of the mountain. She was anxious to cleanse herself of the excessive layers of dust that had left her feeling like a rotting mummy. With a squeal of delight, she dropped her rifle and darted toward the spring. The weapon clattered against the rock and discharged, causing the canyon to echo the sound like a booming canyon. Moriah was finally assured the rifle was loaded!

Reflexively, Devlin dived for cover and then scraped himself off the ground. "Careless fool," he muttered. His keen gaze circled the adjacent peaks. "You may as well have sent a telegraph message from twenty-five miles away! We'll be lucky if an entire party of Apache warriors don't swarm in on us."

"I'm sorry. I didn't think," she murmured in apology.

"Obviously not," he grumbled sourly. "If you plan to survive in these rugged mountains you had better learn to put caution before personal pleasure. Good God, woman, this is not a Sunday-afternoon picnic!"

Ruby had chastised Moriah for the slightest thing she didn't approve of for so long that Moriah naturally snapped back when provoked. She had tried on occasion to hold her tongue but Ruby had pelted her with so much unjustified criticism that Moriah always gave way to the urge to hurl one or two biting rejoinders.

"If I get myself killed, it's no skin off your hide," she lashed out in childish vindictiveness. "That's what you ultimately want, isn't it? For me to get off your mountain? If I get myself killed, the whole damned place will be yours—"

Devlin's hand snaked out so quickly to clutch her

elbow that she didn't see it coming until he manacled her arm and yanked her to his hard, unyielding chest. Her body was molded to his masculine contours and she found herself standing in the shadow of a human mountain that eclipsed the sun.

"Don't sass me, lady," he growled ominously. "If I leave you alone you'd be dead in an hour."

"Legend has it that you are a blood brother of the Apache. One word from you should be enough to protect me from unwanted visitors," she countered, fighting the unexpected tingles that rolled down her spine while her body was pressed full-length to his.

"Blood brother to some, but not all of them," he clarified, stung by the same unexpected sensations Moriah had experienced when they made physical contact. He hadn't anticipated such a fierce reaction to this firebrand. Willfully, Devlin ignored the stirrings that tapped at his nerve endings. "Like the white man, there are a few Apaches who are not to be trusted under any circumstances. Makado and his followers hold me responsible for the bloody confrontation at Ojo del Muerto. They want me out of these mountains and they know no loyalty other than to themselves. Makado has become so bitter that he trusts no one."

Moriah should have been paying more attention to his words and less to the feel of his masculine body imprinted on hers. There was something magnetic and overpowering about this swarthy, bare-chested giant. He triggered sensations that Moriah had never experienced in all her twenty years. She could feel the methodic thud of his heart against her heaving breasts, feel the long columns of his thighs meshed against her hips. For the first time ever, Moriah didn't feel repulsed by a man, but rather *intrigued* by his physical closeness.

Involuntarily, her long lashes fluttered up to focus on the tanned face that loomed over hers. Moriah's attention was automatically drawn to the sensuous curve of his lips. She was stung by the most ridiculous impulse—to feel his chiseled mouth whispering over hers. And considering her aversion to men and her cynicism of the human race, it shocked her all the way to her toes that she would even contemplate kissing him!

Devlin Granger was a man obsessed with revenge. For a year he had eaten, lived, and breathed vengeance. He had been content with his celibacy, thriving on his hatred of injustice. But the granite shell that encased his emotions had unexpectedly cracked when he read the feminine curiosity in this firebrand's sapphire-blue eyes.

In truth, he had been aroused by the picture she presented that first night he had seen her from his lookout point on the towering ridge. He had speculated about what lay beneath the soiled calico gown that had been partially ripped from her breasts. He had wondered if some lusty man had attempted to take advantage of her and he speculated on how she had responded to it. Whether she was pure and innocent, he didn't know. But she seemed the type who preferred a tender touch, even if she wasn't accustomed to having her way with the men in her life.

Devlin hadn't wanted to be affected by the feel of this woman's curvaceous body pressed to his, but he was. His gaze swam over those sparkling blue eyes that were rimmed with long, curly lashes and then dipped to the heart-shaped lips, as soft and pink as the delicate petals of a rose. His senses were fogged by her feminine scent, by the imprint of her supple curves. His body burned in a way that he had almost forgotten it could when he took a woman in his arms.

It wasn't enough that his thoughts of revenge had buckled when he captured this pixie. But Devlin found that his male curiosity was as intense as her female curiosity. He wanted to take her lips under his and explore their alluring pleasures.

"What's your name, tigress?" he murmured, his voice ragged with awakened desire.

"Moriah Laverty," she squeaked, her tone wobbly, her unblinking gaze helplessly fixed on the tempting curve of his mouth.

"Moriah . . . like the restless breeze in this land of storm and wind and fire," he murmured.

There was a fire burning all right. Moriah could feel the unexpected flames searing her flesh when White Shadow's raven head moved deliberately toward hers. For a half-second the accustomed response of kicking a man in his most vulnerable spot struck her, but the thought vanished as quickly as it darted across her mind, and Moriah found herself submitting when warm moist lips rolled over hers. Although this brawny giant was the image of strength and raw masculine force, he had a gentle touch. His kiss was light and inquiring, as if he were allowing her to test her reaction to him while he contemplated his own reaction to her. He took only what she offered; and she wanted what he was giving. The more she offered in return, the more he gave, until the sparks that leaped between them ignited into white-hot fire.

Moriah's heart raced when she felt his muscular arms glide around his waist. Her trembling hands rested on the sleek hair-matted plane of his chest and then glided up to map the lean muscles that covered his massive shoulders.

It would have been a relatively unprovocative movement, if Devlin hadn't been so long without a woman and Moriah hadn't been so inquisitive about this mysterious man. But as it was, each reckless touch burned through both of them like wildfire, making them vividly aware of their explosive reaction to each other.

His second kiss was more demanding, more impetuous, like a flame feeding on the wind, billowing out of control.

Moriah possessed the instinctive powers to arouse a man. And Devlin, a man who had locked his emotions in iron, felt his composure melt down to the consistency of jelly. This defensive wildcat set off an internal combustion that left molten lava channeling through his veins, which had flowed with ice water for more than a year. Devlin was no longer a man obsessed with vengeance, but rather a man of self-imposed starvation who was gnawing with an incredible hunger that demanded appeasement.

He groaned as he clutched Moriah closer. His tongue flicked at her honeyed lips and intruded to explore the soft recesses. His ragged breath became hers and his heart galloped like a runaway stallion. He could feel his strength being absorbed into her pliant body, feel his willpower erode like sand pummeled by the force of the surf. She felt so good in his arms. She was a taste of heaven after a year of hell.

The most remarkable sensations splashed over Moriah when she felt his hands clench into her waist to effortlessly lift her off the ground. She felt the exposed swells of her breasts gliding against his hair-roughened chest, felt her thighs brushing intimately against his bold manhood.

Moriah was utterly rattled by her phenomenal reaction to this muscular lion of a man! No past experience with men had prepared her for the upheaval of emotions that churned inside her. Lightning bolts sizzled through her and sparks leaped from her quaking body to his and back again like a current of electricity that sensitized every nerve and muscle. Shock waves hammered at her. She gasped for breath, but Devlin had stripped it from her lungs, leaving her hanging in sweet, hypnotic limbo . . .

When his left arm curled beneath her hips and his right hand grazed the swell of her breasts, the voice of reason finally shattered the haze of pleasure that fogged Moriah's brain. Warning signals flashed and her conscience stung. With a humiliated squawk, Moriah slapped Devlin's cheek soundly and flung herself away from this man who was most assuredly the devil's own temptation.

In her haste to retreat from danger, she caught her heel in the hem of her gown, and with another startled squeak, she flapped her arms like a windmill to keep herself upright. But White Shadow's arousing kisses and brazen caresses had knocked her completely off balance and she tumbled right into the mountain pool. But even the frigid water didn't cool the fire that burned inside her.

Embarrassed to no end, Moriah floundered to drag her feet beneath her and stand up in the waist-deep pool. Reflexively, her hand went to her lips to wipe away the lingering taste of his intoxicating kiss.

"You shouldn't have kissed me," she sputtered in indignation. "And you never should have touched me, either. For a man who has supposedly sworn off women, you certainly are behaving strangely!"

Deep laughter rumbled in his chest as his gaze drifted over the mop of wet golden hair that was plastered to the sides of Moriah's face. His eyes lingered on the soggy gown that emphasized her delicious curves and swells and made him want what Moriah insisted she had no intention of giving.

"You asked for it, Moriah," he countered with a rakish grin.

"I did not!" she trumpeted in outrage.

"You were wondering what it would be like to kiss me and I merely accommodated you," he had the audacity to say. "Pure feminine curiosity, I suppose, and masculine inquisitiveness on my part. No more, no less."

Moriah hated it when he deciphered all the expressions that flitted across her face. It seemed virtually impossible for her to keep a secret from him unless she learned to mask her emotions behind blank stares. And that was exactly what she was going to have to do if she spent much more time with this mystical man of the mountains. Moriah didn't like what she was feeling for this varmint. He was more man than she knew how to handle!

"Just go away and leave me alone," Moriah all but shouted as she lifted her saturated skirts and clambered from the spring. "And don't you ever touch me again, damn you!"

Devlin was blessed from birth with incredible powers of observation and acute intuition. He had perfected his gift during the year he had spent in the mountains, going about his vindictive business of harassing the Army. It wasn't so much that he *saw* someone in the distance, but rather he *felt* the presence and caught the scent of an intruder. Suddenly his emotions turned to ice and the arousing thoughts stimulated by this golden-haired goddess died a quick death.

Grumbling to himself, as was his habit after spending so many months alone in the mountains, Devlin snatched up his rifle. Pivoting without so much as a backward glance, he strode away. With the agility of a stalking cougar he bounded onto the edge of the boulder and disappeared down the ledge that jutted over the valley below.

Moriah stood there dripping wet, marveling at White Shadow's ability to vanish without a trace. In the batting of an eyelash White Shadow had evaporated into thin air. It was no wonder he had been given that name, for he was as elusive as a shadow.

She frowned at the empty space, White Shadow's lingering image taunting her all the while. She had insisted that he leave and he had left. So why did she feel so disappointed? It was ridiculous. She should have been greatly relieved.

That was what you wanted, Moriah reminded herself as she took a step and water squirted from her shoes. Knowing how magnetically attracted she was to this man she had only met made it doubly imperative that she avoid him like the plague. She knew absolutely nothing about him, except what Clyde had told her, which wasn't all that much. White Shadow dressed like an Indian and sneaked around just as effectively as one, but his golden-brown eyes hinted at white ancestry. Whatever he was, he wasn't the ordinary white man, that was for sure!

Moriah peered around her, trying to put some logic to her puzzling encounter with the man who was the subject of much talk and speculation. Who was this man who had the uncanny knack of reading her thoughts before she could put them to tongue?

Well, she wouldn't think about White Shadow just now, Moriah decided. She would treat herself to the luxury of a bath in the clear spring and swim to her heart's content. This was one of the advantages of solitude in the mountains.

Anxious to enjoy the moment of privacy, Moriah peeled off her soggy gown and petticoats and gave them a thorough scrubbing before draping them over the bushes to dry. The cool water erased the lingering feel of White Shadow's skillful caresses and the taste of his warm, full lips. Moriah fully intended to wash away his memory before it took firm root. What she didn't need was to find herself enamored by a legendary creature who had made it clear that his crusade in life was his sole reason for existence.

It was only the awakening of slumbering desires that disturbed her, Moriah assured herself. White Shadow was her first experience with passion—brief though it had been. White Shadow was right, of course. Feminine curiosity had gotten the best of her, causing a lapse of sanity. But the sinewy giant had come and gone, and now Moriah could pursue her life as a recluse in the Black Mountains. She only wished there wasn't such a devastating diversion prowling about half naked in the chasms and on the rocky crests. She found herself wondering if he could also read her thoughts at a distance, if he knew he preyed on her mind when she was trying so hard to forget their encounter. Criminey, she certainly hoped not!

Chapter 4

Devlin cupped his hands around his mouth and mimicked the sound of a coyote, as was the Apache custom for signaling. Cautious by nature and suspicious by habit, Devlin concealed himself behind the slabs of stone that lay along the canyon rim. Within a few minutes, a lean Apache warrior crept along the rock path in search of him.

Like a genie rising from a bottle, Devlin unfolded himself to gaze down upon Chanos. A quick flick of his moccasin sent a trickle of pebbles dribbling over the lithe medicine man of the Chiricahuas who wheeled with dagger poised in hand, glancing in every direction at once.

"Are you looking for me, Chanos?" he murmured soberly.

The warrior, who was dressed in similar fashion to his blood brother, nodded affirmatively. "I have brought news of Burkhart's patrol."

Cold, hard eyes glittered down on the warrior who weaved his way toward Devlin. The mere mention of Lyle Burkhart's name was enough to stir a boiling rage within him. "What has that murdering butcher done now?"

Chanos crouched down in the soft dirt to sketch Burkhart's location on the west side of the mountains. "He came upon the small village of wickiups of women and children in Doubtful Canyon," he reported grimly. The brave marked the location with an X. "Only a dozen of our people survived to scatter into the Chiricahua Mountains. From what I have learned, a wagon train of white-eyes journeyed across the Butterfield Trail and a woman from the group was murdered. Our people have been blamed for the incident and Burkhart is using it as an excuse to slaughter at will to compensate for the loss of the woman with golden hair."

Devlin's head jerked up to stare back in the direction he had come. Moriah . . .

Chanos sank down on his haunches. "One of the miners from Santa Rita del Cobre proclaims he was visited by the angel of this slain woman and that she has come to confront White Shadow." A wry smile pursed the warrior's lips. "You have touched this angel. I saw you from the summit. Is she an evil spirit or flesh, this woman with the sky in her eyes and gold nuggets in her hair?"

Devlin dodged Chanos's probing stare. Obviously, he had been so preoccupied by his tantalizing encounter with Moriah that he hadn't paid complete attention to his surroundings. Damn, even now his thoughts were tangled with the titillating sensations she had aroused in him.

"She is no evil spirit," Devlin assured the medicine man. "But her powers are strong. She escaped whatever evil sought to destroy her. Perhaps she is a good omen to the Apaches and a curse to Burkhart."

"I await the day that butcher lives no more on this earth," Chanos growled bitterly.

The Apaches did not speak of the beloved family

and friends who had departed from the earth. It was a bad omen. But Devlin knew Chanos grieved for those who had fallen beneath Burkhart's sword as he trekked through the valleys, murdering at will.

Burkhart labored under the theory that all Apaches should be exterminated rather than herded onto the reservations or allowed to roam free. He deemed himself a member of the superior race and labeled Apaches as savages to be hunted for sport and killed without mercy. But one day soon the trap would be sprung and Burkhart would pay for his vile crimes against the Apaches and against Devlin Granger. And if Devlin had his way, Burkhart would die after enduring Apache torture. The man should perish as he lived—cruelly, viciously, heartlessly . . .

"What is to be done with the Angel of the Wind, as the miners have come to call her?" Chanos inquired, dragging Devlin from his pensive deliberations.

"Nothing for now. She wishes to live as a hermit, taking from the mountains only what is needed to survive," Devlin informed him.

A mischievous smile pursed Chanos's lips as he brushed away the diagram he had sketched in the dirt. "Is she to become your woman, White Shadow? You have been a long time without one, even though there have been many Apache maidens who would have accepted you. But there was something in the way you held the white man's angel that suggests—"

"You see too much," Devlin cut in, casting his companion a silencing frown. "The woman means nothing to me, nor I to her."

Somehow Chanos doubted that. White Shadow had been offered several comely maids by Cochise and Geronimo in a display of friendship and brotherhood for his attempt to save the Apaches from Burkhart. But White Shadow had rejected them one and all. His vengeance had been enough to sustain him this past year. Chanos had never seen Devlin display any affection for a woman until today. There was something intriguing about the woman with golden hair and sky-blue eyes, he did admit. Even Chanos had felt the fierce fascination when Holos shined down from the sky to form an aureole around Moriah's head. She was, by both the white and red man's standards, a gorgeous creature. She reminded Chanos of the Apache gold that glittered in the stream of the remote chasm to the northwest.

"Geronimo and Cochise are gathering braves from their *rancherías,"* Chanos announced, casting his musings aside. "I will signal you tonight when we are prepared to retaliate against the massacre at Doubtful Canyon."

Devlin nodded mutely as the agile medicine man trotted back down the ledge and disappeared into the brush. For a long moment, Devlin stared at the sun that hung like a red balloon on the western horizon. Before long he would be totally preoccupied with his crusade and it would consume all his time and energy. But until it was time for him to join his blood brothers in butchering Burkhart's camp, he decided he would teach Moriah to survive by her wits. She had a helluva lot to learn in a short time if she was to become a recluse here. This rugged mountain country tested a man's abilities and preyed upon each weakness.

It wasn't that he wanted to spend time with that feisty she-cat, Devlin tried to reassure himself. Moriah was too much of a distraction. But he knew his mind would wander to her at inopportune moments in the weeks to come if he was concerned about her safety. Once she knew the cunning of the Apache she could go her way and he would go his.

But if he needed her to clear up the unfortunate misconceptions that the Apaches had taken her life, he would use her. And if he could utilize Moriah as a means of getting to Burkhart or to protect the Apaches, he would offer her in exchange. She meant nothing to him, after all. In fact, she would probably be more trouble than she could ever be worth to him.

Burkhart was going to pay for his atrocities against the Apaches and for his betrayal of Devlin. For a year Devlin had been hounding the cavalry every chance he got, refusing to let Burkhart forget that White Shadow was out there watching him, waiting to strike. And in time, Devlin hoped he would have enough evidence against the commander to have him court-martialed, stabbed, hung, and poisoned.

Devlin wasn't sure what he expected to find when he returned to the mesa where he had left Moriah. But he certainly wasn't expecting to enjoy a bird's-eye view of the naked nymph who was frolicking in the pool like a carefree mermaid. There was no man on God's green earth who would have turned his head the other way when so close to absolute perfection, and Devlin did the natural thing. He devoured her with his all-consuming gaze.

Although Devlin had sworn he could feel nothing but bitterness and hatred until his crusade against Burkhart ended, he was aroused by the luscious picture Moriah presented as she cut through the water like a swan. The clear depths caressed her shapely figure, revealing each lovely curve and swell. Her skin resembled silk that was studded with diamonds. The rose-tipped crests of her breasts begged for his touch, and he caught fire and burned at the thought of joining her for a refreshing swim.

Devlin gave himself a mental slap for fantasizing about this seductive nymph. He disliked the way his self-control cracked when he gazed upon her, the way his mind conjured up arousing visions, the way his body tingled with needs that had long gone unappeased. It was all too easy to remember how long he had been without a woman. He didn't want to want this sprite, but damnit he did! Maybe there *was* something to the miner's legend of the Angel of the Wind who had come to confront White Shadow. Devlin felt threatened! Not physically, of course, because he could have crushed that saucy tidbit of femininity with his bare hands, but she struck a fierce emotional chord that served to remind him just how human he really was.

Well, he would simply divert himself from more intimate thoughts by teaching Moriah the valuable techniques of survival. She had left herself easy prey to attack. Her rifle lay too far away from her to be of any use if an unwanted intruder pounced on her. She was oblivious to her surroundings, and she was going to have to learn to pay attention or face the consequences.

Like a prowling lion, Devlin crept along the summit and inched down the boulders that overlooked the spring. It wasn't until Moriah had stretched out on her back to float on the water that she noticed the tower of male invincibility looming over her, eclipsing the setting sun. A shocked gasp gushed from her lips as she tried in vain to cover herself from those penetrating golden eyes.

"How dare you spy on me!" she blustered. No man had ever seen her in the altogether, and she turned every shade of the rainbow at the thought of White Shadow knowing as much about her as she knew about herself!

"You are a fool, Moriah," Devlin snapped, hating himself for being aroused by her. But she could boil his blood, that was for sure, and at close range her naked beauty was even more enticing than at a distance. He looked at her and all his well-meaning lectures to himself went up in smoke. Damn her for stirring him, for making him want more than she intended to give!

He had called her a fool before. She hadn't liked it then and she resented it even more now, especially in view of the fact that he was seeing her in the flesh.

When he stalked over to snatch up her damp clothes from the bushes, Moriah asked vehemently. "What the hell do you think you're doing?" A rash of obscenities followed the question, words Moriah had heard from men but had never before voiced. This seemed the perfect time to voice them!

"Pay attention and learn what I can teach you," Devlin demanded sharply.

To her amazement, he scraped together enough wood and brush for a small campfire and propped a makeshift clothesline above it. Employing the pistol he carried in his belt, he mashed loose gun powder into the barrel, covered the weapon with the skillet Moriah had stolen from Clyde Finnegan, and muffled the discharging Colt. When he removed the skillet, fire crackled on the leaves.

"The loose powder sparks the kindling," he explained in a matter-of-fact tone. "If you have a tinderbox you can use it to ignite your fires. The Apache uses a small fire and sets it in secluded nooks that cannot be seen from a distance. He lingers close enough to enjoy the heat when the cool evening air settles over the mountains. But a large fire attracts trouble, the last thing you need since you haven't the skills to fend for yourself yet."

Moriah was taking his words to heart, but she was still furious. He had stolen her clothes and left her standing in the pool, wearing nothing but a frustrated frown.

Devlin was cautious not to spare the luscious pixie more than an occasional glance while he spoke. He had seen quite enough of Moriah already and his heart was on the verge of exploding.

"Your food is provided from piñon nuts, mescal, and berries. The liquid from the cactus will quench your thirst when you are far from the secluded springs that can be found in the mountains. You must learn the location of each spring, of every canyon and summit. You must be familiar with every path and where it leads—*away* from danger or *into* it."

Forcing himself to focus on her blushing face rather than her appetizing body, Devlin got up from his crouch at the campfire. "If you fear you are being followed, learn to mimic the call of the owl. The Apaches have a special fear of owls; their presence rattles the Indians. They believe the ghosts of the dead rise to inhabit the body of an owl. As I said, there are vicious Indians as well as whites. You must learn to distinguish at a glance which is friend and which is foe. And until you have gained respect and acceptance, every two- and four-legged creature will be your enemy."

Devlin paced like a restless tiger, pausing occasionally to survey the lavender shadows that slid down the eastern slopes of the mountains. "When food is scarce the Apache will eat cougars, lizards, and rats. Although they shun eating fish because it is a bad omen, there are many in the streams hereabout if you are adept in catching them. Neither will the Apaches eat bear meat. Since bears can walk erect, the

Indians believe the creatures might be the reincarnation of an evil person. If an Apache is attacked by a bear and is forced to kill it, he lets the carcass lie."

Moriah gagged on the thought of dining on a skinny rat, but she had no time to dwell on the distasteful dish when White Shadow prowled around, shooting her hasty glances that seared over her exposed flesh like a hot branding iron. Criminey, why wouldn't he just go away and let her wade from the spring with what little dignity she could muster? He was purposely humiliating her, curse him. True, he had a great deal to teach her and she had a great deal to learn, but not while she was standing stark naked in the pool!

"You have to learn absolute independence and become adept with all sorts of weapons if you are to survive," Devlin went on. "Stamina and fortitude are essential in this rugged terrain. You must develop a sixth sense that allows you to anticipate danger. And you must learn to expect the unexpected."

"I want to get out of here!" Moriah finally exploded, her embarrassment triggering her volatile temper.

Devlin pivoted to face her, his golden-brown eyes making a thorough sweep of her luscious figure. "No one is stopping you from coming ashore," he said as blandly as possible, considering her arousing effect on him. "I can't see more of you than I have already seen."

Good God, it was difficult to be reasonable when his male instincts were warring with his logic. He stared at this incredibly lovely vixen and he burned all over. But he would die before he let her know that!

"I am not about to set foot on the bank until you turn your back!" she spouted.

He darted her a devilish grin that revealed pearly

white teeth. "Then you are a fool, Moriah."

"So you keep telling me, damn you," she railed in frustration. "Perhaps you are accustomed to sharing the company of naked women, but I am not accustomed to sharing company when I'm bathing—!"

When the fire began to produce an excessive amount of smoke, Moriah craned her neck around the masculine obstruction that loomed in front of her. To her shock and dismay she watched the only set of clothes she owned go up in flames.

Cursing a blue streak, Devlin spun about to salvage the paltry remnants of the garments he had laid out to dry above the campfire. Now the singed fragments of cloth would serve only as rags.

Moriah employed Devlin's distraction to scurry ashore and crouch beneath the scrub brush, meager cover though it provided.

When Devlin pivoted around, Moriah was nowhere to be seen. He searched the underbrush with eagle eyes. "You have learned your second lesson well," he congratulated as he strode toward her hiding place. "Even the smallest bush can conceal you when danger approaches. Knowing that might one day save your life."

Damn the man! He hadn't even apologized for destroying her only set of clothes. "And just what was the first lesson?" she ground out acrimoniously.

"Never get caught with your breeches down," he replied with a teasing smile.

Had Moriah been dressed, she would have leapt from the bush and strangled the life out of this infuriating rascal. "Thanks to you, I have no breeches, no shirt, no gown. Nothing!" she spewed furiously. "For a man who claims to know everything there is to know about surviving in these mountains, you don't know beans about drying clothes! And don't you dare tell me my charred garments will become my supper. That sounds like something you might say. Everything has its purpose—or some such ridiculous cliché."

"Everything *does* have a purpose," he declared with great conviction.

His golden eyes danced with amusement. Even when this fiery beauty was angry she had the knack of putting a smile on his lips. She was salve for his wounded soul. Still chuckling at Moriah's sassy disposition, Devlin ambled over to retrieve the saddlebag that held what was left of her food rations. To her bewilderment, he hurled the leather pouch over the cliff and out of sight.

Moriah stared at him as if he were a lunatic.

"Now you go fetch it," he ordered before swaggering away. "And tend the fire while I hunt game for supper."

Muttering in exasperation, Moriah peeked around the scratchy bush to ensure that the ornery devil had disappeared before she exposed herself. Knowing him, he would probably slither under a rock to spy on her while she was unaware. What an exasperating man he was! His consideration for her couldn't fill a thimble. And there was something else that galled her beyond belief. He had seen her in the buff and she had no secrets from him, yet she still knew very little about him. Not that she wanted him to strip naked, mind you. She most certainly did not! But for crying out loud, she didn't know what truly motivated this man, where he had come from, or what he was planning. One thing she was sure of was that a man such as he would play every situation to his advantage, if his dealings with her were any indication.

Moriah was relieved that White Shadow hadn't

made an attempt to seduce her while she was so vulnerable. Most men would have taken unfair advantage, but White Shadow had made little of her lack of clothing. He was clearly a man with nerves of steel, a man of unlimited resourcefulness. He could teach her everything she needed to know to survive and a few things about men that she had religiously avoided . . .

She gave herself a mental swat for allowing her mind to detour down such a sordid avenue. White Shadow claimed he didn't want her body to appease his lust. He had kissed the breath out of her, but he hadn't overpowered her when he had the chance. Why hadn't he? Most men would have leaped at the opportunity of stealing more than a kiss if they could get away with it.

And why did he take it upon himself to be the one to instruct her on how to live in the mountains? She certainly hadn't asked for his guidance, only his absence and the right to fend for herself. She supposed she should thank him for what he was trying to do, but she didn't feel grateful when the blundering dolt had burned her only set of clothes and hurled her supplies off the cliff for no other reason than to determine if she had the gumption and ability to retrieve them!

"Fetch them indeed!" Moriah grumbled, stamping a bare foot and then cursing when she trounced on a thorn. Muttering a zillion disrespectful epithets to White Shadow's name, Moriah limped over to snatch up the sheet she had swiped from Clyde. Wrapping the flimsy fabric around her, she managed to create a short toga that stretched diagonally across her chest and tied at one shoulder. The improvised garment was twisted around her waist and hips, leaving her back and legs bare. It was far better than running around stark naked, she reckoned.

When Moriah had slipped on her shoes, she inched over the rim of the chasm to locate the saddlebag. Her gaze fell the full two hundred feet to the valley floor and her stomach leaped to her throat. It wasn't that she was afraid of heights exactly, but she had a great respect for it—the *fall*, that is, not the height.

Mustering her courage, Moriah eased a leg over the ledge and dug her nails into the small crevices in the rock. Her gaze scanned the stone wall below her, mentally plotting the least dangerous path of descent to the pouch that lay some thirty feet below her.

It seemed to take hours for her to inch down the perilous slope, weaving to and fro to avoid a nasty fall. But finally Moriah grasped the saddlebag. A triumphant smile pursed her lips as she slung the pouch over her bare shoulder. She had succeeded in her mission without breaking her neck. Now, if only she could scale the steep canyon wall and return to the spring, she would really have something to boast about!

Arduous though it was, Moriah made the climb to safety. For five full minutes she sat there gasping for breath. It would take time to develop endurance in the higher elevations, to adapt to this unfamiliar way of life. But she *would* adapt, she vowed firmly. If the Lord hadn't wanted her here, he would have seen to it that she was someplace else . . .

A gasp of dismay rushed from her lips when she realized the campfire had nearly burned itself out while she was scaling the canyon wall. Scrambling to her feet, she dashed madly about, gathering kindling to keep the blaze alive until she could retrieve more wood.

In a state of total exhaustion, Moriah collapsed beside the fire as the waning light trickled over the craggy peaks. The blue-violet mountains, which were partly covered with pine and fir, and the orange-brown mesas, now appeared to darken to gray, purple, and brown in the shadows cast by sunset. The twinkle of starlight glittered in the darkening sky.

Moriah sighed appreciatively. There was something pacifying about her surroundings that was helping to smooth the wrinkles from her troubled soul. For the first time in years she was at peace with herself, even though she still harbored a fierce vengeance toward Ruby and Vance Thatcher.

Somehow she would have her revenge, just as White Shadow intended to have his. Moriah had turned the other cheek more times than she cared to count in her dealings with the Thatchers. They would be sorry for what they tried to do to her!

As the last rays of sunshine melted into moonshadows, Moriah propped herself against the boulders that surrounded the spring and conjured up a hundred methods of torture to apply to the Thatchers when she returned to civilization to confront them.

Chapter 5

The muted sound of approaching footsteps sent Moriah diving for her rifle. Rolling over, she braced herself on her elbow and aimed at the unidentified sounds that shattered the silence. Her shoulders slumped in relief when White Shadow moseyed down the path with a skinned rabbit dangling from his fingertips. His astute gaze swept the campsite and he nodded in satisfaction.

"You are learning, tigress," he complimented. "Now, if only you knew how to reload your useless rifle you might be able to protect yourself to some degree." His penetrating gaze roamed over her make-shift toga. "Nice dress," he added with a smirk.

It was irritating the way he flattered her one second and ridiculed her the next. What did he expect, for her to become as adept as he was overnight? And he hadn't even bothered to make mention of the fact that she had scaled the canyon walls like a spider to retrieve her pouch. That in itself was a victorious feat that boosted her self-confidence . . .

Her thoughts trailed off when she noticed the rolled blankets he carried under one brawny arm and the bulging saddlebag that was slung over one granite shoulder. Did he intend to spend the night here . . . with her? No chance! There were enough ridges in these mountains for him to bed down on one of his own!

"This is my campsite," Moriah informed him in no uncertain terms. "You aren't sleeping here."

Unruffled by her terse declaration, Devlin tossed his gear aside and laid the rabbit over the fire to roast. He casually reached into his pouch to fish out the berries he had picked on his way back to camp.

"If you think I'll molest you, you are worrying for naught," he calmly announced. He popped a berry into his mouth and chewed upon it. "I kissed you and you kissed me back. That was more than enough."

And just what, pray tell, was that supposed to mean? That her lack of experience bored him? Left him unmoved? Well, she was twice as bored and unmoved by their embrace as he was. So there!

"Well, thank you very much for the insult," she bit off. "I wasn't all that fond of kissing you, either, if you want to know."

He gave her a hard, probing look that sought out the secrets of her private thoughts. In his estimation, she looked more indignant than relieved. "Make up your mind what you want, Moriah. My body or your unblemished virtues . . . if you have any left to lose, that is."

Moriah realized, a moment too late, that was a foolish thing for her to do. Her arm swished through the air to smack him on the same cheek she had whacked earlier in the day. But this time Devlin caught her arm before she could strike and pressured her thumb backward until she yelped in pain.

"You wouldn't be insulted if your vanity wasn't smarting," he growled, unsure if he was more agitated with her quicksilver temper or his vivid awareness of this saucy wildcat draped in a sheet that did more to tantalize than conceal. "So what if most men are attracted to you, or you to them? You are a beautiful woman. What do you expect? To be ignored?"

"I would prefer it, yes," she spluttered.

"Well, it isn't going to happen," he told her frankly. "You should learn to live with your alluring appearance and utilize men's weaknesses for you to your advantage instead of leaping to a stubborn defense. Use your beauty as a distraction to gain the upper hand. Like this . . ."

He drew her small hand into his own and led her toward him. "Put your arms around my hips." When Moriah eyed him dubiously, he expelled an impatient sigh. "Are you going to learn what I can teach you or behave like a contrary mule?"

Begrudgingly, she did as she was told. But standing this close to this man did incredible things to her. It was difficult to concentrate when her betraying body savored his manly fragrance and she tingled in response to his touch.

"A man is most vulnerable now," he murmured, his voice raspy with desire he didn't want to feel for this fiery nymph. "You could kick me to my knees and I would be incapacitated long enough for you to escape."

"I have done that on several occasions. Thrice this week, as a matter of fact," Moriah bleated, her voice quivering with remembered sensations from their previous embrace. "My stepfather, Lyle Burkhart, and Clyde Finnegan."

Although Devlin never changed expression, the mention of Burkhart's name provoked him to swear to himself. That lusty bastard had obviously forced himself on this stunning minx and she had gouged him in the privates. Good for her.

Discarding the spiteful thought, Devlin gazed down into her clear blue eyes. "Never walk away from trouble and don't let it walk away from you, either. That only gives it the chance to sneak up on you when you are unprepared. Use your powers of observation long before you approach a man or he approaches you. Make note where he stashes his weapons in case you want to relieve him of them." He elevated a quizzical brow. "Where's my dagger?"

"Here," she responded, touching the left side of his hip. She grimaced at the unexpected tremor of pleasure that mere contact with this awesome man aroused in her.

"And my pistol?" he inquired, forcing himself to breathe normally while his heart was prancing around his chest like a flighty stallion.

"Here." She tapped his right hip and cursed her awareness of the man who held her tenderly in the circle of his arms.

Moriah swallowed hard as he reached beneath her chin, forcing her to stare into those tawny eyes that were fanned by thick velvet lashes.

"Kiss me," he commanded huskily. "And take whichever weapon suits you when you feel me let my guard down."

Upon command, she pushed up on tiptoe to compensate for the difference in their height. Moriah had to force herself to concentrate on her objective rather than the erotic feel of his moist lips moving expertly over hers. Employing the technique he had used on her earlier in the day, her probing tongue teased his teeth and then investigated the inner softness of his mouth. She felt his body shudder in response when she took the initiative, felt his hands begin to glide over her hips in an exploring caress.

With the quickness of a striking snake, she lifted her knee as she had done so often in the past. Simultaneously, she snatched the pistol from his belt. With an agonized groan, Devlin doubled over to protect his private parts from another blow. When he did, Moriah clasped both hands around the pistol and her arms shot upward, catching him in the chin. The unexpected blow to the jaw caused his head to snap backward.

In the batting of an eyelash, she leaped back to watch Devlin's knees fold up like an accordion. The color seeped from beneath his deep tan and his breath came in ragged spurts.

"Are you all right?" she questioned. Perhaps the blows she had delivered were more painful than she imagined.

"Hell no, I'm *not* all right," Devlin croaked, his voice one octave higher than normal. Apparently, Moriah had plenty of practice in the art of self-defense. She was quick as a cat. With a bit more instruction she could become her own lethal weapon! Good God, he felt nauseated. Another blow like that and he would be incapacitated for the rest of his life!

"I'm sorry. I didn't mean to . . ." she tried to apologize.

Moriah squawked when she stepped within arm's reach to offer comfort. Devlin grasped her ankle, knocking her legs out from under her. His left hand batted away the pistol and he fell upon her, forcing her breath out in a whoosh. She clutched at his hand, attempting to use the leverage of his thumb and inflict pain on him, just as he had done to her. But she was no match for his superior strength.

To compound her frustration, her body reacted to the feel of his muscular flesh pressing intimately into hers instead of his feigned attack intended to remind her that she was never to let her guard down. She was intensely aware of the sleek columns of his thighs resting between hers, his hips meshed to hers. Criminey, she shouldn't have been so aroused by the feel of his masculine contours!

The gnawing ache in the pit of her belly burned and the peaks of her breasts tingled as his chest glided over hers. Self-defense was suddenly the farthest thing from Moriah's mind. She remembered with shocking clarity how masterfully he could kiss and how intensely she responded to his skillful touch. When his powerful body was half-covering hers, he could tear all thought from her mind and leave her questioning her ability to resist him.

It was unlike Moriah to succumb when she had fought for so long to preserve her virtues. But this sinewy rake made her want things she had never wanted from a man. She couldn't recall ever being tempted to explore the sensual realm of desire, but it seemed natural that this magnificent man who matched these rugged mountains should be the one to teach her about passion. He was, after all, teaching her everything else. At least she would know what she had purposely avoided all these years, she reckoned. She would have experienced all the emotions in the human spectrum—joy, terror, grief, despair . . . and desire.

"The knife, Moriah," Devlin growled when she stared up at him in a way that cut into his very soul. "Take my dagger or perish. I'm your enemy, not your lover . . ."

His lips descended on hers, and more forcefully than before. His powerful body ground into hers, moving suggestively against her, leaving her to burn on a hot compelling flame. His hands speared beneath her makeshift gown, sliding the sheet up to her hip, investigating the silky flesh of her thigh.

Her legs wouldn't move. Her skin quivered beneath his possessive touch and her breath came in irregular spurts. She couldn't think straight when he assaulted her with his bold, persuasive caresses.

What a devil he was! He could make her naive body respond when common sense demanded that she lash out at him. He had somehow broken her barrier of defense. Moriah wasn't sure if the crackling noise that reached her ears came from the campfire or her seared flesh. She felt like dry kindling touched by a blazing torch.

His mouth plundered hers, stealing the last of her breath. His adventurous caresses flooded and receded, leaving more fires burning on her quivering flesh. His hands cupped her breasts, causing her to arch toward him in shameless abandon. A tiny whimper tripped from her lips when she felt herself melting into a pool of frustrated desire.

"The knife, damn you," Devlin muttered, hating himself for feeling so completely out of control.

This was supposed to be a lesson in self-preservation, not passion. But somehow the two had gotten entangled. Suddenly he was wanting to bury himself in this luscious bundle of femininity and call an end to his celibacy.

Moriah's logic came rushing back in the nick of time. With lightning quickness, she grasped the blade and rammed it against his rib. Unexpected tears sprang to her eyes as she shoved against his rock-hard shoulder and used the knife to force him away. With a strangled gulp, Moriah tugged the tangled tresses from her face and rammed her heel into his belly until he pushed back onto his knees.

Devlin stared down at her, watching the conflicting emotions cross her flushed face, noting the trembling of her kiss-swollen lips. Good God, he felt as shaky as a leaf in a windstorm! He could have taken Moriah just now and he wasn't sure she would have stopped him. He knew he would only have been appeasing a need he had ignored for endless months. And he would have discovered if this was her first time with a man. She thoroughly confused him. At times she reacted like a cautious virgin and at other times she seemed a dozen different passions about to erupt.

Panting to catch her breath, Moriah staggered to her feet, battling for hard-won composure. "Damn you," she hissed as she flung the dagger in the dirt and stomped over to tend the rabbit that roasted over the fire.

The man was positively devastating! Even as willful as Moriah had always been, she couldn't quite counter the phenomenal spell White Shadow had cast upon her. What was there about him that crumbled her defenses and broke every rule she had established about men?

"That is the incorrect way to hurl a knife," Devlin pointed out when he recovered his powers of speech. He still felt a little shaky from the aftereffects of their ardent embrace and a *lot* aroused by their intimate contact.

"I don't want to learn any more tonight," she snapped brusquely, refusing to look at him for fear he would decipher the frustrated passion in her eyes.

"Do you want to talk about what just happened?" he questioned as he rolled agilely to his feet.

"No," she muttered self-consciously.

"Good, neither do I." He studied Moriah's shapely figure in the flickering firelight. "Then suppose we talk about who tried to kill you and then blamed the Apaches for the attack."

Her hand stalled in midair. She wheeled, her luminous eyes riveting on his chiseled features. "How did you know about that?"

He shrugged enigmatically. "As the legend goes, White Shadow knows all."

"Just who are you . . . really? Where did you come from?" she questioned.

Devlin hesitated, wondering why he felt compelled to tell her the truth. "The name is Devlin Granger," he finally said, dropping into an exaggerated bow.

He stated his name as if that explained everything. But it didn't—not to Moriah's satisfaction.

"You are a blood brother to the Apaches. That much I know from your headbands, beaded braiding, buckskin clothes, and the other paraphernalia," she smirked. "Tell me something I don't know already about you."

"What is this?" Devlin sputtered explosively. "The Spanish Inquisition?"

"What are you supposed to be, Devlin Granger? The modern-day version of Robin Hood who takes from the whites and gives to the Apaches?" she prodded relentlessly.

"No, damnit—I'm trying to see justice served and ensure that the Apaches are not blamed for crimes they haven't committed, especially after we whites took everything from the Indians that was worth having!" he growled bitterly.

Good God, this woman could put him in a snit so quickly it amazed him. Devlin was usually the epitome of self-control and calculated logic. But his fierce physical attraction to this sprite with her rapier wit and flashing temper unhinged him. He never quite felt in control when he was near her. Luckily, their association would be of short duration, he consoled himself.

"Perhaps I should join up with the Apaches, since we're paddling the same canoe, so to speak." She expelled a heavy sigh. "I feel a little put upon and misunderstood myself."

"What happened, Moriah?"

His tone expressed genuine interest in her plight. Moriah had never had anyone with whom she could share her innermost thoughts or her problems. Ruby had spitefully prevented her from enjoying friendships with girls her own age. There were always chores to do that Ruby considered beneath *her*. Therefore, Moriah was expected to tend to them while Ruby primped and preened herself like a vain peacock.

"My stepfather tried to kill me so he and his wife could keep my inheritance money to themselves," she explained matter-of-factly as she wandered around the spring. "They sold my ranch in Texas before I came of age to assume my own affairs. It was all my stepmother Ruby's idea. She saw her chance to dispose of me and blame the Apaches. My stepfather, Vance, would never have come up with the scheme by himself. He's short of brains.

"When he tried to strangle me, I pretended to be dead and he didn't bother to check my pulse before he tied me to a piece of driftwood and sent me downstream. Fortunately, the clever witch Ruby wasn't there telling him every move to make."

"I'm sorry," Devlin said, watching her shrug off his sympathy as if she had no need of it.

"I didn't ask for their love, only a little consideration," she said dully. "In a way, what they attempted to do to me was a blessing in disguise. I had nothing before and I have nothing now except my cherished freedom. Every sort of refuge has its price, I suppose. I sacrificed my stolen inheritance for the right to live where and how I wish—away from betrayal and my so-called family."

Her thick lashes swept up to survey Devlin's profile in the firelight. "You aren't going to tell me anything about yourself, are you?"

"For your own protection, no," he informed her quietly. "There are those who want my head on a platter, just as I want theirs. The less you know the better."

"My enemy—not my lover . . . not even my friend," she said with a resigned sigh. "I never had one before. I suppose it's a little late to expect to find one now."

Devlin detested the people who had transformed this lovely nymph into such a dreadful cynic—all those insensitive individuals who had made her life a torment. She had been robbed, betrayed, and stifled. It was no wonder her goal was to become a dedicated hermit.

He and Moriah were a great deal alike in some aspects and worlds apart in others. Devlin had known love and friendship and brotherhood until that fateful day more than a year ago when he had been betrayed and played as a pawn. Since that time he reserved his trust only for those who earned it. But unlike Moriah, he did have some place to go—a life he could anticipate when his crusade was over. But both of them were afraid to care for fear of being hurt again, afraid to get too close for fear of the pain that could cut the soul like the sharpest of knives. Trust made a man too vulnerable. Devlin had learned that the hard way. It was glaringly apparent that Moriah had, too.

While they ate, Devlin elaborated on the techniques of enduring in the rugged mountains, explained the signs that alerted him to approaching storms and unwelcome visitors, of all the Apache traditions that could be of use to her.

When Moriah rolled out her pallet, Devlin placed himself a safe distance away, so as not to tempt himself more than he already was . . . He lay with his head cushioned on his linked fingers, studying the Big Dipper that was the timepiece of the Apaches, waiting until he heard Moriah's steady breathing. When he was certain she was sound asleep, he got up, picked up his rifle and ammunition, and stole silently into the night.

Speaking in the Apache tongue, Devlin instructed the party of warriors to descend from the mesa. With Chanos and his braves flanking him, Devlin led his warriors down the shadowed path to the row of canvas tents that gleamed in the moonlight. His objective was to relieve Commander Burkhart of his cavalry mounts and supplies. Although he longed to attack Burkhart and send him on a one-way trip to hell, the incident would provoke the Army to wage a full-scale war on the Apaches. The tribe had steadily dwindled, thanks to the Mexican bounty on Apache scalps, their Indian slave trade, and General Carleton's plan to exterminate or confine every Indian in the territory. Geronimo had grimly predicted that the Apaches would die a slow, agonizing death while they tried to retaliate against the atrocities. But they would continue to fight valiantly for the right to live on land that had been theirs since the beginning of time.

And although it was an uphill battle, Devlin refused to abandon the Apaches until the military officials realized how unjustly they were treating the Indians. No matter what went wrong, the Apaches were accused of evil doing. They were blamed for massacres they didn't commit, accused of stealing livestock when it was, in fact, Mexican and American thieves who swiped the horses and cattle for profit. And one of the worst offenders in the Army was Lyle Burkhart, whose cruel slaughters never reached the proper military authorities. The man wasn't fit to command, and he always blamed the Apaches for inciting battles when it was the other way around.

Devlin longed to run a lance through Burkhart's hard heart. But the time wasn't right, not yet, not until the evidence had been gathered and sent to the authorities to clear Devlin's name and punish Burkhart for his murderous raids on innocent Apache women and children.

Yes, the Indians had killed and plundered in retaliation against the massacres of the tribe, but it was the white man who had invented scalping. No treachery and cruelty had been left unused by whites in their dealings with the Indians. The Apaches had attempted to make peace with the Americans and they were repaid by having Mangas Coloradas tortured and murdered. It was little wonder the Apaches were so wary of the whites, who took without giving in return. Lord, what a misnomer the term "Indian giver" was! It was the whites who made empty promises and went back on their word where the Indians were concerned.

Greedy Americans had poisoned the tribes with strichnine, murdered their women and children, and purposely exposed them to the white man's diseases in order to annihilate the Indians. The word treachery had been unknown to the Apaches until the Americans and Mexicans had taught them the meaning of it.

Curbing his bitter thoughts, Devlin signaled for the warriors to stalk the line of horses. Once the guards had been disposed of by a sound thump of rocks, the braves led the horses away, immobilizing Burkhart's patrol. Devlin also plundered the supply tent to dole out food for the braves who had lost their possessions and loved ones in the most recent massacre.

This was yet another silent skirmish to prevent Burkhart from taking more lives. To Devlin it was meager compensation. But he needed time to gather the evidence against Burkhart without letting the Apaches take the blame for starting another dangerous conflict.

Leaving the white-quilled arrow in taunting reminder of his midnight visit, Devlin and his companions led the horses into the mountains. He would have delighted in seeing the expression on Burkhart's face when he awoke to find his mounts and supplies missing. But in due time they would meet face-to-face, Devlin promised himself. His solace came in knowing the ruthless commander would be cursing White Shadow a dozen times over.

Chapter 6

The crunch of rock underfoot brought Moriah slowly awake. Lying as still as a corpse, she waited to determine the source of the footsteps. A ripple of whispers drifted in the breeze and she reached for the rifle that lay inches away from her fingertips. Her heart skipped a beat when she glanced over to see that Devlin's pallet had been abandoned. Her mind raced frantically, trying to recall everything he had taught her and how she could use the information to her advantage.

The campfire had died hours ago and the moonlight was all that illuminated the area. Moriah cursed the white sheet that had become the only clothing she had. She knew it reflected the light and made her an easy mark for unwelcome visitors. The fact that she had made camp beside a spring was a mistake, she realized. Anyone who traveled the area in search of copper, silver, or gold would probably be familiar with its location, not to mention the Apaches who stalked the mountain passes.

If she survived whatever danger approached, she would make a mental note to confine herself to obscure canyons in the future.

A lump constricted her throat when she heard the rustle of bushes some twenty feet away from where she lay.

Mick Jeffries crouched behind the underbrush beside his partner. He stared in confusion at the delicious form of a woman whose golden hair shimmered with moonbeams. "I swear she looks just like Finnegan's angel," he whispered to his wide-eyed companion.

Kent Hanes nodded in agreement. The white gown that lay diagonally across Moriah's breasts, baring both shoulders, caused a warm throb to pulsate through his loins. It had been a long time since Kent had seen anything quite so exquisite. This vision of loveliness must surely be the Angel of the Wind, he decided.

"What are we gonna do if we catch her?" Kent murmured to his older associate.

A toothy grin split Mick's whiskered face. "If you don't know the answer to that question, boy, you've got a lot to learn."

Kent blinked like a disturbed owl. "We ain't gonna molest no angel! That ain't proper."

"We don't know if she really is one for sure," Mick grumbled as he quietly loaded his rifle. "But you and me is gonna find out. And if she ain't no cherub, I get her first."

The breeze delivered the hushed words of the men to Moriah. Devlin had instructed her to depend on her wits. Now, if only she could stop shaking long enough to think straight! Perhaps if she preyed on their superstitious minds she could escape unscathed. Her only hope was that these varmints were as engrossed in legends and myths as Clyde Finnegan was. If they weren't, she'd *make* them believe in disembodied spirits, she promised herself determinedly.

Humming a soft tune, Moriah rose from her pallet like a spirit rising from the grave. It was her intent to bewitch the unwelcome visitors with a swirling, gliding dance that would make them question whether she was flesh or spirit. She utilized every dance step she had ever learned or seen executed at the few social gatherings Ruby had allowed her to attend.

With sublime feminine grace, Moriah gradually made her way toward the spring, which was protected on one side by huge slabs of rock. Still humming an enchanting melody, she fluttered down behind the first boulder and then hurriedly scuttled along the narrow passage to rise above another stone slab that was located some fifteen feet away.

Mick's mouth dropped open and Kent's hand stalled in midair as they watched the vision disappear and then materialize from nowhere. The moonlight and shadows gave the impression that this captivating siren could reappear at will. Moriah preyed on the illusion—distracting them and then taking flight to rise from the boulders at distant locations around the spring.

The sparkling silver pool enhanced her performance by casting her reflection on the water. For five minutes she executed her mystifying disappearing act, hoping the intruders would be intrigued by the lulling melody and bedeviled by her dance.

Knowing the exact spot where the pool was only ankle-deep, Moriah pretended to dance on the water—pirouetting, twirling and, gliding around the perimeters of the spring like a floating spirit. Momentarily, she disappeared behind a boulder and then rose like a genie vaporizing from a bottle onto a boulder that was situated high above the spring. The trickling spring bubbled between the rocks beside her, tumbling down like a ribbon of silver. The full moon hung behind her like a glowing white ball, silhouetting her curvaceous form, and provoking Kent and Mick to sigh in masculine admiration.

Never in all his life had Kent beheld such an enchanting vision of perfection. This graceful angel was what dreams were made of. Everything Clyde Finnegan had said about her was true! She moved like the wind. She was poetry in motion and she had the voice of a luring siren.

"She can't be human," Kent insisted. "Clyde was right. I think we'd best get out of here before we—"

Mick waved him to silence. If this goddess was an angel, he wanted a closer look . . . a touch . . . Her graceful dance caused tantalizing visions to spin in his head.

"Come on, kid," Mick commanded as he sneaked from the brush to a nearby boulder.

But Kent didn't budge from his spot. To him, there was something sacrilegious about disturbing an angel.

"Come on, coward," Mick snapped impatiently.

Kent gave his unkempt head of hair a negative shake. He wasn't about to bring heaven's wrath down upon himself. There were some things a man didn't do, and molesting heavenly messengers was one of them!

"I ain't goin' no closer than this," Kent said stubbornly.

Moriah noticed the shadowy figure that skulked to the boulder that was clustered with underbrush. Damn, if he ventured too close, she wouldn't be sure of her next move. She raised her arms as if she were testing her invisible wings to soar from her perch above the spring and silently prayed the intruder would keep his distance.

"Who dares approach this angel?" A deep, rumbling voice came out of nowhere and echoed around the canyon like the crack of thunder.

Mick dived behind the boulder and Kent sat down before he fell down. Moriah, who was just as startled by the booming voice, very nearly toppled off her precarious perch.

The sound of pebbles skitted across the empty space that separated Kent and Mick. Kent's eyes bulged when hailstones of gold rained down from the moonlit sky. His heart was thudding so furiously that he swore it would beat him to death.

Even as skeptical as Mick Jeffries was, he was having serious misgivings about sneaking up on the resident angel of Black Mountain. A shocked squeak erupted from Mick's lips when a flame shot across the sky and rustled into the bush beside him. Suddenly the brush was blazing and his only recourse was either to dive to safety or become a human torch.

"Take your treasure and be gone," the ominous voice bellowed out of the darkness. "You have wandered onto ground where only angels tread . . ."

The hokey scheme worked superbly. Darkness and the looming mountains made a perfect backdrop for the angel who was perched on the ridge and the rumbling voice that didn't seem to belong to a human. The smoldering bush that reached skyward like golden fingers weaving incantations in the night lent credence that the spring was inhabited by supernatural spirits.

Devlin had returned from his late-night siege of Burkhart's camp to see two figures prowling Moriah's campsite. He had sat there for a moment, reviewing his choices. When Moriah began her eerie performance, he had smiled and watched with fascinated disbelief. She was indeed a quick learner and had taken Devlin's words to heart, preying upon the weakness of the intruders.

The miners were a superstitious lot who were known to see things that weren't really there and elaborate on what they thought they saw. Devlin had gone into disguise a dozen times to frequent Santa Rita del Cobra and Piños Altos. He had heard the far-fetched tales circulating about White Shadow, as well as the wholloping yarns about miners being visited by skeletons with lanterns dangling from their sunken chests. He had listened to prospectors relate stories about looming spirits that guarded the rich veins of ore that were forbidden to man. He had heard yarns about the mine-dwelling gnomes who supposedly stood two feet high and dressed in leather jackets, peaked hats, and pointed slippers. The gnomes supposedly played spiteful tricks on prospectors who dared to invade their domain and steal their pots of gold. Stories of phantoms who protected Montezuma's treasure and the seven cities of gold ran rampant in the mining camps. The prospectors were wary of the supernatural and they had heard enough tales to leave them wondering if there were such things as gnomes and phantoms and avenging spirits.

At the sight of the flaming bush and the sound of the thundering voice, Mick and Kent scooped up the gold nuggets and took off like discharging cannonballs. They didn't slow their swift pace until they were halfway down the mountain and concealed in the canopy of pine and fir trees.

"I told you we was askin' for trouble," Kent grumbled to his partner.

Mick didn't make a peep. He had scoffed at Clyde Finnegan's tale of the angel with golden hair and sky-blue eyes, just as he had scoffed when the windy prospector claimed to have seen gnomes and leprechauns in his native Ireland. But after suffering a heart seizure and very nearly being burnt to a crisp, Mick was beginning to believe he had indeed been visited by a disembodied spirit at Angel Spring.

Shakily, he unfolded his fist to peer at the glistening gold stones that had laid a path to safety. "Maybe Clyde ain't a bag of wind after all," he mused aloud.

"Maybe?" Kent chirped like a cricket. "There ain't no doubt about it. That was Moriah—Angel of the Wind—who guards the Black Mountains. She scatters gold as she goes and presents it to those who happen upon her, just like Clyde said."

Mick wasn't quite so carried away as Kent, but nor could he discount what he had seen. The vision must surely have been a wandering spirit. A *woman* would never ascend into the mountains of her own free will. Moriah *was* the Angel of the Wind, and disturbing her could bring a man bad luck. Mick promised himself then and there that he would never think an evil thought about the lovely angel ever again!

An annoyed frown knitted Moriah's brow as she inched down the ladder of rocks. "It certainly took you long enough to come to my rescue. Where have you been?" she questioned the shadows.

Devlin rose up above her on the towering precipice and then agilely leaped his way down to the spring. "You didn't need my help," he replied matter-of-factly. "You were doing splendidly without me."

"I was running short on magical tricks," she grumbled as she plopped down on her bedroll to massage her bare feet that felt like human pincushions.

It annoyed her that Devlin hadn't bothered to ask if

she was all right. She should have been accustomed to lack of concern after living with the Thatchers for the past few years. But it still hurt that Devlin didn't inquire about her, just as he hadn't asked if she had had difficulty climbing down the canyon wall to retrieve her pouch. He seemed to just naturally assume that she would meet with success on each endeavor.

"I had some business to transact," he said cryptically.

"I know," she muttered in a begrudging tone. "And I'm not supposed to ask where your nocturnal prowling took you, I assume."

"Precisely." Devlin sank down Indian-style beside her and laid two garments across her lap. "These aren't particularly becoming articles of clothing, but they will have to suffice for a time."

Moriah shook out the white linen shirt and breeches that looked suspiciously like a cavalryman's uniform. She wasn't sure she wanted to know what happened to the man that had once worn them . . .

Her thoughts dispersed when the gentle touch of Devlin's hand cupped her chin, lifting her eyes to his.

"You gave a very convincing performance, angel," he murmured with the faintest hint of a smile. "You're learning. After a few more lessons you really will be ready to test your wings."

His touch always seemed to affect her in the most phenomenal way, no matter how careless or harmless the gesture. It altered her breathing and made her want something she wasn't sure she fully understood. And when this mysterious man was this close, Moriah had difficulty controlling the accelerated beat of her heart and the warm flood of pleasure that surged through her.

To counteract his mystical spell, Moriah pushed

his lingering fingers away. "How did you re-create the burning bush?" she inquired to shatter the electrifying silence and the devastating effect of his nearness.

Devlin's broad shoulders lifted and dropped in a nonchalant shrug. "I merely tied a dried weed to my arrow, lit it from the tinderbox, and shot it into the brush. Nothing very imaginative, but it did serve its purpose," he modestly explained.

"I'll make a note to try your technique in case any other unwanted visitors come prowling around," she said in a flippant tone.

"The first thing you have to do is learn to handle a bow and arrow," he smirked. "You can't always dance your way out of difficulty, light on your feet though you are."

"Don't you ever get tired of being all-knowing and all-seeing?" she grumbled irritably. "I live for the day when I become as proficient in the mountains as you are."

Devlin peered at her curvaceous figure for a long, deliberate moment. "I think you are envious of my abilities." He paused for a moment before adding. "And resentful of this attraction between us."

There he went again, reading her mind. Damn him. She hated it when he was right! She was going to have to learn to conceal her emotions or this man was going to know everything she thought before she even put her feelings to words. Moriah had never been attracted to a man and she wasn't sure how to cope with these tingling feelings. Cynicism made her wary and her past dealings with men made her hesitant to trust what she felt. She knew this swarthy giant had no particular affection for her. He had taken her under his wing to instruct her, but there was no emotional feeling for her. Whatever he felt could be attributed to a man's most noticeable flaw—lust.

From the moment Moriah had awakened to the sound of Mick and Kent's hushed voices and saw that Devlin wasn't there to assist her, Moriah had dealt with the situation herself. And when White Shadow did return from his mysterious midnight prowling, he had waited, allowing her to muddle her way through the encounter as best she could. He had only intervened at the last minute to lend credence to the illusion that spirits inhabited the spring. If he truly felt something for her, he would have leaped to her defense the instant he returned.

Despite what Moriah thought about the relationship between them, Devlin felt a strange, compelling attraction to her. He hated to admit it, but he was fascinated by this inventive elf who moved with sylphlike grace and possessed the voice of a siren. She stirred him, even though it would be folly to let her know it and utterly foolish to strengthen the bond between them. He had to keep his objectives in proper perspective. He had a noble mission. Any intimate association with this blue-eyed enchantress would only distract him. But damn, it was difficult not to stare at her without wanting her in all the ways a man could crave a beautiful young woman.

And before he allowed his male instincts to wage another war against his common sense, Devlin stepped away. "Collect your gear," he said to her. "It's best for us to journey into the remote canyons where white men don't dare go. This spring is on a well-traveled path."

Amen to that! Moriah didn't want to be around when another pair of miners wandered in to disturb her sleep. Dancing on sharp rocks was hard on her feet and it had been difficult to sing when she felt like screaming in pain.

When she had gathered her belongings and changed into the baggy garments Devlin had brought her, Moriah followed in his wake. It would have been best if she hadn't been so aware of him striding silently ahead of her with his purposeful, catlike gait. But it was impossible not to be aware of this vital man, this intriguing, self-disciplined creature. Moriah couldn't help but wonder at his background or marvel at his seemingly inexhaustible abilities. He intrigued her and left her speculating on erotic matters that had no business entering her mind in the first place.

It was a cruel twist of fate, she supposed. All these years she had shunned the dimwitted suitors Ruby had thrust at her. Now she found herself captivated by a man who seemed to resent every association with her. She was a burden to him, an inconvenience. It wasn't flattering to know that Devlin was anxious to send her on her way once she was capable of taking care of herself. After he had polished her techniques of survival he would go his way, too, sparing her no thought. She knew that as well as she knew her own name.

Heaving a dispirited sigh, Moriah trudged up the winding path until she was standing on the lofty summit. Below her lay a sprawling valley that was skirted with timber and brush. The sun had topped the rugged peaks to shade the western slopes in an array of spectacular colors, and Moriah marveled at the panoramic view. She wondered if this was as close to heaven as she would ever come, even if the miners of Santa Rita assumed that she was already an angel. It was glorious to stand atop the world and gaze down at Mother Nature's handiwork.

Devlin caught his breath when he glanced back at

Moriah. The wind had lifted the trailing tresses of her hair and caressed her creamy cheeks. She looked radiant perched upon the rocks, admiring the scenery. Her oversized garments concealed her curvaceous figure, but the sun beamed through the thin fabric of her shirt, outlining her firm breasts and the trim indentation of her waist. Devlin felt a tremor of desire trickling down his spine. Good God, how was he supposed to ignore her feminine charms when she presented such an enchanting picture in the morning light?

A shocked gasp burst from Moriah's lips, jostling Devlin from his musings. He glanced over to see Moriah shrinking away from the tarantula that was taking its own sweet time about crawling over the boulder where Moriah had laid her hand the previous moment.

He smiled reassuringly as he gestured his head toward the hairy spider. "Although tarantulas are poisonous, their bites aren't necessarily fatal, and they aren't overly aggressive toward humans," he explained. "They can, however, jump up to lengths of six feet in the face of danger." To prove his point, Devlin tossed a pebble at the spider and it immediately leaped onto another boulder.

"On some of the ranches in the area, the vaqueros put two tarantulas in a tub and wager on which one will kill the other." His brows furrowed and a teasing smile quirked his lips. "A male tarantula won't attack a female or one of its own relatives. But the female, as in many other species, doesn't know the meaning of loyalty. The female tarantula will bite any other tarantula." His gaze rested heavily on Moriah, studying her for a silent moment. "And you say *you* are cynical of men? Perhaps it is *I* who should be wary of *you*."

Moriah flung him a withering glance. Any idiot would know she wasn't a threat to him. It was the other way around. His mere presence was physically and emotionally disturbing.

Devlin squatted down to scoop up a handful of rocks. "Enough about spiders. It's time you learned to use all available weapons," he announced abruptly.

Moriah frowned in confusion when she surveyed the stones in his large tanned hands.

Devlin gestured toward the flock of turkeys that ambled through the clump of gamma grass below them. "There's our lunch," he murmured. "A rifle exploding in one of these canyons can be heard for miles. Unless you intend to signal that you are accepting guests for a meal, you'll learn to use a rock instead of a rifle to fell your quarry if it's at all possible."

He laid the stone in her hand just so, explaining how to use the flick of her wrist and the projection of her arm to guide and direct the missile toward her intended target. Moriah practiced twice, but Devlin grumbled at her lack of perfection.

"Good God, don't throw like a girl!"

"I can't help it. I am one," she snapped defensively.

As if he hadn't noticed for the umpteenth time already! Moriah had the appetizing curves and swells in all the right places. She always looked dainty and neat, as if she had primped with all the luxuries instead of the barest of necessities. But she was no shrinking violet. Moriah Laverty was the personification of fiery tenacity and undaunted spirit. She was intent on being the mistress of her own fate. She sought to make her own way in this man's world and she was determined to live up to her potential. She was a complicated creature who naturally intrigued and attracted men.

"Well, that's no reason to throw like a woman," he reprimanded, shoving aside his distracting contemplations. He pointed a tapered finger toward the unsuspecting flock of turkeys. "If you miss, we'll be dining on pemmican."

Moriah had choked down enough pemmican and jerky to last her a lifetime. Determined of purpose, she poised herself on the cliff as Devlin instructed her to do. Cocking her arm, she waited until the tom elevated his head. Swiftly, she flicked her wrist and the rock sailed down into the canyon. With a dull squawk, the turkey keeled over in a feathered heap.

It was difficult to tell who was most surprised—the turkey, Moriah, or Devlin. Delighted, Moriah flung her arms around Devlin and then, too late, realized it was not a wise thing to do. Close contact always triggered a rash of sensations that were becoming increasingly difficult to ignore.

Devlin felt as if an unseen fist had plowed into his belly. The feel of Moriah's arms around his neck sent shock waves riveting through every fiber of his being. The radiant smile that captured her elegant features was like the glorious sunrise and it was impossible not to be stirred by it or the feel of her shapely body meshed to his. She was like a breath of spring in the gloom of winter and he felt the blossom of desire unfolding within him.

As if his body possessed a will of its own, it inched ever closer. His arms stole around her trim waist and his betraying hands glided over the curve of her derriere. Devlin could feel the eternal fire feeding upon itself, compelling him to move nearer to the tempting flame. He craved the pleasures she could provide, hungered for the taste of kisses that still lingered on his lips.

The feel of her ripe body moving familiarly against his had been branded on his skin. Each moment he spent with Moriah brought him closer to the threshold and left him teetering on the brink of temptation . . .

Common sense gave Devlin a quick kick in the seat of the pants. Muttering at himself, he stepped away. His abrupt movement threw Moriah off balance—physically as well as emotionally. A frightened yelp escaped her lips when she felt herself wobbling on the edge of the ridge.

It was Devlin's lightning-quick reflexes that spared her from an agonizing fall. When Moriah slid on the loose pebbles, Devlin snatched her to him. After he set her on safer ground he hardly dared to look in her direction. Grumbling at the tidal waves of torment that swamped and buffeted him, he scooped up his pouch and zigzagged down the rocky slope.

"We better fetch our lunch," he mumbled for lack of much else to say.

Moriah's shoulders slumped dejectedly when she realized she had wanted his masterful kiss and that Devlin had denied her the pleasure. For crying out loud, she had practically asked this magnificent creature to kiss her and make love to her, but each time he broke their embrace. And for Moriah, it was anguished minutes before she recovered from the devastating effects of being encircled in his powerful arms.

What was the matter with her? Why couldn't she attract the one man who aroused her feminine yearnings? One look in the mirror assured her that she wasn't an ugly duckling. She had been rather plain as a child, but the awkward caterpillar had transformed into a graceful butterfly. Ruby had resented it when Moriah had matured into a shapely young woman.

Her stepmother had never bolstered Moriah's self-esteem or complimented the metamorphosis, but Moriah's effect on most men assured her that she was somewhat attractive.

Maybe it was her personality flaws that put Devlin off, Moriah mused. She was defensive, quick-tempered, cynical, impatient, and independent. Perhaps she simply didn't appeal to Devlin. Maybe she wasn't woman enough—too naive and inexperienced to satisfy such a man as this.

And why did she even care if Devlin liked her or not? she asked herself. He would be gone soon and she would be on her own. Whatever White Shadow's mysterious purpose, he didn't want her to be a part of it—or a part of his life. Moriah was innocent, true, but she was astute enough to know when a man wanted nothing to do with her. And if she were smart, she would clamp down on her misdirected desires and remember that Devlin wanted nothing more than a brief friendship with no emotional strings attached.

Completely exhausted and thoroughly out of sorts, Ruby Thatcher stared at the crude fort that was constructed of mud bricks. Fort Bowie, Arizona, was located on the slopes of the Chiricuhua Mountains, serving as a link between El Paso and Tucson, defending the route to California. In bleak resignation, Ruby peered at the shabby shacks that constituted the fort. Although she had cleverly managed to rid herself of her biggest headache and threat—Moriah—she was paying restitution by being subjected to this tedious journey through areas where even a coyote had to scrimp to survive.

"I'm not sure I can take much more of this," Ruby

grumbled crankily to Vance. "We've been traveling forever and now here we are in Nowhere, Arizona. Same name different territory! Grains of sand are stuck in my teeth and perspiration turns to mud! God, when is this torment going to end?"

"Tucson is only another week away," Vance comforted her as he lifted her from her perch. "The wagon master plans to spend a few days at Old Pueblo. You'll have the chance to rest and recuperate when we get there."

Ruby preferred to rest and recuperate *now*, not a week down the road! This overnight stop wasn't nearly long enough to satisfy her. Plus, she would be forced to give another description of Moriah to the commander of the fort, as well as the rendition of the incident at the Mimbres River. She just wanted to forget that precocious chit and resume her own life!

Resigning herself to the inevitable, Ruby worked up a few crocodile tears and entered the fort to offer the details of the disaster to the commander.

Confound it, that sassy firebrand's name was still ringing in Ruby's ears, even a week after Moriah's long-awaited departure!

Chapter 7

While the turkey sizzled over the campfire, Devlin set up a target so Moriah could practice with a bow and arrow. Patiently, he instructed her in the skills of archery, never flaunting his exceptional talents, but rather insisting that she perfect hers. He was amazed by her natural ability. She picked up the techniques very quickly and surprised him by being astonishingly accurate.

During their midday meal, Devlin spoke of the ways of the Apaches, leaving her to wonder how long he had lived as one of them. He encouraged her to rely heavily upon her instincts of self-preservation, as the Apaches did. He instructed her to see with her ears as well as her eyes, to tune her senses to the scent of approaching danger, to become like the wild creatures that roamed the hidden valleys, buttes, mesas, and rugged mountains.

Moriah couldn't help herself. She became more enamored with Devlin as the hours went on. She stared into those fathomless amber eyes surrounded by their thick black lashes and her heart skipped several beats. The sound of his deep, resonant voice did incredible things to her pulse and the masculine fragrance that clung to him enveloped her very being. She didn't want to be so consumed by this magnetic attraction for him, but she was. He was nothing like any of the other men she had ever met.

She had the depressing feeling that when this dynamic man walked out of her life she was going to miss him terribly. And that was a crying shame because she knew that White Shadow, the mythical hero of the mountains, would forget her the minute he silently crept away. The simple truth was she didn't matter to this man with his fierce crusade and that to her he mattered more than he should have . . .

"Come, there is much more you must learn," Devlin insisted when he caught Moriah staring at him in ways that made him burn.

Moriah wasn't skilled in concealing her emotions. He could read the confusion and admiration in her thoughts and it frustrated him to no end. It would be so easy to buckle beneath his hungry desires, to take what this luscious beauty had to offer. But the biggest favor he could do for Moriah was to leave her untouched. She was a tormenting temptation and when he ventured too close to her, his noble restraint was placed under an incredible strain.

Devlin wondered if he were the first man to spend so much time with Moriah. Judging by what she had told him about her life with the Thatchers and the loss of her parents, he speculated that she had never enjoyed a complete relationship with a man. She had been hounded by rogues who wanted only her body. Not that he was an expert on deep, lasting relationships, Devlin reminded himself. He had been too much the rogue himself until the previous year when he was betrayed by one of his own kind. Before, he had taken what he wanted from women without feeling any strong attachments. The past year he had basically no associations with women because of his obsessive thirst for revenge and retribution. But spending so much time with this blond-haired hellion made him realize what he had been missing and how . . .

Exasperated with himself for dwelling on thoughts of Moriah, Devlin led her along with him to the canyon. He had to distract himself or he would yield to his hungry needs.

"There are times when you must learn to conceal yourself from danger," he declared as he led her to the lone juniper tree that stood at the far end of the canyon. "In the rocky slopes, you can conceal yourself behind boulders and in caves, but in open spaces such as this, you are vulnerable unless you react quickly and skillfully."

Moriah scanned the area. "Hide here?" she smirked skeptically. "Only a full-fledged phantom could disappear without being detected."

"You think not?" One dark brow lifted in challenge.

Devlin was a mite overconfident, Moriah thought. There was no way he could hide his magnificent body in such a place as this without her finding him—and she proceeded to tell him so.

Devlin braced his hands on her shoulders and turned her around to face the direction they had come. "Walk twenty paces away and then pivot around," he instructed her. A wry smile pursed his lips when she snickered at what she considered a foolish challenge. "I'll lead you to the treasures of Apache gold if you can find me," he baited her.

Two delicately carved brows elevated to an astonished angle. "There is truly a mother lode in these mountains?" she questioned incredulously.

He gave his raven head an affirmative nod. "You

will be the only white woman on the planet who knows where it is if you defeat me at our game of hide-and-seek."

For a moment, Moriah let herself imagine what she would do with a pot of gold. It would be delightful to dream up ways to spend it and to return to civilization to punish the Thatchers for trying to dispose of her.

Determined of purpose, Moriah stepped off twenty paces, gave a shout to signify she was ready, and wheeled about. Her keen gaze swept over the valley floor and a perplexed frown shaded her brow. Where the blazes was he?

Hardly one to admit defeat at the first sign of difficulty, Moriah circled the lone tree and asked herself if she really had spent the past week in the company of a mystical apparition rather than a mortal. Crimi-ney, she was beginning to think White Shadow really was a gifted ghost who could sometimes appear human and sometimes appear to be no more than a floating mirage.

Fifteen minutes later, Moriah was on the verge of losing her temper. Devlin was obviously pulling some ornery prank on her. He must have dashed up the cliff to crouch behind a boulder, leaving her wandering around looking like an utter fool. This was probably another of those valuable lessons about when to trust and when not to.

"You tricked me," Moriah grumbled at the valley at large. "*Devil* Granger, show yourself this instant. I'm tired of your mischievous pranks—"

Moriah knew she had been *had* when something clamped around her ankle, knocking her off balance. To her utter disbelief, she glanced down to see a muscular arm protruding from the thick gamma grass that carpeted the chasm floor.

Devlin's taunting laughter echoed around her as he sat up in the grass. "The devil, am I?" He chortled at the stunned expression on her elegant features.

In a fit of temper, Moriah took a swing at his shoulder, venting her frustration. He had wiggled down into the thick grass like a snake and she had walked in circles for a quarter of an hour without finding hide or hair of him. Blast it, was there nothing this man couldn't do, and do exceptionally well? And damnit, did he have to laugh at her while he did it?

Instinctively, Devlin caught Moriah's hand before she slugged him on the arm for his prank. With a fierce yank, he tugged Moriah down on top of him. When she cursed, he laughed, and that infuriated her all the more. He was mocking her naiveté in the wilds. She couldn't help it if she wasn't as adept as he was! She was trying to emulate his skills, but he had years of experience and she was only a novice.

"You beast," she hissed, tweaking the hair on his bronzed chest. "I await the day that I have the last laugh on you. I'm going to be just like you. When you look at me, you'll see the reflection of yourself and it will scare the living daylights out of you to realize you have molded me into your own likeness! And when you come looking for me, I'll worm down in the grass and trip *you* up for a change!"

Devlin's teasing laughter died into silence. He was already beginning to see his own reflection in those luminous blue pools. He and Moriah had grown more alike with each passing day. He had trained her to act and think like him, to view the world through his eyes. And Godamighty, she was so temptingly close . . .

A wild mane of golden hair tumbled around her, forming a silky cape that framed his face as well as her own. Devlin couldn't see past those delicately sculpted features to view the piling clouds that scraped the northwestern slopes of the mountains. The smell of rain was in the air, but the scent of Moriah was in the wind. She had filled his world and now it was no larger than the space this shapely spitfire occupied. The feel of her body lying suggestively upon his left a gnawing ache that demanded appeasement.

Devlin stared at her as she braced herself upon his chest. He wanted her in all the wild ways he had denied himself since the day he saw her ascending into the mountains. He wanted to feel her satiny flesh gliding provocatively against his, to touch her, to possess her, if only for one glorious moment that burned away time.

His crusade be damned! Fourteen months of celibacy was gnawing at him. He hadn't barely been tempted until he crossed paths with the glorious Moriah. When he looked at her he remembered how breathtaking she had been while she swam in the spring, how enchanting she had been when she danced around the boulders like a fleeting spirit. He knew she was forbidden fruit in paradise, but Devlin's self-control was dangerously close to cracking. He had never spared women much thought until Moriah came along to turn his world upside down.

"You face the gravest danger of all now, Moriah," he growled as his hand glided up her thigh to rest familiarly on her hip.

Moriah had suddenly inherited his ability to read expressions. She peered down into his shimmering golden eyes and fell into their magical depths. He wanted her. His look said it all. She could see the hunger carved in his ruggedly handsome face. He wasn't offering forever, but Moriah wasn't sure she believed in forever. Happiness just seemed to flitter away, and it was impossible to cling to it for too long at a time. Her father had been taken from her mother and her mother had been taken from her. Moriah had learned the hard way that it was best to take one day at a time, to milk what brief pleasure was to be had before it vanished forever. It seemed only natural that Devlin should teach her the meaning of passion, no matter how brief and fleeting it might be. He had, after all, molded her in his image and she had become hopelessly infatuated with him.

Adoringly, she lowered her head, her eyes focused on the sensuous curve of his lips. She had never willingly surrendered to a man and she wasn't quite sure how to go about it since she was far more adept at repulsing advances than responding to them. But passion, she quickly discovered, was something one came by quite naturally. It was an inborn need that unfurled from deep inside to assume control of the mind and body.

Her heart vaulted to her throat when the flood of warm, bubbly sensations channeled through her bloodstream. At the first touch of their lips, Moriah couldn't get enough of him. She resented the garments that separated them, resented her lack of experience in pleasing a man. Moriah longed to share the intense rapture that surged through her innocent body like a tidal wave. She wanted to give and give until these fierce, ardent feelings ebbed, until the burning hunger was appeased.

Devlin groaned deep in his throat when Moriah kissed him with twenty years of pent-up desire and he responded with fourteen months of bottled-up passion. He swore she was a dozen emotions seeking release when her body settled on top of his. And he was like a rumbling volcano that had lain dormant for more months than he cared to count. She touched him, shyly at first, and then with a sense of wonder that had him moaning in unholy torment. And suddenly, he was sinking into a cloud of pleasure that blocked the world from view.

His hand folded over hers, dragging her palm across the thick matting of hair that covered his chest and belly. He ached for her caress. He lived for her dewy kisses. Moriah was a mass of incredible potential that he had just begun to tap. She was the stuff every man's dreams were made of. She looked and felt like an angel who had just enough devil in her to make her hopelessly captivating. And captivated Devlin was! Nothing seemed quite as important as making wild sweet love to this tempting vixen here and now.

He didn't mean to be rough and impatient, but it had been ages since he had lain with a woman, and it had been *never* that he had touched anything quite so exquisite as the silky texture of Moriah's skin. Urgently, he tugged at her shirt, sending buttons flying. He wanted nothing between her creamy flesh and his inquiring caresses—nothing but her warm, pliant body meshed intimately to his.

Lord, she was like a long-awaited banquet and he was starved for her. He ached to explore every delicious inch of her, to seek out each sensitive spot and set it afire. He longed to erase the touch of every man she had known, to teach her the true meaning of lovemaking.

His seeking hands swirled over her ribs to brush the dusky peaks of her breasts and Moriah forgot how to breathe. He drew her to him so that his lips and tongue could glide over the throbbing tips, teasing and arousing her until she burned from inside out.

Moriah gasped to inhale much-needed air but there was none forthcoming. Her naive body burst into sweet flames when he did the most incredible things with his hands and lips. His mouth traveled across her quivering flesh to recapture her lips. His kiss was hard and faintly forceful as his tongue probed deeper, evoking tantalizing sensations that demanded her eager response.

Even the rumble of thunder above them failed to penetrate her paralyzed brain. When Devlin touched her, Moriah forgot who and where she was. All she knew was that she was in this magnificent giant's arms and it felt so right, so wondrous.

When his questing hand trailed over her belly to trace the band of her breeches, another gasp broke from her throat. And when his hand drifted down her thighs, her body instinctively arched toward him, hypnotized by his masterful touch. She hungered for what he offered and she surrendered what he requested in return. He treated her to exquisite caresses and she trembled in response to the sizzling sensations.

Living fire spread through her loins when his fingertips delved beneath her breeches to trace the ultrasensitive flesh of her thighs. He teased her until she cried out in wild, sweet torment. He kissed her until she was lightheaded. Her senses were saturated with him and the needs he had awakened left her arching toward him in total abandon.

Even the brisk breeze that swept down the slope of the mountain didn't cool the fire of longing that taunted her innocent body. It fed the volatile flames until she was on fire for him. Moriah no longer *wanted* this powerful package of masculinity. She *needed* him as she needed air to breathe. His possessive caresses drove her mad with longing, kept her hovering somewhere between fantasy and reality.

When Devlin had peeled away her breeches and shrugged the shirt from her shoulders, he feasted on her tantalizing curves and swells, marveling at the sight and feel of her incredibly soft skin. She was absolute perfection. He yearned to memorize every inch of her body by touch, to pleasure her in all the wondrous ways a man could arouse and satisfy a woman.

His trembling hand curled beneath her chin when she shyly looked away. It embarrassed her to watch him watch her. But Devlin would have none of that. He wanted her to see how lovely she was, how she devastated him when he gazed upon her.

"There is no shame in such elegant beauty," he whispered, his voice ragged with passion. "You are exquisite, Moriah. Looking at you stirs me. Can a woman want more than to arouse a man by the mere sight of her? What greater compliment is there than to be awed by sight, shattered by a mere touch?"

Like an admirer of a priceless sculpture, his hand skied down the slope of her shoulder, drifted over the rose-tipped crests of her breast, and glided over the gentle curve of her hip. "You are a goddess, a masterpiece so perfectly formed, a treasured gift . . ."

His forefinger trailed across her belly to swirl around the full swell of her breasts, making her involuntarily arch toward him again. Absorbed with the sight and feel of her delectable body, he bent his raven head to flick at the taut peaks with his tongue before he took the bud into his mouth to cherish the taste of her.

Moriah felt her body melt into a puddle of liquid fire. She was going to die, of course. Pleasure this fiery and intense demanded supreme sacrifices. Her heart was thundering like the storm that clamored above them in the towering gray clouds. Breathing had long been impossible. Her body shuddered convulsively as his hands and lips left no part of her flesh untouched. His fingers probed and aroused, causing maddening sensations to uncoil inside her and leave her quivering in helpless response.

His intimate fondling only intensified the cravings. Moriah hungered for all this raven-haired rake could give. She didn't understand what she wanted and needed, but neither could she deny its existence. But how could anyone or anything satisfy this phenomenal yearning that shook the roots of her soul? It was beyond her comprehension!

"Devlin, please . . ." Moriah didn't even know what she expected of him, but this masterful magician surely knew how to satisfy these soul-shattering sensations. There was nothing this man of myths didn't know how to do.

"Don't I please you, tigress?" he taunted with a rakish smile. She had no way of knowing how masculine she made him feel when she responded to him in wild abandon. She made him thankful he was a man, made him want all she could give.

"You please me too much," she choked out.

"As of yet, I haven't pleased you nearly enough," he whispered as he bent to devour her trembling lips in another ravenous kiss.

She not only heard his words but she felt them vibrating on her mouth. His lips moved downward, leaving wildfires burning in their wake. His searing kisses drifted over her belly to her thighs and Moriah swore she would go insane if he didn't appease the needs instead of create monstrous new ones. Her body was ablaze and emotions boiled inside her like a simmering caldron that was about to erupt.

Gasping for breath, Moriah watched as Devlin

shucked his buckskin breeches. Her eyes surveyed his muscular chest with delight and descended to marvel at every virile inch of his steel-honed body. He was all solid muscle. The long columns of his legs flexed and relaxed and his shoulders rippled as he stretched out beside her. Moriah couldn't begin to describe the erotic sensations that bombarded her when she felt his masculine body lying familiarly against hers.

Untutored hands roamed over the taut tendons of his back and hips, intrigued by this mass of his strength in repose. Caressing him was like stroking a sleek, powerful jungle cat. He was more than a man. He was a creature of the wilds whom God had labored over with loving care. She could feel her strength being absorbed into him. She could feel the energy rippling through him and flooding into her quaking body.

Like a starved tiger, Devlin ravished her inviting lips. His leg slid between hers, aching for an intimacy he hadn't enjoyed in more than a year. Over and over again, he reminded himself to be gentle with this delicate nymph. He didn't want to rush her or overwhelm her with his ardent needs. Men had obviously abused her in the past, taking what she preferred not to give. Devlin didn't want to hurt or disappoint her, but rather to teach her the joys of passion. If he rushed her, she would be reminded of her previous experiences with men. Moriah knew nothing of love, only lust. He wanted to make a difference, to satisfy her as no other man had.

With a hungry groan, he settled exactly upon her, guiding her thighs apart. He felt her tense at the intrusion of his heavy weight upon hers. When she instinctively pressed her hands to his chest to push him away, he bent to muffle her protest with a breath-stealing kiss. His body surged upon hers and he caught her gasp and then murmured words that assured her he wanted her with every part of his being. Deliberately, he moved away and then uncoiled upon her, waiting until she relaxed beneath him and grew accustomed to the feel of his body.

The patience and tenderness he intended to display crumbled beneath his long-denied desires. He could feel the passions straining against the chains of captivity. He was testing his self-control as it had never been tested and he was losing the battle of mind over body. His senses reeled with the taste, scent, and feel of this lovely nymph and he ached for her in the wildest ways.

A maddening groan rumbled in his chest as the floodwaters of passion engulfed him. Devlin crushed her silken body to his and buried his head in the golden tangles of her hair. He was suddenly moving upon command, appeasing the hungry needs that were as ancient as time. She was his possession and he was famished for her. They were flesh to flesh, a beating, breathing essence that defied reason. His heart hammered against his ribs and his breath came in rapid spurts. He heard her name on his lips as he drove against her, unable to control the fervent cadence of lovemaking.

Huge raindrops splattered against Devlin's back, but nothing penetrated the dense fog of passion that enshrouded him. He was in the throes of mindless desire, a prisoner of his own urgent needs. He could feel himself letting go, feel the wall of flames burning him alive.

Now Moriah was positively certain she was dying, bit by incredible bit. The first stab of pain had ebbed, to be replaced by a rapture that defied description. The velvet warmth of him pulsated inside her, evoking an indescribable brand of pleasure. Torrents of ineffable sensations swamped her body, leading her deeper into the sensual realm of desire. Fervent needs swept her up and then carried her into their swift-flowing currents. Never in her wildest dreams had she expected lovemaking to be so wondrous! She had thought it would be . . . Well, she wasn't exactly sure what she thought, but she never anticipated marvelous feelings like the ones that channeled through her to settle in the very core of her being. And just when she was sure she had enjoyed the most ecstatic sensations imaginable, another deliciously wondrous feeling unfolded within her before it gave way to another and then another . . . as if the pleasure would never end . . .

A trembling gasp burst free when her body shuddered uncontrollably. Moriah dug her nails into Devlin's back and held on for dear life when the sky opened up and buckets of rain streamed into the valley. She didn't care if the floods rolled over her, sweeping her into oblivion. She couldn't move. Intense pleasure immobilized every nerve and muscle in her body, leaving her numb with rapture.

Devlin had been so preoccupied by this gorgeous blue-eyed temptation that he had paid no mind to the approaching storm that could turn the deep chasm between the mountains into a roaring gorge. The thought of how rough and impatient he had been with Moriah left him cursing his own name. He had meant to be tender and gentle, but he had been engulfed by a savage passion. Moriah had shattered his self-control as if it had never even existed!

Still cursing himself, Devlin rolled away long before Moriah was prepared to let him go. She longed to savor the ecstasy she had experienced, to let the sensations fade gradually from her numbed body. The scowl that was stamped on his chiseled features wounded her as nothing else could. She was so unsure of herself and there was Devlin, suddenly muttering a string of expletives. He always had a habit of talking to himself. A hazard of living like a hermit, she supposed. But now that thunderous scowl and those muttered utterances seemed to be directed toward her.

The telltale signs of Moriah's innocence had Devlin swearing several more oaths. It wasn't enough that he had been impatient and lusty, but he had stolen her virginity without realizing it! He had been too caught up in the heat of passion to control himself or to determine whether or not this was her first experience with lovemaking. He had assumed there had been others before him who had used and abused her. She had suggested as much when she mentioned her stepfather and Burkhart. Realizing what he had done made Devlin feel the total cad! Damn his lack of control! Curse his lack of consideration. He had probably turned Moriah's initiation from maidenhood to womanhood into a nightmare!

Was this the way it always was when lovemaking came to its end? Moriah wondered as she watched Devlin yank on his wet clothes and grumble under his breath? Did a man satisfy his needs and then immediately pull away? Was sex the same for him as quenching his thirst or feeding starvation? And why was he still scowling? She must have disappointed him so thoroughly that he regretted their lovemaking.

Moriah choked in humiliation. What had seemed so rare and beautiful now appeared a disastrous mistake. It was as if Devlin couldn't wait to get away from her, as if he resented what had transpired between them.

"Get up, damnit," he growled more harshly than

he intended. "If we don't head for higher ground, we'll be swept up in a flash flood."

Mechanically, Moriah fumbled into her soggy clothes, but she couldn't move quickly enough to suit Devlin, who was mentally kicking himself for his rough handling of Moriah. He refused to glance in her direction and it was as if he were using the storm as a logical excuse to bring their liaison to an abrupt end.

As for herself, Moriah was thankful for the pouring rain. It concealed the stream of tears that rolled down her cheeks. Purposely, she lagged behind as Devlin made a mad dash to retrieve their gear. When he noticed her slow pace, he wheeled to growl at her again.

"Little fool, hurry up!"

That really did it! She knew what an imbecile she was to succumb to him, but he didn't have to keep referring to her as a fool every blessed time she turned around!

"Don't you ever call me that again," she flared, her chin tilting to disguise the anguish and humiliation she was experiencing.

"I'll call you what you are," he snapped as he scooped up their supplies and scurried up the slippery hillside.

Thunder bellowed in the clouds and lightning danced through the shafts of rain. But still the stubborn, pigheaded minx just stood there glaring daggers at him. Not that he blamed her, mind you. He had deflowered her with rough impatience and he deserved every flaming glare she hurled at him. But good God, she should have told him she was a virgin!

"Go ahead then, stand there and get yourself lightning struck," Devlin roared over the resounding thunder.

A half-second later, Devlin was wishing he hadn't voiced that spiteful remark. Someone up there must have heard him. A ball of fire blazed down from the heavens, striking the scraggly tree that was rooted some twenty feet from where Moriah stood glowering at him. He swore he would never forget the electrifying moment, never forget the blinding flash of silver-white light that exploded before him. Moriah's bloodcurdling scream pierced the heavy air as well as Devlin's bleeding heart.

And the world turned pitch black . . .

The smell of smoke curled through the rain-drenched air. Devlin wasn't sure how much time had elapsed when he roused to find himself sprawled facedown on the grass. He could only assume he had been knocked to the ground by the earth-shattering magnitude of the lightning bolt.

He blinked once to clear his dazed brain and then blinked again when nothing but shafts of silver penetrated his eyes. Frantically, he pushed himself up and shook his head to get his bearings. His blurred gaze scanned the valley in search of Moriah. With his heart pounding, he leaped to his feet in a single bound and charged toward the tree that still danced with flames and crackled with smoldering bark.

Moriah lay faceup, some twenty feet away from the smoldering tree trunk. His breath died in his chest when he spied the burns that tarnished her cheeks and eyelids. Grimly, he scanned her limp body, willing her to live. His eyes fell to the gold locket that encircled her throat. It had been charred black.

Devlin let out a howl that was reminiscent of a roaring lion. For half a minute he couldn't think or move. The thought of Moriah dying before his very eyes cut through his soul. She had endured so much. She had been used, abused, and betrayed. Even the one man she had come to depend on for protection and instruction had taken unfair advantage of her. Damn, she hadn't even been able to find consolation and refuge in the mountains when the world turned against her. Hadn't she suffered enough?

Sending a flood of jumbled prayers heavenward, Devlin scooped up her limp body and sidestepped up the hill. He was cautious to avoid the gullies and arroyos that would soon be running level full with water.

There was very little protection from the wind and rain. After watching the tree go up in smoke, Devlin wasn't about to take shelter beneath the canopy of timber and risk being struck by another lightning bolt. He laid Moriah's unconscious body in the hollowed-out niche between the boulders on the hillside and sank back to compose himself. But it took some doing to get his emotions under control. He was so rattled he couldn't think straight. He kept seeing the flash of light, hearing the sizzling explosion . . .

Blast it, he hadn't meant to call the wrath of God down on this lovely sprite! It was anger and fear for her safety and irritation with himself that had put that sarcastic remark to tongue.

Devlin was close to collapsing from exhaustion as the rain speared down from the boiling clouds and the wind wailed and whined as if someone in the mountains was dying . . .

The bleak thought caused him to glance down at the wan beauty who hadn't moved a muscle. A knot coiled in the pit of his belly. Impulsively, Devlin crouched above Moriah to drop a kiss to her unresponsive lips. Silly fool, he scolded himself. Did he think he could kiss her back to life? His was the kiss of death. He had stripped her of her innocence with savage impatience and then he had ridiculed her when he should have turned his frustrations on himself. Moriah had probably cursed him with her last breath . . .

Devlin checked her pulse, wondering if he had only imagined she still had one. It was difficult to tell with the rain pattering and hailstones bouncing over the boulders. Hurriedly, he pressed the heels of his hands into her shoulder blades, forcing her to breathe. For what seemed forever he employed his techniques of resuscitation, but still Moriah didn't rouse.

Suffering all the torments of the damned, Devlin sat in the rain and wind and prayed. And oh how he prayed, willing with all his power for Moriah to survive.

Part II

Chapter 8

Clyde Finnegan took a swig of Taos Lightning and glanced through the open door of the saloon where he sat. Rain drenched the adobe buildings of Santa Rita, turning them to mud. The storm had raged for hours and had refused to let up. Every now and then the thud of hailstones clattered on the roof and thunder boomed like a discharging cannon.

"It sounds as if the Angel of the Wind and White Shadow are clashing in the Black Mountains," Clyde declared to the saloon at large. "It must be one helluva fight."

Kent Hanes and Mick Jeffries readily agreed. Between the liquor they had consumed and the sound effects of the storm, they were certain the angel and White Shadow had declared war on each other. And, of course, there was that incident at Angel Springs to remind them of disembodied spirits flitting from here to kingdom come.

"You should've seen her," Kent chimed in as the other miners congregated around the table to listen to the tales of those who had been visited by the golden-haired goddess of the mountains. "A veritable nymph she was! Her hair was like threads of spun gold and she turned the bubblin' spring into liquid silver when she danced upon the water. And when she wielded her powers, the sky boomed, bushes went up in flame, and gold nuggets rained from heaven."

A murmur undulated through the crowd, encouraging Kent to elaborate. He, like Clyde, found it invigorating to be the object of so much attention. "It was a night I'll never forget, believe you me. The moon was her spotlight and flecks of pure silver trickled from the cracks in the rocks. When she flung her arms upward, the silver pool became twinklin' stars sparklin' in the midnight sky." To lend credence to his testimony, Kent fished into his pocket to reveal the nuggets that had been strewn on the mountain path. "She gave us these as evidence that we had seen her. She must have flown to the Valley of the Eagle to scoop up a handful of Apache gold. That's probably what angered White Shadow," he added, glancing into Clyde's bloodshot eyes as if awaiting confirmation. Clyde nodded in agreement and then another crash of thunder shook the walls like the clash of gigantic cymbals. "And now the two of them are up there havin' it out, callin' upon all their supernatural powers."

"My money's on the angel," Mick announced before downing his Taos Lightning in one swallow. "Anybody who can send balls of fire arching through the sky and set bushes aflame can defy White Shadow." Through the open doorway, lightning sizzled on the towering peaks and the earth shook. "There, you see. She is hurling thunderbolts!"

Someone in the crowd coaxed Clyde into repeating his version of the angel who flew down to his cabin. Clyde spun the best yarn of all and by the time he disclosed the details of his eerie confrontation, he had his angel floating around his shack, making objects and utensils disappear forever. And now that Mick and Kent had returned from their diggings with tales of the angel at the springs and evidence of gold nuggets, there wasn't a man in the place who doubted either the angel's existence or that of White Shadow—the mysterious phantom who had returned from the grave to satisfy his vengeance against Commander Burkhart.

A string of curses tripped off Lyle Burkhart's tongue as he paced about his quarters at Fort McLane, located fifteen miles west of Santa Rita at Apache Tejo. He had been in a huff since the morning he woke to find the supply tent had been cleaned out and the horses stolen. The appearance of the white-quilled arrow that was left behind after the strike on the cavalry infuriated him. He had seen to it that the incompetent guards were whipped for allowing him to be humiliated by those renegade Apaches and Devlin Granger. There were those who claimed Granger had died from the wounds he had sustained that fateful day, but Burkhart wasn't sure of that. All he knew was that he had made a most formidable enemy in Granger—or his avenging ghost.

For the past three months Lyle's superiors had kept a watchful eye on his activities and he feared he was about to lose command of his regiment. That thought spurred him to plan an offensive strike as soon as possible. He had returned to Fort McLane to restock his supplies and to prepare to take the battle into the mountains, where he hoped to flush out the legendary White Shadow and his treacherous Apache brothers.

Upon reaching the fort, he had been handed a message from his superior officer in the department of the New Mexican Army, informing him that charges had been filed against him and that an investigation was underway. He had been ordered to appear in the military court in Santa Fe at the end of two months and been told to prepare the evidence he needed to present his testimony. The news had Lyle cursing a blue streak. It seemed White Shadow had managed to make good his threat, but Lyle was still determined to gather a strike force of seasoned dragoons and seek out the Apache strongholds. His goal was to annihilate as many Indians as possible before he was forced to appear in military court to plead his case in the previous year's incident.

After chugging his third glass of hard whiskey, Lyle stared at the stub of his left arm. His thoughts drifted back to his encounter with Devlin Granger and then to Moriah Laverty. That feisty little bitch! She had deserved to die after she had rejected his advances that day by the Mimbres River. He had used her death as an excuse to launch an attack against the Apache village in Doubtful Canyon and he had spared no mercy on those pesky Indians.

In Lyle's opinion, the only good Indian was a dead one. Unfortunately, not all his superiors agreed with his philosophy, and Lyle was forced to write up reports that indicated he was acting only in defense of himself and his troops. But little by little, the men under his command had resigned their posts because of their aversion to Lyle's brand of killing. And with all the protest to the army authorities, Lyle's activities had fallen under suspicion. He had Devlin Granger's family to thank for all his present troubles. Damn the whole lot of Indian-loving bastards!

His meandering thoughts drifted back through

time to the incident that had triggered the rash of sneak attacks by the Apaches and the appearance of the mythical White Shadow. The legend that had evolved from the massacre at Ojo del Muerto—Spring of the Dead—had come back to haunt him. Lyle had lured Granger, whose family owned a sprawling ranch near Tucson, to lead the cavalry into Apache country to parley after the death of Mangas Coloradas. It had been a trick, of course. Lyle had wanted to inflict another blow on the tribe while they grieved the loss of their respected chief. When Lyle and his men opened fire, the outraged Granger had gone berserk and had turned on him. Lyle had managed to riddle Granger with bullets, but the enraged Indian-lover had kept right on coming.

In a towering rage, Granger had lacerated Lyle's arm so severely that it had required amputation. The painful knife wound in Lyle's belly had slowed him down for six months. Before Lyle could command his men to slaughter Granger, two Apache braves had scooped up their blood brother and carried him into the mountains. Lyle had thought that would be the end of Granger, but—either in flesh or spirit—he had returned to haunt Burkhart. Lyle wasn't sure if Granger had perished and the Apache had kept the legend alive or if Granger was still prowling the mountains. Devlin's family had begun a crusade to have his name cleared of all crimes and to have Burkhart dismissed for his brutal tactics against the Apaches.

The report Lyle delivered to the authorities countered the Granger family's accusations. Lyle stated that the Apaches had launched an attack under a flag of truce and that Granger had plotted with his Apache friends to massacre the cavalry which had only come to urge the renegades to the reservation.

Since the blood-letting at Ojo del Muerto, Lyle had been plagued by some sort of curse. He detested the fact that Granger had become a mythical hero who supposedly prowled the mountain ranges of southern New Mexico and Arizona territories. But Lyle had vowed that no avenging ghost or sneaky Apache was going to make a laughingstock of him. This White Shadow legend was going to come to an end very soon! Lyle would flush out every last one of those renegades and hunt Granger down if he was still alive. The man was said to have as many lives as a cat, but Lyle intended to see that troublemaker dead and buried once and for all.

As soon as the storm ended, Lyle intended to head for Santa Rita and interrogate the miners about possible sightings of the renegades. He was going to demolish every camp and destroy the legend of White Shadow—or the man himself!—if it was the last thing he ever did!

Moriah felt oddly cold and incredibly exhausted when she finally roused from what seemed a century-long nap. The last thing she remembered was hearing a deafening explosion and seeing her life flash before her eyes. It wasn't a pretty picture, either. The fact that Devlin had humiliated her with his mocking taunts and his eagerness to end their love-making had crushed her. The sensible part of her nature wanted to hate him forevermore, but the sentimental part foolishly clung to the memories of the splendor she had discovered in his arms . . .

She groaned in pain when she tried to move. Her body was sluggish and she ached all the way to the bone. And when she pried open her eyes . . .

A terrified whimper bubbled forth as she collapsed back to the ground. No matter how many times she blinked she couldn't see anything except flecks of silver embedded in a world of darkness. She cowered in terror against the jagged rocks that stabbed at her back, feeling them without being able to see them.

Devlin sighed in relief when he saw Moriah regaining consciousness, but a concerned frown wrinkled his brow when he noticed the wild look in her sapphire eyes, surrounded now by singed lashes. She was staring through him without recognizing him.

"Moriah, it's all right," he comforted softly. "I'm here."

She jumped at the sound of his voice and glanced around her, seeing nothing. Her frustration and her temper joined forces, putting bitter words to tongue. "Is that supposed to make me feel better?" she muttered resentfully. "I don't care if I ever see you again—"

A choked sob gushed from her quivering lips when the dismal thought of never seeing *anything* again settled over her like a fog of despair. And before she knew it, she was wailing like an abandoned child—which was exactly how she felt now, and had felt for the last ten years. There was no happiness in this world, only pain and torment and sorrow. If she walked blindly off a cliff Devlin wouldn't care. She was nothing to him but unwanted baggage. She had surrendered to him and he had been repulsed by her naive attempt to satisfy him.

Devlin hated to see this feisty girl reduced to tears. She was a survivor who had been plagued by more pitfalls than one individual should have to endure. But, tears weren't going to solve her problems. And besides, the torrential rains had soaked the countryside quite effectively without her crying a salty river.

"I will have none of that," Devlin insisted curtly.

"I can cry if I want to," she railed at him, and then shed a few more infuriated tears for good measure.

"Not in front of me you won't," he flung back, certain he was the reason for this flood of tears. She hated him. He knew that as surely as he knew there was gold in Eagle Canyon.

"Then turn your back if you don't want to watch. I'm not through crying yet," she all but yelled at him.

She's behaving right strangely, thought Devlin as he watched her feel her way back into the narrow niche. She was staring in every direction except at him. Her face was still seared from the lightning that had hit the tree close to where she had been standing during the storm. She was lucky to be alive. He supposed she deserved to act a little strangely after being robbed of her innocence, not to mention coming within a hairbreadth of being struck by a lightning bolt. But he wished she would stop with those infuriating tears. It unnerved him to watch her sob!

Hesitantly, he reached out a tanned hand to caress her tear-stained cheek. Moriah didn't resist him until the moment he touched her and then she jumped as if she had been stung. A perplexed frown plowed his brow as he attempted to decipher her blank expression.

"Look at me, Moriah," he commanded, his tone softer now.

All the torment and exasperation exploded inside her. "I can't!" she sobbed hysterically. "I can't *see* you!"

A chilling sensation crested on Devlin when he realized Moriah had been blinded by the lightning. How many more trials must this lovely sprite face?

It had been a long time since Devlin had felt anything except obsessive vengeance. But now that Moriah was hurting, he bled for her. And when she cried he cursed himself for making matters even worse for her. She couldn't see his hand in front of her face, she couldn't see the concern in his expression, the deep regret in his eyes . . .

Nothing had frightened Devlin in more than a year. He had become a reckless daredevil who defied death to track down Lyle Burkhart. But imagining the agony Moriah was undergoing shook him to the roots of his soul. He had been scared as hell while she lay unconscious, unsure if she would live or die. Now, the sight of her attempting to cope with her blindness tugged at his heartstrings so fiercely that he could barely draw a breath.

Instinctively, he enfolded her in his arms and cuddled her close to comfort her. "I'm sorry," he whispered against her temple. His lips trailed lower to capture her lips.

Moriah struggled to free herself from his brawny arms. "I don't want your sympathy," she bleated, hating herself for decomposing before his eyes. There was some solace in blindness, she realized. At least she didn't have to see the pity carved on his ruggedly handsome features. "No one has offered me sympathy before. And I don't want it now. Just go away and leave me alone. You've taken all I can give and you have taught me all I need to know, except how to feel my way through the mountains. *That* I will have to learn on my own."

The bitter remark caused Devlin to cringe. He had obviously spoiled her innocent dreams of passion with his urgent lovemaking, his lack of consideration for her naïveté. He had made her even more resentful of men than she had been to begin with.

Damn, she probably loathed his touch and his very presence.

"It was just that I had been too long without a woman," Devlin murmured awkwardly. "If I had—"

Moriah misinterpreted his remark, thinking he was about to give an excuse for making love to her and attempting to smooth over this rejection of her affection. In truth, he had been trying to apologize for stripping her of her innocence with impatient insensitivity. But Moriah was too mortified and frustrated to let him squeeze another word in edgewise.

"Don't touch me and don't speak to me!" she blared at him, shoving him so forcefully that he sprawled back against the rocks. "Don't come near me ever again, damn you. I despise you and the rest of your disgusting breed. Just go away and let me live my life in darkness and in what small amount of peace I can find. I came up here to be a recluse and that is what I'm going to be!"

"I'm not going to leave you alone," he told her firmly. "No matter how much you hate me, you're stuck with me."

She didn't hate him really, but wounded pride and exasperation locked her affection for him deep in her heart. Moriah was certain that all Devlin felt for her was pity and some sort of strange obligation. She was not about to become a burden to him. He had been grooming her to challenge these treacherous mountains and now the challenge was greater than before. But nothing had really changed. She still intended to live life as a hermit to forget the bittersweet memories of his lovemaking.

"If you wish to do something for me, why don't you go tame a wild animal to lead me around?" she suggested, wiping away the scalding tears. "A coyote to guide me would be nice, I think."

The faintest hint of a smile pursed Devlin's lips as he watched Moriah feel her way up the boulder and stand on her feet. No matter how great the obstacles, it seemed nothing could break her spirit, her defiant will to live, or her wry sense of humor.

His admiring gaze roamed unhindered over the damp clothes that clung to her shapely figure. She really was special, but she was determined, headstrong, and perseverant. With her beauty, resilience, and fierce inner drive, nothing would ever stop her from doing whatever it was she decided to do.

"I think I'm falling in love with you," Devlin heard himself say.

And he meant it. From the first moment he had spied this daring beauty alone in the mountains, he had been seized by a strange, undefinable warmth. This blue-eyed blonde had gotten to him as no woman had ever been able to do. He had discovered unparalleled ecstasy in her arms. He had been the first man to teach Moriah the pleasures of passion, even if he hadn't given her the sort of initiation into womanhood that she deserved. But the next time he took her in his arms he would erase her first experience with passion by showering her with gentleness.

Moriah stared in the direction of his hushed voice. Did he really think she believed that nonsense? His true feelings had emerged after they had made love. She would long remember the frown that had been stamped on his face when he rolled away from her. That hadn't been the look of a man in love! That had been the look of a man who regretted submitting to his lusty desires because the woman in his arms wasn't skilled enough to satisfy him.

Now that she had been blinded by the lightning, Devlin felt sorry for her. He had blurted out a confession of love, as if that would make everything right, as if mouthing the words would heal the bitter wounds that left her soul to bleed. The next thing she knew he would probably ask her to marry him so she wouldn't have to be all alone in her dark world! He was accustomed to coming to the aid of those who had been victimized—like the Apaches. He probably saw her as another mission . . .

"Marry me, Moriah," he murmured, reaching out to trace the heart-shaped curve of her lips.

Look who was reading minds now, she thought. She didn't even have to see the expression on his face to know what he was thinking. He was laden with tremendous guilt because she was blind. Now he was sorry he had rejected her after their lovemaking. He was offering marriage because he had compromised the lady who was now blind. How noble of him! she thought furiously. She would become a burden to no man, especially not this raven-haired, guilt-ridden rake.

"The mountains would sooner erode into flat plains," she snapped bitterly, "before I would consider marrying you. Don't try to do me any more favors. You've taught me all I need to know. The survival lessons are ended."

As she inched around the boulder, Devlin lunged to rescue her before she walked off the summit. But Moriah was hardly appreciative. The feel of his body pressed familiarly to hers set off unwanted sensations. She had to forget the pleasure she had experienced in his embrace because she wasn't woman enough to satisfy him. If he ever seduced her again, it would be out of pity and she couldn't bear that thought!

"Let me go," she spluttered in frustration.

"Good God, woman," he exploded. "Your next

step would have been a hundred-foot drop!"

"So what? If I had fallen, you would have been well rid of your burden," she muttered, still worming for freedom.

Devlin was so agitated over the incidents of the past two days that he felt like pulling out his hair strand by strand. He was beginning to wonder if there really was something to the myth that was circulating around Santa Rita about the Angel of the Wind clashing with White Shadow. He had certainly met his match in this sassy, independent beauty!

Well, he wasn't taking no for an answer, no matter how long and loud she protested. Moriah was going with him and she would damned well become his wife. He had stolen her innocence, and because of his frustration over his lack of control, he had inadvertently caused her blindness. If he hadn't snapped at her she wouldn't have been standing there glaring at him when lightning struck. He had a responsibility to her and he was accepting his obligations whether she liked it or not.

Moriah had every right to despise him, he knew, and he would just have to learn to live with her hate. He had never given a thought to marriage before, but this seemed as good a time as any. And when his feud with Lyle Burkhart was over, Devlin would see to it that Moriah wanted for nothing. She would have a home, and servants to wait on her hand and foot.

When his hand shackled her wrist, Moriah stood firm. But Devlin, being as strong as a bull, uprooted her from her spot.

"Where are you taking me?" she demanded to know.

"You'll see soon enough."

"I won't see at all," she clarified.

"I'm taking you to the Valley of the Eagle," he

informed her as he scooped her up in his arms and wound along the precipices.

"It's a little late now," she grumbled bitterly. "Now I won't be able to see the mysterious Old Man in the riddle who supposedly cries tears of gold."

"But at least you can claim to be one of the few whites who has sojourned in the Apache's sacred land," he countered.

"And naturally I won't be able to retrace my footsteps to the legendary gold mine, being blind as I am," she smirked.

Even though Moriah protested, Devlin wrapped rawhide bags around her feet, and his, to protect them from the rugged terrain and then propelled her northwest. Moriah went because she had no choice. Devlin refused to release his grasp on her wrist. He was as determined that she accompany him as she was not to go. But Devlin's superior strength ensured that his stubborn soon-to-be wife did exactly as he demanded of her. But Moriah made it known that she didn't like it one bit. She cursed him every hour, just in case he had forgotten that she was furious with him.

He hadn't . . .

Chapter 9

For two days Devlin prodded Moriah along like a stubborn mule. He reached the Gila Cliff Dwellings that were built into the side of the stone mountains. There he paused to describe to Moriah the ancient Indian abodes that overlooked the sprawling valley below. Moriah responded with a wisecrack about how lovely the view was this time of year.

Devlin reluctantly smiled at her undaunted spirit. Blindness might have affected her eyes, but paralysis hadn't reached her tongue. Despite the tragedies that had befallen her, she had retained her sense of humor, warped though it had become. She could find amusement in almost any situation. It was apparent that she was trying very hard not to take herself too seriously, to accept her handicap. Devlin liked that about her, even if she hated every square inch of him for being so rough and urgent in their first lovemaking encounter. She had accepted her blindness far better than she had adapted to the idea of Devlin becoming her husband. On that point she was dead serious and stood firm in her conviction that there would be no marriage.

Devlin was a self-assured man, but with Moriah,

he found his confidence dimming. Her vulnerability and handicap had become his own and they seemed to rattle him more than they did her. And Devlin had refused to discuss the subject of marriage again. He had decided this feisty spitfire would become his wife because she needed him—and that was that!

To distract Moriah, Devlin explained the legends and myths of the Apaches and related the story of how the Indians had escaped the land of the Fire Dragon beyond the sea and had come to inhabit the buttes and mesas of the Southwest. It didn't resolve the conflict between him and Moriah, but it did prevent them from debating the controversial issue of marriage.

"How is it that you have come to be such an authority on the Apaches?" Moriah demanded, staring blankly in the direction of Devlin's rich baritone voice.

Thus far she had learned very little about this complicated man who despite her protests, had dragged her over hill and dale. For all she knew, Devlin Granger had hatched from an egg, had been raised by a pack of wolves, and had absorbed all his vast and varied knowledge from firsthand experience. And Devlin told her nothing informative, remaining as closed as a clam when she fired prying questions at him.

"I have lived near the Apaches long enough to learn and understand their ways" was all he said before tugging her along beside him. "It won't be much farther to the Valley of the Eagle."

Moriah glanced skyward, attempting to determine the direction they traveled by the warmth of sunshine on her cheeks. As near as she could tell, they were trekking northwest, but she couldn't swear to it and

Devlin wouldn't enlighten her on that or any other subject.

"This really isn't necessary, you know," she grumbled and then stumbled over the stone that obstructed her path.

Devlin caught Moriah before she fell flat on her face. "Isn't it?" he smirked in contradiction.

"I wasn't referring to the fact that you're practically leading me around on a leash," she snapped irritably. "I meant this ridiculous marriage you have in mind and all the attention you're heaping on me."

No answer. Devlin had resolved not to be dragged into an argument on the topic of matrimony. In his estimation, the less said the better until the deed was done.

"I refuse to become one of your responsibilities," she exclaimed when he made no comment. "Just drop me off in the valley and I'll count the gold nuggets and twiddle my thumbs for the next half-century." Hollow laughter tripped from her lips. "I suppose that is the sort of curse that haunts Apache gold anyway. Those who find it never get to spend it."

Devlin paused by a small spring that trickled from the mountainside and offered Moriah a refreshing drink. His gaze wandered freely over her luscious figure, knowing he wouldn't be scolded for devouring her with his eyes since she couldn't see where his lusty thoughts had strayed.

"What would you do with the gold if you had it?" he inquired before taking a drink.

Moriah gulped the much-needed water and pondered his question for a moment. "I would take the gold and build a house that was surrounded by a thick wall to protect me from the cruelty of the world," she decided. "Then I could live out my life without outside influences to frustrate me."

"Ah, what a cynic you are," he said with a chuckle.

Moriah stared in his direction, her expression suggesting he ought to know a cynic when he saw one, since he was one himself. "I haven't found much use for people. Those I've known are deceitful, vicious, and untrustworthy," she declared with assurance.

Remorsefully, Devlin smiled down into her unblinking blue eyes. He reached out to trace the delicate but stubborn line of her jaw. "Even me, Moriah?" She replied to his question by retreating a step.

He frowned at her objection to his touch. "I never meant to hurt you," he murmured softly.

Moriah braced herself, refusing to buckle beneath his tender touch and hushed remark. She was painfully aware that he was only being nice to her because he felt sorry for her. Why, he hadn't even called her a fool for three days! Devlin clearly felt burdened by guilt and he considered himself responsible for her. If she let her guard down and surrendered to him, she knew he would only be going through the motions of affection, just as he had the first time he seduced her. And once again she would feel used and he would be disappointed by her inexperience. Moriah couldn't bear another rejection on top of all else!

Her reaction to his touch assured him that she hadn't forgiven him for seducing her. She resented him. His only recourse was to coax away her hatred and attempt to return to her good graces. It would take time and patience and Devlin wasn't sure he would live long enough to see that happen. Moriah Laverty was stubborn from the top of her golden-blond head to the tip of her toes and all parts in between.

Since she couldn't see it coming, he dropped a quick kiss to her tempting lips. Moriah cursed her instant reaction. When his sensuous lips flitted over hers, goose bumps skied down her spine. It was impossible not to be stirred by this dynamic man. Even though she couldn't see him, his image was branded on her mind and her traitorous body trembled each cussed time they made any sort of physical contact.

"Shall we get on with this journey of ours?" Moriah faltered.

Devlin's shoulders slumped dejectedly. No matter how hard he tried, he couldn't crack the barriers of Moriah's defense. She was hell-bent on hating him.

Heaving a sigh, he clasped her small hand in his and weaved around the boulders toward the obscure valley that lay a few miles ahead of them in the rough, rocky terrain.

Wearily, Moriah sank onto the floor of the cave into which Devlin had led her. According to him, they had reached the Valley of the Eagle. She had to take his word for it since she could see nothing but darkness sprinkled with streaks of silver. She listened astutely as Devlin dropped their gear and the cave echoed with muffled sounds. She heard his footsteps fade into silence and waited expectantly for his return. A few minutes later he ambled back inside to arrange a campfire.

"I'll tend the fire and make sure the meat doesn't burn," she volunteered.

Devlin started to object and then thought better of

it. Moriah was too independent to sit like a bump on a log. "Good, I have a few duties to attend outside." He took her hand, brushing it over the ring of stones that surrounded the small fire. Then he lifted her fingertips to the two quail, set above the fire, that he had snared for their meal. "Call me down when the birds are cooked."

As he strided away, Moriah's quiet voice halted him in his tracks. "Dev?" she asked, hesitating over the familiar way she had shortened his name.

"Yes?"

She glanced down as she memorized the feel of the stones beneath her fingertips. "Thank you for that at least. I don't want to be completely helpless."

"You never were and you never will be, minx." He flung her a wry smile she couldn't see, but she *could* detect the teasing inflection in his voice. "You're stubborn and prone to temper. Other than that, I find no fault with you."

"No fault, my eye!" Moriah scooped up one of the rocks and hurled it at him.

There were some folks whose bursts of temper compelled them to rattle off curses that would singe the ears off a priest. There were other folks who furiously stamped their feet, and others who simply got mad and stormed off. But Moriah threw things to relieve her frustration. She had been forced to stifle her temper when Ruby was around because Vance was always there to punish Moriah. But with Devlin, Moriah was able to unleash her temper at will and she threw the stone at him because he allowed her to get away with it.

Her blind aim, however, missed its intended mark. She hadn't really expected to knock him on the head. Devlin was as quick and agile as a cat. Moriah heard the rock clank against the cavern wall and drop to the dusty floor with an echoing thud.

She knew damned good and well Devlin found fault with her attempt to pleasure him. She would never forget the disgusted look on his craggy features that fateful afternoon. She had found ineffable rapture in his arms and he had walked away, regretting her inability to satisfy him. But of course he wouldn't own up to that now that she was blind and virtually helpless, not to mention alone in the world.

"I'll be outside," Devlin muttered as he stalked off. "I hope your disposition improves by the time I return."

"Chances are it won't."

"I was afraid of that."

When his footsteps receded, Moriah cursed under her breath. Why did everything he said rub her the wrong way? Because she was vulnerable and she was wearing her heart on her sleeve, she decided. It stung her feminine pride to know she wasn't woman enough to please the only man she had ever wanted intimately. Devlin could woo her with sugar-coated flattery, but deep down inside he had been disappointed in her amorous affections.

Her shoulders sagged and a heavy sigh escaped her lips. Criminey, sometimes she swore she had been jinxed! Her life seemed to have been an exercise in frustration. And then along came Devlin Granger—the only man who had awakened her slumbering passions and made her believe she had a chance at happiness. And then before she could revel in her relationship with this special man, she had discovered the torment of rejection and had been struck blind.

Yet, in all fairness to Devlin, Moriah realized her lack of experience wasn't his fault. He had expected more than she knew how to give because she had never informed him that he was her first experiment with passion. There was no hard and fast rule that stated a man was supposed to be hopelessly captivated by the woman who was hopelessly captivated with him. Moriah had tried to make too much of the moment and she was left wanting what she could never have—Devlin's heart-felt affection. Instead, she was offered his compassion. Damn!

While Moriah was battling her despair and scolding herself for taking her frustrations out on Devlin when he didn't deserve it, he was building another campfire to send a smoke signal to Chanos. In Apache country, signals could be seen and relayed up to two hundred miles away and he needed Chanos's assistance. Devlin knew the Apache warrior would come. It was only a matter of time.

Devlin had just smothered the fire when Moriah appeared at the mouth of the cave to announce supper. As wary as a lion tamer entering the cage of a starved cat, Devlin approached. He wondered if this sassy she-cat was in the same frame of mind she had been when he left. Moriah's quicksilver change of moods made it difficult to handle her. She put up a bold front at times, but he knew she was bitter about their lovemaking and that she was struggling to cope with her blindness, but each time he attempted to discuss what had happened, she abruptly cut him off.

Well, there was more than one way to counter her resentfulness, Devlin told himself. He was out of practice after his year of celibacy, but he fully intended to change Moriah's opinion of lovemaking. He refused to allow their first encounter to be the one that lingered in her mind . . .

"I'm sorry," Moriah murmured before chewing on a morsel of juicy meat.

Devlin's brows jackknifed. Damned if she hadn't changed moods again! Just when he had devised a tactic to soften her anger toward him; she switched from feisty to apologetic and he wasn't sure how to proceed without setting her off again.

"I've become a peevish shrew." Brittle laughter bubbled in her throat. "I would do Ruby Thatcher proud. It seems her waspish disposition has rubbed off on me." She glanced toward the heat of the fire. "You seem to think you owe me some stupendous favor after the accident, but you don't," she insisted.

"Riah," he began, liking the musical sound of this intimate form of her name. "I—"

As usual, she cut him short to vocalize her own thoughts, with which she had been grappling for the past thirty minutes. "I am trying to accept what happened between us, and I don't hold you responsible for the accident, either." Her lips trembled and she bit at them before continuing. "It is true that you were my first experience with—" Here she paused to formulate a delicate reference, but she couldn't come up with anything. "With passion. If I had made my inexperience known to you, what happened probably wouldn't have happened. It would have been better for both of us if it hadn't—"

His index finger pressed against her lips to shush her. "Next time will be better, I promise you."

Moriah jerked away. A determined frown bracketed her mouth. "There isn't going to be a next time." She would die before she'd have him make love to her out of pity!

"Oh yes there will," he told her in no uncertain terms. "A man and his wife are entitled to—"

"Entitled?" She bolted to her feet and glared at him. "Husband and wife? Never!"

There she went again, pouncing on his words,

poor choice though they were. "Good God, don't be so damned touchy. I can't say anything without putting you in a snit . . . Where do you think you're going?"

"Outside to take a bath," she grumbled.

"I'll help you."

"I can manage on my own, thank you very much!"

A startled squawk erupted from her lips when she marched forward and stepped into the huge bowl of beans Devlin had set beside him. Muttering curses, Moriah yanked her foot from the clay bowl and flung it against the wall.

"Watch out for the—"

Devlin's warning came too late. Moriah slammed into the low ceiling above the uneven mouth of the cave.

Holding her aching head, Moriah ducked down and wobbled outside, feeling her way along the path.

Sending a glance skyward, Devlin summoned divine patience to deal with this fiery sprite. Hell, they couldn't even have a discussion without it evolving into an argument. But arguments or offense or no, Devlin wasn't about to let Moriah drop off the cliff while she was put out with him.

Despite her protest, Devlin led her down the winding path to the spring that was brimming with nuggets of gold.

"You may leave me now," she dismissed him coolly. Carefully, she bent down to explore the perimeters of the pool.

"It isn't as if I haven't seen you naked before," he muttered at her. "Damnation, Moriah, I don't know why you keep throwing obstacles between us. If we could just talk this out like two reasonable individuals, maybe we could—"

"Can't I have a smidgen of privacy around here?"

she hurled in question. "Kindly take yourself off someplace so I can bathe in peace!"

"Fine, I hope you—" Devlin clamped his mouth shut. The last time he had flung a spiteful rejoinder at the frustrating minx she had wound up blind. He wasn't tempting fate again!

"And don't spy on me just because I can't see you," she added as she listened to his receding footsteps.

Begrudgingly, Devlin stamped around the huge stone pillars that surrounded the spring and filled the valley. Muttering to himself, he stalked back in the direction he had come. He had the feeling Moriah was purposely antagonizing him every chance she got. She thought her quick changes of mood would infuriate him to the point that he would just throw up his hands and leave her to her own devices. But the tactic wasn't going to work; he wasn't going to abandon her or let her go on thinking that passion was nothing more than the impatient encounter he had forced on her!

Although Moriah demanded privacy, Devlin leaned leisurely against a stone slab above the spring and gawked as she peeled off her clothes. He sighed appreciatively when she sank into the clear pool. Lord, she was positively breathtaking. Staring at her satiny flesh stirred his blood. Remembering the intimacy they had shared aroused him. He longed to erase her bitter memories and replace them with a sweet, tantalizing dream of splendor. If he had anything to do with it, she wasn't going to go through life thinking passion was so painful and unpleasant that it should be avoided at all costs . . .

A quiet growl echoed in the soft breeze and Devlin jerked to attention. His keen gaze circled the canyon, seeking the source of the sound. The instant he spied the mountain lion crouching in the brush above the springs, he wheeled to fetch his Winchester. With his heart thumping against his chest, Devlin raced along the path to place himself within rifle range of the crouched beast. His gaze darted to Moriah who had heard the sound and was floundering toward shore.

His name flew from her lips in a cry of alarm as she struggled over to the rocks that lined the pool. Her senses were tuned to the sounds of danger but she couldn't determine what kind of creature had sneaked up on her. She hadn't meant to scream Devlin's name; it had automatically popped from her mouth. It seemed she had come to depend on him more than she cared to admit.

Frantic, Moriah thrashed toward shore, hearing the rustle of bushes above her. What a fool she had been to think she could manage on her own when she couldn't even see what was coming until it was upon her. She was constantly tripping over rocks and colliding with objects she didn't know were there.

Another vicious snarl penetrated her thoughts and she froze in her tracks. Terrified, she tried to scramble away from the sound instead of toward it. The crack of a rifle reverberated around the chasm and suddenly Moriah felt the slash of claws against her bare skin. A horrified screech burst from her throat as she shoved at the hairy creature that had pounced on her. But the cat didn't attack. It slumped against her, causing her to stumble backward on the uneven rocks that surrounded the spring.

While Moriah floundered to heave the lifeless carcass away, Devlin knelt beside her. The strained relationship between them and her near brush with calamity suddenly became too much for Moriah and her composure cracked wide open.

"What did I do to deserve this?" she sobbed, covering herself as best she could. "All I asked was for a little peace and solitude and all I got was blindness and . . ." She groped to determine what animal had attacked her. "And . . . panthers," she finished on a choked breath.

"Mountain lions," he corrected quietly.

"Mountain lions," she amended, still bleeding a sea of tears.

Devlin laid his rifle aside and tugged her into his arms. "It's a sign that you need me, even if you are too proud to admit it. You are much safer in my arms."

The feel of his body molded to hers set off unwanted tingles that Moriah was hard-pressed to ignore, though she made a valiant effort to do so. "Don't touch me!"

Devlin flagrantly disregarded her command. The sight of the mountain lion springing at her had caused the hair on the back of his neck to stand on end. The thought of Moriah being mauled tore his emotions to shreds. And now that he had her back in his arms, he wasn't letting her go. It was time he proved that he was more than an impatient savage who took without giving in return. Moriah might still hate him afterward, but she would know that he could be a tender, sensitive lover.

"Let me be your eyes, Riah," he murmured as he dragged his lips from hers. "Let me be your friend and your lover . . ."

His lips slanted across hers, silencing her before she could refuse his requests. He courted her with a gentleness that was more overpowering than force. He didn't rush her. He waited for her body to surrender to his warm, persuasive assault. His reverent kisses drifted over her tense body, showering her with loving tenderness.

Moriah cursed her lack of willpower. When this mysterious wizard touched her, her brain ceased to function and her traitorous body yielded to his masterful touch. He made her feel cherished and wanted, even though she knew she was nothing of the kind. She was a burden and obligation and he pitied her, nothing more . . .

When his greedy kisses mapped her quaking flesh, she forgot how to resist. He worshipped her with masterful caresses. He rediscovered every inch of her silky flesh, leaving her pliant and submissive in his sinewy arms. Moriah felt herself sinking into a pool of titillating sensations as his hands and lips glided expertly over her body, seeking out each ultrasensitive point. The fear of rejection didn't seem so terrifying when Devlin was weaving his spell of magic on her mind and body. He could make her soul sing and her skin tingle with forbidden sensations.

A soft gasp burst forth when his fingertips swirled around the dusky buds of her breasts. Over and over again, his caresses drifted over her flesh, triggering needs that Moriah had tried to deny to salvage her pride. But there was no resisting Devlin's skillful touch or the tidal wave of pleasure that crested upon her. She longed for his explosive kisses and tingling caresses, yearned to enjoy the intimacy they had once shared, to please him in all the ways he had pleased her.

Moriah twisted away to chart the rugged terrain of his body. She yearned to leave him burning with the same monstrous needs that consumed her. Her hands migrated over his whipcord muscles, measuring the wide expanse of his hair-roughened chest, whispering over the lean flesh of his waist and hips. Although she couldn't see him, she remembered how aroused she had been by the mere sight of his powerful body. Touching him stirred the erotic visions and provided a tingling pleasure all its own.

Moriah let her heart rule her head, let her forbidden feelings for him teach her to please him. She invented ways to tease and tempt him. She wanted to devastate him as thoroughly as he devastated her. Her imaginative touch roamed over every inch of his body, divesting him of his breeches when they inhibited her investigative caresses. She learned him by touch and feel, by spreading moist kisses in the wake of her tantalizing caresses.

Her slow, provocative exploration left Devlin burning on a hot, explosive flame. Her lips and hands greeted every inch of his flesh—his eyelids, his cheeks, his throat and chest and ribs. She wove seductive designs on his belly and thighs, leaving him quivering with needs that threatened to burst out of control.

When the first wave of rapture toppled over him, Devlin groaned in sweet agony. It was difficult to lie there and allow Moriah the freedom to explore his body without clutching her to him and ravishing her. But he had made that mistake the first time and he swore he would let her proceed at her own pace this time, even if it killed him.

The wild, wondrous sensations she evoked with her imaginative caresses shattered what was left of Devlin's self-control as if it was never there at all. He wanted this delicious vixen madly, needed her, craved her like a mindless obsession.

With masculine grace, he rolled above her to treat her to the same sweet torment of intimate kisses and arousing caresses. Moriah melted in a puddle of indescribable pleasure. She had naively thought their first encounter was the epitome of ecstasy, but now she realized that it had only been a stepping-stone that led into the world of sensual pleasure. Devlin aroused her by titillating degrees, leaving her aching for him with every fiber of her being. When he braced himself above her she was eager to give herself to him, to feel his muscular body molded to hers, to share the explosive harmony of all-consuming desire.

Devlin inwardly groaned at the blank stare in Moriah's vivid blue eyes. How he wished she could see the hungry passion in his gaze, see how thoroughly she had devastated him, how desperately he wanted her.

Ever so slowly he guided her thighs apart and brushed his lips over her soft trembling mouth, whispering his need for her. Gently, he came to her, setting the ageless rhythm of love in a slow, hypnotic cadence. He refused to bow down to the ravenous needs that churned inside him. This time, he promised himself, Moriah would experience all the magical sensations of lovemaking. He would give and share his passions without forcing them on her as he had done before.

The warm threat of his powerful body engulfing hers caused Moriah's dark world to sparkle with a kaleidoscope of vivid colors. Devlin didn't take from her; he gave, leaving her wanting all he had to offer, leaving her wondering if even that would be enough to appease this colossal need he instilled in her.

Hungrily, she met his driving thrusts and lost herself to the delirious sensations that channeled through her body. She experienced the most remarkable feelings when he clutched her to him and took complete possession of her body, mind, and spirit. She swore she was flying through space like a shooting star, consumed by white-hot fire. She soared in motionless flight without leaving the circle of Devlin's arms and there was no place in the world she wanted to be except with him.

One battalion of delicious sensations after another assaulted her body as he sought ultimate depths of intimacy. Streams of ecstasy engulfed her and sent her plummeting into swirling fathoms of darkness. Desperately, she clung to him, praying that he was as aroused by their ardent lovemaking as she was, that she wouldn't disappoint him this time.

A muffled groan rumbled in Devlin's chest and he shuddered convulsively. He couldn't seem to control the aftershocks that riveted his body. He couldn't stop squeezing Moriah. Letting her go was virtually impossible when he was in the grips of such overwhelming sensations. He feared he had once again been too rough with her, that his savage passions had caused another round of invisible wounds.

Tenderly, his lips whispered over her kiss-swollen mouth, silently attempting to compensate for any pain he had unintentionally caused her. "Did I hurt you?" he questioned hesitantly.

"No," she rasped, her voice still thick with the afteraffects of indescribable rapture. "Did I please you this time?" she inquired apprehensively.

A muddled frown plowed his dark brows as he glanced down into her sightless stare. "You pleased me the first time," he insisted. "It was *I* who disappointed *you.*"

Blue eyes blinked in disbelief. "I wasn't disappointed one tittle," she assured him. "It was you who turned away because I'm not experienced with men."

Devlin gaped at the tangle-haired beauty as if she had sagebrush growing out her ears. "Is that what you thought?" he asked in an incredulous voice.

Moriah didn't have to look away this time since she couldn't see the expression stamped on his rugged features. "You don't have to pretend you weren't satisfied with me," she murmured. "I saw the look on your face when you turned away then, even if I can't see it *now*."

Lovingly, Devlin nuzzled against her dainty, upturned nose. "Naive imp," he scolded, but his tone was too husky to sound condemning. "What you saw was the look of a man who had, too late, realized he had stolen your innocence and regretted his lack of restraint. I should have been gentle and patient with you. I thought you despised me for being so rough and inconsiderate of you."

A smile to rival the brilliance of the sun lighted her face. Her hand lifted to determine whether Devlin was frowning or smiling at her. His sensual lips were curved into a smile. "You mean I wasn't so bad the first time?"

"You were stupendously wonderful," he growled seductively. "But we could both use some practice. I've been out of touch for a long time and you've just begun to discover what loving is all about . . ."

When his mouth descended on hers, promising to teach her more of the ways of love, Moriah turned her head away. She knew she shouldn't be so prying, but curiosity got the best of her.

"How many women have you had?" she wanted to know that very second.

"Don't spoil the moment with damnfool questions," he grumbled before devouring her lips with a kiss that was meant to strip all thought from her mind. It wasn't one hundred per cent effective, however. Demons of curiosity still had a firm grip on Moriah.

"You know I've never been with any other man. Now I want to know how many women were before me," she persisted.

"What difference does it make?" he whispered

against the sensitive point beneath her ear. "I've already forgotten every woman but you."

The feel of his practiced hands skimming over her flesh made her forget the question. The feel of his masculine body moving suggestively upon hers pushed all curiosity to the far corner of her mind. All of a sudden nothing mattered except the tantalizing sensations that leapfrogged through her every nerve and muscle. And a moment later, Moriah was lost to the sparks that sizzled between his flesh and hers. Helplessly, she gave herself up to the glorious moment, returning his passion kiss for hungry kiss and caress for each possessive caress.

It was a wild, impatient coming together and Moriah found incredible satisfaction in the fact that she had the power to leave him trembling with need. Perhaps she hadn't been the first woman to arouse his male desires, but at least he was hers for as long as his passion for her would last. She still was certain what he felt for her had more to do with pity than love, but at least he had cleared up her misinterpretation of his rejection. Knowing she had pleased him, even if she couldn't compare to the lovers he had known, bolstered her confidence.

Moriah held nothing back this time. She surrendered body and soul to each wondrous sensation that piled upon another. She marveled at each new plateau of ecstasy she discovered in his arms. The explosive harmony of their lovemaking built into a wild crescendo that left Moriah wondering if she could survive such soul-shattering splendor. She held him to her as if she never meant to let him go, riding out the waves of rapture that finally sent her drifting back to reality's shore.

Satiated, Devlin rolled beside Moriah to outline

her heart-shaped lips with his fingertips. "Mmmm . . . I think I'd like to spend the whole night doing this."

"What *this* are you referring to?" she teased with an elfin grin. "Lounging in the grass beside the spring?"

Devlin was amazed and delighted by this new facet of Moriah's personality. Now that one confusing issue had been unshackled; she didn't pounce on his every word. And Lord, what a seductive minx she could be when she wasn't so busy being defensive.

"*This* this," he clarified as his bold caresses wandered over the rose-tipped crests of her breasts, meandered down her ribs, and lingered on the soft curve of her hips.

"Isn't there a limit to how many times a man and woman can make love before they wear themselves out?" Moriah questioned with innocent curiosity.

Devlin took one look at the solemn expression on her exquisite face and burst out laughing. "Why do you ask? Do you wish to set some sort of record?"

Moriah blushed up to the roots of her blond hair. Devlin probably thought she had become an insatiable harlot the way she was behaving, the way she was firing intimate questions at him. "No, I was just curi—"

"*I* would like to set a record . . . but only with you, Riah. I have only to look at you and I feel like loving you again." His scalding kiss blotted all thought from her mind as well as his.

Chapter 10

The soft crunch of rocks roused Devlin from his peaceful sleep. Carefully, he inched away from Moriah's side and crept to the mouth of the cave to see the first shafts of sunlight slant over the jagged mountains.

Chanos regarded his blood brother in silent appraisal and then a wry smile quirked his lips. "I cannot imagine what you need with me, White Shadow," he chuckled, his dark eyes darting to the cave.

Devlin met the knowing grin with a carefully blank stare. "I need you to keep a watchful eye on Moriah while I travel to Santa Rita. She was blinded by a lightning bolt."

At the tragic news, the smile slid off Chanos's bronzed features.

"She is a very independent woman and she tries to fend for herself, even when it proves to be perilous folly," Devlin went on. "But she still needs someone to watch over her until I return."

Chanos nodded somberly as he stared at the entrance of the cave. "I will do as you ask, White Shadow."

"When I say *watch* her, I mean *watch* her," Devlin added with a meaningful glance, noting for the second time where Chanos's gaze had strayed. "She means a great deal to me."

The Apache medicine man assessed his long-time friend. It had been over a year since White Shadow had given much thought to women, as far as he knew. This had been too long in coming, as far as Chanos was concerned. The obsession for revenge was as fierce in Chanos's heart as it was in Devlin's. He had lost his brother because of Burkhart's treachery. Devlin had taken it upon himself to avenge the cruel deaths because he felt responsible for bringing Burkhart to counsel with the Apaches in the first place. That desire for vengeance had been all that had motivated Devlin for more than a year . . . until the woman with sky-blue eyes and golden hair invaded his private domain.

"She will be safe with me until you return," he assured Devlin.

Gesturing for Chanos to wait outside until he roused Moriah, Devlin pivoted around and strode into the cavern. Gently, he nudged Moriah awake and she stretched like a kitten stirring from a nap.

Impulsively, he dropped a kiss to her mouth and patted her shapely derriere. "Wake up, little minx."

The previous night of loving had left Moriah in an amorous mood. Her arms wound around Devlin's neck, knocking him off balance so that he sprawled on top of her. Her body moved suggestively beneath him and the throb of desire pulsed through his veins. Begrudgingly, he reminded himself that Chanos was waiting outside and there was no time for lengthy good-byes.

"Don't do that," Devlin groaned when she arched provocatively toward him. "It's hard enough to go without your teasing me with your delicious body."

She murmured something about setting another record and Devlin moaned in torment.

"Moriah, listen to me," he ordered as he drew her wandering hands away from his shoulders and sat up on his haunches. When her long lashes fluttered up to reveal those shimmering blue pools, he found himself cursing the accident that had left his lovely Moriah blind. "I have to return to Santa Rita."

He didn't say why and that frustrated Moriah. She wanted to be an integral part of his life instead of the time he was killing between battles.

"A friend is going to stay with you until I come back."

A disappointed frown clouded her brow. Moriah had hoped to spend the next few days as pleasurably as they had spent the previous night. But it seemed White Shadow's need for revenge was haunting him again and he had turned his thoughts elsewhere, and, for certain, *away* from her.

"What friend?" she questioned in a sleep-drugged voice.

"He is called Chanos." Urging her to sit up, Devlin assisted her into her clothes. "He's waiting outside to meet you."

Mechanically, Moriah fastened her shirt and combed her fingers through the tangled mass of blond hair that cascaded over her shoulders. When she was decent, Devlin called to his blood brother. Moriah stared in the direction of the muffled footsteps that approached her.

Chanos missed a step as the opening of the cavern admitted the light in its unique design. The dancing sunbeams flitted around the tawny-haired beauty who sat beside Devlin. An aureole of gold circled her head, and eyes as clear and blue as a mountain stream stared unblinkingly at him. For a few moments, Chanos stood there, mystified by the golden rays that silhouetted the bewitching young woman.

A sting of jealousy bit at Devlin when he noticed the rapt expression on Chanos's face. He could see the Apache warrior's eyes roving over the thin shirt that barely concealed Moriah's full breasts. Devlin knew perfectly well what his friend was thinking—the same damned thing Devlin had thought the first time he saw Moriah at close range. Damn!

When Chanos realized Devlin was glaring in disapproval, he broke into a guilty smile. He knew of White Shadow's gift of reading faces. Chanos had been caught speculating about the pleasures Devlin had enjoyed in this enchanting maid's arms!

Devlin scowled at his blood brother before motioning for Chanos to approach.

After the introductions were made, Devlin reluctantly pressed a farewell kiss to Moriah's tempting lips. When he had collected his gear, he ambled outside, Chanos following in his wake.

"You are asking a great deal of me," Chanos grunted. "Even more than I first thought."

"I know," Devlin mumbled as he draped the strap of his rifle over his bare shoulder. "But I trust you with her."

"I'm not sure you should. There is something mystical about that woman," Chanos said frankly. Chanos was always plainspoken and said exactly what was on his mind. "She possesses great powers or she would not have survived all the tragedies that have befallen her. And she is a great temptation to any man."

"I well know all that, and I hope I still have good reason to call you friend when I get back," he muttered as he aimed himself southeast.

"So do I, White Shadow. I would hate to see our long-standing friendship broken because we both want the same woman," Chanos said bluntly.

"Do you have to be so damned honest?" Devlin growled, casting Chanos the evil eye.

Bronzed shoulders lifted in a reckless shrug. "It is my way. And you already read the look of desire in my eyes. It will do neither of us any good to pretend it doesn't exist."

Muttering at Chanos's frankness, Devlin stomped off with the green monster nipping at his heels. He had to put his thoughts in proper perspective. He had already allowed Moriah to distract him more than she should have. Now it was time to channel his energies and efforts into hounding Burkhart. That ruthless butcher had to be stopped and Devlin had to find a way to ensure that the Apaches weren't blamed when Burkhart finally met his downfall. It was time Devlin discovered what Burkhart had in mind for the Apaches this time. It would be easier to prey on the evil commander when Devlin was aware of his plans. Devlin made it a habit of staying one step ahead of Burkhart if at all possible.

While Devlin trekked along the mountain passes, intent on covering as much as seventy miles a day, just as the Apaches did when they traveled the route to battle their Mexican enemies in Chihuahua and Sonora, Moriah sat in the cave. She couldn't help thinking that Devlin had satisfied his male desires and was anxious to put his mind to his mysterious crusade of revenge.

As much as it hurt to admit it, Moriah was sure she was just the woman Devlin trifled with between crusades, just the poor blind woman who needed someone to watch over her.

It had also become painfully apparent that what

she felt for Devlin had evolved from passion into love. And she was chagrined to realize it was one-sided. No matter what Devlin had said the day she was struck blind, he didn't really love her. He loved the challenge of the mountains, craved vengeance against injustice, and he pitied her plight. His confession of affection was only a token of consolation. He had said what he thought she needed to hear.

Moriah heaved a heavy sigh and rose to her feet, finding Chanos there beside her to guide her toward the entrance of the cave. The splendorous interlude was over as quickly as it had begun, she told herself sensibly. She would be a fool to expect more from Devlin than he could possibly give. He had his priorities and she was nowhere near the top of the list.

"Nice view, don't you think, Chanos?" Moriah declared as cheerfully as she could manage. "The sun is hanging above the mountains like an orange balloon, flinging shadows of brown and purple on the western slopes." When the warmth on her face ebbed momentarily, Moriah knew the sun had darted behind the wispy clouds. "But there is the threat of rain in the parade of clouds that marches across the sky," she predicted. Moriah inhaled a deep breath, smelling the hint of moisture in the air. "I suspect we will be plagued with another gully washer by this time tomorrow. I only hope the storm won't be as severe as the last one."

Chanos blinked bewilderedly. "How do you know these things?"

Her hand lifted to pat him on the shoulder. It was a strong shoulder, much like Devlin's. "Just because I'm blind doesn't mean I can't see, Chanos. Come along, let's explore the valley, shall we?"

Thunderstruck, Chanos watched Moriah feel her

way along the winding path. He had expected this lovely sprite to be bitter because of her tragedy, but she was hardly that! And she was, as Devlin had warned him, a mite too independent. Even without her sight, Moriah was all set to explore the Valley of the Eagle.

With a smile of admiration, Chanos followed Moriah to the valley floor. With each passing minute, he understood why White Shadow had become so bewitched by this golden-haired woman. Not only was Moriah the personification of beauty but she was also teeming with undaunted spirit. The combination was staggering, and Chanos had to remind himself that he had promised White Shadow that he would do no more than keep a watchful eye on this nymph who stirred him like the wind that surged through the mountain passes and whispered through the trees and canyons of Apacheland.

"Going on another Apache hunt, are you?" Clyde Finnegan questioned as Commander Burkhart swaggered into the saloon in Santa Rita.

While he was in town, Clyde knew the one-armed commander could be found atop his steed, chasing Apaches and cutting them to shreds, drinking liquor like a fish, or pleasuring himself with as many women as he could get his hands on. Clyde had little use for the man who was the self-appointed god of Southwest New Mexico and Arizona territories. Burkhart was too bloodthirsty to suit Clyde's tastes and contradicted Clyde's philosophy of live and let live.

"Something like that," Burkhart grunted as he settled into his chair and guzzled his drink.

Clyde picked up his cup and invited himself to

Burkhart's table. So much whiskey had spilled on it over the past few years that it was practically varnished with a sticky film. "Well, you've got your work cut out for you if you're going after White Shadow again."

Burkhart's carrot-red head jerked up and frosty green eyes bore into Clyde's mocking smile.

"And with the Angel of the Wind flitting around the Black Mountains, you might find more trouble than you bargained for," Peter Gibson chimed in as he parked himself between Lyle and Clyde.

Lyle took one look at the shaggy-haired miners and decided they were both crazy as loons. "I don't believe in angels any more than I believe in the curses of avenging ghosts," he snorted derisively.

"Well, you oughta," Peter smirked. "Clyde here saw the angel himself. And so did Mick and Kent." He indicated the two miners who were lounging at a nearby table. "They met her, too. And she clashed with White Shadow during the last storm. You could hear 'em bellowing at each other."

A bunch of bonafide loons, Lyle silently assured himself as he stared down his nose at the four miners who had spent so much time in the mountains searching for gold and silver that their brains had been damaged. "If I see your angel, I'll give her your regards," Lyle scoffed before swallowing another glass of whiskey in one gulp.

"You can't miss her," Clyde declared. "Her hair is gold and her eyes are azure blue. Her name is Moriah and she's the prettiest thing a man ever did see."

Lyle, who had poured himself another drink and had taken another gulp, choked on his breath. For a full minute he sputtered and wheezed while Peter and Clyde whacked him between the shoulder blades.

"What was this angel wearing when you saw her?" he croaked.

"You mean besides her wings and halo?" Clyde questioned with a taunting grin. Clyde never met a man he didn't like until Burkhart came along, and he razzed the cocky commander every chance he got. No one who knew Burkhart had much regard for the man. He was frivolous with the lives of his dragoons, merciless with his enemies, and unbearably arrogant.

"Yeah, besides that," Lyle said in a strangled chirp.

"A blue calico gown. But when Mick and Kent happened on her she had changed into the white robe of an angel."

"Saw her where?" Lyle interrogated impatiently.

"At Angel Springs, just to the north," Clyde reported. "At least that's what we decided to name it since her appearance. But as fast as the Angel of the Wind moves, and being able to fly and all, I reckon she could be just about anywhere by now."

Lyle had heard enough. Since he and his men had never recovered that fiery hellion's body, chances were she had miraculously managed to escape. Now she was preying on these superstitious miners and they had made a legend of her as well. Not only could he put an end to the White Shadow myth but he might be able to get his hands on that rebellious sprite who had rejected his advances that night beside the Mimbres River. These fools could spread their fables of angels if they wished, but Lyle had the feeling Moriah Laverty was alive and hiding in the mountains. That was her misfortune because Lyle had a score to settle with her. She wouldn't kick him to his knees again. She would be on her back and he would be satisfying himself with her luscious body!

And after that Lyle didn't care if she really did become a disembodied spirit. Having little regard for human life, other than his own, Lyle didn't give a whit what happened to the feisty blonde after he satisfied his revenge against her humiliating rejection. Women were placed on earth to appease a man's needs, and white men were the superior race of the world. And the sooner those savage Apaches were wiped from the face of the planet, the happier Lyle would be. They had murdered his uncle and cousin five years earlier while the two men were scalp-hunting. Lyle wouldn't be satisfied until every last one of those heathens was frying in hell!

"So when's your next attack?" Clyde quizzed Burkhart, dragging the commander from his spiteful musings.

"I don't attack. I defend," Lyle clarified.

"Yeah, right," Clyde scoffed. "So . . . when are you planning your next defense, Commander? I'll want to make sure I stay out of your way so I'm not mistaken for a renegade."

"I'm taking my regiment and reinforcements into the mountains at the end of next month," Lyle declared. "The Apache problem is getting worse."

Clyde hadn't noticed any problems, only the ones Burkhart conjured up to justify his massacres.

Lyle chugged another drink and then stared hard at his two companions. "Have either of you seen any renegades while you've been digging?"

Clyde nodded negatively. "No. The Apaches don't bother me and I don't bother them. As far as I'm concerned, there isn't a problem. I guess it's mostly between you and White Shadow."

Lyle gritted his teeth and shoved himself away from the table. He didn't have to sit here and listen to these shabbily dressed prospectors mock his noble purpose in life. What did he care what they thought anyway? All he had to do was convince his superiors that he was reacting to a menacing threat. And he would do just that when he was forced to appear before the military court. Damn that Granger family and damn that frustrating legend that was circulating through the West. Well, he was going to put a stop to the Apaches and White Shadow once and for all. Before he was called to court to defend this action, he would wipe out every last renegade!

Drawing himself up to his full arrogant stature, Lyle swaggered out the door, intent on making his rounds to each saloon and posing a few more questions about sightings of Apaches. When he was out of sight, the man who sat inconspicuously in the corner polished off his glass of Taos Lightning and frowned pensively.

Disguised in a sombrero, serape, breeches, and boots, Devlin glanced up from beneath the wide brim of his hat. So Burkhart was making a last ditch effort to attack the Apache strongholds, was he? How interesting. Perhaps Burkhart would be surprised at what he found when he led his regiments and mercenary dragoons into the mountains. The time was rapidly approaching for Lyle to confront White Shadow. The two of them would soon come face-to-face in a battle to the death.

Mulling over that thought, Devlin ambled out of the saloon to track Burkhart to another of his favorite haunts—one of the many taverns that lined the streets of Santa Rita del Cobre. He wasn't leaving town until he knew every move Burkhart intended to make when he launched his offensive against the Apache strongholds.

* * *

"I thought you had your heart set on going all the way to California," Vance remarked as Ruby strutted along beside him, fussing over the new plumed hat she had purchased in Tucson.

"I'm sick and tired of sitting in that dusty wagon," Ruby groused. "Just look around you, Vance."

She raised her arms to encompass the watch-tower walls, sun-dried adobe houses, and the mud-brick pueblos. The caravan of travelers had made a stop to restock supplies at Old Pueblo, and Ruby was thrilled to be off the wagon and on the street.

"There are a half-dozen companies mining copper, gold, and silver in the area. And according to what I've heard, the population is on the rise. There are Arizona Rangers, the Arizona guard, and troops at Fort Lowell to protect citizens from the threat of Indian attack. And the town has the first weekly paper in the area. Why, the proprietor at the dress shop even offered to sell me his business for a price we could easily afford, what with the money we obtained from the sale of the Texas farm. His wife died last winter and he has decided to move back to Colorado to be near his son's family."

Ruby directed Vance's attention to the blacksmith barn which bore a sign indicating help was wanted. "While I manage the shop, you could work with the smithy. He is doing a thriving business shoeing and repairing equipment for the mail stages and wagon trains. With all the gold and silver floating around the area, we could become rich beyond our wildest dreams."

The fact that the travelers on the wagon train had hounded Ruby about her missing stepdaughter was another deciding factor. If she and Vance remained in the prospering town, supposedly to await word about Moriah, no one would be the wiser. No one in

Tucson would even know the Thatchers even *had* a stepdaughter. The community, which retained the atmosphere of a Mexican hacienda, was perfect, and opportunity was staring them in the face. If there was gold in New Mexico, why trudge all the way to California to find prosperity?

"Well, dear, if you're sure that's what you want to do," Vance sighed as he plodded down the street beside his wife.

"That's exactly what I want to do," Ruby adamantly insisted. She gave her lumbering husband a nudge toward the blacksmith barn. "You get yourself a job with the smithy and I'll handle the transaction with the proprietor of the shop. With my knowledge of fashions and fabrics, we will soon be turning gold hand over fist!"

Resolutely, Vance clopped off to do as he was told, just as he always did.

With a triumphant smile, Ruby wheeled back toward the shop with visions of wealth dancing in her head. Now that Moriah was out of the way, things were going splendidly. Her scheme to strip that pesky girl of her inheritance and dispose of her had worked superbly. Soon Moriah would be no more than a bitter page from her past.

No longer did Ruby have to stare into Moriah's enchanting features and lament the loss of her own beauty. That persnickety chit was gone for good. If she and Vance stayed in Tucson, no one would pester her with any more questions. Frankly, she was sick to death of pretending concern for that stepdaughter of hers!

Chapter 11

Moriah had enjoyed Chanos's company far more than she had anticipated. He had led her around the valley that was filled with pillars and slabs of huge stones, showing her the altar of the sun and introducing her to the Old Man of the Mountain, even when she couldn't see who or what she was really looking at.

He provided answers for many of Moriah's questions, and she learned the details of the Apaches' problem with Lyle Burkhart and the other bloodthirsty officers who had broken the peace and put the Apaches on the warpath. Although Moriah was certain there were atrocities on both sides, it seemed to her that the Apaches had just cause to retaliate against the treachery and deceit to which they had been subjected.

According to Chanos, Cochise had been accused of murdering a young boy four years earlier, and an unpleasant incident with the Army had ensued at Apache Pass. Cochise was taken captive under a flag of truce and cut his way out of Commander Bascom's tent, but several individuals were killed on each side before the conflict was resolved to the satisfaction of neither the Americans nor Apaches.

The fact that Mangas Coloradas had been tortured, murdered, scalped, and then decapitated after he had come to make peace with the whites, had put the finishing touches on an already explosive situation. And then along came Lyle Burkhart to teach the Apaches another lesson in treachery.

Chanos predicted it would be many moons before the whites and Apaches could come to an understanding, and he feared the outnumbered Indians would be the ones to make all the sacrifices.

"And how is it that White Shadow has come to your defense?" Moriah pried as she sank down to munch on the rabbit Chanos had snared for their midday meal.

A muddled frown clouded Chanos's brow. "He has not told you of his involvement?"

After Chanos had scorned the deceit of the whites, Moriah couldn't bring herself to mislead him. "I heard bits and pieces from a prospector at Santa Rita, but Devlin refuses to reveal all the details. He thinks I will be safer not knowing. He calls it caution. I call it being unnecessarily mysterious," Moriah sniffed disdainfully. "I have had trouble with Burkhart myself. If White Shadow thinks I would betray him to the beast, he has sorely misjudged me."

After a contemplative moment, Chanos decided to confide in Moriah. He saw no reason why he shouldn't. Being honest and open was the way of the Apache. Deceit was the white man's invention.

"Many moons ago, while our forefathers roamed this country without contact with the white-eyes, Cyrus Granger came to the People in peace and friendship. Devlin's grandfather was bold enough to ride into our camps, setting off smoke signals to announce his approach. He wanted to parley with our chiefs about setting up a trading post near Tucson to exchange animal pelts for supplies. The chief was taken with Devlin's grandfather because of his bold daring and his honesty. He agreed to let the Grangers live beside the Apaches in peace. He leased out land to raise stock and crops, and when the winters were hard for the Apaches, Cyrus gave generous gifts as a token of his continued friendship."

Moriah listened raptly as Chanos explained how the Apaches brought hides, bundles of grass for the livestock, and dry kindling to the trading post to exchange for blankets and food, how the post was handed down to the next generations. The Apaches gave the Grangers ranch land to expand their operation and the family always reciprocated with gifts and friendship. Although the Apaches struck out against those greedy whites who took to their hunting grounds and refused to leave, the Grangers were allowed special privileges.

"Burkhart went to Devlin, asking him to lead the cavalry to parley with the tribal leaders," Chanos went on. "But Burkhart had no wish to speak, only to devastate and destroy. He opened fire at Ojo del Muerto and Devlin turned on him." He paused before adding, "It was Devlin who slashed Burkhart's arm and who would have stabbed his black heart if the other soldiers hadn't been ordered to open fire on him."

Moriah shuddered, imagining the bloody battle, understanding at last the fierce hatred between Burkhart and White Shadow.

"Although my blood brother was critically wounded, we carried him with us to camp and I nursed him back to health. Since that day, White Shadow became a legend of hope for our people. He swore revenge for Burkhart's murders and treachery.

White Shadow's brother and sister vowed to see Burkhart discharged for his ruthless tactics and they have brought charges against the commander while White Shadow leads guerrilla missions against the merciless commander."

"But won't the killing of soldiers only bring down more wrath on the Apaches?" Moriah questioned grimly.

"White Shadow does not take lives. He wants to ensure that the Apaches do not receive the brunt of accusations by making it known that *he* is the one who strikes the offensive. But White Shadow takes only horses and supplies to cripple the Army and makes it more difficult for Burkhart to attack us. When Burkhart meets his end, he will confront White Shadow, not the Apaches. That is the way my blood brother wants it."

Moriah now understood why Devlin had harassed the troops. He knew full well that Burkhart would use any incident to justify more massacres. Without caution and meticulous planning Devlin could instigate a full-scale war between the Americans and Apaches and that was the last thing he wanted.

When Moriah heard liquid splattering she frowned in curiosity. After Chanos folded a tin cup into her hand, she sniffed the aromatic drink. "What is this?" she wanted to know before she took a sip.

"Tiswin," Chanos informed her, urging the cup to her lips. "It is made from fermented corn."

When Moriah declined, Chanos smiled at the bewitching young woman whose fascinating company had made the past few days fly by.

"Tiswin is the Apache's version of whiskey, which is often used in ceremonies. The corn is soaked overnight and then placed in a long trench that is lined and covered with grass. After stirring the

sprouting corn —morning, noon, and night—for ten days, it is ground and then boiled for half a day. The liquid is drained off and once it stops bubbling . . ." He took a slurping sip of the brew. "We drink it." Again, he lifted the cup to Moriah's lips. "At least try it before you condemn it," Chanos insisted.

Moriah took a cautious sip and choked as the alcohol burned its way down her throat to inflame her stomach. Chanos leaned over to pat her back and then chuckled at the expression on her face.

"It is a mite stronger than what I'm accustomed to drinking," she choked out.

"The second and third drink will taste even better," he said with assurance.

And he was right. Moriah wasn't sure if it was the fact that her taste buds were numb or that she had simply adjusted to the fiery taste of the *tiswin*. Whatever the case, she emptied her glass and requested another.

An amused grin slanted Chanos's lips as he watched Moriah lounge casually against the rock wall of the cavern. What a delight she was! So lovely to look at, so full of irrepressible spirit. Mentally shaking himself, Chanos glanced at the pot of mesquite leaves and flax seed that he was brewing over the fire.

"I have concocted a potion for your eyes," he announced as he dipped up the pasty substance and mixed it with the herbs and magical spirit dust that was stashed in the pouch that hung around his neck.

"It's a waste of time," Moriah insisted between sips of *tiswin*. "All I can see is shades of black and gray, sprinkled with shafts of silver."

"My remedy has been mixed with magical spirits which will heal the burns of your eyes," Chanos declared with great conviction. "My people have used these medications since Usen put us on Mother Earth."

Skeptical though she was, Moriah sat still while Chanos smeared the gooey paste in her eyes and then caked her eyelids with it. The pungent aroma took her breath away.

"This smells horrible," she gasped, pulling a face of distaste.

"Take another drink," Chanos commanded. "Soon you won't be able to smell anything at all."

And sure enough, he was right again. The *tiswin* numbed her nostrils as well as her taste buds. And later Moriah was giggling giddishly, unaware that her eyes were glued shut with the foul-smelling potion, unaware of having a care in the world, in fact.

Recklessly, she leaned out to run her hand over the muscled tendons of Chanos's arm. "I want to see what you look like," she slurred with a silly smile.

Chanos was wearing a rather idiotic smile himself, having dipped a bit too deep into the flask of *tiswin*. He sat cross-legged while Moriah brushed her palms over his shoulders and neck. The pads of her fingertips out-lined his copper skin, tracing his angular features, his square chin, his aquiline nose.

"You are very handsome with your strong features," she mused after her inquiring hand glided over the thick black hair that fell to his shoulders. Curiously, she measured the broad expanse of his chest. Except for the lack of crisp hair on Chanos's chest, he was as powerfully muscled as Devlin. They seemed very much alike and yet so different. Devlin never offered more information than was absolutely necessary. Chanos, on the other hand, was straightforward and open.

It was well and good for Moriah to explore her

companion with the sight of her hands, but Chanos felt the tingle of desire pulsating through his loins when her fingertips drifted over his chest and shoulders. Her light touch, compounded with the amount of liquor he had consumed, sent his thoughts wandering off in a most arousing direction.

Moriah's inquisitive touch ascended to map his high cheekbones and the jutting ridges over his eyes. Chanos somehow forgot he had been asked to do nothing more than keep a watchful eye on this dazzling beauty. He had refrained from touching her, but he was still a man and, as Devlin had discovered two weeks earlier, there was a limit to male control when tempted by such a devastatingly attractive female.

Chanos's wife had died three years earlier in an attack by Mexican scalp hunters, and Chanos had been alone too long. He was tempted to satisfy his gnawing hunger for this captivating woman who had become his ward.

While Moriah visualized what the powerful Apache medicine man looked like, his calloused hands glided across her creamy cheeks and traced the soft texture of her heart-shaped lips. When he dared to touch her, Moriah's hand stalled in midair, wondering if she had unknowingly invited him to return her curious caresses. She had wanted to know how he looked, how he compared to Devlin, but it seemed he had mistaken her curiosity for something else.

The fact that her reactions were sluggish from sipping *tiswin* prevented her from retreating when his full lips whispered over hers. Although the feel of his masculine body brushing against her sent a warm tingle down her spine, Moriah knew immediately that it was Devlin who ignited fires in her that could burn out of control. Chanos pleasured her with his tender embrace, but it was Devlin's face that floated above her, his possessive touch that excited her.

A muffled groan rumbled in Chanos's chest as he pressed Moriah to her back. The feel of her honeyed lips beneath his, the feel of her curvaceous body meshed to his, caused a throb of reckless desire to spread through his veins. For the moment, he forgot about White Shadow and Burkhart and everything else.

Devlin froze in his tracks and glared into the cave that flickered with firelight and skipping shadows. He had set a frantic pace, anxious to return from Santa Rita. He had missed waking up to the sight of blond hair glistening in the morning sun and blue eyes sparkling with living fire. Apparently Moriah hadn't missed *him* all that much, judging by what she and Chanos were doing to while away the afternoon.

Damnation, he had spent the past few days assuring himself that he was worrying for naught, convinced that Chanos would observe a respectable distance. Chanos had taken Devlin's request to keep a watchful eye on Moriah to the extreme! Devlin would have trusted Chanos with his life, but he had been a fool to trust the Apache medicine man with his future wife.

And Moriah! Devlin gnashed his teeth and soundly cursed her. If she hadn't wanted Chanos's amorous embrace, she would have fought to escape him. It didn't seem to Devlin that she was putting up much of a fight. The fickle chit! She had warded off men's advances for years and suddenly she was accepting every embrace that came her way!

For an exasperated moment, Devlin stood at the

mouth of the cave, indecision etching his brow. Part of him itched to tear Chanos limb from limb and chew Moriah up one side and down the other. Another part of him wanted to stamp off in a huff, lift a boulder, and hurl it down the side of the mountain to vent his anger. And yet another part of him wanted to pull Moriah into his arms and replace Chanos's fervent kisses with a dozen more . . . until it was the taste of Devlin's kiss that lingered on her petal-soft lips.

Several emotions struggled for supremacy, but finally anger won out. Devlin felt betrayed and yet he well remembered Chanos declaring that White Shadow had asked too much by leaving him alone with hopeless temptation. Devlin couldn't honestly blame Chanos for yielding to his basal needs. Moriah possessed a magnetic attraction, Devlin blamed her for making it too easy for Chanos to succumb to his instincts. If she felt a fierce attachment for Devlin, she would have resisted, wouldn't she? Hell yes, she would have, his male pride shouted indignantly.

"Moriah!" Devlin's deep voice boomed through the cavern and bounced off the walls to come at the cozy couple from all directions.

The fact that Chanos and Moriah had consumed way too much *tiswin* prevented them from reacting quickly. When Chanos finally dragged his lips away to glance over his shoulder, he didn't even look the least bit repentant. That made Devlin mad as hell. To further inflame his temper, Moriah stared at him with a slab of something that looked like a dried potion on her eyes and a ridiculously giddy grin on her lips. That made Devlin positively furious!

When the usually agile Chanos finally wobbled onto rubbery legs, Devlin muttered to himself. It was obvious that Chanos had imbibed in the spirits and was feeling the effects of intoxication. Another mutinous glare at Moriah indicated she had tipped the *tiswin* flask to excess as well. Damn them both! He had nearly run himself into the ground, what with his trip to Santa Rita. And all the while these two were guzzling liquor and . . .

Devlin refused to speculate on what else they had been doing the past few days. The actions he had caught them at red-handed was evidence enough that they had done far more than count the gold nuggets in the canyon!

Chanos, drunk though he was, had no difficulty deciphering the murderous glitter in White Shadow's eyes. With his head held high, Chanos staggered outside—out of earshot of Moriah who was having trouble sitting erect without weaving back and forth like stems of grass waving in the wind. As Chanos meandered out of the cavern, Devlin stalked after him, breathing down his neck all the while.

"I warned you," Chanos mumbled in his native tongue before Devlin could physically attack him.

"And I trusted you!" Devlin snarled, glaring into the medicine man's bloodshot eyes.

"All I did was kiss her a few times," Chanos defended over his thick tongue.

"Didn't you just!" Devlin hissed through clenched teeth.

The fact that Chanos still didn't seem repentant rankled Devlin to no end. "And I suppose if the situation were reversed, you wouldn't be the least bit annoyed to find your blood brother lollygagging with your intended wife." A derisive snort erupted from his curled lips.

"You were foolish enough to leave me alone with her," Chanos reminded him. "I may be your blood brother, but I am only a man, not a pillar of stone. She is too much of a woman, and I should not have to remind you of that fact, White Shadow."

Devlin couldn't argue with that, but it didn't stop him from trying. "Well, it is obvious that I cannot trust you or anyone else to care for her while we prepare for Burkhart's attack. And it appears I can't trust *her* at all!"

Chanos sobered quickly. "He is coming." It wasn't a question. It was a bleak statement of fact.

"At the rise of the new moon," Devlin growled, still fuming to the point that smoke very nearly rolled from his ears. "What I have planned for the butcher will end his long reign of terror in Apachería . . . that is, if you can tear yourself away from my fiancée long enough to help me plot Burkhart's end!"

The warrior's red-streaked eyes circled back to the mouth of the cave to see Moriah propped against the stone wall. He didn't regret taking that curvaceous beauty in his arms. He had been honest with Devlin from the onset. He desired Moriah, and White Shadow knew that. But Chanos was also astute enough to know by Moriah's reaction to him that it was mostly curiosity and whiskey that prompted her to respond. She had been kissing Chanos, but it was Devlin's image that she had conjured in her world of darkness. Unless he missed his guess, Moriah had been comparing the men.

"She is not to blame," Chanos murmured.

"How noble of you to say so," Devlin grunted disdainfully. "From where I stood, she didn't seem to be complaining all that much."

A teasing grin spread across Chanos's bronzed features. "That is because I can be very persuasive. White Shadow is not the only one who possesses legendary powers around here." The smile evaporated when his gaze was magnetically drawn back to Moriah, who looked comical with the medicinal paste plastered on her face. "This woman of the wind who has hair like the sun and eyes like the sky will have to be tamed and won," he whispered. "If not by you, then by me or someone else. If you scorn her, she will not have far to go to find consolation. Do not forget that, my friend."

Having said his piece, Chanos pivoted on his heels to walk away. But Devlin's curt voice gave him pause.

"I'm taking her home," he declared in the Apache tongue. "She will be reasonably safe there until our encounter with Burkhart is over."

Chanos stared at the comely beauty who was having difficulty standing upright. Blindness and *tiswin* didn't mix well. Moriah had no focal point at which to stare to maintain her balance.

"Tell her good-bye for me, White Shadow. Tell her I . . ." His voice trailed off when Devlin frowned disapprovingly. "No, I don't think you will relay that particular message for me. And one day, if you aren't careful, I may have the chance to tell her myself."

Growling at the ambiguous remark that left Devlin to form his own jealous conclusions, he wheeled about to glower at Moriah. In the past, Devlin had never been threatened by competition. But Chanos was a worthy opponent and it was painfully evident that Moriah found the Apache medicine man appealing.

Devlin scowled at the annoying thought. Blast it, he was so irritated with Moriah that he wanted to shake the stuffing out of her! But if he blew up and sent her blindly running away, Chanos would be there to console her.

"Come wash that stinky concoction off your face," he grumbled, roughly grasping her hand and dragging her down the path.

"Chanos thinks it will help the burns caused by the lightning," Moriah slurred out, still too tipsy from the *tiswin* to realize Devlin was annoyed with her.

"Chanos thinks," Devlin mimicked in a high-pitched voice that rattled with sarcasm. "Chanos and his medicine man magic!" He expelled a disgusted snort. "He is hardly a qualified doctor!"

The terse remark caused Moriah to frown. "You don't want me to see again, do you, Dev?" she accused sluggishly.

"What kind of stupid question is that?"

Devlin pivoted so quickly that Moriah rammed head-on into him. He caught her to him when she stumbled and the old familiar fire began to burn at first touch. Devlin had two choices. He could rake Moriah over the coals for betraying him in Chanos's arms or he could accept the challenge to tame Moriah's wild heart. Chanos was waiting to see if Devlin chose the foolish course that wounded male pride demanded or the sensible one. This golden-haired nymph had come to mean a great deal to Devlin. She was the one bright spot in a life that was filled with obsession and vindication. Devlin had grown accustomed to having Moriah around and the thought of losing her left a gnawing ache in the pit of his belly.

"Did you miss me, little imp?" he murmured in a softer tone.

When he tipped her face to his, Moriah melted in his arms. As gentle as Chanos had been, he couldn't replace Devlin in her heart. It was Devlin who had taught her soul to sing, Devlin who made her burn with hungry desire.

Her arms wound around his neck. Her fingers raked through the curly raven hair that capped his head. Her body instinctively arched toward him. Moriah swore she could see sparks flying in the darkness that veiled her eyes. She swore she could hear the enchanting melody of love playing in the distance.

This was where she had wanted to be, even when she had succumbed to Chanos's unexpected kisses. She had tested her reaction and discovered beyond all doubt that this tawny-eyed man of primitive mystery was the one she wanted. He evoked needs that sizzled like a prairie fire. He made her believe in happiness, even though she knew it couldn't be the kind that endured forever.

To Moriah, nothing was everlasting. Time changed like the wind, and life was a succession of phases through which one passed—some good, some not. And because of that philosophy, Moriah clung to the moment. She would revel in the feel of Devlin's muscular body forged to hers for as long as his physical fascination for her lasted, until he grew tired of her and sought out a new challenge.

From the towering ridge, Chanos watched Devlin embrace Moriah. Pain stabbed at his heart when she gave to Devlin what she had not surrendered to Chanos. It seemed White Shadow was the victor of this battle for Moriah's affection. Disappointed, Chanos turned away and silently disappeared behind the stone slabs that were strewn on the slopes of Eagle Canyon.

"I missed you terribly," Moriah admitted, her voice thick with *tiswin* and unappeased passion.

Male pride took hold of his tongue. "Then why did you let Chanos kiss you?" Devlin demanded. "And don't tell me that since you're blind you couldn't tell the difference between him and me!"

Was that the ring of jealousy in his voice? Moriah hoped so. She refused to let Devlin take her for granted. "How many women did you say you had before I came along?" she questioned his question.

Begrudgingly, Devlin smiled, cursing his runaway tongue and wounded pride. Gently, he peeled a layer of the medicinal paste from her eyes. "I don't appreciate watching you kiss other men."

"If you were blind, like I am, you wouldn't have to watch," she flung saucily and then hiccupped. "S'cuse me."

Despite himself, he burst into a chuckle. Moriah was intoxicated and she was all giggles and grins and sassy rejoinders. It was difficult to remain angry with her when he stared into her face that was caked with globs of potion and beaming with impish smiles.

"You are incorrigible," he chided.

"It compensates for my lack of vision," Moriah said sluggishly. Although Devlin was leading her down the slope, she felt incredibly sleepy and would have much preferred lying down to walking.

When Devlin saturated a cloth and wiped the concoction from her face, Moriah lounged against the pillars of rocks that concealed the spring from view. "What mysterious mission took you to Santa Rita?" she queried.

"The same one that will now take you to my ranch," Devlin declared, scrubbing the last of the ointment from her flawless features. "We'll leave at dawn."

"I'm staying here," she informed him drowsily.

"You will be safe at my ranch." Devlin sank down beside her, watching the familiar stubborn expression glaze her face.

"I don't want to go anywhere. I'm staying in the

mountains," she declared, her voice firm.

Devlin rolled his eyes in annoyance. "Good God, woman, I swear you would argue with a wall. If I commanded you to stay, you would go. If I ordered you to go, you would stay, just to be contrary."

"I suggest you try *asking* me instead of *ordering* me about," Moriah flung back at him with an elfin grin.

Devlin expelled an exasperated sigh. "Very well then, will you please stay at my ranch until I return?"

Still grinning mischievously, Moriah reached out to trace his sensuous lips. "For a price, perhaps, White Shadow, oh great sage and avenger of injustice and incredibly lusty rogue of these mountains, I will do as you say."

The mere touch of her fingertips against his lips was enough to send an arousing tingle flying down his spine. "Name your price, sweet witch," he rasped.

Her hands entwined behind his neck, pulling him to her to tempt him with the slightest whisper of a kiss. "I should think this magnificent body of yours wouldn't be a bad bargain."

Devlin was bewitched. He remembered, with vivid clarity, the way her luscious body had responded to his the night before he traveled to Santa Rita. He was painfully aware of the lonely nights he had spent away from her. He ached for this tormenting minx up to his eye-brows. He longed to erase the kisses Chanos had bestowed on her and replace them with his own, to sear his memory on her mind and pleasure her as well as himself . . .

And Moriah was certain she was in love with this golden-eyed, raven-haired mountain of a man. When his body covered hers, sweet flames burst within her. She had missed Devlin more than he would ever know. Her mind kept transporting her back to the night they had made wild passionate love until they had not the strength to move. It had been a glorious night of incredible sensations, of blossoming feelings that had refused to fade.

When his lips devoured hers, Moriah's hand raked over his broad chest, adoring the feel of his muscular flesh beneath her fingertips. Her caresses wandered over him, resenting the buckhide breeches and leggings that concealed the rock-hard contours of his thighs. She wanted to rediscover every powerful inch of him, to spread loving caresses over his hair-roughened skin, to instill the same desperate need in him that engulfed her.

Like a starving man famished for a feast, he ravished her. From the instant Moriah initiated their embrace, Devlin was a creature of instinct and raw emotion. He had accepted the fact that Moriah had burrowed into his heart, but he hadn't realized how deep the taproot ran until he had spent the monotonous days without her and then returned to find her in Chanos's arms.

Perhaps seeing her with Chanos had driven home the realization that he needed her to make his life complete. Or maybe it was the wild, ungovernable sensations that riveted his body that made him so acutely aware of his strong attachment to her. Devlin didn't know for certain. All he knew was that Moriah had come to mean as much to him as his fierce vengeance against Lyle Burkhart. There had been a time when he vowed he would use Moriah as the means of luring Burkhart to his doom. But no longer. The thought of Burkhart abusing her cut him to the quick. And if his plans went awry and he couldn't return to Moriah, at least he would have the memories of this magical moment to carry him through eternity.

A tremulous sigh tumbled from Moriah's lips as Devlin divested her of her clothes and greeted each inch of exposed flesh to greedy kisses and possessive caresses. It seemed as if it had been minutes instead of days since he had touched her. She adored his caresses, reveled in the rapturous sensations that coursed through her, that cascaded over her flesh and into the core of her being like a waterfall of bubbly emotion. She not only heard the words of want and need that he whispered against her flesh but she felt them and responded wholeheartedly.

His tongue flicked at the taut peaks of her breasts and she melted in a pool of fiery desire. His practiced hands glided over her flesh and she burned with a fire that only Devlin could cool. He uncoiled upon her and she arched toward him, aching to be flesh to flesh, soul to soul, hungering with a monstrous need that only he could fulfill.

"Why, Moriah?" Devlin heard himself asking in a husky whisper. "Why did you let Chanos touch you?"

"Because he was safe," she breathed, and then gasped as his muscular body settled exactly upon her. "Because he wasn't you . . ."

"You don't feel safe with me?" he questioned, bracing himself above her, shuddering in anticipation of making her his total possession.

Her arms slid over his shoulders, bringing his full lips back to hers. "With you I'm like a fire burning out of control. Feed this fire, Devlin. I want you madly . . ." she murmured before her lips merged with his.

Her words were like a torch set to dry kindling. He clutched her to him, stealing her breath as he became the living flame within her, igniting a fire so fierce and wild that nothing could contain it. The blaze burned brighter and hotter than the heat of a thousand suns, forging them together. Emotions boiled forth, scalding Moriah inside and out. The flame fed upon itself, needing no other fuel than the fervent sensations that sizzled between her and this man who clutched her against him as if the world were about to explode.

The storm of wildfire billowed over her like a raging thunderhead. And then, without warning, the storm unleashed its fury, leaving Moriah feeling as if she had scattered in a million pieces. She was wild in his arms, gasping for breath, pelted by a multitude of incredible sensations. Her body shuddered against his and his name burst from her lips in a whimper of pleasure and disbelief.

Moriah was a score of fiery passions seeking release. She had not only accepted Devlin's urgent desires, but she equally matched him. And in her selfless giving he found the sublime essence of pleasure and satisfaction. The thought of Chanos discovering what an incredibly skillful lover Moriah had become was a poisonous one to Devlin.

When Devlin mentally reviewed his previous experiences with women he realized how shallow those encounters had been. But Moriah was a complex creature who constantly intrigued and amazed him. It wasn't simply the physical attraction that drew him to her. It was her fierce determination and her relentless spirit that fascinated him as well. When other women would have wallowed in self-pity and despair, Moriah bravely met each challenge, constantly tested her abilities. She made Devlin glad he was a man—the man who had taught her all she knew about passion.

And when this long-standing feud with Burkhart was over and Devlin's name was finally cleared of the charges, he was going to begin a new life with Moriah—if he could convince her to stay with him. He would cherish her as she deserved to be cherished. He would compensate for the pain and misery she had endured over the last ten years. She would want for nothing, he promised himself. And in time, he hoped her desire for him would blossom into a deeper affection. But even if it didn't, he would love her, prove to her that there was one man in this world who wanted her for all the right reasons.

In the aftermath of love, Moriah ran her hand across the scars that marred Devlin's ribs, knowing who and what had caused them. Leisurely, her caress glided over his hips and then receded to retrace the same tantalizing path.

With a growl that was reminiscent of a purring lion, Devlin nipped at her soft lips. He had gone without sleep to make the journey a rapid one, and weariness was catching up with him. He longed to fall asleep in Moriah's arms and wander into erotic dreams that took up where the splendor of their lovemaking left off.

Moriah, who was drowsy from too much Apache whiskey and the drugging effects of passion, nestled against Devlin to follow him into sweet dreams. They were both at peace, feeling the bond between them strengthened. With a hint of a smile on her lips, Moriah's lashes fluttered down and she fell asleep, using Devlin's arm for her pillow. It was the most contented moment she could remember in years. She didn't realize it was only the calm before another of life's storms . . .

Chapter 12

When Moriah stirred from her sleep, she inched away from Devlin and sat up. She could feel the warmth of sunshine at her back, smell the aromas of early evening that she hadn't realized existed until she lost her sight. She had begun to be familiar with the sounds and scents that indicated certain times of the day. Since she had been struck blind, her other senses had compensated for her lack of vision. But she could almost swear there were more shades of gray than black veiling her eyes than there had been before Chanos had smeared the magic potion on her eyes, even if Devlin discounted the remedy as utter nonsense.

Eager to glide across the pool that was formed by the spring that trickled from the mountain, Moriah felt her way toward the familiar rocks. She sighed softly as she sank into the invigorating water and glided across the surface like a swan.

She had no desire to leave this mountain retreat for Devlin's ranch. She was at peace here, far away from the troubles she had known in the past. But she imagined Devlin would bind, gag, and tote her to Tucson, whether she wanted to go or not. It saddened her to think her interlude with Devlin would soon come to an end. Things would never be the same again, she knew. He had been amorous and attentive because he was jealous of Chanos and because he pitied her handicap. But things would change and they would pass into another phase, one in which he would find himself resenting being hindered by a blind woman.

Moriah knew nothing this good could last. It never had before. It seemed whenever she was content, some unexpected event erupted and her life changed drastically. And each time it did, she was given more reason to be cynical and suspicious. She was, quite honestly, afraid she cared too much for Devlin, afraid she was halfway in love with him already. She knew the pain of losing those she loved, and she feared becoming too dependent on him. Becoming too hopelessly involved with him would only bring heartache.

Devlin would tire of her and her handicap and his physical attraction to her would fade. He wasn't the kind of man to be satisfied with just one woman. If he were, he would have married long before now, she reckoned. The fact that he had been a recluse in the mountains for more than a year was all that had lured Devlin to her. She was convenient and she was a female. She had quenched a need that he had denied too long, that was all. His pity for her was another factor, but in time his sympathy would turn to apathy and his obligation would become a burden. He would view her as an anchor that weighed him down and his roving eye would lead him astray.

The eerie rattle somewhere in the not too distant perimeter of the springs caused Moriah's heart to skip several beats. When she pricked her ears, she heard the unnerving sound again, except this time there was a chorus of rattles and hisses. Moriah had never heard that sound before, but she had the uneasy feeling it was that of a snake—or more specifically, a den of them.

Attempting to swim away without causing even more disturbance, Moriah groped to locate the rim of stones and feel her way back in the direction she had come. But suddenly the hissing sounds seemed to surround her. Her hand collided with a sharp rock and Moriah instinctively shrieked, certain she had been bitten.

Her terrified scream jolted Devlin from sleep and he jerked upright. His eyes flew open to see the light reflecting off the water. For an instant he couldn't determine what had caused Moriah's alarm, couldn't even see her in the bright light. Shading his eyes with his hand, he scanned the springs.

His heart climbed the ladder of his ribs and clogged his throat when he spied the slithering vipers that had been curled in the shade of the stone wall. Moriah had unknowingly disturbed more than a dozen rattler of all sizes that wove around the water's edge.

Cursing, Devlin snatched up a nearby stone, wishing his pistol and rifle weren't lying in the cave, doing him no good whatsoever. Hurriedly, he sailed the rock at the huge sidewinder that had shot forward to protect its brood. Then he assaulted the other hissing serpents with a barrage of pebbles—anything he could get his hands on to discourage them from attacking Moriah.

Moriah panicked. She could hear rocks bombarding the water and the surrounding stones. She could hear the angry rattles and hisses that came at her from all directions at once. She was starkly aware of how helpless and defenseless she was and she hated that feeling, hated not knowing which way to turn to find safety.

Devlin's breath froze in his throat when the five-foot-long sidewinder that had appointed himself the protector of the nest coiled and prepared to strike at Moriah who had wandered into its path.

"Don't move," Devlin commanded as calmly as he could.

Without taking his eyes off the snake, he groped for a larger rock and hurled it just as the viper lunged. The blow caused the dazed serpent to recoil and Devlin frantically bombarded him again and again, until the snake finally collapsed, its slimy body winding around the rock that had landed a fatal blow.

Devlin didn't even remember vaulting to his feet to circle the spring. But he was there, yanking Moriah from the water before another self-appointed protector slithered up to strike.

Fear transformed to desolation. Moriah's entire body shook and shiny tears spilled down her cheeks. "You should have let them have me," she sobbed hysterically. "First the mountain lion and now snakes! I hate this darkness!"

Moriah was strong-willed and perseverant, but facing unseen predators frustrated her and she resented her inabilities. It wrenched Devlin's soul to see her decompose and it tore him apart each time she confronted calamity.

"Damnit, don't even think such things," he bellowed at her, shaking her with violent force that lent testimony to his own frustration. A waterfall of wet golden curls tumbled around her and spilled over his taut arm. "You have me to watch over you."

Devlin might have been trying to shake some sense into her, but all he succeeded in doing was shaking loose her temper.

"Criminey, you don't have to shout. I'm blind, but I'm not deaf!" she flared through the streaming tears. "And for how long will I have you, Dev?" Shimmering blue eyes peered up at him, seeing nothing but shades of gray and speckles of silver. "How long will it be before you wish to shake off your helpless shadow? How long before you regret this burden? Even now, when you are planning to do whatever it is you intend to do to Burkhart, you have decided to bring me back to your ranch so I won't be in your way. And what then? What will you do with your burden? Shove her off on your unsuspecting family? And what am I supposed to do when another woman comes along to distract you? Blind as I am, I won't be able to see your indiscretions."

"You're talking crazy," Devlin growled at her. "And how do you know about my family and my feud with Burkhart?"

"Chanos told me all of it. He trusted me with the knowledge, you clearly wouldn't. It only proves that you are tolerating me because you think you have to," she snapped at him. "I'm something you toy with between battles, while you're plotting your revenge."

"That isn't true!" Devlin all but shouted at her.

"It is, too!" she loudly protested.

"Is not!" he boomed.

When Moriah wheeled to dash away, her bare foot slammed against the uneven stones, wrenching her ankle. With a squawk, she fell into the pool, and this time Devlin was too infuriated to help retrieve her.

"A simple thank you for saving you from several deadly rattlesnake bites would have been nice," he snorted, watching her flounder to gain her footing.

"Consider yourself thanked," she muttered in a

tone nowhere near appreciative. Moriah reached down to scoop up the pebbles on the spring bed and flung them at him. Devlin found himself hammered by a barrage of gold nuggets, and smiled that Moriah didn't know what she was throwing at him. "Now go away and leave me alone. The snakes and I would like a little peace and quiet!"

Devlin scanned the spring to ensure that the vipers had slithered away—except for the one that would eventually become their supper. Reaching down, he scooped up the serpent that was still reflexively winding this way and that.

"Fine, Madam Atilla," he growled sarcastically. "When you finish your bath, you can make your own way back to the cave."

"I should have no trouble locating it," she sniped. "No doubt you'll be up there fluttering around with the rest of the bats."

Devlin drew himself up after being slapped with the insult. "Sometimes, woman, I wonder why I put up with you. You have the disposition of a viper. No wonder they congregated around you. They thought you were one of them! Leave it to a snake to recognize one of its own kind!" With that, Devlin stalked over to retrieve his clothes and hastily shrugged them on.

"Oh yeah?" she sniffed in childish vindictiveness. "Well, it's better than being a shadow, and a white one to boot! Whoever heard of a white shadow anyway? What a ridiculous name you bestowed on yourself. White shadows, pink elephants, and red herrings!"

"But how aptly the miners named you," he bit off testily. "Angel of the Wind." He expelled a derisive snort. "Only it should have been Witch of the Wind, if you ask me. You can change temperament faster than the wind changes directions. And come to think of it, you remind me more of a cyclone blustering about!"

"Well, it's still better than being a stupid shadow," she parried with a smirk.

"Women!" Devlin exploded as he zigzagged around the huge stone mounds and towering pillars to retrace the path to the cave.

"Men!" Moriah grumbled, slapping at the water that surrounded her. "I would have been much happier if the good Lord would have placed all of you on another planet."

"Now I remember why I swore off women a year ago," Devlin scowled loud enough for her to hear him. This was the first time he gave verbal voice to his private thoughts. "Trouble. That's what they are, they always were, and they always will be!"

As his footsteps died into brittle silence, Moriah scowled under her breath. Her emotions had been on an even keel when Chanos was around, she realized. She didn't love him, but neither did he frustrate her the way Devlin did. With Devlin, her emotions flew up and down like a seesaw. First they were loving the hours away and the next thing she knew they were fighting. Sometimes he meant the world to her and sometimes she couldn't think of one nice thing to say about him. Well, if Devlin had his way, it wouldn't be long before she was out of his sight and mind. He would dump her at his ranch for his relatives to watch over and he would turn his thoughts to his revenge.

She was going to have to start making some plans of her own, she decided. She couldn't keep clinging to whimsical dreams. She didn't want to be around when Devlin got over feeling guilty and sympathetic and sought out another feminine conquest. It would kill her to know she was still carrying a torch for him but he had finally come to his senses and realized he had mistaken affection for pity. Somehow, some way, she was going to have a life of her own, blindness or no!

On that determined thought, Moriah walked ashore and spent ten minutes trying to locate her clothes. She swore Devlin had moved the garments, just to be ornery and spiteful. And she was right. He had!

With her head held high after she had slammed into the low-hanging rocks that formed the mouth of the cavern, Moriah marched toward the sound of the crackling fire in stiff, precise strides.

"Are you over being angry yet?" Devlin questioned. His tone indicated *he* wasn't.

"No," Moriah informed him icily, refusing to do him the courtesy of glancing in his direction.

"Neither am I," Devlin grunted as he plucked the meat from the fire and sliced it into bite-size pieces.

Moriah munched on her meal from the plate Devlin had dumped in her lap. "This is quite good," she begrudgingly complimented. "I'm not familiar with the taste. Is it something different from the meat we usually have?"

"Yes. It's rattlesnake steak," he announced with wicked glee. He knew the revulsion would cause her to choke on the piece she had popped into her mouth and she did.

"You should have told me," Moriah croaked, her face purple. "Is this the same snake that very nearly had *me* for supper?"

"Yep." When Moriah made another distasteful face, Devlin broke into a devilish grin. "Look at it this way, witch. He could have taken a bite out of you or you out of him. Either way, it probably would have killed him, knowing what a nasty bite you have."

So they were going for the throat, were they? Well, she could fling insults with the best of them.

"At least I have an excuse for being testy. I can't see my hand in front of my face, not to mention a nest of vipers sunbathing by the spring—"

"They were lounging in the shade," he clarified with a haughty smirk.

"Whatever." Moriah shrugged off his sarcasm. "I have learned to live with my blindness, but I don't like it. I don't like depending on you or anyone else. And I am getting very tired of your pity that turns sour without the slightest provocation."

"Don't worry, honey, you aren't getting any sympathy now," he growled at her. Damn, sometimes she annoyed him so thoroughly that he wanted to shake her until her teeth fell out. "I think a temporary separation is just what we both need."

"A permanent separation would be best," Moriah declared with great conviction. "Time isn't going to change the way you are—*spiteful!* And by the way, that was a rotten trick, moving my clothes so I had to hunt them down. Only the lowest form of life would play cruel games on a blind person. *Arrogant!* You seem to think you have all the answers to all the questions. This legend of disembodied spirits flitting around the mountains has obviously gone to your head. *Tight-lipped!* You refuse to let anyone close enough to know what you're thinking, feeling, or planning. It's as if the rest of us are dimwits who can't be trusted with your all-important secrets."

Moriah paused to inhale a quick breath and then plunged on. "And for your information, I would like to see Lyle Burkhart's reign of terror stopped. He may be ruthless in his attempt to annihilate the Apaches, but he is also rough and abusive with women. I can attest to that from firsthand experience. And if you think I wouldn't condone your vengeance, then *you* are the fool, *Devil* Granger!"

"If you're finished lambasting me, I have a few observations to make about you," he muttered.

"I'm not finished," Moriah announced with her nose in the air. "If you will allow me to take a few gold nuggets from this canyon, I will rent my own room in Tucson and find work as a maid at a hotel. If nothing else, I could make a bed in the dark and fill basins with water."

"No." Devlin's sharp tone invited no argument. Moriah, however, needed no invitation to debate with him.

"I'm not staying at the ranch with your brother and sister," she told him in no uncertain terms.

"And I suppose I have Chanos to thank for telling you about my brother and sister," he grunted. "Did he also reveal the tales of my wayward youth?"

"No, he did not. But he saw no reason for all this secrecy," she countered. "You're so suspicious that you think someone will betray you to Burkhart."

"I only refused to divulge any of my past or the purpose of my mission to protect you," Devlin growled. "But, having the curiosity of a cat, you probably coaxed information out of Chanos with a few kisses—and only God knows what else you offered in exchange for information!"

"You idiot!" she flared. "I do not dole out affection to gain information!"

"Well, you could have fooled me. You suddenly seem to know all there is to know about me," he snapped brusquely. "I returned to find you plying Chanos with kisses." He glared accusingly at her. "I was gone four days. I hate to hazard a guess as to how many times the two of you were sprawled on the ground together!"

A flash of memory spurred Devlin's temper. "That seems to be a new tactic of yours, come to think of it. Three hours ago, you agreed to come peaceably to my ranch if, and I repeat your exact words, you got this magnificent body of mine in the bargain."

Moriah's jaw dropped. How dare he twist her words around and employ them as evidence against her!

"I did no such thing with Chanos! I had a mite too much *tiswin* to drink and so did he. That was all there was to it!" she defended, and then spitefully added, just to get his goat. "And I'm beginning to wonder if he isn't the one I should have experimented with in the first place. I have earned Chanos's respect. All I have is your pity."

Sure enough, she got his goat. Devlin's amber eyes sparked fire. Their attempt to needle each other had evolved into a full-blown argument and Devlin couldn't even remember what insignificant remark had instigated this shouting match.

"What do you care if you receive respect or pity from me?" he scowled as he dumped water on the fire, leaving the logs to sizzle. They had nothing on Devlin. He was sizzling himself. "You have nothing to give a man in return anyway. All you have ever wanted is to be left alone to fly your flag of independence. You are incredibly stubborn, quick-tempered, and sharp-tongued. You don't want to need anyone and you don't know beans about love or commitment or compromise."

"As if you do!" Moriah sniped.

"I know it isn't something you drag on and off when the mood suits." The walls flung back his roaring voice. "And this debate is officially over. I'm taking you to the ranch and you had damned well better be there when I get back or I'll hunt you down and throttle you like I should have done every time you defied me for one flimsy excuse or another."

"I have had good reason to rebel," Moriah all but shouted as he jerked her to her feet and shuffled her toward the mouth of the cave. "You appointed yourself my guardian and shepherded me hither and yon when all I asked was for my own space in these mountains."

"Watch out for the—"

Her forehead smacked into the jutting rocks.

"Low ceiling," he finished a second too late.

"There, you see? You aren't even that much help to me," she smirked, massaging her aching head.

Devlin flung her a withering glance and hustled her along the path that led toward the mesa to the southwest. Moriah was the most exasperating woman he had ever met. She touched each and every emotion he had kept locked beneath the surface for more than a year, but she kept erecting invisible partitions between them. Good God, sometimes he wondered why he did put up with her.

Muttering to himself, Devlin stalked off. He should let this hellion strike out on her own, just to prove to her how much she really did need him. Then she would come crawling back to him, humbly requesting his forgiveness.

That would be the day, Devlin thought bitterly. Moriah's knees wouldn't bend to take her down to begging. No man would ever tame her wild heart. She had encountered too many men who had soured her on the entire male species. She refused to trust them. Devlin had confessed to care for her once and she reduced his admission to sympathetic guilt. And when Moriah formed her opinions, even a sledge-hammer wouldn't crack them. And Devlin wasn't even sure he did love her anyway. She had him so confused and frustrated he didn't know what he was feeling. He didn't realize how lucky he had been when he had flitted from one shallow sexual encounter to another. At least he hadn't had to endure the emotional turmoil Moriah caused!

There had been dozens of women before Hurricane Moriah swept into his life. Other women would have leaped at the chance to take his name and become his wife. Hell, a few of the more persistent females had practically run him down in an attempt to trap him. But not Moriah. She constantly kept showing him the door, dreaming up excuses not to stay at his ranch or to marry him. Dreamed them up, mind you! He had been noble and compassionate and she flung his virtues in his face as if they were failing graces. Criminey! he grumbled, unaware that he had used Moriah's favorite expression. If he hadn't been as stubborn and determined as she was, he would have thrown up his hands, stalked off, and left her to the mountain lions and rattlesnakes.

What had gone wrong? Devlin asked himself an hour later. He had found splendor in her arms that afternoon and suddenly their relationship had turned sour. She refused to be reasonable, he reminded himself huffily. He knew what was best for her and she was too contrary and belligerent to accept her fate! Women were, without a doubt, the most frustrating creatures. Just when he thought he had Moriah figured out, she changed like the wind and he was left to wonder if it wasn't simply the physical attraction that bound them together.

Chapter 13

Exhausted, Moriah plunked down in the middle of the path, refusing to take another step. They had walked for hours, paused briefly to rest, and then walked another fifteen miles or so. The sun had come and gone three times and still Devlin refused to stop for more than a few hours at a time.

"If you intended to prove that you have more stamina than I, it worked," she resentfully admitted. "And why must we travel all through the night? Although day and night look the same to me, I would appreciate a little rest!"

"Because the sooner I drop you at the ranch, the sooner I can return to organize our attack on Burkhart," he told her tartly.

Devlin had ears like a fox. And the fact that, from her point of view, he was doing exactly as she predicted, irritated him. He supposed he would have reacted the same way if she had been leading him around instead of vice versa.

"You'll like my brother," Devlin said, striving for a cheerful tone and purposely avoiding a rebuttal to her comment, which would undoubtedly instigate another argument. She was baiting him and he damned well knew it. "Barrett is even-tempered, gentlemanly, and well mannered."

"The exact opposite of you. How fascinating," she replied flippantly. "He does sound charming. I'm sure we'll get along fine during my *brief* visit."

Devlin punished her with a glare that had no effect on her whatsoever. Valiantly, he sought to control his temper, which had been sorely put upon the past several days. "And Jessica will be pleasant company for you. They will both make you feel right at home . . ."

The howl of a coyote caused Devlin's words to trail off. He glanced in the direction of the sound. "Stay here. I'll be back in a minute."

"If I get bored, I'll walk off the side of the mountain," Moriah smirked.

When Devlin's footsteps faded, her shoulders slumped. Criminey, why wouldn't he listen to reason? Because he was a billy goat of a man, that's why. Couldn't he see that she wanted her freedom before his lust for her faded into disinterest? Blind though she was, she still had her pride! Loving Devlin as she did made her terribly vulnerable and sensitive. She was afraid if she buckled to the emotions that churned inside her that she would become overly demanding of his time and affection.

Sooner or later he would come to resent her. He would feel tied down—as if he had an albatross draped around his neck and shackles on his ankles. Why wouldn't he just let her go? They were already hurting each other with spiteful jibes and cutting insults, and it would only get worse if Moriah allowed her love to show and then had it crushed.

The sound of trickling pebbles jostled her from her dispirited musings. "That didn't take long. What was—?"

A hand clamped around Moriah's mouth and she was jerked off the ground and clean off her feet. She was slammed against a rock-hard chest, and arms like steel bands fastened around her. The shuffle of more feet caused Moriah's heart to patter like driving rain. Although she wiggled and squirmed, she couldn't free herself from whomever had latched onto her. When she was bound and gagged, she was flung over a sturdy shoulder and carried away like a sack of grain.

What now? she asked herself miserably. It had proved to be three frustrating days. Devlin had returned to scold her for the harmless kiss she had bestowed on Chanos. And just when they had resolved one conflict, she had wandered into a den of snakes and that had incited another argument. Then Devlin had tried to punish her by dragging her through the mountains at an exhausting pace. And now, out of nowhere, here came more trouble. She didn't know if it was some of Burkhart's scouts who had a hold of her, or vagabonds, outlaws, or Apaches.

Well, this was one way of freeing herself from Devlin, she supposed. It was a mite drastic and probably disastrous. But then, as she had come to realize, every sort of refuge had its price. Moriah was left to wonder just what it was going to cost her to escape this latest calamity. She had the inescapable feeling the price would be a steep one!

Devlin scowled when he climbed atop the ridge and saw that Moriah wasn't where he had left her. Instinctively, he strode over to the cliff to see if she had thrown herself off the mountain just to spite him. Seeing no sign of her mangled body, Devlin glanced first in one direction and then the other. He had gone to investigate the sounds that had seemed too human to be a four-legged coyote howling at the moon, but there had been no one there. And when he returned, he couldn't find hide nor hair of Moriah. It was if an invisible hand had reached down from the sky and plucked her off the mountain.

Talking to himself, as he had a habit of doing the past year, he paced back to the spot where Moriah had been sitting. Squatting, Devlin traced the footprints in the loose dirt. Being an experienced tracker who was armed with the Apache's skill of reading footprints, by the depth of the tracks Devlin determined that Moriah had been carried off. Moccasin prints, four sets of them, were everywhere. Either the Apaches who had heard their approach hadn't realized it was White Shadow or he had happened onto warriors who had little regard for him. One Apache in particular came to mind—Makado. He had been at Ojo del Muerto the day of the ambush. Makado had lost his father and younger brother and he blamed Devlin for the killings. Makado had rejected the idea of a conference in the first place and he preferred war against the Americans to their treacherous brand of peace.

That was all he needed, thought Devlin as he followed the footprints until they ended on the slabs of stones that lay against the mountain slope. If Makado had Moriah, he wouldn't be eager to give her up, especially to Devlin. There was no love lost between the two men. Makado had organized expeditions against the whites, giving the Army just cause to hunt down the renegades. While Devlin tried to harass Burkhart without taking lives, Makado sought an eye for an eye with every dragoon who was foolish enough to scout his domain.

Grimly, Devlin inched down the steep slope,

hoping his premonition proved false. If Moriah fell into Makado's hands, she would be left to wonder who was more abusive, Makado or Lyle Burkhart. Devlin felt that Makado wasn't ruthlessly vicious, only confused. It was Makado's fierce dislike of Devlin that prevented the two men from developing a tolerable friendship. Like Moriah, Makado had been soured on life and he had come to despise the white men. Women, however, were in a separate category. To Devlin's knowledge, Makado had never met a woman he hadn't wanted. And if he had taken Moriah captive . . .

After Moriah was dumped unceremoniously on the ground, she braced herself on her elbow, wide luminous eyes blinking at the voices that whispered in the darkness that floated in front of her. She didn't wait to determine what was to become of her. She rolled to her feet and ran for her life. A mutinous growl erupted from Makado's lips when he realized his captive dared to escape him. He flung himself at the shapely blonde who was garbed in a cavalry uniform and yanked her back by the hair of her head.

Moriah's pained yelp was muffled by her gag. She stumbled back against Makado's heaving chest. In hopes of frightening her into submission, Makado whipped out his knife, waving it threateningly in front of her face, but there was no hint of fear in her eyes. She exhibited her spunk by gouging him in the midsection with her elbow before wheeling to lift her knee, striking him in the groin.

The unexpected blow caused Makado's breath to come out in a whoosh and he involuntarily dropped to his knees. Infuriated, Makado snaked out a hand to clasp the foot that was aimed at his chin.

A muffled squawk vibrated on her lips when she was flipped off balance and wound up on her backside. Before she could bound to her feet and sprint away, Makado was upon her. He shoved the heel of his hand to her chest and straddled her.

Certain it was rape that her captor intended, Moriah blindly struck out with her bound fists, catching Makado in the jaw. Like a growling panther, he clenched the front of her shirt, sending buttons flying. Again he brandished the dagger in front of her, as if he meant to carve her face to bloody shreds. And again there was not one hint of fear in those flashing blue eyes that reflected the moonlight.

A muddled frown etched his brow. He had confronted white women before, but none of them had put up such a fight and all of them had cowered in fear when finally subdued. This one did not. She was like a captured Apache who was never more dangerous than when he was wounded or surrounded. The Apache fought valiantly with his last dying breath, determined to take as many of his enemies with him when he left Mother Earth to join Usen and the other great spirits.

His dark eyes fell to the exposed swells of Moriah's bosom and so did his hand. But the moment he touched her, Moriah bucked and struck out with a blow that sent him reeling sideways.

"Get off me, you big ape!" Moriah spluttered when she managed to tear the gag loose from her mouth.

Makado liked this feisty hellion who proved her courage and spunk even at the risk of death. She would be a conquest worth taking. Determined to exhibit his strength, Makado dropped the dagger and shackled her wrists above her head. His knee wedged between her thighs, forcing her legs apart. With a victorious grin, he bent to take her lips, stealing her breath and muffling her outraged outburst.

"Argh!" Makado howled when his captive bit into his lip.

Moriah raised her leg, gouging her knee into his hips and knocking him partially off balance. But her only award for attempting to unseat her captor was his amused laughter.

"You are a sassy one, Sunflower," he chortled as his muscular body slid over hers, situating himself intimately upon her and drinking in the alluring sight of her heaving breasts. "You will please me and I will pleasure you . . ."

The thick accent assured Moriah that her assailant's second language was English. He was an Apache, she guessed. He spoke with the same stilted brogue that Chanos had used, only Chanos was more adept with English and far more of a gentleman by anyone's standards!

"All that will please me is being free of you!" Moriah spat in defiance.

The arrogant smile slid off Makado's lips and his mouth twisted in an indignant sneer. "I'll take you or you will die," he growled into her snapping blue eyes.

"I'd gladly die than suffer your abuse," she said boldly. "You are not a man. You are a beast . . . Ouch!"

His hand twisted in her hair, yanking her lips to his. When Moriah struggled, she felt the discarded dagger beside her hip. With an abrupt jerk, she loosed her hands from his grasp and snatched it up.

Like a striking snake, Moriah attacked, slicing a gash in his arm. Makado let out a squawk of pain that rumbled through the chasm. He clasped his wounded arm with the other hand and shrank away.

Moriah, having turned the knife to cut her wrists free, made another swipe with the sharp blade. The Apache brave leaped to his feet in retreat and prepared to wrestle away his own knife. Before he could lunge at Moriah she scrambled to her feet. A booming voice thundered through the night air, carrying Makado's name like an evil curse.

The Apache swung about, flanked by his three companions. Dark eyes flashed with recognition when Devlin leaped from the boulder like a pouncing tiger.

"It is my woman you have dared to touch," Devlin's ferocious snarl froze the four Apaches in their tracks. His eyes darted to Moriah who had crouched to point the dagger in every direction, as if she anticipated an attack at any moment from any corner. "Come here, Riah." His voice softened when he called to her.

Shakily, Moriah aimed herself in the direction of Devlin's voice. The way his words echoed around the canyon, it made it difficult to know exactly which way to walk.

Another yelp erupted from Makado's lips when Moriah rammed him broadside and the point of the stiletto grazed his ribs. It was not until Devlin stretched his hands out to guide her to him that Makado realized why the golden-haired tigress hadn't batted an eyelash at having a dagger flashed in her face. She couldn't see the threat of the blade! Stunned, Makado gaped at the daring spitfire who had countered his assault and left her mark on him—twice.

The thunderstruck expression on Makado's face—and those of the other three warriors—put a mocking smile on Devlin's lips. "You have tangled with the wrong person, Makado," he chortled, pulling Moriah possessively against him.

Makado scowled furiously. "She is blind. If she could see you, she would know how treacherous you are, especially to the Apache. And because she cannot see, you keep her as your prisoner. She is the only kind of woman a man like you could have," he taunted. "Sunflower depends on you so you do not have to fear that she will leave you. Blind loyalty—the kind my foolish brothers extended to you before you betrayed us at Ojo del Muerto."

Criticizing and ridiculing Devlin was an exclusive privilege that Moriah reserved for herself. It was one thing for her to lash out at Devlin and quite another to have this abusive savage mock Devlin. Moriah found herself automatically coming to his defense, even though Devlin was more than capable of responding to the intimidating remark.

"White Shadow is everything you are not," Moriah fumed. "He can be fierce or gentle, but you know nothing of tenderness. You know how to take, but not how to give."

"White Shadow wanted peace for your people and his. It was Burkhart who plotted the treachery and if you weren't such an arrogant, muleheaded brute you would know that!"

Makado's English was rudimentary at best and Moriah was firing words at him like a barrage of bullets. It took him a minute to translate the rapidly spouted words. When he finally caught up with her, he expelled a derisive snort. "Not only does this woman display her blind loyalty to a traitor but you allow her to speak for you as well, White Shadow."

His gaze flooded over Devlin's massive form, wishing there was something more about him to criticize. "Your friend Chanos misnamed you. I shall call you He-who-hides-behind-a-woman's-skirt." In the customary gesture of taunting the enemy, Makado slapped his backside to emphasize his ridiculing contempt.

The comment didn't have the expected effect. Instead of snarling, Devlin broke into a goading grin. "And your family made a poor choice in naming you, Makado. I will call you He-who-suffered-defeat-by-the-blind-woman's-hand."

Makado looked as if he had been clobbered by a doubled fist. The blow to his pride left a noticeable dent. He puffed up with so much indignation he nearly burst at the seams. Before he could erupt in a flurry of insults, Devlin spoke first.

"I have no fight with you, Makado. My battle is with Burkhart. And when I bring him down, you will know that I did not betray the Apache. I would call you my friend, but you cannot accept me as your blood brother. I promise you that Burkhart will pay for his merciless killings with his own blood. And his death will come at my hands so that none of your people will be blamed."

Makado harbored an intense hatred for Americans, but his dislike of Devlin Granger was tempered with grudging respect. This brawny giant had lived with the Apache and there were those who counted him as a friend. But Makado refused to be convinced that Devlin was sincere until he proved himself worthy.

His assessing gaze drifted to Moriah, whose silky hair shimmered in the moonlight like a waterfall of pure gold. He begrudged White Shadow's hold on this dazzling young beauty who possessed the heart of a tigress. He had wanted to possess her, but she was as crafty and cunning as the Apache. Granger had taught her well. Her blindness inhibited her to some extent, but it was as obvious as the gash on his arm and the puncture on his rib that Moriah was as bold as she was beautiful. Makado wanted her. She would make a much-envied wife.

"We will wait to see if White Shadow again speaks out both sides of his mouth. And if he does, he will fall with Burkhart, and the woman will be mine," Makado declared.

"Over my dead body!" Moriah snapped. "I wouldn't let you touch me again if you were the last man on earth!"

"I do wish you'd learn when to keep quiet," Devlin growled in her ear. "We stand a good chance of walking out of here without a fight if you'll kindly be silent."

Moriah compressed her lips and clutched her gaping shirt together. Devlin could be diplomatic if he wished, but she was the one who had come within a hairbreadth of being molested, and she wanted it known, here and now, that she would have nothing more to do with this baboon.

Clamping his fingers around Moriah's forearm, Devlin strode toward the narrow path that wound up the mountain. For a long moment, Makado stared at the departing silhouettes. And even when Moriah vanished from view, he could envision the feisty beauty lying beneath him. She had aroused him with her curvaceous body and challenged him with her spirit. When he had his chance, he would take her as his own, Makado vowed to himself. And he would prove to her that he was even more of a man than White Shadow was—because Makado was born Apache!

Part III

Chapter 14

After following the Gila River into Arizona Territory, Devlin trekked southwest. He paused only when Moriah looked as if she were ready to drop from exhaustion. Devlin had the encouraging feeling she cared more about him than her intractable pride would allow her to admit. The fact that she had leaped to his defense when Makado had ridiculed him lent testimony to that.

Devlin sighed, thinking that his emotions were once again swaying like a pendulum. When they began this jaunt several days earlier, he was ready to throw up his hands and cast Moriah off as a reckless encounter he'd had after his long abstinence from women. When Makado captured Moriah, the thought of losing this captivating minx forever cut a gash in his soul. Devlin knew Moriah wanted her freedom and yet he couldn't let her go. The attraction was still there, just as it had been in the beginning. The trials they had endured together strengthened the bond she fought so hard to break.

"I think you like me more than you are willing to admit," Devlin announced out of the blue.

Moriah missed a step and very nearly tripped over

her own feet. "I think I am going to like you better when we won't be seeing each other," she insisted with a stubborn tilt to her chin.

A wry smile bordered his lips. He surveyed the tangle-haired beauty for a thoughtful moment. After Makado had popped the buttons from her shirt, Moriah had tied the garment beneath her breasts, leaving the creamy swells exposed to his appreciative gaze and revealing the trim indentation of her waist. Moriah wasn't aware of how tantalizing she appeared in her makeshift garments and Devlin wasn't about to tell her. Contrary as she was, she would probably wrap a blanket around her and deprive him of the delectable view.

"If you are anxious to be rid of me, why did you spout those glowing accolades about me to Makado?" he teased as he drew Moriah over to a small boulder and placed her on it.

Moriah glanced toward the warmth of the setting sun. She was so tired, so weary of walking toward the horizon and never seeming to get there. She was also weary of putting up this proud front to protect her bleeding heart. Perhaps it was time to bare her soul to Devlin. Soon he would leave her behind and they would probably never see each other again. She might as well tell him how she felt and clear the air.

For all his faults, Devlin Granger was still the only man she had ever loved and probably ever would. But he was too dynamic and vital to be saddled with a blind woman who would someday become a resented burden to him. Heaving a forlorn sigh, Moriah glanced in his general direction. "You are a most impossible man, Devlin Granger," she said with a semblance of a smile and a tone that was too gentle to be scolding.

Devlin lapped his arms over his bronzed chest, crossed his feet at the ankles, and grinned at her. "And you are a most infuriating woman, Moriah Laverty," he countered.

"I know," she replied without taking offense. "Another of my many faults."

A bemused frown puckered Devlin's thick brows. He marveled at Moriah's mood, for he had expected her to become defensive the way she usually did when he teased her.

"I'm going to be honest with you . . ." she began, formulating a tactful way to put her thoughts into words.

"When haven't you been?" he mocked dryly.

"Not often enough, I'm afraid." Moriah massaged her aching thighs, thankful for the fuzzy shade of gray that veiled her eyes from his facial expressions. "You may as well know the truth now that we are so close to Tucson."

Devlin tensed, afraid they were about to pass into another phase in their rocky relationship, but Devlin didn't have the foggiest notion whether it would be for better or worse. Moriah had become an expert at concealing her feelings and he could no longer decipher the expressions in her azure-blue eyes.

"Something that I didn't want to happen has happened," Moriah announced, mustering her courage. "And it would have been better if it hadn't."

"For one who is usually direct and to the point, you are certainly beating around the bush," Devlin grumbled impatiently. "What could possibly have happened that I didn't notice? And how is it that you can see it when I can't?"

"Because I refused to let you see" was all she said in reply.

"Good God, woman, spit it out! The suspense is killing me!" Devlin's voice was growling louder by the syllable.

"Don't shout at me. This is difficult enough as it is," Moriah muttered uneasily.

Revealing her innermost feelings was something she had never done in all her life and she found it to be more painful than tearing off an arm. She had never before told a man she loved him, and the words were virtually impossible to push off the tip of her tongue. They simply stuck there.

Devlin reached over to pull Moriah to her feet, situating her between his outstretched legs while he leaned against the boulder. He clamped his hands around her elbows, forcing her to look straight at him, even if she couldn't see him.

"What the hell is wrong?" he demanded to know.

Remorsefully, she reached out to trace his chiseled features, memorizing the feel of his roughened skin beneath her fingertips. "I didn't want to fall in love with you, especially not after I lost my sight and you were hovering around feeling sorry for me and blaming yourself for the accident. But the truth is, it was my stubbornness that left me standing in the valley like a lightning rod. I don't hold you responsible for my plight and I expect no compensation."

Wonders never ceased! Of all the possible things he thought she might say, that wasn't even on the list. All this time Devlin had sworn she resented their attraction to each other. She had hidden her feelings beneath the surface, employing harsh words as a protective shield. "You're behaving as if your love for me is a fate worse than death," he chortled before dropping a kiss to her lips. "That isn't very flattering, you know. I'm really not such a bad fellow, aside from the fact that I'm wanted for murder and conspiracy by the Army and I can't show my face anywhere in New Mexico or Arizona Territory without concealing my identity behind a disguise for fear of being captured by bounty hunters."

"A wanted man and a blind woman," Moriah laughed hollowly. "What a miserably matched pair we are, Dev. And *that* is the point."

A wary frown knitted his brow. He had the unshakable feeling this conversation was going from good to bad.

"Loving you isn't enough," Moriah told him with sensible conviction. "Your crusade to clear your name and avenge Burkhart's dastardly crimes are your missions in life. The very fact that you intend to shunt me off to Tucson so I won't be in your way is an indication that I don't fit into your life."

"I'm only trying to protect you from—" he tried to protest.

Moriah pressed her index finger to his lips to shush him. Unfortunately, her aim was a little high and she poked him in the eye.

"The day you said you thought you were falling in love with me, I knew it was only your guilty conscience and sympathy speaking. You were trying to make me feel wanted and needed, to lift my sagging spirits. For that I thank you. But it is you who must face the truth and realize that you spoke to me out of pity, not out of love. The fact that you never uttered the confession again in the weeks we have been together signifies you spoke on impulse."

"I'm certainly old enough and intelligent enough to know what I feel," Devlin contested, blinking the eye in which Moriah had accidentally poked her forefinger.

"If I weren't blind you probably wouldn't have said it. If I could see and you repeated that confession

I might even allow myself to believe it. But I *am* blind and I cannot believe your possessiveness is more than guilt over my condition."

This conversation hadn't gone from good to bad. It had headed straight to terrible! Moriah had confessed to love him. But before he could enjoy one smidgen of satisfaction or revel in her long-denied affection, she had rejected his feelings for her. The woman was absolutely impossible! In her warped opinion, there were two sides to every issue—her side and the wrong side. Her deeply ingrained mistrust of men prevented her from giving Devlin credit for experiencing any emotions other than guilt and lust!

"And just what, dare I ask, is this lengthy explanation leading up to?" Devlin questioned flippantly.

Moriah tunneled her fingers through the shaggy raven mane that capped his head. His tone of voice indicated that he was annoyed with her, but she was determined to express her thoughts before he deposited her at his ranch and trotted on his way.

"I will consent to stay at your ranch for a few days while I attempt to find work to pay my passage back to Texas," Moriah compromised.

"No." His adamant rejection of her plans didn't deter her, but he really wasn't surprised.

"And when I can afford a ticket for the stagecoach, I don't want you to come after me because you think it's the thing to do."

"You aren't going anywhere."

"There are homes for the blind in Texas."

"You won't need one because you'll have me."

Moriah heaved a heavy sigh. "It will never work between us. I don't want to be around when your pity finally fades and you realize you want more from life than I can offer you. I don't want to be there to watch you turn to another woman when you tire of your burden and of me."

When Devlin started to object, Moriah held up a hand to forestall him, accidentally catching him in the chin, which made him bite his tongue. While he groaned in pain, she continued. "I watched my mother turn to Vance Thatcher to ease her loneliness and to provide what she thought would be security for us. But she died deeply regretting her mistake. I won't allow myself to repeat my mother's actions. I lived through the agony of watching my mother wither away, knowing she should have gone on alone without complicating her life and her emotions."

An adoring smile hovered on her lips as she cupped Devlin's face. "I have shared your passion because of our close proximity the past few weeks, but I could have been any other woman. It wouldn't have mattered to you, not really. And when you leave Tucson it will be over between us. It has to be, for both our sakes." Her voice cracked and tears glistened in her luminous blue eyes.

"You have never in your life been a bigger fool than you are now, Riah," Devlin scowled at her. "You are giving me no opportunity to convince you how I feel about you, and you damned well know I have other commitments right now. I can't offer you happiness until my name is cleared and you aren't willing to wait to let me prove that I think what is between us can last!"

"We have a few days left," she reminded him as her body brushed provocatively against his, aching to recreate their few precious memories of splendor. "Just let me love you until it's time for you to go. Let me cherish this precious time together—a time that cannot be a part of our future lives . . ."

The feel of her delicious body gliding suggestively against his was Devlin's undoing. He wanted her as desperately now as he had the first time and the glorious times thereafter. Knowing she loved him was agony and ecstasy. She was willing to offer her body and her love, but she had every intention of leaving when he wasn't around to stop her from going.

"I do love you, Riah," he rasped as his hands drifted across her shirt to free the taut buds. His lips whispered over the dusky peaks and his hushed words hovered on her sensitized skin. "Don't leave me. Give our love a chance . . ."

"If you love me, even a little, you'll let me go," she whispered as she brought his lips to hers. "I can't bear the thought of watching my love for you become your burden. Just give me today . . . now . . ."

"Damn you," he growled in frustration and unappeased passion. "I should bring you up and stake you to a tree to ensure you're still here when I get back—"

His words transformed into a tormented moan when her titillating caresses swirled over his chest to trace the band of his breeches. Her fingertips delved beneath the fabric, caressing him, teasing him until he was so on fire for her that he could think of nothing else.

What a seductress she had turned out to be, he mused as Moriah urged him to the carpet of grass that lined the mountain path. He had taught her far too well to pleasure a man. She knew just where and how to touch to spin his nerves and his thoughts into tangled twine. She could make him forget everything except the moment of rapture that her kisses and caresses promised.

Her touch was embroidered with love. She glided

her hand over his rock-hard flesh, mapping each taut tendon, every whipcord muscle, each rippling contour of his body until she had committed every inch of his flesh to memory. Her soft lips fluttered over his male nipples and the scars on his ribs. She melted his bones and muscles to mush, leaving him receptive to her adoring touch. *I love you* was in each tender kiss and gentle caress. *I love you* was conveyed in the way her body brushed wantonly against his.

For once, Moriah let her every feeling show and showered him with heartfelt affection. She had spent agonizing weeks concealing her love for him. If this was to be their last intimate encounter, she vowed it would be a time that would be emblazoned on his mind and branded on his body forever. In years to come, she wanted him to look back on their weeks together with remembered affection. She longed to be the quiet smile that grazed his lips when no one else was around. She wanted to be the sweet memory that burned through him, bringing her vision to mind. They couldn't have forever, but they had now. It would have to be enough.

Devlin swore he had been deprived of oxygen when Moriah spread a sea of cresting kisses in the wake of her adventurous caresses. Her loving touch was like a rolling tide tumbling ashore. He was swamped by a floodtide of living fire that left him to burn on a scorching flame.

With lithe grace, he rolled sideways, forcing her to her back, causing the golden tendrils to tumble about her like molten lava. His caresses streamed over her supple flesh like a meteor leaving a path of sparks trailing behind it. His kisses fed the flickering flame that leaped from her exquisite body to his and back again. His hands and lips were everywhere at once—teasing, arousing, exciting. His caresses migrated over the gaping garments and then tunneled beneath them, removing each one as he went until she lay naked in the grass.

His heated gaze poured over her, relishing the sight and feel of her deliciously formed body, treating her to worshipping caresses that displayed a hunger tempered with loving patience. His tongue encircled the buds of her breasts while his hands trailed over the satiny terrain of her abdomen and thighs. He adored the way she responded to his touch, marveled at the way her honey-sweet lips parted in invitation.

Devlin wanted to savor and devour her. He wanted the moment to burn away time and span eternity. He yearned to carve his name on her heart and soul. And when she left him, the compelling memory would bring her back to him, even if her willful determination sought to keep her away.

She was so cussed sure that it was guilt and sympathy that controlled his emotions. But thirty years of wondering if he would ever meet his match in a woman supplied him with the foresight to know when he had. And Devlin had most certainly found his destiny with this Angel of the Wind, whether she believed it or not. Fate had brought them together and Devlin longed to make her realize she would be half a person, not a whole one, without him in her life. And for those few days before he returned to the mountains he would give her a glimpse of the future they could enjoy together. He would reveal their private paradise to her and she would lament leaving him . . .

His thoughts disintegrated when Moriah's hand folded around him and she whispered her need for him. The sweet hot ache of passion burned holes in his mind. He crouched above her, watching the potent effects of desire engulf her elegant features. He wished with all his heart that she could see the love blazing in his amber eyes. If she could see him now she would know that it was far more than pity and lust that consumed him. This was a love so fierce and wild that it could endure until the end of time. And it was hers for the taking.

"I love you," he murmured as he came to her. "I need you . . ."

Moriah let herself believe him for that splendorous moment when they were one beating breathing essence unto each other. She was the candle and he was the warm flame that spread a beacon light through her world of darkness. She could feel her body melting with the wondrous sensations that his skillful lovemaking evoked. She adored the feel of his muscular body blending into hers, reveled in the ecstasy of being one heart forging with another.

A soft gasp tumbled from her lips when the cadence of love sent her dark world spinning furiously about her. Moriah struggled to catch her breath before she entered the heavenly world of passion. Time stood still as desire swamped her, leaving her reeling in sublime ecstasy.

Devlin felt the tidal wave of passion tumble over him. Helplessly, he shuddered with the sensations that spilled from his body like sparkling champagne cascading over the rim of a crystal goblet. He was numb with indescribable pleasure, devoid of strength. He cradled Moriah in his arms, drunk on the scent, taste, and feel of her body molded to his.

"You're going to be sorry, stubborn sprite," he breathed against her flushed cheek. "I swear you will."

A melancholy smile tripped across Moriah's lips as

she glided her hand over his powerful shoulder and drew lazy circles down his spine. "I have no doubt of that."

"And you're going to miss me terribly," he whispered as his body moved suggestively against hers.

"More than you'll ever know," she sighed in agreement.

"You'll have no one to argue with. Ah, what a dull, dreary existence you'll endure," he grumbled against her ear.

"There's no question about it."

Mustering his strength, Devlin rolled away, frustrated to no end. When she argued with him, it infuriated him. Now she was agreeing with everything he said, and it exasperated him!

"Of all the women in all the world, I had to fall in love with the most stubborn female on the planet!"

"Dev, don't . . ." Moriah tried to protest before he broke the magical spell of contentment.

His breath came out in an exasperated rush. The nearby juniper tree would be just as receptive to his reasoning. "All right, damnit, have it your way. You usually do," he muttered sourly. "My pity turned to passion and my guilt transformed into desire. I wanted you because you were convenient. It had been ages since I had touched a woman and I lost control. That's all it was and that's all it will ever be. Never mind what I really think and feel. That's what you want to hear!" His loud voice was punctuation in itself.

"You and I will get along much better if you accept the truth of your emotions instead of trying to pretend you feel something you don't," she murmured as she reached over to smooth away his agitated frown and wound up poking him in the other eye.

"Good God, woman, you're making me crazy!" Devlin growled, clutching his hair as if he meant to yank it out.

Moriah leaned out to press a kiss to his pouting lips. And this time she didn't miss her mark. Her kiss melted his anger. "I love you, crazy though you are . . ."

A reluctant smile bordered his lips. He wanted to shout and curse at her for being so determined to let what they had fade away like a forgotten memory from another lifetime. And yet it was impossible to stay angry with her when she had finally confessed to love him. He would simply have to find a way to convince her that his love was true. *He* believed *her*. Damnation, why couldn't she trust in him enough to believe *him?*

You've got four days, Granger, Devlin reminded himself sternly. *You damned well better make the most of them or you'll wind up losing the one woman you've ever really wanted.* He only hoped this wasn't some kind of divine punishment for dismissing the score of women he could have had in the past and taking them all for granted.

"Okay, minx, you win," Devlin sighed in defeat. "You do what you think you need to do and I'll do the same for my own best interests."

"I really do love you," she murmured before groping for her discarded clothes.

"I'll try to remember that when I return to Tucson to find you gone. I'm sure that will be of great comfort to me in my dotage," he smirked sarcastically.

"You'll forget me soon enough," Moriah predicted.

"And if I don't, I'll hold it over you for the rest of your natural life," he snorted. After stuffing his legs into his breeches, he stood up. None too gently, he tugged Moriah up beside him. "Come on, stubborn woman, we still have a long walk ahead of us."

Without complaint, but with an aching heart, Moriah allowed Devlin to lead her away. She would have preferred to tarry in the Dragoon Mountains a few more days before this phase of her life was over. This was one chapter she didn't want to see come to an end. It meant she would never see Devlin again, never feel his protective arms enfolding her, never travel that intimate journey through the sensual world of passion.

As well, Moriah reminded herself glumly. She had always known that nothing good lasted very long. It was a depressing fact of life and it would do no good whatsoever to wallow in despair.

Chapter 15

Devlin paused on the gentle slopes to stare across the valley. To the north, the Santa Catalina Mountains were cloaked with lavender shadows that hung in the tree-choked ridges. In the distance he could see the Santa Cruz River shimmering like a silver snake in the morning light. The spires of San Xavier de Bac Mission, The White Dove of the Desert, reached toward the cloudless sky, silhouetted against the backdrop of the mountain range. He stared pensively at the walled city of Tucson that graced the valley and then he focused on the ranch that lay to the south beside the glistening river.

Moriah's hand slid into his and her eyes lifted toward the faint glint of light that filtered through her private spectrum of darkness. "What's the matter?" she questioned.

"Nothing except we're almost home and when I leave I'll probably never see you again," Devlin mumbled acrimoniously. "Never before has coming home caused such a mixture of emotions."

"I rather doubt that, but thank you for being kind enough to say so," Moriah replied, attempting to appear lighthearted, even though her spirits had nose-dived to the foothills.

"I'm not being kind, only honest," Devlin muttered as he wound through the canopy of trees. "You refuse to believe it, but you have become a habit I'll have difficulty unlearning."

He was only being nice to her because this was the beginning of the end, Moriah speculated. Devlin could say anything he liked, but he was still going to leave her to ensure that his most important crusade in life met with success.

If he really loved her, he would put her before his revenge against Burkhart, wouldn't he? If given a choice between repaying the Thatchers for their betrayal and remaining with Devlin, Moriah would take Devlin without question, revenge and her inheritance be damned. In light of her love for Devlin, nothing else seemed to matter as much. She would never be Devlin's first consideration. More than anything, he wanted to clear his name and bring Burkhart to his knees. And although it was a noble purpose, it made Moriah realize that what they shared wasn't quite as important to him as he wanted her to believe.

She was actually doing him the greatest favor a woman could do for a man, she mused as they paced across the fertile valley, hearing the whinny of horses and the lowing of cattle in the distance. Moriah had erased Devlin's choices for him so he could focus on his dedicated purpose. He really should have been grateful that she was unselfish and understanding instead of scolding her for leaving him. She knew he was meant for better things than catering to a blind lady he happened onto . . .

The instant Moriah heard the thunder of approaching hooves, she stopped stock-still. Her heart shriveled in her chest when Devlin unloosed her hand and trotted forward. The giggle of feminine laughter reached Moriah's ears.

Jessica Granger yanked her steed to a skidding halt and leaped to the ground to squeeze the stuffing out of Devlin. "Four months and not a word," she chided as she hugged him to her. "I'll never forgive you for staying away so long this time."

Devlin combed his hands through the ebony strands that whipped around her face and then dropped a kiss to her forehead. "Outlaws can't waltz around free as a bird, pet," he reminded her. "I come when I can."

Jessica sighed happily. She had always worshipped the ground both her brothers walked on. She had missed Devlin terribly and cursed the unfair charges that had placed a price on his head. She was anxious for the day Thomas Havern, the family lawyer, took the case to the military court in Santa Fe and exonerated Devlin.

Her dark eyes drifted around Devlin's broad shoulder to study the shapely young woman whose unconventional garb revealed more of her figure than was decent for a lady to expose. Jessica took one look at the blue-eyed blonde and disliked her on sight. This hussy was no lady, not the way she was dressed! The fact that this Jezebel was traveling with Devlin aroused Jessica's darkest suspicions. Moriah's skin was tanned from hours of exposure and Jessica shuddered to guess just how the wild-haired witch had gotten that tan and how much flesh it covered!

With Devlin's dashing good looks, wealth, and primitive lusty appeal, women had always chased after him like kittens on the trail of fresh milk. This chit was no different from the rest of them, except that she obviously came from a lower class. She had undoubtedly provided the physical pleasure that no man could deny when faced with the devil's temptation.

While Jessica was sizing Moriah up, Barrett screeched to a halt. His sparkling hazel eyes lingered momentarily on his brother, but it was only a tenth of a second before they landed squarely on the voluptuous beauty whose full breasts lay temptingly beneath her white shirt. Her bared midriff left Barrett to visually measure the curvy indentation of her waist. The outrageous garments did little to conceal the woman's undeniable charms and Barrett's temperature rose just gawking at her.

Lord, Devlin always did have the most appealing females on his arm. Even though he had been in hiding for over a year he obviously hadn't lost his touch. This blue-eyed blonde had the most arousing effect on a man!

Barrett mentally shook himself and dragged his eyes back to Devlin. "I've got good news, big brother," he announced, his gaze betraying him by darting back to Moriah. "Thomas Havern has finally gathered all the evidence and persuaded the Army to set a date for the trial. With any luck at all your face will be off those wanted posters in less than two months."

Devlin certainly hoped so. But even if he were acquitted, there still remained Burkhart's forceful attack against the Apaches. He had so much to contend with while he was left to wonder what Moriah was doing and where she was. Damn, why couldn't he confront just one obstacle at a time instead of having them bombard him from all directions?

"Jess, Rett, I want you to meet Moriah Laverty," he announced, casting aside his troubled musings.

To Jessica's chagrin, Devlin slid a possessive arm

around Moriah's bare midsection. The fact that Moriah didn't protest his familiarity with her did not set well with Jessica. It galled her to see this harlot stealing Devlin's attention.

"The pleasure is all mine, Moriah," Barrett murmured as his gaze flooded over her bewitching figure, counting her assets. When he stretched out his hand, Moriah didn't reciprocate by lifting hers to his proffered handshake. She merely smiled cordially and stared at the air over his head.

Awkwardly, Barrett let his arm drop loosely by his side. "We welcome you to our ranch, my dear."

Oh no we don't! Jessica thought huffily. But she didn't dare voice her complaints while Devlin and Barrett were ogling this blond harpy as if she were the meal they were about to devour.

When Devlin swept Moriah in his arms and deposited her atop the horse Barrett had brought for him, Jessica silently fumed. And to her further irritation, Devlin swung up behind the harridan and rested his left hand on her thigh as if it belonged there. Jessica was seeing various shades of indignant red!

For as long as she could remember, Devlin and Barrett had lectured her on what was proper behavior for a lady when she was in the company of a man. Devlin wasn't practicing what he preached and Barrett kept darting lusty glances at Moriah. Jessica was supposed to behave like a sophisticated lady while her two brothers slobbered all over this blonde who didn't even scold them for staring so brazenly at her! Jessica fumed. Decent young ladies were to guard their virtues while it was acceptable for men to dally with females who would allow them to take what they wanted in exchange for monetary favors and other compensations.

Jessica was not having Devlin's paramour under their roof! And she would tell him so the first chance she got! And Barrett, curse his hide, was gawking at Moriah as if he itched to be next in line when Devlin finished taking his turn with her. It was positively scandalous and both of her brothers were making complete asses of themselves!

Sullenly, Jessica rode past the family trading post and returned to the sprawling hacienda that was located beside the Santa Cruz River. She was crushed by Devlin's lack of attention. He had always showered her with affection when he returned from his long seclusions in the mountains, but suddenly Jessica was the unnoticed doormat he walked over as he shepherded his new mistress into the house.

Even Barrett didn't seem to remember he had a sister! He engaged himself in conversation with Devlin while he drooled over Moriah. Jessica wanted to club both of them over the head until they came to their senses.

"Jess, go fetch us something to eat and drink," Devlin commanded as he guided Moriah into the elaborately furnished parlor and parked himself beside her on the sofa.

What did he think she was, one of the servants? Jessica silently smoldered.

"Bring me a brandy, Jess," Barrett requested without taking his eyes off the stunning blonde.

"Furniture!" Moriah sighed appreciatively as she nestled into the padded couch. Her hand brushed inquisitively over the rich velvet upholstery. "I almost forgot what a luxury it is to sit down on something besides a rock." Her gaze drifted toward Devlin. "What color is it?"

"Gold," he informed as he raised a strand of her hair and let it trickle over his fingertips. "Not as exquisite as this, I'm sorry to say."

A muddled frown clouded Barrett's brow. He glanced from Moriah's sapphire-blue eyes to Devlin's bronzed face. It suddenly dawned on him why Moriah hadn't bothered to shake his hand and why she had inquired about the shade of the upholstery. She was blind and he had been too busy devouring her appetizing figure to notice!

The stunned expression on Barrett's handsome face put a teasing grin on Devlin's lips. "Your powers of observation need polishing, little brother," he mocked lightly. "It certainly took you long enough to notice."

A wave of sympathy and newfound respect for Moriah flooded over Barrett. He couldn't begin to imagine how this young woman had survived in the rugged mountains where Devlin took refuge to elude bounty hunters and army scouts.

Devlin had been vividly aware of the attention Barrett had been paying Moriah since he laid eyes on her. His twenty-seven-year-old brother had looked a little too interested in this feisty beauty to suit Devlin's tastes. Now it was even worse. Barrett was visualizing himself as Moriah's new protector while Devlin was off battling Burkhart. Damn.

"Food and drink," Jessica announced as she sailed into the parlor like a flying carpet. "Will that be all, maharajah, or may I join you?"

The sarcastic remark caused a shade of vexation to cloud Devlin's brow. Jessica had always been a bit rambunctious and high-spirited but she had never exhibited such rude behavior in front of a guest. She had been taught better than that. What had gotten into her?

His discerning gaze fastened on Jessica's face, reading the irritation of her thoughts. Mumbling a thank-you and shooting his sister a reproachful frown, Devlin placed the glass of brandy into Moriah's hand and then offered her some bread and cheese.

It still hadn't dawned on Jessica that Moriah was blind. She was too busy seething and thinking mutinous thoughts about Dev and Rett.

"You have a grand home," Moriah complimented, tossing Rett an elfin smile. "I've never seen a lovelier or larger mansion."

After counting the number of paces from the threshold of the front door, through the wide foyer and across the spacious parlor, Moriah had speculated the house was gigantic. Her calculations were correct and her comment provoked Barrett's chuckle. It was clearly evident to Barrett, as Moriah had hoped it would be, that she had accepted her handicap and intended to make light of it. She wanted no pity, only the right to be treated equally.

"How kind of you to notice and to say so," Barrett teased her back with typical Granger charm. "What do you think of the emerald-green drapes? As for me, I think they're a bit too much with the gold couch and royal-blue tuft chairs."

Moriah liked the sound of Barrett's voice and his willingness to indulge her. He, like Devlin, had a refreshing sense of humor. Moriah had discovered there were a few good men in the world who didn't introduce themselves and then start pawing at a woman.

"I find the rich color combination very elegant and pleasing to the eye," Moriah insisted with a mischievous grin. "I prefer bold shades to pale pastels. Sunrise and rainbows provide enough of the lighter spectrum."

This was the most idiotic conversation Jessica had

ever been forced to endure. She was fed up with her brothers ignoring her presence and showering this indecent doxie with such exaggerated consideration when she didn't deserve it. Her brothers had always pampered her and spoiled her. And the minute they dragged home this Moriah woman, Jessica was completely forgotten.

"Will you be staying for supper, Moriah?" Jessica managed to question without grinding out the words. Her inquiry suggested correctly that she was anxious for the unwelcome baggage to tote herself off.

"For supper, and as long as she wishes to remain at the hacienda, enjoying our hospitality," Devlin declared, flinging his ill-mannered sister a condescending glare.

Well, if that didn't beat all! Next, Devlin would probably shuffle Jessica out of her elegantly furnished bedchamber so Princess Moriah could enjoy all the luxuries that weren't to be found in the guest room. Or, worse, he and his harlot would have the audacity to share the master bedroom! Now, Jessica was seeing crimson red!

"How nice," Jessica grumbled, her tone implying it was nothing of the kind.

Moriah glanced toward the voice that vibrated with the chord of distaste. It was glaringly apparent that Jessica didn't approve of her, and Moriah knew she must have looked a fright. "I will only impose on your hospitality until I can find work in Tucson," she informed Jessica.

Devlin clamped his lips together, fighting the urge to voice a protest. But he and Moriah had been through this before and she had made up her mind to leave once she had seen to the necessary arrangements.

Astonished, Barrett gaped at Moriah and then caught himself the split second before he blurted out some stupid remark about the impossibility of finding a job when she couldn't even see. Judging by the depth of character this dazzling young woman displayed, Barrett decided Moriah possessed the will to find a way to acquire a job, even sightless.

Of course, Jessica knew perfectly well what type of employment a soiled dove would seek out—the kind that kept her on her back in bed, the kind that required no stylish wardrobe. The look she flung Moriah said as much, but Moriah couldn't intercept it. However, Devlin did, and he made a mental note to chastise his disrespectful sister when he got her alone.

"While Moriah bathes and changes into one of Jessica's gowns, you can brief me on the case Havern has compiled for court," Devlin suggested.

Jessica silently burned herself into a pile of furious ashes. She would not have this woman prancing around in her dresses! How dare Devlin offer her garments to this floozie!

Barrett glanced at his fuming sister and quickly volunteered to escort Moriah upstairs while Devlin had a private word with Jessica. She looked as if she were sorely in need of it. Her piercing glares indicated she had no wish to open their home to Devlin's remarkable guest.

"I'll have the servants fill the tub and I'll show you the way," Barrett insisted, appointing himself her guide. "I'm sure you'll like the decor upstairs," he added with a grin and a light squeeze on her wrist. "We just redecorated in white and royal blue."

"I can't wait to see the upper level," Moriah replied with an impish smile.

"You amaze me," Barrett complimented as he veered toward the steps.

"You flatter me." Moriah curled her hand around his elbow, allowing him to guide her. "How many steps are in the staircase?"

A blank look slid over his face. "To tell the truth, I don't know. I never had reason to count them before."

Anticipating great enjoyment from Moriah's stay at the hacienda, Barrett counted his way up the steps and then indicated where each bedroom was located. He led Moriah into the guest room at the head of the stairs and paced over the six steps between her room and the banister so she wouldn't miscalculate and tumble down them by accident.

Meanwhile, Devlin had cornered Jessica and was in the process of handing down a lecture to his misbehaving sister.

"You know better than to treat a guest in our home with discourtesy." Devlin gave his sister a look that was as hard as rocks. "That display was beneath you. Surely you don't begrudge Moriah wearing a few of your gowns until I can purchase some for her!"

Surely she did! "Purchase?" Jessica squawked in outrage. "How dare you bring that hussy in here in the first place! Buy her a wardrobe? You had better not!" She snorted in disgust. "I will not wait on your strumpet as if she were the visiting queen until you come back home to fetch her! She is leaving the instant you can secure a room for her at the hotel in Tucson."

Devlin leveled his sister a blistering glare. "Moriah will leave when she is damned good and ready to and not one instant before. And until she wants to go you will treat her with the respect and courtesy she deserves."

"I have already treated her with the exact amount of respect she deserves." Jessica stared at him with challenging directness. "None whatsoever. And I shall continue to do so until she takes the hint and makes herself scarce!"

Devlin loomed over Jessica like an ominous thundercloud. "You will do precisely as I say, young lady," he boomed. "And if Barrett tells me that you have been rude and surly, you will have hell to pay when I get back."

"I'd rather take the beating," she flared in rebellious defense.

"You'll take a beating now if you don't do what I tell you." Devlin's voice was reminiscent of the crack of thunder. "Moriah has no one to turn to. You have been behaving like such a spoiled brat that you couldn't even stop being huffy long enough to notice she's blind. I want this ranch to be one place in this world that she can call her port in the storm, the one place she longs to return to when she realizes she needs me."

"Blind?" Jessica parroted, blinking in stunned disbelief. "She never said so."

"Of course she didn't," Devlin smirked. "She is proud and independent and determined to make her own way through the darkness. She has already been through all kinds of hell and I want her to enjoy the time she spends here. And I want you to become her confidante and friend. Heaven knows she's been deprived of even *that* the last ten years!"

For a long, frustrating moment Jessica studied the expression on her elder brother's face. So that was it, she decided. Devlin, who always had a soft spot in his heart for stray cats, lost causes, and underdogs, felt sorry for Moriah. And no doubt that cunning trollop had milked his sympathy for all it was worth. She had undoubtedly cried a few crocodile tears, offered him her body, and told him her sad little story, which probably wasn't true. The fact that Moriah was blind must have been the clincher, Jessica speculated. Devlin had been taken in by the attractive blind floozie with her hard-luck story that was designed to tear a man's heart out.

Jessica could see it would be up to her to break the spell Moriah had cast on Devlin. He had been alone in the wilds much too long, that was all. It had taken forever for her and Barrett to contact the men who had resigned their commissions under Lyle Burkhart and urge them to testify against him. Some of them were afraid to speak out for fear Burkhart would retaliate. And in the meantime, Devlin was left to tromp through the mountains, shunning civilization. Moriah had happened along and he had clung to her because there simply was no one else.

Making up her mind to deal with Moriah in her own subtle way after Devlin left, Jessica nodded in compliance, begrudging though it was. "Very well, I will try to befriend your harlot."

"She is not a harlot," Devlin snarled.

When he thrust his scowling face in hers and close to bit her head off, Jessica added, "And she can have some of my dresses, though I doubt they will be a proper fit. I'll just have them burned when she has no more use for them," she added flippantly.

Devlin wagged a finger in his sister's belligerent face. "I'm warning you, Jess. If I hear one snide remark or catch one spiteful glance, I'll have you over my knee so fast it will make your head spin," he vowed stormily.

"I'm too old for a thrashing," she flung back at him and then tilted a dignified chin.

"You're never too old for a throttling if you deserve one," he muttered, struggling for composure. "What is between Riah and me is none of your concern, and you had better not poke your nose in places it doesn't belong or it's liable to get clipped off."

"I can assure you that the less I see of your—" She didn't say the word because Devlin looked as if he was considering paddling her on the spot if she dared. "Your 'new friend,' the better," she finished waspishly.

"And now that we have that settled and out of the way, march yourself upstairs and select a suitable gown for Moriah. You will also offer Moriah perfume and whatever toiletries she might like. She's been forced to survive on the barest necessities instead of having all the luxuries you've taken for granted because Barrett and I have done you the disservice of spoiling you rotten."

Devlin had never scolded her so severely or criticized her so harshly until that blond-haired strumpet showed up. Jessica was incensed. No, she decided after giving the matter second consideration, she was positively outraged! Devlin had always been warm and loving with her. Now he was cold and cutting, and it was all Moriah's fault. That devious witch had put a curse on Devlin and soured his good disposition. She brought out the worst in him, and Jessica swore she would remove Moriah from Devlin's life for his own good.

Devlin had suffered enough because of Lyle Burkhart's betrayal. He would not be brought even lower by a scheming shrew who used her blindness as a weapon against the man she had bedeviled.

"If you are quite finished, I will adjourn upstairs

to gather the duchess's new clothes," Jessica said smartly.

"You had damned well better be the perfect hostess at supper," Devlin threatened. "One false move and you'll wish you hadn't disobeyed me."

Jessica squared her shoulders, elevated her proud chin, and stalked out with her back as stiff as a flagpole. Silently, she wished that blond-haired harlot out of her home and into perdition!

While the servants scurried about filling the tub, Barrett acquainted Moriah with the arrangement of the furniture and the terrace door that led onto the balcony that encircled the back of the house. When they were alone again, Barrett blessed the shapely beauty with a smile.

"Just make yourself at home," he insisted as he strode toward the door.

Barrett glanced back, noting there were no towels or wash cloths on the commode. Absently, he pushed the door shut and pivoted toward the adjoining entrance to Devlin's room to fetch the other supplies Moriah would need.

Hearing the creak of the door, Moriah presumed she was alone. Innocently, she peeled off her soiled shirt and had just begun unfastening her breeches when Barrett ambled through the short hall that joined his brother's room with the guest room. With towels in hand and jaw gaping, Barrett froze in his tracks.

The thick carpet prevented Moriah from hearing his approach. As she tossed her shirt aside, Barrett stood there like a marble statue, devouring the creamy swells of her breasts and the low-riding breeches that revealed her narrow waist and the gentle curve of her hips.

Damn, if that brother of his didn't have all the luck! Moriah was perfection in the flesh, a living, breathing goddess who could fulfill a man's most arousing fantasies. Although Barrett cursed himself for behaving like a lovestruck schoolboy, he didn't back down the hall and take his leave. Quietly, he reached around the corner to set the towels on the commode and devoured every inch of Moriah's luscious figure until his guilty conscience sharply reprimanded him.

While Barrett stood there ogling Moriah, Jessica breezed down the hall to voice her complaints to Barrett. She had glanced into Devlin's room to see Barrett poised between the two chambers. Wearing a muddled frown, she walked in to catch him gawking at Moriah.

Clamping her lips together, Jessica spun on her heels, knowing it would be a waste of time to plead her cause to Barrett. He was as bewitched as Devlin! Brooding over this most infuriating situation, Jessica stamped off to retrieve a gown for the witch who had taken up residence at the Granger ranch.

Oblivious to the fact that he had been caught peeping at Moriah, Barrett quietly backed out of the corridor and into Devlin's bedroom. As he tiptoed away, he scolded himself for drooling over Moriah, but what man wouldn't have savored her tantalizing charms? Barrett rationalized.

With wayward visions dancing in his head, Barrett ambled down the hall to consult with his brother. But he had the tingling feeling he was going to be a bit too preoccupied to make a good listener. As it turned out, Barrett was right.

Chapter 16

The abrupt rap at the door at eight o'clock in the morning sent Devlin bounding out of Moriah's bed and streaking back to his own room in a flash. Drowsily, Moriah fumbled to retrieve the shirt Devlin had loaned her to use as a makeshift nightgown. She barely had time to shrug the garment on before the door banged against the wall and the unidentified intruder burst in.

"Forgive me for barging in on you. I hope you don't mind," Jessica declared as she stamped forward with the breakfast tray Barrett had insisted she cart up the stairs to Moriah.

No one sounded less in need of forgiveness than Jessica, and Moriah minded quite a bit actually. But instead of snapping back at Jessica, she forced a smile and allowed her thoughts to center on the lingering memories of the previous night. She had been awakened from a deep sleep by the touch of skillful hands and the warm draft of arousing kisses. And all through the night Devlin had been beside her, sharing his passion, cradling her in his protective arms . . . until the rattle of the door had sent him darting back to his own room.

The clatter of dishes and the aroma of steak and eggs assured Moriah that Jessica had brought her breakfast. "It is kind of you to bring me a tray," Moriah murmured, discreetly checking to ensure her shirt was properly buttoned. "But it isn't necessary. I could have made my way down to the dining room."

Jessica surveyed the rumpled bed. "I trust you slept well," she said, her voice dripping false honey.

"Like a baby," Moriah sighed. "It's been ages since I have had the pleasure of sleeping on a bed."

And the last time she did, it had probably been with a score of different men, Jessica thought mutinously. Her scorning gaze scrutinized the pillow beside Moriah. From the look of things, Jessica speculated that this shameless hussy had been entertaining Devlin. Damn her.

With her fingers clenched around the tray, wishing all the while that she had a stranglehold on Moriah's neck, Jessica set the breakfast dishes in her guest's lap. "Barrett thought you might enjoy having breakfast in bed this morning."

Moriah's brows knitted at the undertone of venom in Jessica's voice. She had noticed it at supper the previous evening as well as this morning. Jessica fiercely resented Moriah's intrusion. Moriah didn't know why, but Jessica's voice betrayed the turmoil that was boiling through her veins.

"That was very considerate of Barrett. He seems to be very much the gentleman. And there are so few of them around," Moriah added, her cynicism creeping into her tone.

The comment had Jessica gnashing her teeth. Women like Moriah probably had little occasion to meet men like Devlin. That was why she had latched onto the eldest Granger. This gold digger might be blind, but she could probably hear a man's wallet opening and shutting and she knew just which men could keep her in a manner to which she aspired. And if Moriah knew she had corrupted Barrett by letting him gawk at her before she stepped into her tub, she would no doubt use her wiles to bedevil him as well as Devlin.

When Moriah tentatively brushed her hand over the tray, Jessica smiled wickedly. "The tomato juice is on the left."

Moriah reached out and took a sip. A pained gasp trickled from her lips when scalding coffee burned her tongue and dribbled down her chin.

"I'm so sorry," Jessica apologized. She wasn't the least bit sorry actually. "The juice was on *my* left, not yours."

"It's all right," Moriah assured her. "I should have smelled the difference, but I wasn't paying attention." The fact was that all her senses were still filled with Devlin's masculine fragrance and her mind was still adrift in the tantalizing memories of spending their first night together in a real bed.

"How old are you, Moriah?" Jessica inquired as the bewitching blonde groped to locate her fork and stabbed at her egg.

"Twenty," Moriah replied before nibbling on the oversalted egg. "And you?"

"Twenty-three," Jessica answered, smiling devilishly as Moriah reached for the tomato juice to wash down the highly seasoned steak and eggs. "My brothers and I have been together a long time. In case you hadn't noticed, I'm exceptionally fond of both of them." Although Moriah couldn't detect it, Jessica punished her with a mutinous glare. "I want nothing but the best for them. And when they are in danger, my protective instincts take over."

Moriah had the feeling Jessica was subtly warning

her away from Devlin. Jessica knew there could be no match between them. It was a shame Devlin wasn't as perceptive as his sister.

"While you finish your meal, I'll fetch you another of my dresses," Jessica volunteered, smiling in wicked glee when Moriah burned her tongue a second time on the scalding coffee. For spite, Jessica had boiled it before bringing it upstairs.

When she was alone, Moriah choked down her breakfast, wondering why the cook had used such a heavy hand on the salt and pepper. Moriah was sure she would have to drink water like a thirsty camel all day after consuming such highly seasoned food.

Grinning triumphantly, Jessica breezed down the hall to retrieve a gown for her annoying guest. Now for phase two, Jessica mused mischievously. She was going to make Moriah anxious to find a room at a Tucson hotel. Jessica didn't want her around when Devlin finally returned to take his rightful place on the Granger ranch.

After Moriah finished her breakfast and sank into the tub, she shivered uncontrollably. The water was too cold to be relaxing, but it was invigorating. The fact that Moriah found even minute pleasure in her tub would have chagrined Jessica, who had seen to it that only a minimal amount of heated water had been added to the bath.

When Moriah fastened herself into the red gown Jessica loaned her, she brushed her hand over the daring neckline and its tight bodice. It fit her like a leather glove. Ah well, beggers weren't allowed to be choosers, Moriah reminded herself as she struggled with the lacings. But she would have preferred to wear the high-collared garment Jessica had lent her the previous night.

After combing her hair, Moriah paced off the six

steps from her bedroom door and aimed herself toward the banister. But the unexpected wrinkle in the rug that lined the hall caused her to trip. Although she wasn't close enough to the staircase to tumble down, she was left to flounder in an attempt to regain her balance.

Composing herself, Moriah located the banister and descended the steps without further mishap. She didn't have the faintest notion that the wrinkled carpet was another of Jessica's attempts to make Moriah's sojourn as brief and unpleasant as possible.

Hearing Devlin and Barrett's voice, Moriah propelled herself through the wide vestibule and veered into the spacious study that was paneled with pine and polished to a glistening shine. Her appearance brought the men's conversation to an abrupt halt.

The bright red dress that Jessica had selected for Moriah caught both men's attention and left their mouths gaping. The garment clung to Moriah's curvaceous figure like a second set of skin and exposed the full swells of her breasts. Although Devlin was aroused by the tempting display of creamy flesh and the vivid curves and swells that were accentuated by the scarlet-red dress, he did not appreciate the way Barrett was devouring Moriah with hungry eyes. As always, Moriah's stunning appearance drew a man's undivided attention. The fact that it was now his own brother who ogled Moriah with bold fascination had Devlin grinding his teeth.

And damn that Jessica and her ornery prank, Devlin scowled under his breath. She had purposely selected a garment that emphasized all Moriah's alluring assets just to instigate trouble. She had her heart set on hating Moriah and was trying to cause conflict between the brothers. It was annoyingly apparent that Devlin was going to have to have another chat with that mischievous sister of his. The first lecture hadn't made much of an impression on her, it seemed. To spite him, Jessica had loaned Moriah a dowdy gown the previous night. This morning she had decked their guest out in flaming red. That ornery little minx!

"You are breathtaking," Barrett chirped, his hazel eyes sweeping over her appetizing figure.

"Am I?" Moriah chortled lightly. "What color am I wearing?"

"Bright pink," Devlin declared, casting his brother a warning glance.

Barrett stared at Moriah and then at Devlin's sour frown. Suddenly it dawned on him that Jessica was trying to make her opinion of Moriah known by offering her a daring red gown that should have been worn to an evening social gathering, unless the woman in question held the lowly position of a calico queen or a prostitute.

"You look fetching in pink, Moriah," Barrett complimented as he rose to full stature. "Dev wants to show you around the ranch and trading post this morning. I'll join you after I have a word with Jessica." That remark was directed more toward his brother than the fetching blonde.

Moriah listened to Barrett's retreating footsteps before she heard the click of boots pacing across the tiled floor toward her. A warm flood of pleasure rippled through her, sensing Devlin's approach.

"I trust you slept comfortably last night, Señorita Laverty," Devlin drawled in a thick Spanish accent. His index finger sketched the plunging neckline that had a most arousing effect on him.

One delicate brow arched inquisitively when Devlin lifted her hand to brush his lips over her wrist. Curiously, she wiggled her fingertips free to map his broad chest. Devlin was garbed in a serape. A bandoleer that was lined with bullets was draped diagonally over his shoulder and ribs. Her hand glided up his chin to note the fake mustache that had been pasted on his upper lip. Smiling in amusement, she investigated the wide-brimmed sombrero that shadowed his handsome face.

"Sí, señor." A provocative grin hovered on the corner of her mouth. "It was a most pleasurable evening . . ." Her voice trailed off as inviting lips slanted over hers. "You are traveling incognito, I see, Señor Shadow," she murmured when he granted her a breath of air.

Devlin smiled into her radiant features. "I hope the mustache doesn't tickle, *chiquita,"* he rasped as his lips grazed the swanlike column of her throat. "When a man is wanted by the law, he must have many faces."

"That mustache cannot remain," Moriah purred as her adventurous fingertips tunneled beneath the serape and shirt to make stimulating contact with his hair-matted flesh.

"It won't be there tonight when I steal into your room to show you all the tantalizing ways a man can pleasure a woman." His hands drifted over her derriere, pulling her full length against him, letting her feel his ardent desire for her.

Devlin had become incredibly charming and seductive the past two days, making it even more impossible to think of leaving him forever, even if they *were* wrong for each other. Moriah had vowed to savor these last few days together, to reap every pleasure, treasure every precious moment. But when the time came, she had to go her own way.

"I see there is a new man in my life," she whispered as she swayed toward him. Her brazen caress slid over his lean hips, feeling the double holsters that held two Colts. "First it was the half man, half wolf who stalked the rugged mountains." Her titillating caress traced the band of his breeches. "Now it is the dashing vaquero who is armed to the teeth and devastatingly appealing in his Spanish attire."

Devlin's heart leapfrogged around his chest when Moriah caressed him and teased him with tempting kisses. "I think I prefer to retire to your room instead of touring the ranch," he growled suggestively. "The scenery in your room is better."

Moriah graced him with a seductive grin. "I think you would look just as fascinating lying beside the river as you would in my bed, Señor Shadow. You provide all the scenery I require. Even though my world is a fuzzy shade of gray, I can still see you lounging in the gamma grass in the canyon, just as you were the very first time we—"

"Come along, vixen," Devlin cut in, his voice ragged with desire. Moriah's mention of a time that had long lingered in his dreams triggered a maelstrom of sensations. He yearned to make today just like the very first time, except better. "If I don't get you all to myself and quickly, the servants will have something scandalous to gossip about."

"And I don't think I'm as anxious to see your ranch as I am to spend a few hours alone with you," Moriah confessed as she slipped her hand into his.

Devlin murmured his husky agreement and then practically dragged Moriah along with his swift, impatient stride in his haste to get her alone and shower her with his affection. He had only two days left to convince this stubborn creature that she meant the world to him.

* * *

While Devlin was retrieving a horse from the stable and visualizing the two of them making wild sweet love beside the river, Barrett had pounced on his sister in the parlor and let her have it with both barrels.

"Neither Devlin nor I found your prank the least bit amusing," Barrett scowled at Jessica, who suddenly looked so angelic that he expected her to sprout wings and a halo any second.

"Whatever are you talking about, Rett?" Jessica questioned, batting her big brown eyes and flashing him a cherubic smile.

"You know damned well what I'm referring to. Devlin and I forbade you to wear that revealing red velvet gown in public because it is too suggestive and revealing for a proper lady! And you had the nerve to loan it to Moriah."

Jessica shrugged off his reprimand and absently toyed with the tassel on the drapes. Her gaze strayed out the window, watching Devlin and Moriah trot across the pasture. "I thought it was befitting our guest."

An angry scowl was plastered on Barrett's face. "You have no right to sit in judgment, Jess," he said. "Moriah is a very remarkable woman who deserves your consideration and respect."

Jessica blinked wide-eyed. Good Lord, not both of them! Now Barrett was scolding her like a misbehaving child, too. He had never uttered a cross word to her until Moriah came along. And suddenly both Rett and Dev were leaping to that blond harlot's defense. She had bewitched both men.

"You have no room to talk," she retaliated tartly. "I have seen the way you flutter around Moriah and gape at her as if you were waiting to have her all to yourself. We both know what she is." Jessica expelled a distasteful sniff. "Remarkable? Only in bed, I'll wager. I'm sure she has had years of experience in perfecting her skills in the boudoir."

Barrett snapped up his head and glowered at his sister. "You mind your tongue, young lady," he growled, hazel eyes flashing sparks.

"You are counting the days until Devlin leaves so you can have Moriah all to yourself," she hurled in accusation. "Well, if you intend to stoop that low, you will not do it under this roof! You can do so at the bordello where Moriah will undoubtedly be renting a room to service her other customers."

Barrett had never struck his sister, but at the moment he would have liked to. He itched to slap that haughty smirk off her face and shake her until her teeth fell out.

"I'll be watching your every move, Jess," he muttered in threat. "If you do one more thing to insult Moriah, if you make one derogatory remark, I'll paddle your backside so hard you won't be able to sit down for a week!"

That was the second time Jessica had been threatened with a beating and all because of Moriah. That woman had to go. She would play one Granger against another, doling out sexual favors until she decided which one of them she wanted to latch onto permanently.

"The gown you offer Moriah tomorrow had better be one that is fit for a lady," Barrett demanded through clenched teeth.

"Why should it? Moriah certainly isn't a lady, not by any stretch of the imagination," Jessica scoffed sarcastically.

Barrett knotted his fists, visualizing how his sassy sister would look with his fingers clamped around her throat. "Devlin plans to take Moriah into Tucson to purchase her own garments tomorrow and she had damned well better be dressed like a lady when she goes!"

Damnation, that sorceress had Devlin paying for his favors by furnishing her with an expensive wardrobe. What other lavish gifts would the Granger men bestow on her, just to sample her charms? Jessica hated to venture a guess. It wasn't *her* behavior that was in question here. It was Devlin and Barrett's, and yet Jessica was the one who had been subjected to these harsh scoldings!

"You better watch your step, Jess," Barrett snapped. "I won't tolerate your ridicule or disrespect. And despite what you want, Moriah will stay here until *she* decides to go, not when *you* decide you want her out of our house."

This lecture sounded infuriatingly similar to the fire-breathing sermon Devlin had delivered the previous afternoon. Jessica felt like an outcast in her own home and she held Moriah solely responsible for all her woes.

Jessica was no longer receiving her brother's warm, loving attention. She was being ignored for Moriah. Jessica had longed for Devlin's return, prayed for it. But he hadn't given her the time of day since he arrived at the ranch. Moriah was monopolizing his time and the affection that rightfully belonged to Jessica. She resented every frustrating moment. She was not going to lie down and let that harpy waltz all over her! She was going to fight back until she had successfully routed Moriah from the hacienda!

Contentedly, Moriah stretched in the midmorning sun, her body aglow with the memories of the lovemaking she and Devlin had shared on the riverbank. They hadn't seen all that much of the sprawling ranch and hadn't set foot in the trading post where the Apaches came to barter for much-needed supplies.

While Moriah stirred like a graceful kitten and nestled against him, Devlin studied her enchanting features. The past two days had been a foretaste of heaven. He had vowed to make their time together a delicious dream that would burn with tender memories. He hoped to persuade Moriah to remain in Arizona until his feud with Burkhart ended. Devlin had discarded vocal arguments, employing a more tantalizing tactic to prove what kind of future Moriah could anticipate if she waited for him to return.

"I could spend the entire day loving you," Moriah sighed as she traced the whipcord muscles of his arm.

"I could spend the week," Devlin chortled before dropping a kiss to her petal-soft lips.

Moriah's smile evaporated and she became pensively silent. Ah, if only they had a week, a lifetime . . . If only she had time enough to transform Devlin's guilt-ridden pity into love—the kind that would endure forever.

Moriah chided herself for her wistful thoughts. Happiness had always eluded her. It was always long in coming and hasty in retreating from her grasp. Devlin had been born to great accomplishments and she had been born to woe. Clinging to whimsical dreams would only torment her more than she already was. She had to be sensible! When Devlin returned to the mountains to plan his strategy against Burkhart she had to put the past behind her and continue with the rest of her life, tormented though it might be . . .

The thunder of hooves sent Moriah and Devlin

scrambling for their clothes. They jumped into their garments with frantic haste and tried to appear engrossed in nothing more than harmless conversation when Barrett cantered toward them.

"Here you are at last," Barrett declared. His astute gaze assessed Moriah's flushed features, kiss-swollen lips, and tousled blond hair. Devlin looked a mite ruffled himself, Barrett noted. The lucky rake. Barrett had pitied his older brother's plight for the past year, but at the moment he would have eagerly exchanged places with Devlin. "I was hoping to join you for a tour of the ranch."

"We were waiting for you," Devlin mumbled awkwardly, aware of his brother's scrutinizing gaze.

Barrett didn't believe him for a second. "Weren't you just." He muffled his snicker behind an artificial cough. "Let's show Moriah the trading post that has been handed down through the generations," he suggested, biting back a grin.

While they rode east, Barrett repeated the tale of his grandfather's trek from Tennessee to Arizona. He explained Cyrus's first encounter with the Apache and the respectful peace and trust that had lingered through the decades until too many greedy white men attempted to take from the Indians without offering anything in return. Cyrus Granger had imported supplies and food in the harsh winters to accommodate the Apache and he bought hides and pelts to sell in the East. Cyrus was generous in sharing his profits with the Apache, offering gifts of beef, blankets, and trinkets in a gesture of continued friendship and steadfast loyalty.

Moriah listened in admiration while Barrett spoke. He, like Devlin, was a defender of justice, a man with a fierce sense of obligation to a tradition. Her opinion of men in general improved after her association with the Grangers. It was a shame Ruby Thatcher had thrust the worst miscreants in Texas at Moriah when she was younger and more impressionable. Perhaps Moriah would have met more honorable men like Devlin and Barrett. She might not be so cynical if she hadn't been forced to contend with the Lyle Burkharts and Vance Thatchers of the world.

"These stables boast some of the best-trained horses in the country," Barrett declared, forcing Moriah from her contemplative deliberations. "They have been trained by Apaches and the Mexican vaqueros who work at the ranch. We have sold many of them for staggering prices."

Moriah was duly impressed. The Grangers had built an empire in the fertile valley and had kept Cyrus Granger's tradition of good will to the Indians alive.

A clomp of hooves once again jolted Moriah from her musings. She felt Devlin's arm slide protectively around her and then drop away when he recognized the approaching guest.

"I'll take Moriah inside while you greet Thomas," Devlin murmured to his brother.

Nodding agreeably, Barrett leaned against the planks of the corral, waiting for the family lawyer to rein his buggy to a halt. Thomas Havern bounded to the ground and displayed a greeting smile that was as wide as the Santa Cruz River. Thomas was a wiry little man of fifty-five or thereabouts. His hair had turned silver-gray years ago and what hadn't turned gray had turned loose, leaving a bald spot on the crown of his head.

"Our case against Burkhart is in order," he announced with great enthusiasm. "I have telegraphed the witnesses from Burkhart's regiment who have agreed to testify about the incident at Ojo del

Muerto. They have each accepted your generous offer to pay their expenses for the trip back to Santa Fe. In a month, Devlin's name should be cleared of the charges. Burkhart doesn't stand a chance."

Thomas Havern burst into another grin. "And to celebrate the upcoming trial and reinstatement of Devlin's good name, my wife and I have planned a party for you tomorrow evening." His eyelid dropped into a wink. "You know who Regina is. She employs every excuse to entertain. I only wish Devlin could be there to share the evening with us."

Barrett was greatly encouraged by the news, but he wished the military court hadn't allowed Burkhart so much time to prepare his defense. The ruthless commander might browbeat his dragoons into testifying as he demanded or face the penalty of death.

"Even Devlin will be attending your party, but in disguise," Barrett declared, casting his worrisome thoughts aside.

"He's here now?" Thomas glanced anxiously around him. "Good, I want to personally deliver the news to him. I should insist that he give himself up to the sheriff in Tucson, you know." Thomas displayed a mischievous grin. "But considering the way the Army has protected that Burkhart fellow, I wouldn't want to see Devlin retained in custody while that maniac is running around loose. There are times when the law victimizes the innocent and this is one of those times. As far as I'm concerned, I haven't seen hide nor hair of Devlin in over a year."

"I'm sure my big brother will be relieved to hear you don't expect him to rot in jail pending trial," Barrett murmured with a grateful sigh.

"Sometimes the laws have to be bent, and it infuriates me that the Army has dragged this conflict with Devlin and Burkhart out as long as they have. They should have investigated Burkhart's activities months ago!"

While Devlin, Barrett, and Thomas Havern conferred in the study, Moriah puttered around her room and paused to stare out the window. Ever so slowly, the haze of black that curtained her eyes had transformed into cobwebs of gray and silver shadows. It was too much to hope that she would completely regain her vision, but there had been times in the past few days that Moriah could detect glints of light, such as now when she passed the window. She still couldn't see images, but it was a vast improvement over the pitch-black veil that had once shielded her eyes.

In the privacy of her room, Moriah allowed her thoughts to circle to Devlin, and she grinned at the stimulating memories of their morning beside the river. Devlin had been playfully amorous and marvelously passionate as they loved the hours away. Those glorious moments would form the perimeters of her dreams. In the days to come she would savor her memories and pluck out those especially sweet, arousing fantasies.

Crimineyl It was going to be difficult to imagine a life without Devlin Granger. But Moriah had promised herself to stand firm in her logical convictions and ignore her romantic sentiments. Devlin was catering to her out of sympathy. He had been so long without a woman that he had naturally turned to Moriah when there were no other women around.

She probably shouldn't have confessed her love for him because he had used it as a weapon against her, trying to persuade her to stay. In addition to becoming his weapon for argument it was also another burden of responsibility for him to bear. He would probably come to regret her love for him one day, she reckoned. But she hadn't been able to keep the silence any longer. Her affection for Devlin was bursting out all over and she couldn't hold the confession from him. Pretending she didn't care had been tearing her to pieces.

Two more days, Moriah mused as she raised her eyes to the warm sunshine that sprayed through her window. She would make these two days last an eternity. She would reap every ounce of happiness from her hours with Devlin, and the glorious memories would warm her aching soul during the long, lonely years to come.

She would never have to know when Devlin finally settled down and took a wife. But he *would* have children and a capable woman to watch over his sons and daughters. And while he was settling into his future life, Moriah would count the memories of days gone by, cherishing a love that wasn't meant to be.

A single tear slipped down her cheek. Oh, now she wished she could have been the mother of Devlin's children. She would have loved them as dearly as her parents had loved her, as fiercely as she loved this dynamic man with the amber eyes that glowed like molten lava when he was angry and shimmered like wild mountain honey when he was in one of his gentler moods.

The thought of never bearing Devlin's child tore Moriah to shreds, bit by excruciating bit. She would never know the joy of staring down into a tiny face that was framed with hair as black as a raven's wing, never know the pleasure of watching their child grow and change and become a man who was the spitting image of his father.

Moriah gave herself a mental slap and wiped the

tears away. She had to remain strong and determined. She couldn't indulge in these bouts with self-pity. They would do her no good whatsoever. She would become the mistress of her own fate and she would make her own way without Devlin's pity. She would do what was best for both of them.

Letting go when she longed to cling to him forever would be the most difficult task she had ever undertaken. It would tear her soul in two to watch him go. But one day he would realize what she had known all along, that his feelings for her were born of guilt and pity. And Moriah knew, deep down in her heart, that Devlin would forget her years before she ever got over loving him.

Ah, such was her life, Moriah reminded herself gloomily. When one was born under a black cloud, one really shouldn't expect sunshine, should they?

Chapter 17

Moriah sat on the buckboard between Devlin, who was still disguised as one of the Mexican vaqueros, and Barrett. Their destination was Tucson, even though the hint of rain hung in the air. Moriah could smell the moisture, feel the sticky perspiration that clung to her skin.

"Anything that meets your whim is yours today," Barrett declared with unlimited generosity and an affectionate pat on Moriah's hand.

"You are too kind," Moriah teased him. "What if my whim exceeds your wallet?"

Jessica sat in the back of the wagon. There was no room on the seat and Moriah had been offered *her* customary place between Dev and Rett. Jessica had silently smoldered. Barrett's boundless generosity would cost him dearly, she predicted. Moriah would bleed him and Devlin dry before she was through with them.

"I'll find a way to pay for whatever you wish to buy," Barrett chuckled as he playfully flicked the tip of her dainty nose.

Devlin could see his brother becoming more infatuated with Moriah with each passing hour. It galled him to speculate how Barrett would behave when Devlin was away from the ranch. If Barrett's present attention toward Moriah was any indication, the competition for Moriah's love was going to be damned stiff. His own brother, for crying out loud!

Although Devlin was envy green, Jessica was angry red and had been since Moriah showed up. Once upon a time Barrett had made those offers to her. Now, neither Devlin nor Barrett was aware she even existed! She may as well have remained at the ranch, for all her brothers cared. They were fawning all over that blue-eyed trollop and Jessica was developing a toothache just listening to the sticky sweet conversation.

"I appreciate the offer, Rett," Moriah replied. "But my needs are relatively few."

Now Barrett would insist and, with a little coaxing, Moriah would give in, Jessica speculated. That's how scheming women operated.

"I want to buy you something," Barrett insisted, just as Jessica knew he would.

"Thank you, but no," Moriah said firmly. "Whatever clothing I purchase, I intend to repay when I find work."

Jessica frowned. This must be some revolutionary new tactic that would earn Moriah even more extravagant gifts than Barrett had originally offered. Wily women like Moriah had their cunning ways of obtaining exactly what they wanted.

When the wagon rolled into town, Barrett assisted Moriah to the ground. Jessica wriggled from the wagon bed and begrudgingly flanked Barrett who still hadn't noticed she was there and couldn't have cared less since he was hypnotized by the shapely blonde who looked stunning in the pale-blue satin gown Jessica had been forced to loan her.

Devlin lagged behind the threesome in the manner of a humble servant. He would have preferred to take his place beside Moriah, especially since Barrett seemed all too eager to act as her escort. Damn, not a day would pass while he was stalking the mountains that he wouldn't wonder just how friendly Barrett would dare to become with Moriah. Barrett was enamored, that was for sure.

Humming a light tune, Vance Thatcher picked up the foreleg of the bay gelding he was shodding for a waiting customer at the blacksmith barn. Within a few minutes he had nailed the last shoe in place and led the horse outside to collect his fee. He had just lumbered around the corner when the Grangers and their guest aimed themselves toward the dry goods store to purchase weekly supplies.

Vance's face bleached white as flour when he spied the young woman who could have passed as Moriah's identical twin. His heart hung in his chest like a ton of lead and his jaw dropped off its hinges.

"It can't be!" Vance croaked like a sick cricket. Moriah was dead. She had been strangled and drowned in the Mimbres River almost two months earlier.

Battling to rewind his unraveled composure, Vance peered around the horse he was employing as his shield. When Moriah giggled at some clever remark one of her companions made, Vance's face froze in an expression of terror. He hadn't heard Moriah laugh all that much the past few years but he *had* heard the sound often enough to recognize her voice. It *was* Moriah! Holy hell! If she saw him or Ruby they would both be swinging from the gallows.

Handing the reins to the customer, Vance clambered toward the alley and scuttled toward the back door of the dress shop Ruby had purchased. He had to warn Ruby, and quickly! If Moriah happened into the shop, pandemonium would break loose.

A perplexed frown creased Ruby's brow when she glanced up from her ledger to see Vance clomping toward her, his face chalky white. "What are you doing here in the middle of the afternoon?" Her frown settled deeper into her caked makeup when Vance craned his neck around the office door to scan the shop. "What the devil is wrong with you?"

"We've got serious trouble," Vance whispered as he flattened himself against the wall and cautiously inched back to Ruby's cluttered desk. "Moriah is in Tucson."

"Moriah?" Ruby croaked. "That's ridiculous. She's been dead and gone for two months." She clucked her tongue at Vance. "You have been out in the sun too long. The heat has melted your brain."

"I know it was her," Vance proclaimed with firm conviction. "She and her companions were headed toward the dry goods store."

Ruby flung her husband a withering glance. Intent on proving him wrong, she breezed through the shop and stepped onto the boardwalk. Her eyes bulged from their sockets when she spied the mane of golden hair through the window of the adjacent store. Ruby gaped at the young woman again. Gasping for breath, she clutched her heaving bosom and scurried back inside.

"I told you. Didn't I tell you?" Vance rattled nervously. "It's her. She's here. It has to be her. Why is she here? Maybe she knows where we are and she's comin' to scare the daylights out of us before she has us hustled off to jail. That's got to be it!"

"You stupid dolt," Ruby railed, glaring murderously at her babbling husband. "You swore she drowned in the river. How could you have botched that up? I told you every move to make!"

Vance wrung his hands and paced back and forth like a horse clomping impatiently around its stall. "She looked dead enough to me when I tied her to the driftwood and set her afloat."

"Well, obviously she wasn't *quite* dead enough!" Ruby spumed. "Damnit, Vance, can't you do anything right?"

Vance shrugged helplessly and darted an apprehensive glance at the front door of the shop. "If she comes in here and sees us, we're the ones who are goin' to be as good as dead!"

Expelling an agitated breath, Ruby shuffled her husband back into the office. "Dorita can wait on the customers if they should walk in. Moriah needs never know we own the shop or that we live in Tucson. But you—" She poked his chest with a long finger. "You are going to have to dispose of her. And you had better not foul up again. Moriah will make sure that we hang high! And I for one am enjoying the prosperity of our life in Tucson. I'm not leaving here. That girl has to go!"

Vance swallowed the lump that constricted his throat and nodded in glum compliance. "We'll find out where she's stayin' and I'll dispose of her . . . somehow."

"We'll make it look like a robbery and assault," Ruby plotted, pacing the office in quick nervous strides. "We'll draw her out and you can finish the deed." She jerked up her head and stared at Vance who was still wringing his hands in front of him. "Go back to the blacksmith barn and, for heaven's sake, stay out of sight. I'll find out where she's staying and then I'll plan the when and where."

Nodding gloomily, Vance skulked out the back door and trotted down the alley.

Scowling to herself, Ruby wheeled around to request that Dorita wait on any customers who happened in while she tended her bookwork. Leaving the door slightly ajar, Ruby plunked down and drummed her fingers, nervously wondering if Moriah would wander into the shop. The minutes dragged by at a snail's pace and Ruby swore her overworked heart would pop out of her chest before this dreadful crisis passed!

"And now let's see about your wardrobe," Barrett insisted, grasping Moriah's elbow to lead her back to the street. "Jess can help you select all the proper paraphernalia."

Wonderful! thought Jessica. She would have much preferred to have Moriah fitted with a sturdy noose.

"Devlin and I will help you decide which color of gown best complement your beauty, although I can't imagine any shade that wouldn't suit you," Barrett murmured.

"A mite thick on the flattery, aren't we?" Devlin smirked.

Moriah simply smiled to herself when she heard Devlin's quiet comment to his brother. She had come to realize Barrett was only acting the gallant gentleman he truly was. Devlin had no reason to pretend jealousy. He knew she loved him. She had conveyed her affection with words and deeds the past two days.

When the foursome ambled into the shop, Ruby shrank away from the door and held her breath until she turned blue in the face. She could hear Moriah's melodic voice as she chatted with her companions.

For what seemed forever Ruby crouched under her desk just in case Moriah walked back to the office. Thank God Ruby hadn't had the chance to change the name of the shop! Moriah would have known immediately that the Thatchers had left the wagon train to open their new business with her inheritance money.

"This is a stunning gown," Barrett remarked as he lifted the garment from the rack.

"It's a bit out of style," Jessica interjected as she snatched the gown from Barrett's hand and shoved it back to its place on the rack. "This is far more suitable for Moriah." She indicated the slinky black gown, the neckline of which could easily have been mistaken for a waistline.

Devlin's fingers bit into Jessica's arm until she grimaced in pain. "I think this would be more to Señorita Laverty's tastes," he said with a thick Spanish accent and a silent snarl to his sister.

Moriah ran her hand over the garment Devlin held up for her inspection. Her fingertips skimmed the soft eyelet ruffles that adorned the neck and then she investigated the puffy sleeves that were cuffed with matching ruffles. "It feels pretty."

"And you will look lovely in lavender," Barrett assured her. He reached over to retrieve the emerald-green velvet gown that was trimmed with delicate white lace—the very one Jess had yanked out of his hands. "How do you like the cut of this dress, my dear?"

After Moriah inspected the garment with her fingertips, she nodded agreeably. "I hope neither of these gowns is too expensive. It will take me weeks to repay you."

"No, as a matter of fact, they are exceptionally reasonable," Devlin lied through his teeth. He spared

Dorita a discreet glance, reminding himself to stay out of her way so she wouldn't recognize him. "Pick three more and we will—"

"Three?" Moriah bleated, aghast. "I couldn't. I will be indebted forever."

Of course she could, Jessica mused sourly. The Granger brothers' insistence increased in direct proportion to Moriah's feigned protests. The tramp, Jessica silently seethed. She was skilled at getting exactly what she wanted and allowing her male admirers to think they were the ones who had encouraged her to make the extravagant purchases.

"*Four* more," Barrett insisted. "The last one will be my gift to Moriah since she herself refused to select an item as a token of our friendship."

Jessica wheeled away in disgust. No one had bothered to ask if she might like to have a new gown or a necklace or a drink to wash away the taste of sour grapes that clung to her palate.

Under Devlin's observing eye, Jessica was forced to select the necessary undergarments for Moriah, and that galled her beyond belief. An hour later, after Devlin had insisted Moriah model every gown, and both men showered her with compliments, the foursome ambled back to the street and aimed themselves toward the restaurant. To Jessica's outrage, Moriah was outfitted in one of the new gowns Devlin had selected for her.

Since Thomas Havern had informed the Grangers of the celebration he'd planned for the evening, Devlin had seen to it that Moriah was dressed fit to kill. No doubt half the town would be at the gathering. When the Haverns threw a party it was the highlight of Tucson's social season.

Jessica's only consolation was that she could distract herself with several of her own beaux. And she hoped her two brothers, who were making such idiotic fools of themselves, found a long line forming behind Moriah. With any luck at all, this conniving adventuress would latch onto one of the other wealthy ranchers or businessmen in Tucson and leave the Grangers alone!

In fact, Jessica would make sure Moriah was never without a dance partner. The spiteful thought provoked her to smile deviously. Nothing would make her happier than to see Moriah surrounded by eligible bachelors. As long as it wasn't one of the Granger brothers, Jessica quickly tacked on. And none of *her* suitors had better fall beneath that blond's spell, either! That would positively be the last straw!

On weak knees, Ruby wobbled into her dress shop to interrogate Dorita who had been born and raised in Tucson and who knew everybody who was anybody. That was, after all, the main reason Ruby had kept Dorita as a clerk. Dorita was cheerful, well liked, and an excellent seamstress who had been with the former owner for seven years.

"We certainly turned a tidy profit with those customers," Ruby remarked when Dorita handed her the tally.

Dorita nodded her head and smiled enthusiastically. "The Grangers have expensive tastes," she volunteered without Ruby having to pry out the customers' names. "Barrett was very generous with his houseguest and she certainly complemented the exquisite garments he purchased for her."

"You seem to know everybody in the county." Ruby sighed before darting Dorita a discreet glance. "It will take me forever to learn my customers' names and where they live. Luckily, I have you to assist me."

Accepting the compliment, Dorita proceeded to dole out the information Ruby wanted. "The Grangers own a large ranch and trading post south of town. You will never have to fret about extending credit to them, either. The family is one of the pillars of society."

A remorseful frown clouded Dorita's brow. "Barrett's oldest brother hasn't been around the past year. He had some sort of clash with the Army and is wanted by the authorities." She shrugged carelessly. "But I'm sure there must have been some mistake. Devlin is as fine a man as his brother. According to reports, the Grangers have compiled evidence to have the charges against Devlin rescinded. I'm sure Jessica and Barrett will be greatly relieved when their brother can return home without worrying about being arrested."

Personally, Ruby didn't give a tinker's damn what problems the Grangers had. All that concerned her was drawing Moriah out and disposing of her. As long as Moriah was alive and roaming the streets of Tucson, the Thatchers were in grave danger of being spotted.

"It is a shame that—" Dorita intended to inform Ruby that the Grangers' house guest was blind, but the older woman cut her off to return to her office to make her plans for Moriah's demise.

If Ruby had the patience and courtesy to let Dorita finish, she wouldn't have been in quite such a stew. But Ruby didn't know Moriah couldn't point an accusing finger unless she identified voices. As it was, Moriah wouldn't have recognized the Thatchers if they had passed face-to-face on the street!

Chapter 18

Jessica had mixed emotions about the commotion Moriah's presence caused at the party and dance that was held on the lawn and in the street beside the Haverns' home. At first the competition for Moriah's attention amused Jessica. Devlin was forced to cling to the shadows for fear of being recognized by the soldiers who milled about. Barrett had to wait in line to dance with the comely blonde. But suddenly Jessica wasn't quite so amused when three of her favorite suitors left her side to pay their respects to the remarkable young woman who had taken Tucson by storm.

"It appears Moriah Laverty has become the belle of this ball" came one teasing remark that set Jessica's teeth on edge.

"Considering her reputation with men, I'm not surprised she's attracting so much attention," Jessica muttered, tossing the cascade of ebony curls over her shoulder.

The four men who were hovering around her were taken aback by her insinuation. "Well, it's true," Jessica defended tartly. "If Barrett wasn't so generous of heart, that woman would probably have a room at the bordello and men would be paying to do far more than dance with her."

If Devlin and Barrett had heard Jessica, they would have cheerfully choked her. Lucky for Jess, they didn't. But the damage had been done. Rumors, whether true or false, spread like wildfire. The line of men who waited their turn to dance with Moriah suddenly doubled.

Moriah found herself passed from one pair of eager arms to another. And all the while she longed for one man—the one who would soon be out of her life forever. But Devlin was being inconspicuous and cautious, just as he had been at the shops and restaurant that afternoon. Moriah knew he was around somewhere, but he remained on the sidelines of the party. She didn't know why he wanted her to mingle with society. He knew she would have preferred to be in her room. More specifically, in his arms . . .

"You dance exceptionally well," her partner complimented before pulling her closer than necessary. "So the story goes, dancing isn't the only thing you do well, honey."

A muddled frown puckered Moriah's brow. "What are you implying?"

The young man's eyes slid over the delectable décolletage of her gown and his hand wandered to her derriere to give her a playful pinch. "Name your price, sweetheart. I'll be only too happy to pay it. We can stroll off through the trees and—"

Moriah struck out like a rattlesnake, emblazoning her handprint on the man's clean-shaven cheek. Her assault caused her companion to clutch her hands, bending her into his body.

"You have no need to pretend to be insulted, minx. We both know what you are," he breathed down her neck.

Barrett snapped to attention when he saw Moriah strike out at her companion. Bowing his neck, he made a beeline toward the couple to come to Moriah's defense.

"Easy, little brother," Devlin's hand clamped on Barrett's taut arm, jerking him backward.

"That scoundrel must have made some snide remark to offend her," Barrett growled. "You can't come to her rescue without risking being discovered, but I certainly can!"

A faint smile pursed Devlin's lips. He had seen Moriah in action before. Though blind, she could take care of herself. "Let's wait out this sparring match, shall we? You may find you have sold the lady short."

Barrett stared at his brother as if he had a bolt loose in his brain. But since Devlin refused to unloose his arm, Barrett was forced to stand aside and watch. To his mute astonishment, Moriah countered the bear hug with a knee to the crotch—discreet but effective. She struck so quickly that those around her didn't realize she had inflicted a blow that caused her companion to bend at the waist and choke to catch his breath. Looking white as a sheet, the man hobbled away, walking carefully as he went.

"Well, I'll be damned," Barrett snickered, silently applauding Moriah's tactics. The amused smile evaporated and he turned an inquisitive frown to the shadowed face beneath the concealing wide-brimmed sombrero. "Where did she come from, Dev? I think I should know something about her before you leave her in my care."

The miners from Santa Rita would have replied that she came from heaven. But Devlin knew he would have to be more specific with his brother. Devlin revealed very little information to anyone, but his brother was the exception. They had always been confidants and friends. And considering Barrett would soon be Moriah's guardian, he decided to tell what he knew.

"Moriah's life has been hard," he said as he propped himself against the tree. "When her parents died, she was left in the care of stepparents who sold her farm in Texas and then tried to kill her so they could take possession of her money."

Through Barrett's gasps and curses, Devlin continued. "After an unpleasant encounter with Lyle Burkhart, and God knows how many other lusty men she had to ward off, she sought refuge in the Black Mountains. That's where I met her."

His gaze flooded over the graceful beauty who had wound up in another pair of arms. "All Moriah wanted was to be left alone." A pained expression crossed his dark features. "I was with her when lightning struck a nearby tree and singed her eyes. For two days I wasn't sure if she would live or die. And for the past month I have lived with the torment of knowing she would have her sight if I hadn't scolded her and left her standing there so vulnerable, cursing me for my lack of sensitivity."

Devlin didn't bother with the intimate details of that day. Barrett knew what he needed to know—that Devlin considered himself to blame for the accident. "If Moriah would have had her way I would have left her alone to fend against her blindness and the elements in the rugged mountain ranges. And as capable as she is in hand-to-hand combat, she can't see danger until it's upon her. I couldn't leave her alone up there, not with Burkhart making plans to attack. He damned well intends to go out in a blaze of glory, even if he is stripped of his medals and forced to resign his command."

Devlin shifted from one foot to the other and stared thoughtfully at the tawny-haired beauty who had been handed to yet another partner. "She came within inches of being clawed to shreds by a mountain lion. She unknowingly waded into a nest of vipers and she was captured by Makado. In short, she has been through hell."

Barrett shook his head in dismay. "It's a wonder she hasn't thrown up her hands and cursed all men and life in general. She would certainly have her valid reasons."

"She has the most incredible spirit and resilience I've ever seen," Devlin murmured quietly. "I wanted her to stay at the ranch until this ordeal is over, to become my wife. But she insists on striking out on her own, despite the obvious obstacles."

"And you're going to let her go?" Barrett asked in disbelief.

A muted chuckle rumbled in Devlin's chest. "Little brother, I have never *let* Moriah do anything that she feels inclined to do. I have, on a number of occasions, tried to *stop* her from doing what she has taken a mind to do, but I haven't had much success. Even with her handicap, she is infuriatingly headstrong and independent."

Barrett stared at his brother's veiled features for a long moment. "You are in love with her, aren't you, Devlin?" The man who'd had more women than bees had honey was truly in love? Lord-a-mercy, wonders never ceased!

Devlin nodded, but only slightly and his voice was barely more than a whisper when he spoke. "In love to the point that I can't force her to wait for me when she has her heart set on leaving. She thinks it's best for both of us."

"But why?" Barrett gaped at him.

Devlin exhaled a heavy sigh. "She swears it's guilt-ridden pity that draws me to her. I call it love."

Barrett's eyes swung back to the proud beauty. "Yes, I suppose a woman like Moriah would have doubts about your feelings for her. She probably doesn't even know what it's like to be loved, just for herself."

"I can only hope she'll realize she needs me one day. But knowing her fiercely stubborn spirit, I don't think she'll ever let herself believe we could have a future together. And the most maddening thing of all is that her blindness is what is keeping us apart. She has learned to cope with it, but she refuses to let me share her burden because she believes that her handicap is already an obligation I will soon tire of contending with."

"You know, I've been envious of you since you brought Moriah here," Barrett admitted. "But now I almost pity you, big brother."

"So do I, Rett, so do I . . ." Devlin pushed away from the tree and glanced toward the shapely blonde who constantly commanded his attention. "I never wanted anything or anyone so much in my life. And I have never been so certain I can't have it. That is the hell of it."

His shadowed gaze darted back to his brother. "I'm counting on you to convince Moriah that all men aren't the treacherous creatures she believes them to be. And yet I'm not so sure you wouldn't like to have her all to yourself. I don't blame you, Rett, but I can't bear the thought of losing her . . . period!"

When Devlin disappeared into the cluster of trees, Barrett stuffed his hands in his pockets and ambled across the lawn. He had the feeling Moriah's monumental pride and determined spirit would bring her more unhappiness in the years to come. With a troubled past like hers, she had come to expect the worst and resigned herself to it. A pity that Devlin had never openly admitted to loving a woman. And the one time he did, the stunning lady in question was not only blind, but she was also deaf to Devlin's confessions. That was a crying shame because Devlin wasn't the kind of man who would dare to love again after he lost the only woman he ever really wanted. Moriah might have thought she was doing both of them a favor, but she would wind up making them both miserable.

Thoroughly perturbed at the last three partners who had propositioned her in the middle of a dance step, Moriah ground her heel in the most recent offender's toe and demanded that he lead her toward the refreshment table before she rammed her knee in his groin and left him chirping in a high-pitched voice for the rest of his life.

The rude remarks Moriah had endured, thanks to Jessica's spiteful declarations, solidified Moriah's opinion that most men's brains were situated below their belt buckles and they allowed their basic urges to do their thinking for them. Except for Devlin and Barrett, Moriah generously amended. As far as she was concerned, the rest of the males on earth were a disgusting breed who deserved no consideration whatsoever.

Moriah tried to feed her frustrations by munching on the tarts and cool her temper with the punch the Haverns had provided. But nothing helped.

"Enjoying yourself, *querida?*" came the amused voice that hummed with a thick Spanish accent.

Moriah glanced in the direction of the sound. "If you thought to show me a good time by dragging me here, you failed in your mission," she muttered crabbily. "You have managed to remind me why I had my heart set on living like a hermit."

"You didn't find another man who pleasures you more than I?" Devlin questioned as he moved directly behind her.

So that was what this was all about, she realized. He wanted her to make comparisons in hopes of convincing herself that Devlin was the only man she needed. If she hadn't known better she would have accused him of bribing her dance partners to voice those lurid propositions!

The question wasn't whether she loved him enough to await his return. She had told him a hundred different ways that he was the only man who meant something to *her*, but the point was, there were probably a score of females flittering around the party who would have made him a suitable wife.

All Moriah had wanted was seclusion. But Devlin was trying to teach her a lesson when, in fact, he was the one who had an important lesson to learn! Blind women and bold, dynamic men were mismatched.

When the music of harmonicas, Spanish guitars, and tambourines once again filled the air, Devlin's hand emerged from beneath his serape to sketch her ribs and drift over her hip. "Come dance with me, Riah. I've never held you and swayed to the rhythm of music playing in the distance . . ."

His familiar caress ignited memories of all they had done together, things they would never do again because, come the early hours before dawn, they would go their separate ways.

Devlin slid his arm around her waist and glanced discreetly around him before drawing Moriah into the canopy of trees that lined the street. She went without protest. And when he turned her in his arms, she rewarded him with a steamy kiss. Her kiss carried enough heat to melt the bandoleer that was wrapped across his chest and leave him dripping in a puddle of desire.

At long last Moriah found herself in the right pair of arms, dancing to a melody that played only for them. She had maintained a respectable distance from her overeager suitors, but she pressed wantonly to Devlin, letting her body convey her desire to do more than dance cheek to cheek.

A tormented groan vibrated in his throat when Moriah's delicious body glided in perfect rhythm with his. So little time, he thought maddeningly. So much he wanted to say and couldn't because he had promised Moriah that she could do what she thought she should do. To await his return had to be her decision. Good God, what else could he do to persuade her that he cared deeply, that it wasn't only pity and guilt and physical attraction that motivated him!

The rumble of distant thunder caused Moriah to flinch. The threat of the approaching storm that had lingered on the horizon all afternoon had triggered unpleasant memories of a time she preferred to forget—the terror, the anguish.

Damnit, why tonight? Devlin muttered to himself. He had envisioned slipping into Moriah's room to spend what was left of the evening with her before he returned to the mountains. He had wanted to make their hours span eternity, wanted every moment to be perfection. But she would hear the thunder and smell the rain and she would remember why she felt the need to leave him. Damnation!

Another crack of thunder sent the guests scurrying toward home. Scowling at the untimely interruption, Devlin clutched Moriah's hand and led her through the trees. Since Jessica was the closest one to him, he gestured for her to assist Moriah back to the wagon that was heaped with supplies.

Begrudgingly, Jessica marched over to clutch Moriah's hand while Devlin circled the crowd of soldiers and familiar faces. The fact that Moriah and Devlin had stolen off into the trees galled Jessica to no end. She had hoped to foist this chit off on one of the other eligible bachelors at the party, but no such luck.

Well, at least the truth had been told, Jessica consoled herself. And once Moriah set up housekeeping in Tucson, she would have a considerable number of clients who were anxious to pay her visits. She would find someone else to replace Devlin soon enough. And when he returned, he would see this heartless hussy for what she really was!

To Jessica's annoyance, she was again shuffled into the wagon bed with the sacks of flour while Moriah was bookended on the seat by Dev and Rett. Frustrated, Jessica glanced heavenward, wishing lightning would strike this wicked witch. Had she known that was what had destroyed Moriah's vision in the first place, she might have been more sympathetic. *Might have.* Jessica's wounded vanity and resentment had a fierce hold on her. The adoring attention that her brothers usually heaped on her was now being piled on this blue-eyed trollop, and this lack of consideration and attention was killing her!

Another clap of thunder echoed in the clouds and Moriah instinctively clutched at Devlin's arm. She had never had a fear of storms until she had awakened from the cloudburst to find herself staring at a world of darkness.

The smell of rain saturated the breeze that whipped past her face. She could envision the ominous clouds swallowing the moon and stars. She knew that, at any moment, the lightning would knife across the sky and strike the earth like an electrified spear. Criminey, she didn't even want to think about the chances of being struck twice!

Aware of Moriah's anxiety, Devlin popped the reins over the horses, sending them lunging into their swiftest gait. Jessica was hurtled helter-skelter in the bed of the wagon as they raced over the bumpy road. The rough ride fueled her already smoldering temper.

By the time Devlin slammed on the brake and screeched to a halt in front of the hacienda Jessica was in a full-fledged snit. Because of the scathing lectures she had received from her two brothers she held her tongue, but she was positively furious for a number of reasons and she resembled a ticking bomb awaiting the perfect moment to explode.

To make matters worse, Devlin ordered Jessica to assist Moriah up to her room while he and Barrett unhitched the team. Jessica cursed the fact that the servants had all retired to their quarters, leaving her to tend this conniving witch. If there had been even one servant within shouting distance, she would have shoved Moriah at him and stomped off.

Although Moriah courteously thanked Jessica for the assistance, she was met with a terse "Good night." A muddled frown knitted Moriah's brow as she reached out to detain Jessica. "Have I done something to upset you?" she questioned curiously.

Jessica snatched her arm away as if she had been stung by a wasp. "Your very presence here upsets me," she bit off. "You are preying on my brother's pity and generosity. You must know that all Devlin feels for you is sympathy."

The brutal remark struck a sensitive nerve. Moriah

was all too aware of Devlin's pity. He had been the picture of manly devotion since her accident. Even Jessica could understand Devlin's motivation, and she refused to let him settle for less than he could have with another woman.

"In case you have forgotten, I'm twenty-three years old and I'm perfectly aware of what kind of hold you have on my brother," Jessica spumed. "I know you have doled out sexual favors to ensure his loyalty."

Moriah gasped at the biting remark. For the past few days she had sensed Jessica's hostility and the thread of contempt in her voice. It was obvious Jessica thought Moriah was using her handicap to bleed Devlin for whatever she could obtain.

"You are sorely mistaken about my feelings for Devlin," Moriah declared, and none too gently.

"Am I?" Jessica scoffed caustically. "Then prove it. If you want what is best for him, you will walk out of his life forever. You will bring him nothing but trouble and heartache if you stay and he has enough of that already trying to remain one step ahead of the bounty hunters who would love to collect the thousand-dollar-reward on his head. And he has to live with accusations of crimes he didn't commit." She raked Moriah with scornful mockery. "But you don't give a flying fig about his woes, do you, Moriah? Women like you are only concerned about themselves. You play men like gambits for your own selfish purposes."

Moriah knew Jessica had Devlin's best interest at heart and that she was striking out to protect the brother she loved so dearly. But the insults were hard to swallow without retaliating in the same ridiculing tone.

"I expected nothing from Devlin and it seems the biggest cross he had to bear is his sister who thinks she has to defend him like a mother hen," Moriah countered, leaving Jessica muttering in shock. "I can assure you that Devlin is more than capable of taking care of himself. You should channel your efforts into improving your testy disposition and stop trying to run your brother's life."

Jessica drew herself up after being slapped by the insult. "I don't want you in my house," she hissed poisonously. "The only reason I have tolerated you at all is because Devlin and Barrett demanded it. Men are blinded by your good looks, but I can see through you well enough."

Bitter laughter bubbled from Jessica's curled lips. "I'm sure you amuse yourself with the technique of blinding men and letting them think *you* are the one without vision. You are even trying to pit brother against brother. Poor Barrett has fallen beneath your spell. You have him hungering for what Devlin has and you're causing friction between them. I'm sure that delights a cunning trollop like you."

Moriah punished the snippy shrew with a flaming glower. Her tone more than compensated for her inability to visually communicate her disdain. "I pity you, Jessica. There is no one as blind as she who refuses to see. I know perfectly well that Devlin feels sorry for me. But despite what you want to believe, I care more for him than life itself. And because I do, I have every intention of walking out of his life as soon as he leaves for New Mexico."

"I'll help you pack," Jessica volunteered in a sarcastic tone. "I will even drive you into town and pay a week's rent for your room at the bordello until your clientele is established."

Moriah pivoted to feel her way into her room. There was no sense going another round with Jessica. She believed the worst about her unwanted guest and no amount of explanation was going to convince her that Moriah's affection was sincere. "I don't want your charity, thanks just the same," she muttered over her shoulder.

"It isn't charity," Jessica growled at the back of Moriah's head. "It's bribe money to get you out from underfoot. I would gladly pay a king's ransom if I could spare Devlin from a woman like you. As capable as he is, there are times when he has to be saved from himself."

Dispiritedly, Moriah eased the door shut, just as the storm they had outrun rolled over the hacienda. Thunder clamored overhead like the peal of doom. Moriah's spirits had already scraped rock bottom, knowing Devlin would be gone before dawn. Finding herself on the receiving end of Jessica's blistering tirade, compounded by the tormenting memories triggered by the thunder and rain, did nothing for Moriah's mood. She felt so alone and unwanted in this fuzzy world of gray that shaded her eyes.

Even if she foolishly changed her mind and decided to wait for Devlin to return from his clash with Burkhart she wouldn't be welcome at the ranch. Jessica would make life unbearable and before long Devlin's pity would evaporate. The situation would become as anguishing as enduring all the tortures of the damned. Moriah had to strike out on her own, now more than ever!

Muffling a sniff, Moriah shucked her gown and huddled beneath the quilts as the sky opened and shafts of rain speared against the window pane. The last time she had endured the ravages of a storm, her sight had been stripped away. This time Devlin would be stripped from her arms. And she would be walking under a black cloud until the end of her days.

Chapter 19

With a melancholy smile, Barrett handed his brother a brandy. "To better days," he murmured, lifting his glass in toast.

Devlin peeled off his mustache and sombrero and sipped the snifter of whiskey. "I hope to be back within a month," he remarked, his gaze drifting toward the hall. "And if I'm not—" He fixed his amber eyes on his brother. "Take care of her for me as best you can, Rett. I don't want to have to worry about Moriah while I'm dealing with Burkhart."

Barrett nodded in compliance. "She will want for nothing. You can depend on that," he promised faithfully.

Devlin expelled a disheartened sigh. "I only wish I could depend on her to be here when I get back."

"I could tie her to the bedposts and lock her in her room," Barrett offered.

Although he managed a meager smile, Devlin was not amused. Absently, he studied the contents of his glass. "Moriah is much too contrary to be cornered and forced into submission. If she comes back to me, it has to be of her own free will."

"So you keep telling me." Barrett sighed heavily

and then poured himself another drink. "But I still think staking her down is the only answer. I'll get a rope."

Barrett's attempt to humor Devlin out of his glum mood fell short of its mark. Devlin felt as if he were about to lose a vital part of himself. The gnawing emptiness in the pit of his belly was already eating him alive. Time was so damned short, Devlin mused dismally.

With nothing but Moriah on his mind, Devlin ambled through the foyer and ascended the steps. How did a man go about doing all his living in the course of a few hours? And how did a man make the one loving memory of the past four days sustain him for the rest of his life?

Devlin growled under his breath. Bringing Burkhart to his knees wouldn't heal the pain of losing Moriah and having the charges against him rescinded wouldn't keep his soul from bleeding each time her haunting memory rose from its shallow grave to torment him. The wind would whisper Moriah's name to him all the rest of his days. He would see the streaming golden tendrils of her hair in each sunrise and sunset. He would stare into her luminous blue eyes each time he glanced skyward. Her memory would be there, calling to him like the twinkling stars that hung a million miles out of his reach.

The flash of lightning splintered through the window, paving a silver path across his room. Devlin paused only long enough to shed his bandoleer and serape before he strode silently through the door that adjoined Moriah's room to his. This was one storm that would bring Moriah splendor instead of anguish, Devlin vowed to himself. The storm of passion he brewed for them this night would far exceed the one that raged outside the hacienda. He would give all of himself to her in hopes that she would someday realize that he did love her. Hopefully, she would come back to him. And if she didn't, she would leave with a burning memory that would brand his name on her heart for all the endless days to come.

A rueful smile pursed his lips as he towered over Moriah's bed. Lightning sizzled across the black sky, illuminating her room, spotlighting the golden spray of hair that spilled over her pillow. She reminded Devlin of a frightened child huddling beneath the quilts. She was so strong-willed and yet she looked so vulnerable lying there with her fists clenched around the sheet, listening apprehensively to the raging storm.

When Devlin shucked the rest of his clothes and sank down on the edge of the bed, Moriah glanced toward the faint flash of silver that penetrated the hazy darkness that shaded her eyes. "Will it be over soon? I hear the thunder and I keep remembering—"

He slid into bed beside her, cuddling her quaking body comfortingly to his. He felt the tears that streamed down her cheeks, unaware that Jessica's tirade and the grim realization that she could never come back to him had caused most of her torment. Devlin assumed her tears were provoked by the terrifying memories of the last storm that had caused her blindness.

"This love storm has only just begun," he whispered before his sensuous lips took warm possession of hers. "Love me, Moriah, for all the tomorrows when I reach out to you and you're not there . . ."

His kiss was as intoxicating as wine and his words drove home the depressing point that this was their last good-bye. Moriah surrendered mind, soul, and body to the tidal wave of pleasure that crested upon her. Bubbly sensations channeled through her blood, sending her pulse leaping in triple time. Devlin's skillful caresses massaged away her anxiety of the storm and the sting of Jessica's biting words.

Moments before, Moriah had felt so cold and all alone. But this strong, invincible giant made her feel wanted and needed. As his gentle hands skied over her shoulder to encircle the throbbing peaks of her breasts, Moriah melted into sentimental puddles.

There was a time and a season for all things, she reminded herself. This was the very last time she could communicate her affection for the only man she had ever, would ever, love. She wanted Devlin to cherish her memory in the years to come, to gaze back through the window of time with fondness, remembering a love that could never be because fate had thrust so many insurmountable obstacles between them.

Uncontrollable shudders rocked Moriah's soul as Devlin's explosive kisses stole her breath. His masterful touch freed every emotion that churned just beneath the surface. The whisper of his greedy kisses drowned out the rain and wind that hammered against the window. Moriah quivered as his moist lips tracked along the column of her neck to the rose-tipped peaks, igniting internal fires that seared her inside and out.

Moriah gave herself up to the hypnotic magic of his kisses and caresses. She coveted each wild tingle of splendor, cherished each intimate touch. The thunder and pelting rain that rattled the windowpane was no match for the storm of passion that burst between them. She was oblivious to all except Devlin's arousing caresses. In his gentleness she found immeasurable strength. In his ardent need for her she found undefinable pleasure.

Waves of rapture undulated through her body as

he plied her with more intimate caresses and heart-stopping kisses. The agony of leaving him and the ecstasy of loving him with every fiber of her being made their last night together as precious as all the gold that lay in the Valley of the Eagle. Moriah would have given the entire treasure if she could make this night last forever, if she never had to wake from this erotic dream.

Moriah savored each wondrous sensation, marveled at the heady feelings that riddled her body. She would love this lion of a man as he had never been loved before. She would make the world shrink to fill a space no larger than they occupied while they sky-rocketed through a sea of swirling stars.

When Moriah twisted away to return his touch, kiss for tantalizing kiss, caress for titillating caress, Devlin shuddered uncontrollably. Moriah had become a skillful lover who was sensitive to his needs, vividly aware of what drove him mad with wanting. Each moment of their lovemaking was even better than the one before and yet it was always the same. That wild, breathless excitement was always there, threatening to shatter his composure. His hunger for her had never ebbed in the time they had been together. It was a constant thing, a craving that fed upon itself, an obsession that demanded appeasement again and again and again . . .

Devlin gasped for breath when her fingertips trickled down the dark matting of hair on his chest and belly. He could feel her moist breath skimming his sinewy flesh. Her tantalizing kisses and caresses mapped the rugged terrain of his body until she transformed him into smooth submissive planes. Her arousing touch was his undoing and his body was enslaved by a gentleness that was more overpowering than brute force.

A husky moan escaped his lips as she investigated every inch of his hair-roughened flesh, over and over again. She teased and aroused him to the limits of his sanity, made him question his self-control. Like the surf rolling onto the sandy seashore and then receding, she engulfed him with splendorous caresses.

"Don't leave me, Riah," Devlin whispered raggedly.

"I will always be here," she murmured against his ribs. "In all the tomorrows to come, you have but to close your eyes and I will be there, loving you as I do now . . . with every beat of my heart."

Her quiet utterance tore his emotions to shreds. Rolling away, Devlin effortlessly drew her beneath him. He was starved for her, tormented by thoughts of losing this enchanting nymph forever. His mouth came down hard on hers—slanting, twisting, devouring. His knee eased between her legs to guide her thighs apart. When Moriah arched toward him, a groan of unholy torment erupted from beneath his ravishing kiss.

Gentleness bowed down to the savage passion that surged through his taut body. Devlin no longer merely wanted this blue-eyed enchantress. He *had* to have her, *had* to feel her supple flesh forged to his, *had* to encircle her in his arms and hold on to her before she escaped him forever.

His body became hers as he came to her, conveying a love she refused to believe existed. His strength was hers. Sparks sizzled like the zigzagging streaks of lightning that slashed across the sky. His love for her poured out like the torrential rains that bombarded the hacienda. Instincts as ancient as time itself flooded between them and they held nothing back. The explosive harmony of their lovemaking was as fierce and potent as the whirling winds of a hurricane.

A maelstrom of sensations piled upon them like towering clouds, and then the storm collapsed like forceful currents of air gushing along a windswept path. Devlin clutched Moriah to him as the wild, riveting feelings swept through him, leaving him a mass of shudders. His breath came in ragged spurts and the monstrous ache that had claimed his body transformed into the quintessence of ecstasy.

For countless moments, Devlin cradled Moriah in his possessive embrace, memorizing the exquisite feel of her luscious body molded intimately to his. They were like a living puzzle that made no sense at all unless they were of one body, heart, and soul.

"You're going to take the sun, moon, and stars with you when you go," he rasped before his lips rolled over hers again. "Nothing will quench my thirst the way your kisses do. Nothing will ever touch me again the way you have, Riah. You leave me defenseless . . ."

Adoringly, Moriah combed her fingers through the thick raven hair. Carefully, she traced his dark brows and the spidery lines that sprayed from those tawny eyes that were surrounded with black velvet lashes. "I miss you already, my love, and you haven't even gone."

"Then wait for me," Devlin demanded huskily. "When I come back, we will begin our life all over again. We will make our own special place in the sun."

"There is no sun," Moriah contradicted, her tone thick with remorse. "There are only shadows. But there is tonight and I want to make it last forever. Grant me that much, Devlin. For it is more than I ever even dreamed I could find."

Her hand curled around the corded tendons of his neck, bringing his lips back to hers. Devlin wanted to scream and shout in protest, to make demands on her, to get down on his knees and beg as a last resort. But Moriah's tempting kiss entangled his thoughts and fed the eternal flame of passion. He couldn't refuse her soft request any more than he could change her mind. He could only love her for as long as the night would last.

Although the legends that circulated around Santa Rita del Cobre praised White Shadow's unconquerable strength and supernatural powers, he was no match for this lovely angel's determined will. Danger Devlin could face unafraid and emerge the victor. But in this tender battle of emotions Moriah reigned supreme. Forcing her would accomplish nothing, Devlin reminded himself bleakly. She had to see for herself that facing the world without him would make both of them miserable. He would enshroud her in glorious memories that called to her through her sea of darkness. This love he felt for her would bring her back to him, even against her will and her firm resolve. It had to. The thought of never seeing her again was killing him!

Once again Devlin showered Moriah with the love she couldn't see, communicating his need for her in warm, compelling kisses and butterfly caresses. Tender and savage emotions became entwined as passion reared its head to consume them again. The fire blazed hotter as Moriah gave herself up to the desperation of knowing the hours were ticking by, threatening to close the door on these past two months of her life.

Moriah relished each breath-stealing kiss and possessive caress, reveled in the miraculous sensations that engulfed her quaking body. This was her eternity and she cherished each second, each wondrous moment that turned her inside out. Loving this golden-eyed renegade was her one reward in life. This brawny giant of a man made all the trials and adversity and torments she had endured worthwhile. She had discovered the unique pleasures of loving a man to distraction and nothing could take these glorious memories away from her. They would be hers to keep until the end of time.

Quietly, Jessica eased open the door to Devlin's room. She gazed fuzzily at the unoccupied bed as distant lightning flickered across the room. The muffled sounds of voices wafted their way through the door that joined Moriah's room to Devlin's. Jessica had come to bid her brother good-bye and now she had been deprived of even that because of Moriah!

As Jessica wheeled around in the hall, bitter rage rose inside her. She was not going to let Devlin leave without saying farewell and she wasn't going to let that witch have the last word, either! Knowing how cunning Moriah was, Jessica was certain she would tattle to Devlin. Jessica feared she would receive another tongue-lashing from her brother, but this time she was going to take her battle into her enemy's camp.

With determined stride, Jessica stamped toward Moriah's bedroom door. She didn't care if she did get a thrashing from both her brothers. She was going to air her outrage and rout Devlin from his concubine's bed!

Devlin clutched the sheet protectively about them

as the door unexpectedly banged against the wall. A furious scowl erupted from his lips when the lantern light from the hall framed Jessica's rigid form.

"Get the hell out of here, Jess," Devlin snapped at his fuming sister.

"Why? So you can dally with your harlot until it's time for you to leave?" Jessica blared. Her dark eyes raked Moriah with barely constrained fury and blatant contempt. "You and Rett have lectured me on the proper behavior between men and women for years, but you don't practice what you preach! I am supposed to portray the genteel lady while you tumble this witch who wants nothing more than to milk your sympathy and steal whatever wealth she can gain from this sordid liaison!"

Devlin's jaw fell off its hinges as he gaped at his sister. He couldn't believe her audacity. Good God, had Jessica lost her mind? "Damnit, Jess, you don't know what you're talking about. Go to your room and I'll be there shortly to tell you what an idiot you're making of yourself," he all but yelled at her.

"You're the one who is behaving like an idiot," Jessica snapped back.

Devlin swore viciously. He wanted to bound from the bed and throttle Jessica until she had blisters on her bottom, but she held the advantageous position and he couldn't get up without exposing himself. Damn.

"You're letting this strumpet prey on your pity and your male instincts. You have lectured me on not becoming *her* kind of woman and yet you are cavorting with her. And she isn't the first, even if you and Rett have tried to make me think the two of you didn't go looking for sexual favors from her type," she spluttered furiously. "I know you've had more than your fair share of women, even if I'm supposed to avoid intimacy with men. I have tried to overlook your promiscuity, but I will not tolerate having this whore in our house!"

"Jessica!" Devlin bellowed, wishing his arms were twelve feet long so he could strangle his ranting sister without bounding from bed.

Moriah said not one word in her own behalf. Embarrassed though she was, she knew it was for the best that Jessica expressed her opinion. Devlin needed to know it would be impossible for her to remain at his ranch. Jessica clearly despised her, and Moriah had no intention of coming between brother and sister. This humiliating confrontation only made Moriah more determined to leave and never come back.

"What the devil is all this shouting about?" Barrett blundered in after hearing the booming voices that clamored down the hall like a clanging bell.

"Get her out of here," Devlin growled at Barrett.

"Jessica, you have no right to intrude." Barrett clamped his hand around his sister's taut arm, but she stubbornly refused to budge from her spot. "You should be ashamed of yourself for voicing such cruel remarks! What has gotten into you?"

"Ashamed?" Jessica looked Barrett up and down and scoffed disdainfully. "The only reason you are leaping to that witch's defense is because she cast her spell on you, too. I saw you standing in the doorway the first day Moriah arrived. She was preparing to take her bath and you were gaping at her while she was unaware. Don't talk to me about intruding on someone's privacy, you lecher! You are the one who should be ashamed of himself!"

Barrett sorely wished the floor would open so he

could drop out of sight. He cringed at the shocked expression on Moriah's face and the murderous sneer that twisted his brother's mouth. If Devlin had not been confined to bed without a stitch, Barrett was positively certain he would have stomped over to give him a taste of beefy fist.

With a frustrated grunt, Barrett roughly uprooted Jessica from her spot and dragged her toward the door, despite her furious protests. In swift angry strides he propelled Jessica down the hall, shoved her into her room, and slammed the door with his boot heel.

"I have never in my life wanted to clobber a woman as much as I want to clobber you at this very moment!" Barrett snarled into Jessica's face. "But no one deserves it as much as you do. Damn you, Jess! How could you have done such a thing!"

"Go ahead and strike me if you wish," Jessica hurled at him, her eyes blazing. "But you know I have just cause to voice my accusations. And I will not tolerate that woman's presence in our house for another day. She is poison! The next thing I know, you and Dev will be fighting over her. She will tear our family apart and I have only dared to try to stop her before that happens. We have enough turmoil with Devlin being hunted by bounty hunters and Army officials. I will not have another ordeal piled on top of that!"

While Jessica was loudly voicing her complaints in the room down the hall, Devlin scrambled into his clothes and stamped toward the door. This family problem could not have come at a worse time. He had to leave in a few hours and now Jessica's tirade had spoiled the moment, as well as Devlin's wish to offer Moriah a peaceful refuge from the cruel world. When he got through with Jessica and Barrett they would both be bowing at Moriah's feet, begging for forgiveness!

"Devlin, let it be," Moriah pleaded as the tears streamed down her cheeks. She pushed up against the headboard and clutched the sheet around her, her misty gaze imploring him to return to her. "Jessica only stated what she felt. She is entitled to her opinion. Even she can see what binds you to me. It would never have worked between us anyway. And Jessica might have become so angry and bitter that it would drive her from her own home. This is *her* house, too, and I'm the one who has to go!"

Devlin clamped a stranglehold on the doorknob and leaned heavily upon it. The fact that Jessica had dared to voice such crude remarks infuriated him. The fact that Moriah forgave that termagant exasperated him. As for himself, he was mad as hell at Jessica and Barrett and at Moriah for wanting to leave him in the first place.

"Jessica is not old enough to throw her weight around and spout off insulting remarks," he fumed. "Barrett has been spying on you and that is inexcusable. And if you had agreed to marry me, this wouldn't have happened!"

Moriah tensed at the sound of his blistering voice. "Jessica is twenty-three years old," she rasped out, unable to control her own temper. "She is older than I am! I think she is entitled to express her feelings! And I'm sure Barrett is mortified by what he did. And as for me, I told you I couldn't marry you, but you insisted on dragging me here anyway. If you are looking to lay the blame on someone, blame yourself! I would still be in the mountains if not for you. I certainly didn't ask for this!"

"Twenty-three?" Devlin croaked. "Is that what Jess told you?" A mutinous growl tumbled from his lips. "For your information, Jessica just turned fifteen this summer."

Moriah collapsed against the headboard. "Crimdeparture, that's even worse!"

Moriah well remembered how impressionable she was at that age—her exact age when Ruby was thrust into her life. Moriah had thrown a few tirades herself and Jessica was simply acting true to her age. Jess had every right to be upset.

But why had Jess lied to her? Moriah wondered curiously. Perhaps Jessica wanted to make Moriah think she was her equal. Or was it just another of the spiteful pranks Jessica had played on her? During the past two days, Moriah had begun to wonder if the scalding coffee, highly seasoned food, and cold baths were Jessica's ways of making her stay unpleasant. It seemed Jessica had been trying to strike back with her own subtle techniques, hoping Moriah would pack up and leave.

When Moriah heard Devlin whip open the door, her heart twisted in her chest. "Dev, please, don't—"

"I am still the master of this house," he growled, unable to keep from taking his frustration out on Moriah, even if she was the last person who deserved to be barked at. "Things are going to change around here. And if I have to, I'll run my idiotic sister and brother out of here and deed this place over to you! They are going to be eternally sorry for what they've done!"

As the door slammed shut behind him, the entire house shook as if it had been besieged by an earthquake. When Devlin stormed off in a towering rage, Moriah's shoulders slumped. She had hoped her last night with Devlin would be a sweet dream. But then she reminded herself that heartache and trouble had always followed in her shadow. Fate had frowned on her again. She had learned to accept the philosophy that if there was even a remote chance that things could go wrong they would. Times never seemed to get better for her.

Chapter 20

When Devlin stalked into Jessica's bedroom, fit to be tied, both his brother and sister were simultaneously flinging insults at each other. Noting the venomous scowl on Devlin's face, they clamped their mouths shut and instinctively took a retreating step. Angry though Jessica was, she cowered behind Barrett and peeked around his broad shoulders to survey the man whose venomous snarl left her wondering if she really knew him at all. She shrank back another step when Devlin loomed over her like an ominous thundercloud.

"If you weren't my sister, I would toss you out of this house on your ear!" he boomed. The windowpane rattled.

Jessica mustered her courage and tilted an indignant chin. "Why? Because I caught you abed with your paramour? Didn't you think I knew what you were doing each night since she has been here?" Her dark eyes flashed, even though she knew she risked being snatched up off the floor and shaken until her teeth rattled. "Let he among us who is guiltless cast the first stone!"

Barrett valiantly refrained from striking his hysterical sister, but Devlin could no longer control himself and jerked Jessica to him, shoved her over his knee, and paddled her backside, not once but thrice. A whimper bubbled from her lips when the sting of Devlin's hand pulsated on her derriere. The forceful swats jolted Jessica to her senses and she clamped down on her runaway tongue. Sobbing in great gulps, she wilted onto the edge of the bed, sitting carefully on her wounded posterior.

"I have never thought I could be so disappointed in my own flesh and blood!" Devlin growled at Jessica who now sat with her fists clenched in the folds of her gown and her head downcast. "First you lied to Moriah to make her think you were her elder. You deceived her for pure spite, didn't you, Jess? I shudder to think what else you did to goad her when you were told to mind your manners and your own business."

"Didn't she tell you?" Jessica sobbed, crushed by Devlin's repeated blows to her backside and his biting tone.

"No, she didn't," Devlin snapped brusquely. "That's the difference between a woman and a selfish child who was obviously rebelling because she wasn't getting her way, because she wasn't getting all the expected attention from her usually doting brothers." His tawny eyes burned fire and brimstone. "Now what exactly *did* you do to make Moriah's stay as unpleasant as possible, besides humiliating her by bursting in on us and calling her every disrespectful name in the book?" he wanted to know that very second.

Jessica grimaced, refusing to speak. Devlin reached over to give her a fierce shake, spilling the words off the tip of her tongue. Jessica began by confessing about the scalding coffee and salted food and cold baths. Then she admitted she had wrinkled the carpet so Moriah would trip. Reluctantly, she revealed the fact that she had selected undergarments that were either uncomfortably too tight or too loose. She finished, and quite hesitantly, by divulging the comments she had made to Moriah's secret admirers at Haverns' party.

Devlin couldn't believe what he was hearing! He wanted to choke the life out of Jessica, but he refused to yield to the temptation until his sassy little sister knew how wrong she had been about Moriah. Jessica's brothers had spoiled her since the death of their parents six years earlier during the cholera epidemic, and they could now see the error of their ways.

"Of all the women you know, Jess, Moriah is the one you should have strived to emulate. She is proud and independent. She is above petty spite. Your life has been a bed of roses compared to hers, and she has forsaken her own security and happiness in her belief that I couldn't love her because of her handicap."

"You do pity her," Jessica said with a muffled sniff. "You feel sorry for her, just as you pity the Apaches who have been unjustly accused of crimes they didn't commit."

"Pity?" Devlin scoffed at his naïve little sister. "I love Moriah as I have loved no other woman. I wanted her to be my wife. I wanted her to await my return so we could find a little happiness together. But she refused me. Why? Because she thought I deserved more than to cope with her blindness. Because she didn't want to be a responsibility and a burden. But love makes all the difference, Jess. I care about her and I want her in my life. Blind, destitute, and even cynical. It doesn't matter. I'll take her any way I can get her!"

Jessica blinked bewilderment and raised misty eyes

to Devlin's frustrated expression. "You really do love her that much?"

He nodded affirmatively. "She has not worked her cunning wiles on me as you accused. But rather I have done all within my power to convince her of my affection and my desire to have her as my wife. With no help from you, I might add!" He flung Jessica a condescending glare. "Moriah's stepfather tried to kill her to gain control of her inheritance. She felt so betrayed she might have remained in the mountains and perished."

Jessica gasped in astonishment.

"You have lived in the lap of luxury, Jess. Rett and I have granted your every whim and showered you with love and affection. Moriah has known only rejection and betrayal. I have tried to make her believe in love and friendship and you have undermined my efforts. Moriah didn't give herself to me to gain favors. I compromised her. I was the first man she'd known and I took what she might not have given if I hadn't been persistent . . ."

His voice trailed off, letting Jessica draw her own conclusions. That wasn't a good thing, for Jessica had an active imagination and she could visualize her brother doing all sorts of horrible things to Moriah.

"I forced her to remain with me when she would have gone her own way. I watched her fall beside a lightning bolt and I suffered all the torments of the damned, wondering if she would survive the ordeal. I told her how I felt about her, but all she could see was the darkness and another cruel twist of fate. All she had asked from life was to escape those who had hurt her and suddenly she couldn't even see which way to run!"

"I have been feeling sorry for you, but I should

have pitied her," Jessica muttered. "And you should have told me."

"I shouldn't have had to, and you had no right to judge anyone by your inexperienced standards, Jess. You should have had enough respect for my judgment not to question my authority," Devlin growled at her. "Moriah never asked for your pity. She doesn't want mine or Rett's or yours. She only wants the chance to regenerate her spirit before she sets out in the world to find a haven of peace, to put aside the treachery and disappointment and try to live her life. She expected nothing more than your consideration and a little respect and you called her my whore!"

Devlin's voice rose to a roar and he breathed down Jessica's neck, venting his pent-up frustration. "I do not have to answer to you, Jessica. And I shouldn't have had to tell you this, even now. You should have opened your heart and your home to one who is so richly deserving of admiration and one who needed to be loved to make up for all the years that she was mocked and scorned by her evil stepparents."

He inhaled a steadying breath and trying to clamp a tight grip on his smoldering temper. "Put yourself in Moriah's place for just one minute and speculate on how you would have reacted to the hell she has been through. Could you have coped with all of it? With any of it? Moriah lost her parents, too, and you damned well know the pain of losing someone you love. That was only the beginning of Moriah's nightmare and you have made it worse! And the most pathetic thing about it is that you could go to her and apologize and she would probably forgive you, even when you don't deserve it."

"I couldn't face her after the terrible things I've said and done," Jessica squeaked. "I resented the fact that she monopolized all your time. I've waited months for you to come back and Moriah was suddenly the object of your attention and you didn't even remember I was alive!"

The anger drained from Devlin's body as he watched Jessica's shoulders shake with heart-wrenching sobs. "I'm sorry if I neglected you, pet. I didn't mean to. I was fighting to keep Moriah, trying to prove to her that she meant something very special to me. But it took all my time and effort to persuade her when she has been so long without love. She doesn't trust what she hasn't had and doesn't understand. And in some ways she is still a little girl—naïve and unsure of what it means to be a woman who is desired by many men."

"And I have made a complete mess of things by assuring her that all you felt was *lust* and sympathy."

"I wish you would quit throwing that word around," Barrett grumbled. "A fifteen-year-old young lady shouldn't talk about such things."

A faint smile pursed Devlin's lips as he peered down at his young sister who was bleeding tears. "I think Jess has grown up a great deal these past few days. I think she is beginning to realize that the world doesn't revolve around the space she occupies."

Rounded eyes lifted to Devlin. This seemed the perfect moment for that little chat Devlin and Barrett kept saying they needed to have with her about the birds and bees. They had told her what proper ladies shouldn't do, but they had deprived her of the intimate details in the relationship between a man and woman.

"If Moriah doesn't know when a man really loves her, how am I supposed to know when the right man for me comes along? If my beau says he does and I think I do, would it be all right for us to make love the way you and Moriah did? And if we shouldn't, why did you seduce Moriah if she wasn't that kind of woman?"

Devlin looked around for a hole to crawl into. As fate would have it, there wasn't one.

Barrett was no help whatsoever. He propped himself against the wall and grinned broadly. "Do by all means, big brother, explain to Jess when it is permissible for a woman to succumb to a man without being labeled 'that kind of woman.' Since you are so worldly, you would be far better at clearing up this mystery of when to allow exception to the rules than I."

Devlin flashed his brother a contemptuous glower. "I will do my best to differentiate between the two. And when I'm through, you can explain why it is disgraceful to play the Peeping Tom who spies on a woman when she thinks she has been granted absolute privacy."

The well-aimed barb wiped the teasing grin off Barrett's handsome face. Properly put in his place, he slinked over to the chair and sank meekly into it.

Heaving a sigh, Devlin rammed his hands into his pockets and paced the floor while he formulated his thoughts. He had dreaded this conversation for years and had stalled it as long as possible. But Jessica needed answers and she deserved to know what went on between a man and woman. Unfortunately, Devlin didn't want to have to be the one to tell her. In the past, he had spoken in generalities, but the time had come to reveal the particulars.

"Sometimes courtships don't proceed in idealistic order and things don't fall neatly into place like a romantic fairytale," he began awkwardly. "I hope you will be courted by gentlemanly suitors who do not make demands on you. It is true, I suppose, that those of us of the male persuasion—" He tossed

Barrett a quick glance. "Your brother and I included, I'm sorry to say, do occasionally overlook propriety in our need to satisfy natural urges."

Jessica couldn't swear to it, but she thought she detected a slight blush creeping into Devlin's tanned cheeks, the first one she ever remembered seeing.

Devlin nervously cleared his throat and plowed on. "Men are a bit more daring and they have a tendency to take what they think they can get from those females who are free with their charms."

"So you are saying that a proper lady should resist a man, even if a gentleman refuses to deny himself physical pleasures if he can find them elsewhere," Jessica paraphrased, her tone noticeably sour. "Who made up these stupid rules anyway? Some arrogant man who wanted a chaste wife while he was sampling the various spices of life?"

Devlin muttered under his breath. "I didn't say it was right, only that that is the way it is with men. They are not always as discriminating as they should be. And when it comes to women, a man's willpower isn't always what it should be either. Perhaps it is male pride that goads them. Ask your brother. Maybe he knows what provokes him to go tomcatting around town."

Barrett shifted uneasily in his chair when he found himself on the hot spot. "I suddenly find myself ashamed to be a member of the male gender," he mumbled, refusing to meet Jessica's probing stare.

"Quit hedging," Devlin grunted. "I shouldn't have to do all the talking. You're Jessica's brother and guardian, too, you know."

"And you quit tossing the toughest questions in my lap," Barrett shot back. He glanced briefly at Jessica, who impatiently awaited an answer. "Male pride is a fragile, troublesome thing at times. I guess a man thinks he has to prove his virility to women and prove that he is a man to other men. There are times when we men allow physical desire to do our thinking for us. We want our wives to be pure and our lovers to be—"

Barrett tugged at the collar of his shirt to relieve the mounting tension. "We sometimes take women for granted, thinking only of our own pleasure without considering the woman's feelings and the repercussions she might face. But er . . . that is to say, a . . . a—"

Devlin interrupted while Barrett floundered to express himself on the awkward subject. "But sometimes a very unique female comes along who not only incites a man's basic instincts but also compels him to explore a deeper, more meaningful liaison. It makes him wish he had waited, that he had shunned passion for passion's sake. Then he finds himself wishing that this special woman was his very first experience, just as he hopes he will be hers."

"Do you understand what we're trying to tell you, Jess?" Devlin asked gently, shifting from one foot to the other, very uncomfortable with this intimate conversation.

Jessica gave her head a shake. "No, I still don't know when I should accept a man's affection and when I should reject it," she said in exasperation.

"Perhaps if you and Moriah become friends she can find a better way to explain—woman to woman," Devlin suggested. "If I tell you not to trust any man's intentions until you are wearing his wedding ring I have condemned my own actions with Moriah. And if I allow you to believe you should submit without a commitment, then you risk being hurt. You also have to deal with the possibility that your suitors are liable to say and do anything to marry into your money. There are all sorts of pitfalls into which you can stumble if you trust blindly and allow your feminine curiosity and innocent heart to lead you."

"Lord, I never realized how difficult it was to be a woman," Barrett groaned. "I think we're mixing poor Jess up worse than she already is."

"You've certainly got that right," Jessica grumbled. "From the way you make it sound, men aren't to be trusted in affairs of the heart. Men will take whatever a woman will give, whether her intentions are sincere or whether she seeks only monetary compensation for doling out favors. If she is chaste she is labeled an ice maiden and if she is generous with her affection she is tainted for life and no 'respectable' man would want her for a wife!"

Jessica glared scornfully at her two brothers, suddenly seeing them as men rather than brothers. "Why Moriah would believe a man's intentions toward her were honorable after all you've told me is laughable. With her dazzling good looks men are naturally attracted to her and attempt to take what they can from her. According to Dev, she was abused and mistreated by men." Her dark eyes drilled into her eldest brother. "And then you came along to compromise her virtues and confuse her all the more. She is probably just as baffled by the inconsistency in men's characters as I am. How could she possibly know whether a man loves her for herself or for her alluring appearance? And how can I know when a man wishes to deflower me just to carve another notch on his bedpost and bolster his male pride? If I were Moriah, I would be of the opinion that it was lust and sympathy that prompted your confession of affection . . . if you have even bothered to voice one."

Here she paused to glare daggers at Devlin, and

then she punished Barrett with a glower for spying on a blind woman who was oblivious to his presence. "As for me, I don't think I will be so naïve and gullible again. I will not trust a man's intentions toward me. I think women are better off if they steer clear of males," she finished on a bitter note.

This discussion had dragged on longer than Devlin had intended. But this was not the time to drop the sensitive topic of conversation, not when Jessica had turned as cynical and mistrusting as Moriah. Good God, where had he fouled up? he asked himself. Jessica kept flinging glances at Dev and Rett as if they were disgusting two-legged rats.

"For God's sake, Dev, state your explanation before Jess thinks we are the worst scoundrels in a condemned breed," Barrett muttered.

"Why don't you redefine what I have been trying to say," Devlin scowled. "I keep digging myself in so deep I can't crawl out. It wouldn't hurt you to jump in and try to save me!"

Barrett pushed onto the edge of his chair. "Now look here, Jess . . ." he began, praying the right words would leap to mind to save him from another disastrous blunder. They didn't. "You have to decide what kind of woman you want to be—the kind a man beds or weds."

Devlin rolled his eyes heavenward. "I'll call the doctor to see if he can surgically remove the two feet you just crammed in your mouth."

Jessica blinked bemusedly. "You mean a man doesn't expect to do both with his wife? He intends to keep mistresses when he's married and only seduce his wife to produce heirs? That makes a wife sound like a brood mare that is selected only for propagating the species!"

She crossed her arms over her chest and stuck out

her chin. "I don't ever want to get married if that is the way of things. My God, how did my poor mother endure life with Papa? What degrading humiliation did she suffer? And poor Moriah. She probably thinks Devlin wanted to marry her just because she was blind."

Devlin took one look at his fuming sister and he could read all the contemptuous thoughts that were chasing through her head. "Thanks one helluva lot, Rett," Devlin scowled acrimoniously. "Now my own sister hates me. Next she'll be trying to talk Moriah out of marrying me for an entirely different reason than the one she had before we got into this confounded discussion!"

"That's for sure," Jessica snapped tartly. "You have kept Moriah as your mistress since you first met her. I know you feel sorry for her, but you've been preying on her handicap. I'd gladly help her leave to make a fresh start after what the two of you told me." Hollow laughter bubbled from Jessica's lips. "Why would Moriah want to stay here with a Peeping Tom gawking at her every chance he gets and a lusty rake creeping into her bedroom every night, whether she wanted him there or not."

"I happen to love her . . . a lot!" Devlin flared.

"Well, you couldn't prove it by me, horrible man! Women aren't safe on this planet. Men should be locked behind bars," Jessica spewed.

"Jeezus!" Devlin threw up his hands in frustration. What had he said to draw such an adverse reaction from his sister?

"Jess, you're getting the wrong impression," Barrett jumped in head first. "A man's basic makeup and philosophies may be different from a woman's, but there are many honorable men in this world."

"But unfortunately my brothers aren't among them," Jessica finished for him as she glowered at Dev and Rett. "It seems to me that men should post signs on their chests to let the female population know which ones of them should be avoided. I'm ashamed to say that I live with two of the worst womanizing rogues on the Continent. And if Moriah consents to it, I think I'll run away with her. I will be her eyes."

"You're talking nonsense," Devlin growled.

"I'm talking perfect sense." Jessica bounded to her feet and stormed toward the door in stiff, precise strides. "If you two lusty heathens will excuse me, I'm going to fling myself at Moriah's feet and beg forgiveness for treating her so abominably when it was the two of you I should have protected her from. And if she still wants to leave, I'm going with her!"

When she buzzed by like a disturbed hornet, Devlin grabbed her arm, intent on shaking some sense into her.

"Don't touch me, you . . . you animal!" Jessica shrieked, worming for freedom. "Moriah was right. There is no one as blind as the one who refuses to see. But now I see very clearly and I have developed an aversion to men and their detestable motives—my brothers included!"

"You damned well better apologize to Moriah, but don't you dare try to convince her to leave," Devlin warned through gritted teeth. "And for heaven's sake, ask her to explain the birds and bees to you through a woman's eyes before you leap to any more wild conclusions!"

Flinging her nose in the air, Jessica whipped open the door and disappeared into the hall, but not before flashing her brothers a militant glare.

"Women to bed or wed?" Devlin scoffed disdainfully at Rett. "You call that tact?"

"You weren't doing so great yourself," Rett defended sourly. "What was all that malarkey about Moriah being the first time you wished it were your first time? What female is going to believe that nonsense with all the experience you have under your belt?"

Devlin puffed up with so much indignation he very nearly popped the buttons off his shirt. "You'd know exactly what I meant if you had ever met a woman who made you wonder what you had been doing for the past several years—because it wasn't anywhere near the same thing you had been doing with her," Devlin bit off. "You have more lady friends than a dog has fleas. Jess is fully aware of that. Now she thinks we're both rounders and hypocrites."

Barrett slumped back in his chair and exhaled a long sigh. "I only hope Moriah can convince Jess that she has a distorted picture of men. Thanks to your confusing explanation," he added resentfully.

Devlin plopped down on Jessica's bed to await his sister's return, exasperated that his time here was so short. Damn, he should have left an hour ago. "That should be a most interesting conversation. A skeptic trying to explain the facts of life to a would-be skeptic." Long lashes swept down to flutter against bronzed cheeks. Devlin emitted a deflated sigh. "I've lost her, Rett. I can feel it in my bones."

Barrett had the inescapable feeling Devlin was right. After the humiliation and torment Moriah had endured during the course of the evening, not to mention her ordeals the past decade, she wouldn't want to remain at the ranch with a bunch of lunatics like the Grangers. Who would, for crying out loud? He had transformed into a Peeping Tom and Jessica had undertaken a crusade to have all men burned at the stake!

A few minutes later Jessica reappeared in the door. Huge tears glistened in her dark eyes. Guilt and regret were written on her lovely features in bold letters. Devlin knew what his sister was going to say before the words stampeded off her tongue.

"She's already gone."

Her words dropped like stones in the silence.

A muffled scowl tripped off Devlin's lips as he vaulted off the bed and shot toward the door. He didn't have time to chase Moriah down and yet he was worried about her, knowing she was probably suffering nine kinds of hell after her confrontation with Jessica, who had now turned over a new leaf and at the ripe old age of fifteen, had sworn off men. Devlin should have left yesterday as it was. But he had wanted to savor every possible minute with Moriah, knowing it would be his last. Now he had tarried so long that there wasn't a minute to spare. Damnation.

When Devlin stood indecisively in the hall, Jessica glared at his broad back. "For her sake, let it be over," she muttered bitterly. "Wherever she is, she's probably thankful to be rid of all of us. She thinks I despise her. She thinks you feel sorry for her and she knows Rett is a pervert."

"I am not a pervert!" Rett loudly protested. Clamping down on his temper, he stared at Devlin's drooping shoulders. "I'll find her and explain things to her. She can't have gone far."

Devlin dragged in a depressing breath of air and stalked back to his room to gather his gear. Why was it that when things got as bad as they could get, they always managed to get even worse? This evening had evolved into a nightmare. Jessica, who had once worshipped the ground he walked on, now despised him because he was a man. And there was no telling where Moriah was or what sort of trouble she had gotten herself into this time. She not only had an uncanny knack for attracting trouble but she attracted men who attracted trouble.

And damn her hide, she hadn't even bothered to say good-bye. It was bad enough that he had a week of trekking through rough country ahead of him. Knowing Moriah had vanished would torment him every step of the way.

"Don't worry about her," Barrett consoled his brother. "Just take care of yourself and watch your step with Burkhart. I want you to live long enough to see your name exonerated. Jessica and I will find Moriah and apologize. She'll be here waiting for you when you come back."

"No she won't," Devlin grumbled as he slung his saddlebag over his shoulder and pushed past Barrett. "The Grangers have given Moriah just cause to think she is better off alone. And I can't honestly say that I blame her. If I were her, I'd aim myself toward parts unknown without ever looking back."

Barrett had never seen Devlin quite so surly or dispirited. He was usually a tower of strength who rose to meet each challenge and crisis. Now he was reminiscent of a wounded lion who had been abandoned by his lioness.

"I'll tear Arizona upside down to find her if I have to," Barrett vowed fiercely. "She will be here when you get back."

"Sure," Devlin scoffed sarcastically. "And donkeys fly."

As he strode down the hall, dressed as an Apache,

Jessica sent him off with a cold shoulder that dripped icicles. "Do something with that girl," Devlin muttered to his brother who was one step behind him.

"Tar and feather her, perhaps?" Barrett smirked after he received the cold shoulder treatment as well.

"You might try convincing Jess that men aren't the scum of the earth."

"You always leave me with the impossible tasks," Barrett muttered resentfully. "Here you go tripping off to the mountains and I'm left to straighten out Jessie and chase down Moriah. If you would have handled Moriah properly in the first place we wouldn't be stewing in our own juice now."

"I'm beginning to think Moriah was right," Devlin grumbled as he stalked out the door. "Living as a hermit in the mountains is the only way an individual can find any peace! I may not come back!"

With that, he stomped off. Devlin was feeling as miserable as one man could get.

Chapter 21

The moment Devlin had marched down the hall to scold Jessica for her hysterical tirade, Moriah had wriggled into her breeches and shirt and fled from the house, burning bridges behind her. She had wanted her last few hours with Devlin to be perfect but they had been anything but! She had overstayed her welcome at the Grangers' ranch and it was time for her to move on.

Wallowing in dreary thoughts, Moriah had retrieved a horse from the stable. The storm had passed, and for that Moriah was grateful. Swinging onto the steed, Moriah allowed it to choose its own direction. It didn't really matter which way she went or where she wound up. Anywhere without Devlin was going to be hell.

An hour later, Moriah saw the hint of lights through the gray shadows that stared back at her. She assumed the steed had taken her to town. When she heard the murmur of voices and the piano music that clamored through saloons until all hours of the night she was sure she had been carted back to Tucson.

When the steed paused, Moriah heard the whinny

and braying of livestock. Horses, it seemed, had an affinity to other horses and, by the smell of it, her mount had delivered her to the blacksmith stable.

Sliding to the ground, Moriah felt her way toward the wide door, moved quietly past the stalls, and led her mount into an empty one. Deciding to bed down in the straw, Moriah inched past the livestock to locate the narrow stairway that led into the hay loft. A pile of hay wouldn't be the most comfortable place to sleep, but she had certainly endured worse, she reminded herself. And first thing next morning, she would find some sort of job to earn enough money to buy herself a ticket on the stage bound for . . . anywhere.

She wondered if Devlin had already aimed himself toward the mountains to prepare his confrontation with Burkhart. He was now free to fight his crusade because she had taken the responsibility of herself away from him.

And with any luck at all Moriah would forget the powerfully built renegade with amber eyes and jet-black hair. *You'll forget him in a couple hundred years or so* came the whispering of her heart. And on that depressing thought, Moriah fell asleep, allowing her dreams to offer her what harsh reality had not been able to grant her.

Vance Thatcher lumbered inside the blacksmith shop at the crack of dawn to begin another work day. He wasn't in the best frame of mind, though. Ruby had been in a huff since the moment she discovered Moriah had miraculously returned from the dead to torment the Thatchers for their sins. They had conjured up and discarded a hundred schemes of disposing of Moriah. Now that Ruby had sunk the inheritance money into the shop and Vance was holding down a job, she had no intention of being uprooted. Moriah, Ruby had loudly proclaimed, had to go.

Ruby had given Vance instructions to be on the lookout for their stepdaughter in case she returned to town. And whom did Vance happen upon the first thing that morning? He froze in his tracks when he climbed the steps to fetch hay for the livestock. Moriah!

Vance choked on his breath when he spied the sleeping beauty curled up in the corner of the straw. Vance simply stood there gaping at her. His footsteps on the stairs had awakened Moriah and she slowly roused from sleep. When she began to stir, Vance shrank back behind a mound of hay, trying to decide which of Ruby's plans would best suit this situation.

In mute amazement, Vance watched Moriah sit up and glance around her. A muddled frown puckered his brow when she groped to locate the wall and then pulled herself to her feet and his jaw dropped when she felt her way around the loft to locate the railing to the steps.

Blind? She was blind? Vance blinked in astonishment. Dull-witted though he was, Vance was smart enough to realize opportunity was staring him in the face. As Moriah started down the steps, Vance unfolded his bulky frame from his hiding place and charged after her.

The rustle of straw startled Moriah. She swiveled her head to see a blurred image among the hazy shadows that curtained her eyes. Frightened by the muted growl that tumbled from the man's lips, Moriah clutched at the rail and scuttled down the steps.

Slow as he was, Vance was quick enough to apprehend his fleeing stepdaughter. Shoving his hands against her back, he sent her stumbling down the steps. A terrified shriek burst free as Moriah's shoulder slammed against the railing. Frantically, she tried to upright herself, but Vance was upon her, knocking her off balance. Another yelp erupted when she felt herself hoisted over the rail and hurled through space.

Vance waited, thinking the fall would be the end of Moriah. But she seemed to possess the legendary nine lives of a cat that always managed to land on its feet. The pile of straw beside the stairs broke her fall and, groaning, she scrambled to her knees to feel her way around the wall.

Vance scurried down the remainder of the steps to reach her. Although momentarily stunned by the jarring fall, Moriah regained her footing. Her senses came to life and she groped for anything that might serve as a weapon against this unidentified assailant. Her hand folded around the pitchfork that was propped in the corner and she thrust it at the rustling straw and shuffling noises.

Vance cried out in pain when the sharp prongs grazed his arm. As Moriah lunged again, Vance clamped his hand on the handle, yanking her improvised weapon from her grasp. But Moriah pounced on him, knocking the pitchfork loose before he could turn it upon her.

Moriah tried to remember everything Devlin had taught her about self-defense. As Vance crushed her in a bear hug and lifted her up from the floor, Moriah's hands slid down his ribs to check for a weapon. With lightning quickness, she snatched the pistol from his holster and slammed the butt of his Colt against his head.

The unexpected blow stunned Vance, but Moriah wasn't taking any chances with the big baboon who had latched on to her. Moriah walloped him again and then hit him a third time for good measure. When she felt her attacker loosen his grasp, Moriah raised her knee to deliver another painful blow to his crotch.

After Vance wilted with a muffled thud in the straw, Moriah rummaged through the man's pockets to retrieve the coins he carried, unaware that she was stealing her own money from her stepfather. Hurriedly, Moriah felt her way along the top planks of the stalls. She opened the gate quickly to retrieve the steed she had borrowed from the Grangers.

Moriah supposed her attacker was one of the spiteful men against whom she had retaliated at the dance for making lurid propositions. It seemed she was no longer safe in Tucson; she had made some male enemies at the dance and she was definitely unwanted baggage at the Granger ranch. Jessica despised her. There was only one place she could go to escape all the bitter memories of her past—the mountains.

Blinking back the tears of torment and frustration, Moriah clung to her steed as it trotted out of the stable. She glanced at the light in the east and aimed herself toward the sunrise. Things weren't as bad as they once were, Moriah consoled herself. During the past month, the curtain of darkness had begun to lift. Now she could distinguish faint images and differentiate between light and darkness. It gave her hope that she might eventually be able to identify shapes and perhaps even colors. Even now, as she stared toward the sun, she could detect the hint of bluish gold among the streaks of gray.

Somehow she would find her way into the mountains from which she had come—and where she should have stayed! She preferred to challenge the rugged mountains than the torment of civilization. If she remained anywhere near Tucson, Jessica would surely drive her away. And there was always the possibility that she would run into another vindictive suitor like the one who had very nearly pushed her to her death in the blacksmith barn.

Her only recourse was to wander through the mountains, attempting to retrace the path she and Devlin had followed. And if she perished in her attempt to seek refuge in the mountains, at least she would die trying to outrun her fate. It was for certain that she wouldn't have lasted long in Tucson. Her would-be assailant wanted her dead!

Riding hell for leather, Moriah aimed herself toward the sun. And if what little luck she had held out, she might survive grizzly bear and cougar attacks, not to mention the risk of encountering unfriendly Apaches like Makado.

Moriah realized, at that moment, as she mustered her courage and fought down the apprehension of confronting all sorts of unseen catastrophes, how much she had come to depend on Devlin. Life hadn't seemed quite so bleak and burdensome while he was beside her. She had been able to keep her spirit, knowing he was there to pick her up each time she stumbled. Now she had no one.

Well now, Miss Laverty, Moriah told herself with a rueful smile. *We're about to see if you are made of stuff as sturdy as you thought.* Talk was cheap when Devlin was there to back her up. Now she was alone with the memories of a love that was over and done with. She had to think in terms of life without that raven-haired renegade. She could never go back. Jessica had spoiled any chance of that.

The past two months were a closed chapter of her

past and now she had to forge ahead as best she could—half blind and missing Devlin to the point that he permeated every thought. Falling in love with that mountain of a man had been the easy part. Forgetting him . . . ? Now that was going to take some doing!

Seeing double, Vance wobbled through the alley to the adobe home he and Ruby had purchased from the former proprietor of the dress shop. He dreaded giving the news to Ruby that he had again failed to dispose of Moriah. She would be furious.

The rattle of the back door caused Ruby to wheel about. She was just preparing to leave the house to open her shop. The unexpected sound took ten years off her life. She knew it was Moriah, come to seek her revenge. That chit was all Ruby had been able to think about since she had seen Moriah on the streets of Tucson.

Cursing vehemently, Ruby snatched up the figurine on the table and positioned herself beside the door. The instant it swung open, she leaped out to smash the statue over Moriah's head. Only it wasn't Moriah's blond head. It was Vance's—which already had three knots on it!

With a muffled groan, Vance folded up at the knees and pitched forward on the doormat. Ruby gasped in disbelief as she stared at the limp form of her husband.

"What the devil are you doing back at the house?" she muttered in question. "You are supposed to be at the stable. It serves you right, you blundering idiot!"

Vance didn't reply. He had a blinding headache that refused to permit Ruby's scathing words from penetrating his spongy brain.

Scowling, Ruby stamped over to fetch the pitcher of water and dumped it on Vance's throbbing head. She offered not one tittle of sympathy when he pushed onto all fours to get his bearings.

"What in hell did you do that for?" Vance bleated.

"I thought you were Moriah, come to blow me to smithereens," Ruby snapped. "You should have announced yourself."

"She wouldn't have been able to find you," Vance sighed, trying to hold his aching head in a position that didn't hurt. There wasn't one. "She's blind as a bat."

"What!" Ruby crowed in astonishment.

Vance nodded affirmation. "I found her sleepin' in the loft at the stable this mornin' and I shoved her down the steps."

Ruby's taut body sagged in relief. "Thank goodness. That should be the end of that one."

"It wasn't," Vance reported gloomily. "She grabbed a pitchfork and tried to run me through after she fell."

Ruby's face turned a remarkable shade of purple.

"That girl is the scrappiest fighter I ever did see, blind and all. Before I could choke the life out of her and make it look as if she fell and broke her neck, she clubbed me with my own pistol. Hell, I don't even know how she managed to get ahold of it."

"You moron!" Ruby screeched, on the verge of hysterics. "Can't you do anything right? How could you let that mere wisp of a woman best you?"

Vance glared at the double image of his fuming wife. "If you think you will have better luck, then you take after her. When I woke up, she was thunderin' off on horseback. If you can catch her, you deal with her, since you're so damned smart!"

Muttering a string of epithets to Moriah's name,

Ruby hooked her arm around Vance's elbow and hoisted him to his feet. They were doomed to live in constant fear, wondering when Moriah would return. Ruby was already as jumpy as a grasshopper. Now she was like a gunshy rabbit that anticipated being attacked from all directions at once. She would have to remain on constant guard, afraid of her own shadow. Until they disposed of that troublesome chit both their lives were in jeopardy.

Ruby was relieved to hear that Vance had had the presence of mind not to speak to Moriah. At least she wouldn't have recognized him during their fracas. Somehow Ruby would devise a way to remove Moriah. She wanted the girl gone! She and Vance had put down roots in Tucson. They weren't packing up and leaving. Ruby vowed to find a way to discreetly dispose of Moriah if it was the last thing she ever did!

Barrett sighed dispiritedly as he stood by the watchtower walls of Tucson. For two days he had hunted high and low and he hadn't turned up even one clue.

Barrett was worried sick. He had checked every hotel in town and had even stood like a posted sentinel all day to determine if Moriah had taken a room under an assumed name. But no one he had interrogated had seen the stunning blonde. Even the blank-faced baboon who worked at the blacksmith stable insisted he hadn't seen Moriah. That was a lie, of course. Vance had three knots on his head to prove it, plus a fourth bump that Ruby had given him. It had come as a great relief to Vance that Moriah had lit out for parts unknown without informing her host of her destination. Now Vance and Ruby could breathe a little easier . . . at least for the time being.

The fact that Barrett hadn't found Moriah in Tucson or at the abandoned town of Tubac, which lay to the south of the ranch, sent his spirits nose-diving. Barrett hated to venture a guess as to what had happened to her. If she had stumbled into disaster, she wouldn't even have been able to see it coming. She might have decided she was doing the Grangers a favor by removing herself from their lives, but she was tripping on the borderline of catastrophe. Thanks to Jessica, who had reversed her low opinion of Moriah and now hailed her as some sort of martyr, the comely nymph had spirited off into the night. Jessica felt terrible about the incident and she was taking her irritation out on every man she encountered. When one of her suitors came to call, Jessica lambasted him with accusing insults and sent him skulking away with his tail tucked between his legs.

Barrett pitied the man who set his sights on that ebony-haired hellion. Jess had always been a handful. Now she was unmanageable. And that was the fault of Devlin and Barrett. They had done a miserable job of explaining the facts of life and had made men seem like insensitive, despicable creatures. But blast it, how was man to caution a young woman on the dangers of romantic affairs without cutting his own throat? Damned if Barrett knew. All he and Devlin had accomplished was making Jessica as stubborn and cynical as Moriah.

Heaving a heavy sigh, Barrett reined toward the trading post. Since Devlin had become a hunted man, Barrett had full responsibility of the post and the ranch. He was meeting himself coming and going. Fretting over Moriah, Devlin, and Jessica wasn't helping matters. He longed to cuddle up to something soft and feminine and forget his troubles for a few hours. But he couldn't even do that, not with the raging Jessica underfoot. She had already referred to him as a lusty, lecherous philistine four times the past two days.

Devlin had his share of troubles, but he had nothing on Barrett! Lord, he would be glad when Dev could return home to assist with the duties of the post and ranch and, more important, Jessica! But Barrett doubted his older brother could settle into the life he had enjoyed before Burkhart's treachery. Even if the charges were dropped, his soul wouldn't be free. Devlin would be a haunted man, wondering what had become of the golden-haired beauty who had wandered into his life and galloped away with his heart. If Barrett couldn't discover what had happened to Moriah, Devlin was going to be hell to live with! Barrett dreaded the thought of giving Devlin the news that his exhausting search for Moriah had turned up nothing.

Part IV

Chapter 22

"You are here in body, but not in spirit, White Shadow," Chanos observed as he watched his blood brother stare off into space.

Since White Shadow had returned to the Apache stronghold near Devil's Park, as the white-eyes chose to call the rugged peaks and plunging arroyos in the mountains of Apachería, he had been remote and preoccupied. It seemed Moriah's memory kept climbing up from the depths of his mind to torment him.

While they traveled over the rocky paths to reach the location which Devlin had designated the tribal conference, Chanos had been forced to repeat himself several times because White Shadow was too distracted to listen to the conversation.

Devlin's mood had become darker with each passing day. He had trekked northwest to fulfill the vow he had made to Chanos, Geronimo, and Cochise, but his heart was wherever Moriah was. How Devlin hoped Barrett had tracked her down. And damn her for not waiting to say good-bye! That galled him to no end.

Moriah had taken nothing but a steed from the

barn. She had no money, no food, nothing. How did that little minx think she could survive? And worse, had Jessica's harsh words cut her so deeply that Moriah no longer cared if she lived or died?

"White Shadow." Chanos gouged him in the ribs when his question not only went unanswered but didn't even register in Devlin's distracted brain.

Devlin surfaced from his deep thoughts. He glanced up to see the somber faces of Cochise and Geronimo as they weaved silently down the path that led into the Valley of the Eagle. Behind the two powerful chiefs were the leaders of the Warm Springs, Pinals, Mimbres, and White Mountain Apaches. In grim silence the procession treaded down the mountain like a winding snake to council at the altar of the sun in the sacred canyon of their gods.

Willfully, Devlin pushed all thoughts of Moriah to the corner of his mind and concentrated on his purpose. He had to ensure that the Apaches understood the gravity of this encounter with Burkhart and followed his instructions to the letter. If not, a full-blown war would erupt and the government would send scores of well-armed dragoons to attack the Apaches.

His solemn gaze swept over Cochise's six-foot frame. The Indian leader of the Chiricahuas was broad and stout and possessed a Roman nose that was situated amid strong commanding features. His obsidian eyes bore the look of a man who had seen enough sorrow, pain, and betrayal to last him a lifetime.

Geronimo was the smaller of the two warlords, standing five feet seven inches. His chest was massive, and muscles rippled beneath his copper flesh. Thick brows set above dark, penetrating eyes, and his hawk's beak of a nose and dominant cheekbones gave him a foreboding appearance. His straight, thin mouth had not quirked in a smile in so long that Devlin wondered if Geronimo still remembered the gesture. Neither he nor the Apaches had found little amusement the past year.

The only pleasure Devlin had known had escaped him when Moriah spirited out of his life. But he wasn't going to think about that right now. He had plans to discuss, he reminded himself sternly.

"I have promised to keep my solemn vow to the Apaches . . ." Devlin began, pausing to stare into each chiseled face. "But I must have Burkhart all to myself or the People will pay with the loss of more lives."

"It is to be another trap," Makado grunted sourly. "You led our people into the valley of death once before and we will not follow you again."

Devlin studied the belligerent warrior for a long moment. It appeared that the wounds Moriah had inflicted on Makado had healed, but the brave's pride was still smarting. Makado had come to stir trouble.

Cochise raised his hand to silence the rebellious outburst. "White Shadow has proved his loyalty. For years he and his family have bought our herds of cattle and horses for fair prices. He has treated us with respect and kindness. I do not think he is a traitor."

Begrudgingly, Makado clamped his mouth shut and swallowed the half-dozen accusations he had intended to voice. He had wanted to warn the Apaches that White Shadow was a curse not a blessing, but Cochise and Geronimo were omnipotent leaders and White Shadow had deviously persuaded them to trust him.

"Speak, White Shadow, and we will listen,"

Geronimo encouraged him, flashing Makado a condescending glare. "What is it that you ask of us, if not to slash the cavalry to shreds?"

Calmly Devlin unfolded his plan, explaining his reasons for such a plot against Burkhart. He informed the Apaches that Burkhart was gathering a strike force, intent on bringing the battle to the mountains. The commander had boasted that he had handpicked seasoned soldiers for this attack.

"We must let Burkhart prove his evil ways to his own men. We must let the soldiers see that it is not retaliation Burkhart wants, but rather brutal murder. If we hand Burkhart the knife, he will slit his own throat," Devlin prophesied.

Cochise frowned bemusedly. "If you take sole responsibility for Burkhart, what is to be our purpose, if not to lessen the odds?"

A wry smile pursed Devlin's lips. "The Apache warlords will provide intimidation to make the cavalry think twice about their chances of emerging from the Apachería alive."

Devlin then went into extensive detail, outlining each phase of his plan. When he finished, even Geronimo managed a sly smile. "You are too wise to be a white man," he chuckled. "You should have been born Apache."

The praise heaped on White Shadow soured Makado's stomach. The white man pulled more weight at the tribal council than Makado himself did, and he was Apache through and through! Displaying his displeasure with the scheme that did not avenge the lives of those who had perished beneath army bullets and bayonets, Makado gathered his warriors and stalked off.

Devlin frowned warily at Makado's departing

back. The warrior could cause serious trouble if he decided to launch his own offensive while Devlin was luring Burkhart deeper into the mountains.

"I do not care if you refuse to participate," Devlin declared, halting Makado in his tracks. "But if you interfere and bring the wrath of the Army down on your people, you will be labeled the traitor, not I."

Makado's face twisted in a scowl when the dark, probing eyes of the other tribal leaders riveted on him.

"Betray our purpose, Makado, and *you* will become my crusade after Burkhart receives his just reward," Devlin said ominously.

The threat hung heavily in the air. Glaring daggers, Makado pivoted around and stomped off.

"When will Burkhart come?" Cochise wanted to know.

"When the moon is full and he can ensure that the night will not conspire against him. He is a vicious murderer, but he is not a fool. He will be followed by a cloud of dust, but it will become his cloud of doom."

After Devlin said his piece, the tribal leaders dispersed to gather their forces of warriors in preparation for the assault against Burkhart. Devlin paced beside the bubbling spring like a restless tiger. He couldn't afford to take Makado for granted. The rebellious warrior would like nothing better than for Devlin to fall from the Apache's good graces. It would take only one human error to set off an incident that could explode like a keg of blasting powder. Devlin had taken every detail into consideration, calculating his every move like a chess player weighing his options and analyzing his countertactics. One false move could cause an avalanche of disaster.

Damn, he had waited almost eighteen months to have his revenge on Burkhart. Makado had better not ruin things!

After two weeks of trekking through the mountains, Moriah had all but regained her sight. Day by day, the hazy shadows had evaporated, revealing the colors and shapes that she had never dared hope to see again. It had been six weeks since the accident, six weeks of blundering in the darkness. Regaining her vision was a wonderful blessing, but Moriah would have gladly sacrificed her sight if she could have acquired Devlin's love in the bargain. But even if she could have her wish, she knew she would only cause dissension at the Granger Ranch. Jessica didn't want her there. Jessica didn't want Moriah in the territory!

Pausing briefly on the summit, Moriah glanced back in the direction she had come, contemplating the past two weeks. She had come upon a small farm during her journey east. The good Samaritans who lived there had consented to sell her much-needed supplies and an extra set of clothes—a cream-colored flannel shirt and black breeches their son had outgrown. Laden down with supplies, and armed with the outdated rifle the farmer insisted he could spare, Moriah had propelled herself eastward on horseback until the terrain became too difficult for the winded steed.

Turning the mount loose, Moriah slung her knapsack over her shoulder and ascended into the craggy peaks, trying to chart the identical course she and Devlin had followed. Often Moriah would pause to close her eyes, attempting to recall the sounds, smells, and sensations she had experienced when she was blind. She had come upon two Apache villages nestled in the valleys and reflected on the fact that Devlin had mentioned their existence when they had passed this way.

Now that Moriah had regained her sight, she had decided what she was going to do about her future. She fully intended to return to the Valley of the Eagle, if she could locate it. She would scoop up enough gold nuggets to get her back to Texas and begin her new life. Although she yearned to travel to California and have her revenge on the Thatchers, she decided it best to take no action. She should be thankful to be rid of them once and for all, she reckoned. Having them out of her life forever was her reward . . .

The crunch of rocks beneath moccasined feet jostled Moriah from her silent reverie. Like a coiling snake, she crouched behind the slab of rock that rested beside the Apache trail.

And then there was silence. Warily, Moriah waited for a sound to alert her to danger. Minutes passed. Finally, she rose from her hiding place, certain whatever danger had approached had wandered away. But Moriah had forgotten the firm declaration Devlin had once made. "Nobody can outwait an Apache," he had once said and it seemed he was right.

Damn, of all the Indians in all the valleys in all these mountains, Makado would have to show up! Moriah knew it was he the instant she heard his rumbling laughter and mocking voice on the ridge above her.

"White Shadow has taught you well, Sunflower. But neither you nor he is Makado's match," he boasted.

Moriah had only the element of surprise on her side. Makado didn't know she had regained her sight or that she was armed to the teeth.

Like an agile cougar, the bare-chested brave leaped down to the boulder beside Moriah. She was careful to maintain a blank stare, even while she sized up her challenger. Makado was not tall, but he was as graceful and sly as a tiger. Moriah gave him full credit for being a cunning and resourceful Apache. As Devlin had once said, "It is best not to underestimate one's competition unless one plans on meeting with defeat."

"If you dropped down to pay your respects, Makado, consider them paid." Moriah groped along the boulder like the blind woman she had once been. "I bear no grudge against you. All I want is to be left alone to live beside your people in peace."

Makado admired this blond-haired wildcat's courage and unflappable spirit. She was bold to a fault and afraid of very little, it seemed. With a taunting chuckle, he snaked out a hand to grasp her forearm. Moriah didn't flinch. She merely glanced at him with a well-disciplined stare.

"And I want you, Sunflower." His voice dropped to a seductive growl that left no mistake as to his meaning.

"Why? So you can say you've had me?" Moriah had the audacity to scoff at him, but she felt she had nothing to lose in acting the reckless daredevil who defied every danger.

Another chortle rumbled in Makado's chest. "White Shadow was right about you. You do not know when to hold your tongue. I could introduce you to tortures you never imagined if you continue to challenge me."

"Worse ones than being raped by a man who doesn't know how to treat a woman like a lady?" she smirked.

Makado gnashed his teeth. Other white captives had begged for his mercy, but Moriah purposely provoked him, just to see if she could get away with it. Why he let her get away with it baffled him. But Makado vowed to have his sweet revenge. He knew forcing himself on this brazen wildcat would bring him no satisfaction. Making her want him the way she wanted White Shadow would be his ultimate goal—one that would bring Granger to his knees as nothing else could.

"We shall see which one of us is more of a man when it comes to pleasing a woman," Makado declared haughtily. "I will make you forget White Shadow, traitor to the Apache."

"I doubt that," Moriah retaliated.

After expelling a wordless growl, Makado barked an order in his native tongue. Three braves materialized from the rocks and scurried down the slopes. Moriah found herself shackled by two warriors and followed by the other while Makado led the way along the weaving path.

Just what she thought. If she had attacked Makado, she wouldn't have gotten very far. His companions would have descended on her like a swarm of angry hornets. There was naught else to do but stumble along, pretending to be blind, and wait for the braves to put their guard down. When she had the chance she would beat a hasty retreat.

Setting a swift pace, Makado strode along the towering precipices toward his destination. He intended to keep a bird's eye view on White Shadow's activities in case he was plotting to trap the Apaches. And when the moment was ripe, Makado would strike to save the all-too trusting tribal chiefs from more of White Shadow's treachery. And with this blue-eyed Sunflower as bait, Makado would lure White Shadow into a trap, instead of it being the other way around!

In pensive silence, Devlin watched the curl of dust rise from the distant canyon. Burkhart and his seasoned soldiers had begun their march from Santa Rita. The stage had been set.

"The dragon comes," Devlin murmured.

Nodding mutely, Chanos pulled a piece of flint from his pouch and built a small fire to send the signal to the other bands of Apache warriors who were positioned along the jutting peaks that lined the winding chasms to the northwest.

"I hope to hell Makado doesn't come back to cause us trouble," Devlin muttered sourly. "That mistrusting fool could be the death of all of us."

Chanos grinned wryly. "He has a personal vendetta against you, White Shadow. He resents your relationship with Geronimo and Cochise. And after what you told me about your confrontation on the way to Arizona, I think he would like to have the Angel of the Wind as his own."

"I'm thankful Moriah isn't anywhere near here," Devlin grumbled, flashing Chanos an accusing glance. "If she were, I would have to worry over which one of you would be trying to take advantage of her."

The medicine man shrugged off the disparaging remark and grinned again. "No man can capture the wind, White Shadow. But many of us would like to try, just as you did, and apparently without success. I do not understand why you take offense because many men are attracted to Moriah. She is a rare woman who challenges a man. Women were only a pastime for you until she came into your life, were they not?"

Chanos didn't wait for Devlin to reply. He continued with a reckless chuckle. "If this unique woman stirred the heart of a man such as you, why then is it so surprising that she arouses other men?"

Devlin fell silent, his gaze drifting back to the legion of soldiers that plodded toward them. Chanos had driven home the depressing point that had hounded Devlin for more than two weeks. There were some things in life that a man couldn't have, no matter how fiercely he tried. The elusive wind and the golden-haired, blue-eyed Moriah Laverty were two of them. Damnit, he hoped she was happy, wherever she was. Devlin himself was angry and frustrated and miserable.

The thin fingers of smoke that rose from the timbered rim of the canyon provoked Burkhart to bring his regiment to a halt. Narrowed green eyes focused on the black wisps of smoke, wondering what messages the savages were relating to each other.

"They know we're here," Captain John Grimes murmured to his superior officer.

"Of course they know we're here," Lyle snorted sarcastically. "Those cussed Apaches know when anything moves or invades their domain. But even with their ammunition and weapons, they are no match for us. When they attack, we'll be ready and waiting. They will confront more gunfire than they know what to do with."

But the Apaches didn't strike. They merely communicated by smoke signals throughout the day. And when the flaming red sun sank behind the rugged peaks that blocked the horizon, the regiment of soldiers began to grumble uneasily.

"They must have decided to wait until dawn," Lyle speculated as he paced around the campfire, flinging sporadic glances at the looming mountains. "It's just like them to play these cat-and-mouse games, leaving us to wonder what they're planning."

"And what if White Shadow commands them to strike at night?" one of the dragoons muttered in question. "We'll be sitting ducks in this canyon."

"Apaches don't attack at night," Lyle countered in a ridiculing tone. "They think evil spirits stalk the darkness and they huddle together like cowards and await the sun."

"Injuns are a lot of things," somebody smirked from the crisscrossed shadows. "But they ain't cowards."

"If you recall, Commander, White Shadow and his braves sneaked up on us several times at night to steal your mount and our supplies," John Grimes piped up and then wilted when Lyle flashed him a mutinous glare.

"That wasn't an attack," Lyle growled in contradiction. "It was all Granger's doing."

"I heard Granger died a long time ago," came another unidentified voice from the perimeters of the camp.

"I heard he was charmed and that no bullets or arrows could bring him down," someone reported.

"I don't think you know the Apaches and White Shadow as well as you think you do, Commander," one of the dragoons muttered.

"I don't like this waiting game," another soldier grumbled nervously. "We could all be dead if you try to second-guess those renegades. If you ask me, we should—"

"I'm the one who gives the orders and makes the decisions!" Lyle bellowed at his troops. "I have been fighting the Apaches long enough to understand their ways. We're safe until dawn. And when the sun comes up we can expect those murdering savages to pour down from the slopes like a flash flood rolling through a ravine. But they will be the sitting ducks, not us!"

"I think Burkhart is a little too confident and a lot crazy," one of the soldiers said confidentially to Captain Grimes.

Grimes didn't second that opinion verbally, but he was thinking the same thing himself. Burkhart had become so obsessed with this mission that he had taken to talking to himself since they left Fort McLane. For the past month Burkhart had been in a most irascible mood, cursing the Granger brothers for bringing charges against him, swearing vengeance on every redskin on the continent. The one-armed commander had been drunk more than he had been sober and he cursed the legend of White Shadow that threatened his commission in the Army.

Scooting down onto his pallet, Captain Grimes left Burkhart to pace back and forth while the regiments slept. Still scowling, Lyle smacked five of his men on the shoulder and ordered them to stand guard during the night. Annoyed, he plopped down on his bedroll and glared at the full moon and stars. Lyle knew the Apaches would take advantage of the opportunity. He had purposely halted in this valley that provided a natural fort at one end. The huge slabs of rocks would serve as a shield from which the Army could blast the Apaches to smithereens when they tried to descend the rough terrain. The timber line was on the higher elevations and the lower zones offered the Indians little protection from being spotted. Even as skilled at hiding as the Apaches were, they couldn't evaporate into thin air and materialize at will. Not here, not in this bowl-shaped chasm.

The Apaches would come, Lyle assured himself arrogantly. And by the following evening, the riddled bodies of those savage heathens would be strewn in the grass. That satisfying picture put a sinister smile on his lips. When he was finished with the bastards the Army would heap medals on him instead of dragging him to a court-martial!

Chapter 23

Lyle Burkhart yelped in shock when the rattle of a snake jerked him from his restless sleep. In the dim light of dawn, Lyle stared at the sidewinder with its spiked horns above its gleaming black eyes. Panicked, he reached for his Colt and fired at the quilt over his feet where the viper lay coiled to strike. If he hadn't been a crackshot he would have blown off his toes.

The sound of the discharging weapon echoed around the chasm and brought every soldier straight out of his bedroll. Gasping for breath, Lyle watched the snake flip onto its back before the eerie rattle died in the silence. Bracing himself on the stub of his left arm, Lyle burst into a string of profanity. There, beside the serpent, lay the white-quilled arrow that indicated White Shadow had been prowling about.

Grimly, Captain Grimes ambled over to pluck the arrow from the ground and then twirled it in his fingers. "It seems to me that White Shadow is after you, Commander. He could have slit any number of throats when he crept into camp, but he singled you out."

Lyle muttered a few more salty curses and rolled to his feet. "Our mission is to search out the Apache strongholds and relieve the white settlers and miners in the area of these menacing savages." He stabbed the captain with a blunt-end finger. "And you, Grimes, are not being paid to speculate, only to fight."

While Lyle stalked over to ensure that his saddle-bags hadn't been sabotaged with scorpions and snakes, the other men glanced morosely at one another. To them, the incident with the viper and arrow suggested the Apaches were toying with them. Burkhart, however, was obsessed with his purpose, and they feared his eagerness to massacre the Apaches would get them all killed.

As the sun peeked above the canyon wall to paint shades of lavender ánd gold on the jagged slopes, the regiment waited with bated breath, expecting to be attacked from all directions at once. Still the Apaches didn't come.

Scowling at the tactics of the cunning savages and their Indian-loving blood brother, Lyle rapped out the order to mount up. If the Apaches wouldn't come to the Army, then the Army would take the battle to the Apaches! Sooner or later those heathens would fight. But as Moriah had discovered, nobody could outlast an Apache or the legendary White Shadow. It took Lyle a while, but he finally began to realize that he was dealing with an enemy far more patient and crafty than he was. What a blow to his stupendous pride to admit it!

As the hours blended one into another, curls of smoke spiraled into a sky while fleeting clouds paraded above the looming granite shoulders of the mountains. Lyle followed the smoke, winding deeper into the rocky terrain and timbered slopes that could leave a man feeling lost and disoriented.

"If you ask me, the Apaches are taking us exactly

where they want us to go," Captain Grimes murmured, glancing apprehensively at the faces in the rock formations that seemed to be smirking down at him.

"I didn't ask you," Lyle growled irritably. He was spoiling for a fight, and the Apaches refused to give him one. Damn, what did it take to lure those son of a bitches out? This waiting and wondering was turning his mood black as pitch.

When the sullen procession of soldiers veered around the sharp bend that led into a steep-walled canyon, the men began to grumble and stare uneasily around them.

"It's a trap," someone in the rear of the regiment declared.

Lyle jerked his steed to a halt and glowered at his insolent dragoons. "I'll have the whole lot of you court-martialed when we return to headquarters if I hear another outburst from the ranks!"

If Lyle would have requested a show of hands, he would have been the only one who believed the cavalry had a snowball's chance in hell of riding out of this valley of death alive. But Burkhart didn't have the courtesy to take a survey. He was out for blood and he didn't care how many soldiers' lives it cost.

"Commander, look up there!" Grimes shouted when he saw the movement behind the boulders.

In eerie dread, the dragoons watched the white stallion that had been stolen from Burkhart three months earlier clomp down the narrow trail. Beads and feathers adorned the rope halter, and white-quilled arrows dangled from the saddle blanket like ornaments. Sitting upon the steed's back was an effigy that was stuffed with grass and leaves and garbed in a double-breasted frock coat with golden epaulets and shiny buttons. The jacket looked exactly like the one Burkhart was presently wearing. The white sack that served as the rider's head was capped with cascading tufts of dyed buffalo hair that resembled the color of Burkhart's carrot-red mane. Upon the ghastly-looking head of the effigy was a dashing Napoleonic hat that was adorned with gold studs and plumes.

Knowing White Shadow and the Apache renegades were mocking Commander Burkhart wasn't half as bad as the emotional blow provoked by the white-quilled arrow etched on the uniform with blood that protruded from the jacket—right smack dab through the heart.

The appearance of the missing stallion and its doomed rider sent a wave of murmurs undulating through the ranks. "It looks as if White Shadow intends to settle his score with you," someone had the nerve to say.

Lyle swore fluently and wheeled his steed around to glare at his disobedient men. "Curse your souls to hell!" he roared. His voice thundered through the chasm like a booming cannon.

"It looks like our souls have already been cursed" came another disgruntled voice.

Despite the reluctance of the men to proceed, Burkhart barked the command. Sitting tall and straight in the saddle, Lyle marched forward, leading the wary procession of soldiers who would have preferred to be anywhere except under Madman Burkhart's command in the very heart of Apacheland!

A devilish smile bordered Devlin's lips as he watched the regiment pick its way through the V-shaped canyon. Burkhart's arrogance was turning him into every kind of fool, Devlin thought as he stared at the leader of the troops. If Devlin wanted to launch an attack, he could have massacred the cavalry here and now, even though the Apaches were outnumbered four to one. Geronimo and Cochise, who had several axes to grind with the Army, would have delighted in settling old scores. But out of respect for what White Shadow was trying to accomplish, they had consented to direct the fight to the man who had instigated so many ruthless massacres against their women and children.

Trekking along the towering slopes, Devlin and his rank of warriors trailed the dragoons. The soldiers were sipping from their canteens as if water were a limitless commodity. The sun beat down on them and the towering walls blocked off the wind, leaving not a breath of air stirring in the chasm.

Very soon the dragoons would wish they had been more sparing with the precious water, Devlin predicted. Still sporting a wicked smile, Devlin motioned for Chanos to crouch beside him. From behind the boulder that overlooked the small spring they listened to the scouts inform the troops that water lay ahead.

The sight of the water sparkling in the late-afternoon sunlight caused the plodding procession to quicken its pace. But when they reached the spring, their anticipation turned to gloomy dread.

A murderous sneer swallowed Lyle's homely features when he spied the bleached bones of the skeleton that was propped beside the spring. Upon the skull sat another plumed chapeau that resembled the one Lyle was wearing. Another white-quilled arrow protruded from the ribs of the skeleton. To make matters even worse, a skull and crossbones had been placed upon the slab of rock directly in front of the springs, indicating contaminated water.

Another grumble of voices erupted from the regiment when their hopes of filling their canteens were dashed. Lyle snarled and brandished his fist at the unseen enemy who had led them through this valley of hell and then taunted them with poisoned water.

The horses pranced under their riders, anxious to slurp from the spring, but not one soldier dared to risk his steed or himself to test the purity of the water.

"I think we should turn back," Captain Grimes declared. "Without a water supply, we don't stand a chance. The Apaches know the location of every spring in these mountains. But we could scout for days without finding one. Even if we did find one, our scouts probably wouldn't live long enough to return with a report. We should abort this mission and—"

"Silence!" Lyle bellowed, his green eyes spitting flames. "We will find another spring to refill our canteens—all of us together! And we are not now, nor will we ever, turn tail and run from these goddamn Apaches!"

"It's wishful thinking to believe we'll find another spring" came a muttered voice from somewhere in the center of the ranks. "We'll die before we quench our thirst."

To lend credence to that gloomy remark, the Apaches suddenly appeared on the ridges that lined three sides of the chasm. No shots were fired from the precipices, even though there were dozens of itchy fingers resting lightly on hairpin triggers. Every bow had been drawn and aimed at blue-coated targets, but not one shower of arrows sliced through the air to cut down the dragoons. The Apaches merely stood in grim reminder that the regiment which had invaded their domain was a pack of fools who blundered in where not even angels feared to tread.

The soldiers shifted skittishly in their saddles as the parade of Apaches wound along the narrow trails like slithering snakes. The howl of coyotes fluttered in the breeze and the methodic beat of a distant drum hammered in rhythm with the thudding hearts of the dragoons who were bottled in the sweltering canyon.

"If this ain't hell, it's as close as I ever want to be," one of the men scowled, hooking his finger in the collar of his jacket to relieve the pressure that made him feel as if he were about to choke.

With the sharp command for silence, Lyle gestured toward the spiral of smoke that curled from the timber to the northwest. Grimly, the dragoons followed the maniac who took the warning signs as a challenge instead of a hint to get out while they still could. Thoughts of mutiny flickered through every man's head. They all knew their hours were numbered, but no one could convince Burkhart of that. He wanted to settle his feud with White Shadow and exterminate every Apache renegade from the face of the earth.

To Moriah's chagrin, Makado and his braves didn't pause for more than a few minutes to rest. She had hoped she would have the opportunity to slip away long before now, but it had been a full day since she had encountered Makado and not once had he or his warriors left her alone long enough to dare an escape.

When Makado finally did stop for the night to make camp, Moriah became apprehensive. If it was rape he intended, he was the one with all the opportunity. The thought of being subjected to his degrading abuse made Moriah's skin crawl with repulsion. She wanted no other man's touch, not after she had known the pleasure of Devlin's caress. She had planned to go to her grave with the memory of only one man on her mind and in her heart. It looked as if she wouldn't be granted even that wish. Another of her dashed hopes, she mused dispiritedly.

Makado watched the golden-haired beauty like a hawk, visualizing himself in her arms, imagining himself taming her wild heart. But threatening her into submission was a waste of time, he knew. Makado had tried that once before.

Pensively, Makado glanced at his three companions who had crouched down beside the fire to roast the rabbit one of them had snared. Now was his chance to woo his stubborn captive and melt the wall of ice that encased her heart. Determined of purpose, Makado strode over to the pallet where Moriah sat staked to the ground to prevent her escape.

Careful not to look up and alert Makado that she could see far better than he thought she could, Moriah stared off into space. When Makado plunked down, brushing his arm against hers, then and only then did she flinch.

Gently, he lifted her face to his. "I am not always the heathen you believe me to be, Sunflower," he murmured in his most persuasive voice.

"Thank you for clearing up my misconception," Moriah sassed, slapping his hand away as if it were a pesky insect.

Grinding his teeth, Makado tried again. "I have no wish to hurt you, only to pleasure you. But you must meet me halfway."

Moriah wasn't meeting him period! Her raised chin and clenched jaw said as much.

Giving way to temptation, Makado took her lips under his and pressed her to the ground. The urge to defend herself from his amorous assault warred with logic. Moriah forced herself to lie there like a stone slab, feeling nothing, giving nothing in return.

When she didn't respond, Makado levered upon an elbow to peer down at the stubborn beauty who was staring at the starry sky. "Is White Shadow's memory so strong?" he scoffed. "If you are trying to be faithful to him, you waste your time, Sunflower. I was with White Shadow only a few days ago at council. There are Apache maids who have pleasured him since he let you go. You grasp at straws."

The remark cut like a dagger. Moriah told herself she had no hold on Devlin now. He thought she was gone forever. She couldn't expect him to pine for her the way she pined for him. He didn't love her the way she loved him, after all. The bitter truth was that Devlin was probably thankful to have her out of his life, but knowing he had turned to other women so quickly hurt her as nothing else could.

Suddenly, Moriah didn't care if she perished in her escape attempt. The frustration caused by Makado's remark made her blood boil. All she knew was that she wanted to be alone to wrestle with this anguishing ache that burned in the pit of her stomach. She had to devise a way to do that even though Makado and his companions were hovering around her, barely allowing her to breathe.

"Do you want me because of White Shadow or for myself?" Moriah quizzed him.

The Apache renegade trailed a bronzed finger over her exquisite features, marveling at the satiny texture of her skin. "Both," he admitted.

"And you would take me, staked to the ground, like a wild mustang to be broken?" Moriah muttered at him. "Surely you know by now that the tighter I am tied, the harder I fight."

Makado's English, meager at best, failed him when Moriah rapidly delivered her comments. "Again, Sunflower," he insisted. "But slower this time."

"Must I be tied like a wild creature who rebels against captivity?" she summed up.

An amused smile traced his lips. "You *are* a wild creature," he contended.

"And I defy the chains. A woman does not feel put upon when she is free to give, not *staked* to *take!*"

Makado considered this for a long moment and then pulled his dagger from his moccasin to slash the rope that bound Moriah's right wrist.

Criminey, now what? Moriah asked herself nervously. She needed his knife to ensure that it didn't spear into her back when she dashed for freedom. Her mind wrestled with alternatives.

"Where are your companions, Makado?" she asked, even though she could see perfectly well where they were. "Will you humiliate me by letting them watch us? Will I also be expected to pleasure them when you have no more use for me?"

"You will be mine alone," Makado assured her. "You will be my woman." His lusty gaze flicked over the trim-fitting flannel shirt and breeches that hugged her curvaceous figure like a second set of skin. "You will need no other man, Sunflower."

"Are there trees nearby where we can have privacy from gawking eyes?" She knew there were, but Makado didn't know she knew, and Moriah preferred to keep it that way.

A smile of hungry anticipation glistened in his obsidian eyes as he wrapped his hand around hers and hoisted her to her feet. After rattling a request in his native tongue, Makado led Moriah into the thicket. When he encircled her in his arms and bent her into his muscled contours, Moriah concentrated solely on her plan of escape.

As Makado drew her to the ground, lost to the throb of passion that dulled his brain, Moriah slid her hand down his leg, which was draped over her thighs. Her supposed caress suddenly transformed into lightning-quick reflexes. Before Makado realized the kiss she offered was only a distraction, Moriah reached into his moccasins to swipe his dagger. And even more quickly, the stiletto lay at Makado's throat, threatening to cut loose his vocal chords if he dared to yelp for help.

Staring frog-eyed, Makado watched Moriah worm her wrist from the rope. When she ordered him to roll onto his belly, he did as he was told. Makado knew full well that this she-cat could and would attack. He still bore the scars on his arm and rib as proof. The naked steel of his own dagger lay on his back, making him starkly aware that Moriah would run him through if he moved a muscle. Swiftly, she secured his wrists. The rending of cloth suggested Moriah had ripped the hem of her shirt to employ it as a gag that would keep him silent.

When Makado was bound and gagged, Moriah slashed the leather strap that hung diagonally across his chest and used it to stake his foot to the tree. Rising, she smiled triumphantly at the warrior who didn't realize he'd been had until it was too late.

"You were willing to offer your trust and gentleness," Moriah told him. "I do appreciate that, I really do. You proved you do have a heart deep down beneath the bitterness and mistrust . . . Am I going too fast for you, my friend?"

The disgruntled warrior muttered into the gag that was thick with Moriah's alluring scent and shook his head in reply.

"But I cherish my freedom, just as you do. I wish to pick and choose a man, not to be coerced to gain favors from you," Moriah murmured as she backed into the shadow of the trees. "I cannot be your woman, Makado. I will never belong to any man, not even White Shadow . . ."

And then she was gone and Makado mentally kicked himself for forgetting how cunning the vixen was. But she was a fool if she thought she could elude him forever. He could pick his way through this labyrinth of mountains blindfolded. They would meet again, he promised himself fiercely. And next time she would be his. He would refuse to fall into another of her cunning traps!

Flouncing like a fish out of water, Makado flopped onto his back and yelled for assistance. But his companions misinterpreted the meaning of the muffled sounds and merely snickered to themselves while they sat beside the fire, sipping *tiswin*. After ten minutes of listening to the muted noises, they grew suspicious and crept over to investigate. The instant they spied Makado, they rushed to free him. Mortified, Makado growled the order for the braves to scatter and retrieve the devious hellcat who had eluded him.

To the Apache, trickery was more highly prized than bravery. Although Makado resented being made to look the fool in front of his warriors and was infuriated that he had been outfoxed, he admired Sunflower's keen wit. She had issued a direct challenge that he had to accept to save face. He would find her, Makado vowed as he searched the canopy of trees. And the last intimate victory would be his!

* * *

The Apaches, who naturally assumed Moriah had fled through the valley, gave chase. But the fact was, Moriah had employed the tactic Devlin had taught her of burying herself in the grass. She had wriggled down, only fifty yards from the clump of trees. As soon as the coast was clear, she sneaked back to the campfire to fetch the roasted meat and her supplies. Since the braves had headed south, she propelled herself up the eastern slope to follow the trail that skimmed the peaks.

Moriah didn't gloat over her successful escape. She was too busy cursing Devlin for turning to another female the moment she was out of his life. That rake! In memory of what they'd shared the past two months, the least he could have done was to observe a few weeks of celibacy. But no, White Shadow was spreading himself thin at the Apache villages. Damn that man! He had proved his affection for her was only passion deep, just as she thought all along. Now that she was out of his life, he had taken to seducing any female within reach.

Moriah stamped through the mountain passes, refusing to rest until she had put a safe distance between herself and Makado. Men! They were all alike. All they wanted from a woman was a warm body and a few moments of physical satisfaction. Moriah assured herself she was better off without any of them. She would haunt these mountains until she found the Apache gold in the Valley of the Eagle. And then she would carry off enough nuggets to keep her in a modest manner. She wasn't going to have any contact with the male of the species for the rest of her life. They were worse than a colony of lepers!

Chapter 24

Lyle gave out with another yelp of shock when he woke to find a family of scorpions crawling on his chest. A white-quilled arrow had been slipped into his hand during the night, the infuriating reminder that White Shadow had put a curse on him.

Swatting the deadly insects off his blanket, Lyle rolled to his feet to stamp the pests into the ground. A raft of curses floated through the canyon as the sun spilled over the towering precipices like molten lava rolling from the crater of a volcano.

The incessant murmur of voices caused Lyle to pivot around. He glared murderously into each grim face that stared back at him. "Mount up!" he ordered ominously. "It will take more than a few scorpions and snakes to deter me from my mission."

"We took a vote last night and it seems to us that the Apaches don't want to fight," one dragoon dared to say. "We've been wandering around this maze of mountains for three days and our supplies and waters are low. We think it's best to turn back."

Lyle puffed up with so much indignation that he resembled an inflated bagpipe. "Those bastards will fight when we get close to their stronghold." He inhaled a furious breath. "Poltroons! That's what all of you are!" he said through a twisted snarl. "I order you to mount up and fall into procession."

Grimly, Captain Grimes stepped forward to confront the raging commander. "We all agree this is a waste of time and lives. The men have put me in charge of the regiment."

"*I* am still in command of this legion," Lyle blared, his voice ricocheting off the walls. "You will do what I tell you *when* I tell you, Captain!"

John Grimes shook his head. "Not this time, Burkhart. You're letting vengeance overrule logic. This battle is between you and White Shadow. The fact that the Apaches refuse to engage us bears evidence of that."

Blind fury overcame Lyle. He whipped his pistol from his holster to gun down his traitorous junior officer. John Grimes and every dragoon within fifteen feet of him dived sideways to avoid being blown to kingdom come by the raging lunatic.

While Grimes grabbed his wounded leg and stared incredulously at his snarling commander, Lyle backed away, wildly aiming his pistol every direction at once. "Lily-livered cowards," he hissed. "You bastards! None of you are fit to serve with me." Green eyes blazed over the stunned faces of the cavalry. "Desert me if you wish, but you will go without your weapons, food, and canteens."

When he gestured for his men to make a mound of their pistols and rifles, as well as their water-dry canteens, the soldiers obeyed. In Burkhart's frenzied state of mind he would be firing without provocation and John Grimes wouldn't be the only one nursing a wound.

Lyle made wild gestures with the stub of his arm

and spewed venomous curses. "Go crawl onto your mounts and slither off like whipped pups," he growled. "Those murdering Apaches will cut you down and leave you to the buzzards after they torture you."

Better left to the Apaches and buzzards than this crazed maniac, John Grimes reckoned as he hobbled off on his bloodied leg. Not one man volunteered to follow Burkhart into the canyon of doom. They tramped along in Grime's wake, casting glances over their shoulders to ensure that Burkhart didn't drill bullets into their departing backs.

Lyle cursed a rabid streak while his men mounted their steeds and turned back in the direction they had come. Scowling at the legend of White Shadow and Apache cunning, Lyle gathered as many rifles and pistols as he could stuff in his belt and jacket. After slinging several canteens over the pommel of the saddle, he swung onto his horse. He vowed to confront White Shadow face-to-face before he returned to Santa Rita. He had nothing to lose, thanks to Devlin Granger and his relentless pursuit. But they would settle this feud once and for all—if the bastard was still alive!

Lyle followed the puffs of smoke that led him through the labyrinth of chasms. With each plodding step his mount took, Lyle swore to blow that Indian-loving son of a bitch to bits!

A relieved sigh escaped Devlin's lips as he watched the dragoons retreat through the canyon. At long last he had Burkhart right where he wanted him. The past few days Devlin had scanned the towering peaks, expecting to see Makado and his warriors appear to instigate a battle. But Makado hadn't come. Devlin had no way of knowing Moriah had inadvertently assisted him in routing the cavalry without incident or that Makado was too busy trying to hunt down the elusive sprite to reach the canyon and cause trouble for White Shadow.

"You have proved your skills as an Apache," Cochise murmured. "You kept your promise and we will keep ours. Burkhart is yours to avenge."

Devlin nodded gratefully as the Chirachua warriors clustered around him. "I cannot bring back the lives Burkhart cost the Apache, but I will ensure he sheds no blood other than his own."

"And when you have settled this feud, you will have more than repaid the debt you felt you owed to us," Geronimo chimed in. "We tried to befriend the Americans and they repaid our trust with treachery. There are too many Burkharts in the cavalry. The Apache will never know peace until the white-eyes give us back the homeland they threaten to take from us. We will not suffer the degradation of being herded onto reservations like cattle. We will fight for our pride and our home until we have no more strength to fight, even though I fear we face a losing battle."

Devlin knew that Geronimo possessed the powers of precognition. No doubt his grim prediction of continuous war would come true. The Apache battle had only begun. Devlin couldn't fight all their wars for them, but he could lend support and provide supplies to sustain this proud clan when winters were harsh and food was scarce.

"We leave Burkhart to you," Chanos whispered, clasping Devlin's arm in a gesture of friendship. "You will always be welcome in Apachería, even if the other white-eyes are not. With you, the Apaches will always live in peace."

Scooping up his rifle, Devlin tracked along the trail to remain far enough ahead of Burkhart to lead the murdering bastard into the Valley of the Eagle. The trap for Burkhart had already been set and waited to be sprung. Wearing a triumphant smile, Devlin trekked past the Gila Cliff Dwellings, confident that he would have his revenge after a year and a half of plotting and waiting. They would meet again—alone. . . .

Frowning, Makado crouched down to press his hand upon the footprints he had discovered after a full day of wandering back and forth through the maze of chasms and rocky ravines. Moriah had been here, and not too long ago, he speculated. Although his warriors had gone to hunt game before returning to the village of wickiups in the White Mountains, Makado had been obsessed with finding Moriah. He had intended to keep a watchful eye on White Shadow, but his personal pride was at stake and Sunflower's tormenting image lured him. Twice, the fiery she-cat had made him look the fool. Now Makado wanted more than revenge. He wanted Moriah.

It amazed him that she could weave through these perilous passes blind as she was without tumbling to her death. Had he known she had also deceived him about that, he would have been even more mortified than he already was.

Agilely, Makado rose to his feet to follow the tracks that disappeared and then reappeared on the stony trail. He had vowed not to return to the village in the

White Mountains until he recaptured the blue-eyed vixen who had lured him with her beauty and undaunted spirit. She would be his—the possession that even White Shadow had not been able to claim. Taking what had once been White Shadow's for a time sweetened the challenge of conquest for Makado. Furthermore, he resented White Shadow's relationship with Geronimo and Cochise and wouldn't be satisfied until he had White Shadow's prestige and the one woman who met each challenge as competently as any man.

An agonized groan tripped from Moriah's lips as she propped herself up on one elbow. She had weaved through the mountains to elude Makado, pausing occasionally to close her eyes and allow her other senses to determine if she were following the trail that led into the Valley of the Eagle.

The scents and sounds had become her compass, and she had found herself standing upon the ridge of the Gila Cliff Dwellings, seeing them as Devlin had described them to her a lifetime ago. She had relied upon the feel of sunshine on her face and recalled the downward descent they had made from the dwellings. The prevailing wind had always been on her cheeks as they trekked toward the Valley of the Eagle and Moriah followed her instincts, hoping they would lead her to the legendary treasure.

Three times the past day, Moriah thought she had finally located the mythical valley of gold that was located beside the temple of the sun. She had ventured into one cave that she swore was identical to the one in which she and Devlin had stayed. But there had been no eagles soaring over the valley as the legend suggested. Neither had there been any rock formations that resembled the temple of the sun that Chanos had described while they wandered around the valley during Devlin's absence.

Moriah, perseverent and determined though she was, was getting a mite discouraged. She began to wonder if she would be able to retrace her footsteps to the Apache gold. If she failed in her mission, she vowed she would live as a recluse as she had first planned to do when she fled from the Thatchers.

Bewilderedly, Moriah blinked at the sunshine that sprayed through the opening of the cavern where she had spent the last hours of the night. Her jaw dropped in astonishment and she gaped at the configuration of stone that formed the mouth of the cave.

"Beyond the Moons of winter skies
The eagle of the valley flies—
Until all battles have been won."

Moriah murmured the first stanza of the legend and then laughed in delighted realization. The bird to which the poem referred was staring her in the face! The eagle that soared forever didn't refer to the winged fowl that glided across the sky, but rather to the formation of rock that surrounded the entrance of the cave! There, like a graceful eagle in motionless flight, composed of morning sunlight that sprayed into the cavern, was the legendary eagle of the valley. When Moriah was blind she had actually bumped her head on the low-hanging stone that formed the curve of the eagle's neck!

Astonished, Moriah twisted around to see the sunlight cast its golden image on the rock wall behind her. And sure enough, there was another image of an eagle in flight, burning against the stone and surrounded by the shadowed walls of the cave.

Moriah was on her feet in a single bound. She scurried down the winding path to the valley below.

> "The heart on fire forever lies
> Hot beneath Old Man Mountain's eyes
> At the lost temple of the Sun."

Over and over again, Moriah recited the second stanza while her heart raced in anticipation. Chanos had taken her to the sacred altar and Moriah had felt the towering stone slabs. But the canyon was a complicated maze of wrinkled rock formations. Some of the boulders resembled the Egyptian sphinx and others were reminiscent of carved totem poles. Huge mounds of weatherbeaten rocks even looked as if they had been staked upon each other by the hands of a strong and powerful mythical god.

It was no wonder the Apaches considered this obscure valley the sacred home of the great spirits. The fantastic rock formations certainly staggered the imagination and left one wondering if some supernatural forces had conspired to build this stone garden in the remote regions of the Southwest.

Moriah had felt her way along this spectacular valley, but seeing it at close range boggled the mind! How would she ever determine which massive formation was the temple of the sun when there were so many incredible towers of stone?

And then she saw it, and her legs very nearly folded up beneath her. The slanting sunlight beamed over the spiraled pillar of stone that rose from the canyon floor. The spire wasn't the tallest one in the chasm, but rather the fingerlike monument that stood between two ominous mounds of rock. The sun was at just the exact angle to leave a stream of light glinting down into the valley like a beam that pointed direction. Moriah followed the phenomenal beam of light that lanced off four parallel slabs of stone that leaned against the face of a vertical cliff.

"The heart of fire forever lies . . ." Moriah whispered, spellbound. There, between the two six-foot-tall slabs that lay closest to the face of the looming mountain wall, was the image of a burning heart, created by the slanting angle of sunlight that curled around the rim of the jagged stone slabs. "The heart of the sun, forever on fire," Moriah murmured, astounded by the miraculous effect created by the sunlight and shadows.

Moriah crouched to scan the looming walls of the canyon and repeated the last stanza of the legend.

"Apache Gold—the white man's prize—
Bleeds in the tears the Old Man cries—
Until the Spirit rain is done."

Where the devil was the Old Man of the Mountain that the legend kept referring to? Her gaze circled the surrounding cliffs. And where was the spring in which she had swum before she disturbed the den of vipers? She knew it had to be here somewhere among these phenomenal slabs and mounds of rock.

Moriah swore she had lingered beside the heart of fire for well over an hour, surveying the rocky peaks without seeing the resemblance of a human face etched in stone. But lo and behold, as the sun made its regal ascent, diminishing the heart of fire until it disappeared into shadows, the glittering light slashed across the northeastern slopes.

With a gasp, Moriah watched the sun reveal what looked to be the jutting brows and long straight nose of a wrinkled face. The shadows against the rugged cliff formed the dark eyes and the curved mouth of the mystical Old Man of the Mountain. His angular features and somber eyes seemed to stare down over the valley where the legendary eagle soared in eternal flight. On each side of the wrinkled stone face, piñon and juniper trees trailed downward like braids of hair.

Scrambling through the rugged terrain of boulders and monstrous stone slabs, Moriah approached the Old Man. She blinked in amazement when the sun revealed the sparkling rocks in his stony face. Veins of gold streamed across the Old Man's cheeks and disappeared into the hump of rock that resembled the breast plate of a knight from days of old.

There, hidden from view by the looming mounds of stones, was the spring beside which Moriah and Devlin had made wild sweet love. The thought stabbed at Moriah's heart like a dull knife. So many splendorous memories, so many bitter nightmares of a love that couldn't survive.

Her blindness and Devlin's obsession of avenging Burkhart had torn them apart, Jessica's cruel accusations had severed their fragile bond, and Devlin's betrayal of turning to other women when Moriah walked out of his life had flung them apart permanently.

Moriah could understand that Devlin had succumbed to his primal desires now that their relationship was over and done, but she could never forgive him for sleeping in another woman's arms so soon after they had parted. Damn him. He had lived a life of celibacy while he plotted his revenge against

Burkhart, but he didn't return to that chaste way of life when Moriah left. Curse him! The fact that he yielded to lust assured her that his affection for her was nowhere near as enduring as his need to seek vengeance on Burkhart.

Willfully, Moriah flung the bittersweet memories aside and ambled around the gigantic mounds of stone that stood beside the spring. Cautiously, she inspected the area for snakes that might be lounging in the shade beside the cool water. In her haste to descend into the valley, she had left all her weapons behind. If she stumbled onto a nest of vipers only a speedy flight from the area would save her from a painful bite.

A curious frown knitted her brow when she glanced down into the clear depths of the pool. In the middle of the rippling spring that was surrounded by a circle of stones were glittering gold nuggets and a bleached skull. Where the eyes should have been were two huge nuggets. Encircling the skull was a ring of sandstone upon which sat . . .

Moriah frowned again. She couldn't be sure because of the ripples caused by the trickling water, but it almost looked like a gigantic necklace of gold nuggets bound together by a rope.

Fascinated, Moriah waded out into the pool to investigate. Standing inside the circling necklace of gold nuggets, Moriah tried to pluck up the skull and retrieve the gigantic nuggets. Lifting the skull took a great deal of strength. With a grimace and a fierce heave, Moriah managed to move the skull that had been weighted down with rocks.

A startled gasp burst from her lips when the necklace of rope and gold nuggets bit at her ankles. Too late, she realized she had walked into a booby trap!

The temptation to reach for the largest nuggets had wrought disaster. The skull that was filled with stones held the rope that was tied to the bent juniper tree that formed part of the Old Man's braid. When Moriah sprung the trap, she was dragged across the pool, unable to grasp anything that would prevent her from being yanked up with the recoiling rope. Her shoulder slammed against the slab of stone that resembled a warrior's shield, causing her to groan painfully. Moriah was left hanging upside down, staring up at the Old Man, whose smile was growing ever wider as the sun climbed into the sky, casting its brilliant light on the wrinkled stone face above her.

Damn, whoever set this cunning trap had preyed upon her greed for the egg-size nuggets that had been implanted in the anchor of a skull! Moriah cursed the mastermind who had designed this ingenious snare. She would probably hang here forever, becoming the gloomy omen that warned other seekers of Apache gold away from the unexpected pitfalls and the curse of the valley.

Blood rushed to her head, and Moriah swore at the face of stone that grinned tauntingly down at her. Of all the rotten luck! It was true that he who solved the riddle of the legend could never emerge from this obscure canyon to tell of the riches to be found. If the rattlesnakes that ventured to the spring didn't get her first, starvation and hanging in this upside down position eventually would. Moriah sighed dismally. Her future looked grim . . .

And there she hung for what seemed hours, tormented by the spring from which she couldn't drink, haunted by the glittering nuggets of gold that remained just out of her reach. The Old Man silently mocked her foolish greed, and Moriah dreaded the late-afternoon hours when the vipers arrived to cool themselves in the shade of the jutting rocks. Her eyes fastened on the sparkling nuggets of gold that had fallen from the rich vein that formed the tears the Old Man shed when the winter snows melted in the sun.

What bitter irony I have discovered in the Valley of the Eagle, Moriah mused dizzily. She had come so close to the Apache gold. Now she might as well have been a thousand miles away for all the good the gold would do her. This was the beginning of the tormenting end, she reckoned. Her fate was to suffer until the final veil of darkness dropped over her.

Chapter 25

Lyle Burkhart scowled through parched lips as he tripped over the loose pebbles that lined the path he had been following. He had been forced to release his mount the previous night because the terrain had become too rough and the animal had turned up lame. The soles of Lyle's boots were so thin from scraping against the sharp rocks that he swore he was walking barefoot. But Lyle had foregone every comfort and convenience in his maddening pursuit of Devlin Granger.

Lyle knew for certain the bastard was still alive. Three separate times, he had appeared on the towering ridges above him, taunting Lyle until he was swearing in fluent profanity. But each time Granger had positioned himself with the sun at his back, making it impossible for Lyle to blow the looming giant off the mountain. The blinding light was Granger's shield. Although Lyle had fired his Winchester, he hit nothing but rock. To infuriate Lyle to the extreme, Granger's laughter rang through the chasm before he vanished into thin air.

"Curse your soul!" Lyle bellowed, only to have the

cliffs and vertical walls of the chasm fling his words back in his face.

"You want me, Burkhart?" came Devlin's echoing voice from only God knew where. "Come and get me. If you are the victor of this battle, then the Apache gold is yours. And if I emerge the conqueror, I'll feed your poisoned heart to the mountain lions!"

"You son of a bitch, you've cost me my commission and my regiment," Lyle growled as he stalked toward the taunting voice that eluded him. "You protect those bloodthirsty savages as if they were your own flesh and blood, but you will die just as they have. This time I'll fill you with so much buckshot that no Apache medicine man can bring you back to life!"

Like a bounding mountain goat, Devlin sprang into the rocks that lined the entrance to the Valley of the Eagle. His mocking denials lured Lyle along the rugged path. Very soon, Burkhart would be left to explore the valley and to test his avarice. Devlin smiled devilishly at the thought of Burkhart falling into his well-laid snare at the springs. Lyle would wander around a day or so before he stumbled onto the spring. The gold would be his downfall. And when that murdering bastard was hanging upside down by his heels, Devlin would introduce him to the Apache brand of torture that was befitting the cruel violence Burkhart had practiced on the Indians. The malicious commander would die by the code by which he lived. Burkhart would endure the same hell he had forced on the Apache men, women, and children.

The resounding voices drew Makado's wary

frown. Like a stalking tiger, he approached the rim of the remote canyon. Clutching his rifle, Makado leaped from the path to crouch behind the slabs of stone.

Although none of the three men knew it just yet, they had formed the three sides of a triangle that left them equal distances apart in the Valley of the Eagle. Below him, Makado could hear the one-armed commander tripping over the obstacles of sharp stones and swearing epithets. In the distance, the trickling of rocks suggested there was someone else darting around the canyon. Makado wasn't certain who had stumbled into the chasm since he could see no one. He assumed it was a couple of soldiers from Burkhart's troops. White Shadow had probably led the Apaches into another trap and two of the dragoons had gone in search of Apache gold while his cohorts scalped every warrior who had fallen beneath White Shadow's treachery.

While Makado was thinking vile thoughts about White Shadow, Devlin was scuttling around the mounds of rocks below the cave. He glanced up to see that the Old Man of the Mountain, who traditionally wore a smile while the morning light shined down on him, was now wearing his late-afternoon frown. The sun slanted across the wrinkled layers of stone revealing the other faces that seemed to materialize from the rock formations at particular hours of the day.

Devlin licked his lips in anticipation. Soon Burkhart would exhaust his water supply and go thirsty until he stumbled upon the pool of gold. When he reached for the huge nuggets that formed the eyes of the stone-filled skull, he would spring the trap and Devlin would enjoy the final victory . . .

"Show yourself, bastard," Lyle snarled impatiently.

Makado, thinking the degrading remark was intended for him, sprang from his hiding place and crouched behind another boulder.

The tumbling pebbles provoked Burkhart to fire in the direction of the sound. The buckshot splattered against the cliff and ricocheted around Makado like a swarm of bats.

At the sound of the discharging Winchester, Devlin catapulted himself to the bottom of the canyon. The rock slide he caused was followed by another explosion of Burkhart's rifle.

Devlin's brow puckered as he craned his neck around the stone slab to see Lyle crouch behind a boulder. Why in hell had that lunatic fired at the opposite wall first? Devlin wondered. There was supposed to be only the two of them in the canyon. Chanos had announced he was returning to his village and so had Geronimo and Cochise. They had promised to let him handle Burkhart in his own way. So who the devil was here?

Keen amber eyes scanned the rocks that lined the lower rim of the canyon, but he couldn't see anything except boulders and gnarled roots of trees that protruded from the massive walls. The sound of boots scuffling around the mounds of stone jostled Devlin from his musings.

"Show your face, coward," Lyle challenged with a mocking sneer.

"Show yourself, white-eyes," Makado snarled at what he assumed to be another personal insult.

Devlin blinked in disbelief. Unless he missed his guess, Makado had arrived upon the scene. That cynical renegade had come to put an end to both Burkhart and the legend of White Shadow. Damn, just what he didn't need right now—an Apache he couldn't trust!

Cursing Makado's intrusion, Devlin scooped up a rock and heaved it against one of the looming pillars that stood beside the temple of the sun. Two rifles simultaneously exploded and all three men scrambled for position. Devlin scuttled up to a higher vantage point, only to see the dark head of Makado sinking behind a protective boulder. Burkhart's blue chapeau with its golden plumes disappeared behind another slab of stone, giving his position away.

Moriah, who had been hanging upside down like a duck roasting above a campfire, roused to the sound of discharging rifles. Her head throbbed in rhythm with her thudding heart. She was so lightheaded from drifting in and out of consciousness that a pained whimper trickled from her lips. Her voice disturbed the family of rattlesnakes that slithered into the shade beside the pool each afternoon. The eerie rattles caused Moriah's eyes to fly wide open. She tilted her head so she could peer down at the vipers that swarmed over the rocks, sending nuggets of gold dribbling into the water. Her long tresses dangled above the nest of rattlers and Moriah screamed when one of them coiled and struck at the cascading tendrils of her hair.

Devlin had once informed her that vipers could strike at distances of two-thirds of their own length. But who was to say that one of the guard snakes in the nest wouldn't slither onto a higher rock to take a bite out of her face? Moriah had already crossed her arms over her chest to prevent being struck in the hand, but her head could easily become the target of the vipers that ventured onto a higher rock.

Her terrified shriek caused the entire nest to coil and slither along the rim of the spring. Moriah yelled at the top of her lungs when another daring rattler struck at the tangled tendrils that were draped over the vertical slab of stone. Damn, she wished she could have remained unconscious! The threat of being bitten was enough to scare the living daylights out of her. The real thing would be a hundred times worse!

When Moriah screamed, all three men leaped from their hiding places. Devlin's face was as white as flour when he recognized Moriah's voice. Makado was thunderstruck and Lyle was snarling in rage. Devlin had tricked him. White Shadow wasn't alone in the valley. He had obviously brought along one of his Apache friends to tip the scales in his favor.

And there the three of them stood with their rifles braced against their shoulders, pointing at first one deadly enemy and then the other. Each of them had been captured by position and didn't dare trust the other two challengers. There was no hope of victory or even retreat. Devlin knew full well that if he gunned Lyle down, Makado would drop him in his tracks.

Lyle was certain that if he blew Devlin to smithereens the growling Apache warrior would riddle him with bullets before he could swing his rifle to fire a second time.

Makado was sure that Burkhart would pellet him with buckshot if he dared to blast away at White Shadow.

Not one of them could trust the other two. And all the while they stood there glancing from one murderous face to the other, Moriah was squealing in horror and none of the men dared to move first, certain they would draw fire.

Devlin felt as if there were a team of horses strapped to each of his arms and legs, pulling him every which way at once. He knew Moriah was in trouble, but he couldn't see her because of the huge pillars of rock that blocked his view of the springs. How she had managed to return to the Valley of the Eagle baffled him. The last time he saw her she had been blind, but somehow that resourceful sprite had made her way to the valley and had apparently fallen into the trap he had set for Burkhart. Damn.

A wary frown knitted Devlin's brow when another thought skipped across his mind. He couldn't rule out the possibility that Makado had somehow captured Moriah and had strung her up for some vile brand of torture. The grisly picture that leaped to mind provoked Devlin to glower at Makado before darting Lyle a cautious glance. If Makado had captured Moriah, there was no telling what he had done to her! Double damn.

Whatever was happening to Moriah was going to have to wait a little longer, Devlin decided as he peered into the snarling faces of Makado and Lyle. Not one man had moved from his position. They stood like monuments of killing fury tempered with wary trepidation. Devlin had it figured that whoever moved first would draw fire and risk death. Apparently Lyle and Makado had arrived at the same conclusion. The first one to advance or retreat would set off a chain reaction and pandemonium would break loose.

With that in mind, Devlin glanced at Lyle while keeping a watchful eye on Makado. "You won't walk out of here alive, Burkhart," Devlin taunted with a satanic smile.

"Neither will you," Lyle sneered. "This Apache

seems as cautious of you as he does of me."

Makado stared at the one-armed commander. "Do not be so sure," he growled, still studying White Shadow with consternation. "I hate all whites, but you, I hate the worst!"

"He lost part of his family at the massacre at Ojo del Muerto," Devlin growled at Lyle. "Tell Makado how you schemed to lure me in with your talk of peace and good will, how you forewarned your troops to open fire and murder as many Apaches as they could shoot before the smoke cleared and the Indians scattered. You used me, you son of a bitch." Devlin focused his attention on Lyle for a half-second when the haunting memories came rushing back to torment him. "You murdered the people who had been my friends, just as you tried to murder me!"

Something inside Burkhart's tangled mind snapped at the harsh accusations. Facing the vicious Apache and the Indian-loving white man who had returned from the dead to place a curse on him caused Lyle's composure to crack. "I wish I could have killed you as I had planned that day," he sneered contemptuously.

Lyle's green eyes glazed over with murderous fury, making him reckless in his hunger to put an end to the White Shadow curse once and for all.

Just as Lyle swung his rifle toward Devlin, Moriah's piercing scream clamored through the canyon like a pealing bell of doom. Three rifles simultaneously discharged. Devlin leaped sideways, rolling over the rocks. A pained grimace twisted his lips when he felt the sting in his left thigh. Hurriedly, he cocked his Winchester, but he had no need to fire a second time. His first shot had found its fatal mark and so had Makado's.

The Apache, when faced with the choice, preferred

to see the end of Burkhart rather than the death of the legend of White Shadow. When it came right down to it, neither Makado nor Devlin had considered the other the deadliest threat. Their only purpose was killing Burkhart, no matter what consequences they risked by discarding all thoughts of their other challenger. At the last second, they had combined forces to ensure that Burkhart never rose again.

Felled by two well-aimed bullets to the chest, Burkhart dropped to his knees. "You son of a bitch of an Indian-lover," he growled with his last ounce of breath.

A strange look passed across his puckered features and he pitched forward, landing in a lifeless heap. After eighteen months of cruel, merciless killing Burkhart's reign of terror had come to an end. Devlin only wished that he could say the same for all the other Burkharts in the world who had vowed to see the Apache become an extinct species.

Makado stared down the barrel of his rifle at Devlin and then dropped the weapon by his side. He walked toward the man who had deliberately moved first and provoked Burkhart into firing at him. The bits and pieces of conversation Makado had picked up, plus the fact that Burkhart had aimed solely at White Shadow, spoke for themselves. Makado had the feeling he had misjudged this daring white man.

Squatting down on his haunches, Makado loosed the leather strap around his arm and tied it around Devlin's leg like a tourniquet. "You kept your word to the Apaches," he murmured humbly. "You managed to lure Burkhart out and put him to death." His black eyes drilled into Devlin's pinched features that testified to his pain. "How many of my people lost their lives so you could bring Burkhart to his fitting end?"

"Not one shot was fired," Devlin hissed as he pushed himself up to his knees. "The cavalry turned back to Santa Rita." He stared long and hard into Makado's bronzed features. "I bear you no malice, Makado, and I have never had any quarrel with you. All I wanted was to repay Burkhart for using me as a device to get to the Apaches. I wanted to avenge the injustice at Ojo del Muerto. It has always been your mistrust of me that placed insurmountable obstacles between us."

Makado peered at the rumpled body of Burkhart for a long moment. "If I had fired at Burkhart first, would you have defended me or aimed at me, White Shadow?"

"I think you know the answer to that, Makado. I had my sets on Burkhart. I would have even taken your bullet through the heart if it meant the death of that menace," Devlin assured him somberly.

Devlin touched his wound with his hand and then raised it in a gesture of peace and friendship. He etched a cross of his own blood on Makado's wrist. "I consider you my brother, even if you do not reciprocate." When Makado frowned at the unfamiliar word in his second language, Devlin translated into Apache. "Even if you do not wish to call me friend, I want peace. You will always be welcome at my ranch. The horses your clan trains will always receive a fair price in exchange for the food and supplies you require. The Apaches need all the friends they can get."

The faintest hint of a smile curved Makado's lips upward. "Friends perhaps," he conceded. "But challengers for Sunflower's affection. The blue-eyed woman is too great a prize, White Shadow. In that arena we will always be in fierce competition."

Makado gripped Devlin's hand firmly and then

assisted him to his feet. Before Devlin could warn Makado that no man could ever win Moriah's cynical heart, her bloodcurdling voice reverberated through the canyon.

Makado and Devlin may have shaken hands and made peace, but Moriah was still in quite a predicament. Her horrified screams and the exploding of nearby rifles had put the nest of vipers in a frenzy. Devlin had always said that snakes only struck as a last resort to being threatened and cornered. That may well have been true of one viper fending for himself, but it was not the conditioned response of a den of vipers who felt threatened. Apparently, the serpents became courageous warlords who fought side by side to protect themselves from what they assumed to be a deadly attack.

Rattlesnakes were swarming everywhere at once, crawling over the boulders to strike at the dangling waterfall of hair that trailed across the great slab of stone that formed the Old Man's shield of armor.

Moriah could only curl up and hold her head out of the viper's reach for just so long before the pull of gravity and screaming muscles forced her to drop back into her upside-down position. The world kept fading and then flashing at her, taking her from consciousness to a trancelike sleep that left her immobile.

Although Moriah didn't have the slightest idea who was waging war on the other side of the stone mounds that concealed the spring, she sorely wished someone would answer her cry of alarm. The suspense of wondering if she was to become this vipers' nest evening meal was driving her insane.

Another frightened cry burst from her when one of the serpents shot across the vertical rock in attempt to strike before it fell back into the stirring nest. Moriah wondered why she was trying to remove herself from the path of the snakes. The rattles and hisses were an impending death knell. Sooner or later they would inflict their deadly bites.

Why not get it over with? She couldn't hold out much longer anyway. She might as well resign herself to a battle lost and murmur her last prayer while she still had the chance.

On that dismal thought, Moriah slumped against the rock and awaited her destiny.

Chapter 26

Devlin and Makado gasped simultaneously when they veered around the stone pillars to see Moriah dangling upside down, her back resting against the vertical rock slab, her head dangerously close to the disturbed nest of rattlers.

When Makado yanked his rifle to his shoulder to fire at the serpents, Devlin clutched his arm. "If the buckshot ricochets off the rocks it could hit her," he muttered, cursing Moriah for getting herself into such a precarious situation. Damn, that trap had been meant for Burkhart, not this daring nymph!

When Moriah whimpered and slumped into unconsciousness, Devlin gestured for Makado to follow him. Together they crept along the rock-rimmed spring to forcefully rout the vipers. Some of them slithered off of their own free will, but the more courageous ones put up one helluva fight, continuously striking at the barrels of the rifles that nudged them on their way.

"Good God!" Devlin growled when the granddaddy of the entire nest, the biggest damn sidewinder Devlin had ever seen, slithered over the jutting slab to make another strike at Moriah.

In the batting of an eyelash, Devlin yanked his dagger from his moccasin and flung it at the lunging snake. That split second in time seemed to span eternity while Devlin watched the serpent hurl itself toward Moriah's neck. The dagger found its mark in the nick of time. The viper's deadly jaws were only scant inches from Moriah's throat when the blade plunged into its triangular-shaped head and sent it plummeting to the rocks below. The eerie rattle shattered the brittle silence and the viper's spineless body twisted and curled around the stiletto.

Devlin didn't take time to breathe a sigh of relief. His probing gaze scanned the surrounding rocks, wondering if there was another snake waiting to launch an attack if the patriarch met with defeat. Once the area was deemed reasonably safe, Devlin positioned himself directly below Moriah's dangling body.

Since Devlin was wounded, Makado had volunteered to scale the stone slab and cut Moriah's ankles free of the rope that left her hanging upside down. Bracing himself, Devlin raised his arms to catch Moriah when she dropped like an anchor. Devlin groaned when his injured leg threatened to buckle beneath him. Devlin staggered to maintain his balance as Moriah's dead weight dropped into his arms, but he caught his heel on a rock. With Moriah clutched to his chest he kerplopped backward into the pool, completely dousing both of them.

The cold water brought Moriah awake with a start. Her eyes flew open to see the flash of silver-blue flooding over her. Dazed, she watched an image materialize above her and felt a hand clamp around her wrist, jerking her up from wherever she was. The hands that shackled her arms caused her to writhe for freedom. When she tried to inhale a breath, she choked on water and sputtered and coughed to suck air into her lungs.

When Moriah was dragged from the pool she recognized Makado's blurry image looming over her and she fought even harder to loose herself from his grasp. She had tried so hard to elude this persistent warrior and here he was again, anxious to make demands on her. She supposed she should have thanked him for delivering her from the pit of snakes, but considering the kind of gratitude he probably expected, Moriah didn't feel all that generous.

While Makado tried to pull the hysterical wildcat to safety, Devlin was being gouged and kicked underwater. Moriah had yet to realize Devlin was beneath her and she was all flying fists and kicking feet. Devlin was painfully aware that Moriah was putting up a fight when she knocked the breath out of him twice and jabbed him in the groin thrice.

Effort though it was, Makado finally managed to capture Moriah in his arms, allowing Devlin to snatch a breath of air and flounder from the pool. "Calm down, Sunflower," Makado growled, giving Moriah a fierce shake.

"Let me go!" she railed, unable to see the bronzed face above her because her tangle of blond hair had completely covered her face.

"Good God, woman, you nearly drowned me!" Devlin muttered, dragging himself from the spring. "We saved your life. And this is the thanks we get?"

The unexpected sound of Devlin's voice momentarily took all the fight out of Moriah. She twisted in Makado's arms and shoved the dripping tendrils from her eyes. She gasped in shock when she spied the bloodstained water and the tourniquet that was tied around Devlin's thigh.

Since there were only the two men present, Moriah

naturally assumed that Makado had inflicted the wound on Devlin. She turned on the Apache, delivering a blow that caused him to slam back against the rocks. Although it had become second nature to defend the man she loved, Moriah quickly reminded herself that Devlin had betrayed her with another woman . . . or women. Criminey, there had probably been so many that they would have to be listed in alphabetical order!

"If I had known you were there, I would have drowned you when I had the chance," she snapped at Devlin.

Devlin gaped at her in astonishment. "Me? What did I do except save your life?" he snorted derisively.

As if he didn't know, the lusty scoundrel! Flinging her nose in the air, Moriah stalked away, leaving both men's mouths hanging open wide enough for a crow to nest.

After watching Moriah storm away without tripping over or ramming into the stone pillars, Devlin swiveled his head around to peer at Makado, who was massaging his stinging jaw. "She can see again."

Makado had arrived at the same conclusion and frowned curiously, wondering when the miracle had taken place. Shaking his head to rid himself of the stars that twinkled in front of his eyes, he strode over to assist Devlin to his feet. Lagging a safe distance behind the fuming female cyclone, the two men veered around the huge mounds of stone.

Moriah pulled up short and stared down at Burkhart's lifeless body. When realization dawned on her, she wheeled to stare at the Apache brave who had offered Devlin a shoulder to lean on. "You didn't shoot Devlin. Burkhart did," she concluded.

Makado nodded affirmatively.

Her baffled gaze bounced back and forth between

Devlin and Makado. For whatever reason, it appeared Makado's animosity for Devlin had evaporated. "I'm sorry, Makado, I shouldn't have struck you. I thought—"

A faint smile brimmed Devlin's ashen lips as he shot the warrior a quick glance. "He has decided I'm not as treacherous and deceitful as he first believed. It's nice to have *one* friend around here."

Moriah was glad to hear that, she truly was, but she was still peeved at Devlin for cavorting with other women the first chance he got. His lack of respect for the memories they'd made struck a fierce blow to her feminine pride.

Even though she'd had ten years scared off her life during the ordeal with the vipers, she was still determined to follow through with her plans. Squaring her shoulders, she reversed direction and trounced past the two men, intent on gathering as many nuggets as she could cram in her pockets.

"That is Apache gold," Devlin grumbled when he realized her intentions. "It stays where it is."

"I only want enough to start a new life in Texas," she declared.

"If you go back to Tucson with me, you won't need it," he insisted, miffed at her aloof attitude toward him. He didn't have the foggiest notion what had put her in such a snit.

"I can't and I won't go back to Tucson," she declared, refusing to meet his piercing glare.

"Why the hell not?" he demanded.

"Jessica, for one reason," Moriah reminded him tartly. "And you for another."

Devlin's brows jackknifed. "Now what did I do to upset you?"

"You have already forgotten I exist," she spumed. "I didn't expect you to remain loyal to my memory forever and ever. But, for crying out loud, you could have waited at least a month or two!"

Moriah's rapid delivery in English flew over Makado's head, but Devlin caught every word. He didn't understand her insinuation but it wasn't because his English was faulty.

"What the blazes are you babbling about?" Devlin shouted in exasperation. "Waited a month for what . . . ?"

Those were the last words Devlin was able to get out before the loss of blood left him so lightheaded that he folded up at the knees. Once the shock of being shot and then rescuing Moriah from disaster wore off, Devlin succumbed to the blistering summer sun. Makado staggered to keep him upright, and despite her irritation, Moriah rushed over to assist. Together they dragged Devlin up the winding path to the cave.

They had just reached the ridge when Chanos appeared from out of nowhere. The Apache brave had declared that he was returning to his village, but he hadn't stated specifically *when* he was leaving for home. The fact was, he had wanted to be around to see how the confrontation between Burkhart and White Shadow turned out. He had no time to question Makado or Moriah's presence in the canyon. The instant he saw his blood brother hanging limp, he rushed down the trail to attend his wounded friend.

When the threesome finally hauled Devlin into the cave, Moriah dashed back outside to fetch wood for a fire. After Chanos sterilized his knife, he cut away Devlin's buckskin breeches to inspect the wound. While he performed primitive surgery, Makado offered his rendition of the encounter with Burkhart. Once the wound was cleansed and Chanos mixed a concoction of wild herbs, roots, and magical healing dust from the pouch that hung around his neck, he smeared it on Devlin's leg.

"You deceived me twice, Sunflower," Makado murmured, casting her a wry smile. "It seems I was the one who was blinded by your trickery."

"Thanks to Chanos's magical powers, I have gradually regained my sight," she confessed with a grateful smile to the medicine man.

Entranced by the impish grin that captured her features, Makado ambled over to squat down beside Moriah. Gently, his fingertips outlined her exquisite face. "I want you to come away with me, Sunflower. I will prove to you that I can be tender," he murmured softly. "I want—"

"You are taking unfair advantage," Chanos grunted, flinging Makado a condescending glance.

Although Makado was annoyed by Chanos's interference, he begrudgingly backed away. When it came to White Shadow and his influence over this blue-eyed vixen, Makado wanted to take any kind of advantage he could get. When White Shadow roused, Makado feared he would have no chance to plead his cause.

"Sleep, Angel of the Wind," Chanos encouraged her. "We will watch over White Shadow for a time."

Exhausted, Moriah sprawled on her pallet while the Apache warriors stood vigil over their patient. Devlin's entreating words to stay with him kept ringing in her ears, but she knew she couldn't return to Tucson, even if she forgave him for his infidelity. And yet she couldn't leave him until she knew he had recovered from his injury.

Heaving a weary sigh, Moriah closed her eyes. She tried to forget the nightmare with the vipers, to forget the fierce hold that golden-eyed renegade had on her heart. She hadn't wanted to leave Devlin—ever. But she had no other choice. They could never find happiness together. If she returned to the Granger Ranch she would only instigate trouble with Devlin's family. And if Devlin had forsaken her with the Indian maids it would only be a matter of time before his roving eyes led him astray. Once a rake always a rake, she reckoned.

On that dismal thought, Moriah drifted off to sleep, wishing for things she knew she couldn't have.

Chapter 27

Devlin's muffled groan roused Moriah from a deep sleep. When she pried one eye open she found that Makado and Chanos had vanished, leaving her in charge of her fevered patient. Crouching beside Devlin, Moriah lifted his tousled raven head onto her lap and offered him a few sips of water. Although he did manage to gulp some down, he mumbled in slurred sentences that made no sense whatsoever. Occasionally her name flooded from his bone-dry lips, but for the most part Devlin was oblivious to anything that transpired around him.

Throughout the day and into the night, Moriah watched over him, comforting him during his delirious ravings. Finally, after midnight, Devlin slumped into peaceful slumber and Moriah managed a brief nap. And to her relief, she awoke at dawn to hear Devlin's grunts and growls. The fever had broken, leaving him conscious but in a sour mood. When he tried to prop up on an elbow, Moriah shoved him back down.

"You have lost a great deal of blood and the infection caused a high fever," she told him. "The best thing for you to do is stay where you are until you have regained your strength."

"I'm perfectly fine," he muttered irascibly.

"Of course you are," Moriah smirked. "That's why your face is as white as a sheet and there are dark circles under your hollow eyes. You look a great deal like the legendary ghost the miners in Santa Rita believe you to be."

"So naturally, the guardian angel of Black Mountain consented to remain by my side until I recover enough to stand on my own two feet," he grumbled grouchily. "I'm surprised you didn't gather all the gold you could carry and trot off on your merry way while I was too weak to protest." He glared at her. "Why didn't you? Because of pity?"

"Compassion," she clarified.

"There's a difference?" Devlin snorted in question. "There wasn't any difference when you were blind and I sympathized with your plight." He muttered to himself for a half a minute before focusing his disgruntled glare on Moriah. "You have been able to see for a long time now, haven't you?" His waxen lips puckered in a scowl. "You were just waiting for me to go back to the mountains so you could make good your escape from the ranch! I'm sure you had a good laugh at my expense. You and your confessions of love. Bah! It was a clever ruse. You were biding your time so you could come back for the gold, only you fell into the trap I designed for Burkhart, greedy witch that you are!"

His harsh accusations hit her like a sledgehammer. "That isn't true!" Moriah protested. "I loved you from the very beginning, despite my better judgment, and I never used you for any purpose. It has only been the past two weeks that I have gradually regained my sight. I left the ranch because I had no choice! I came back to the mountains out of sheer desperation!"

"Oh, you had a choice all right," he grunted, glaring accusingly at her. "You just didn't care about me as much as you wanted me to believe. You were just letting me know in a gentle manner. How noble of you."

"That isn't true, either!" she spumed. "You're the one who couldn't wait to get me out from underfoot so you could dally with every Indian maiden between here and Tucson."

"I did no such thing!" Devlin growled in self-defense. "There has been no one else."

"Makado says there have been dozens of somebody elses!" Moriah bit off.

Devlin rolled his eyes in disbelief. "You would take the word of Makado over mine? He wants you all to himself, in case you have yet to figure that out. And so does Chanos and even my own brother, for God's sake!" He heaved an exhausted sigh and plunked back to his pallet. "Why the hell am I arguing with you? It won't do me an ounce of good, stubborn as you are."

Devlin refused to glance in her direction but gestured his head instead toward the mouth of the cave. "Go, if you have your heart set on leaving me. I've recovered from wounds far worse than this. Since you're so sure it is only our pity for each other that holds us together, we may as well call it quits once and for all. You don't have enough trust to believe the truth when you hear it and you damned sure don't believe *in* me. If you want to go, then go. I'm through trying to stop you."

Moriah bristled at his scathing tone. "My, you have certainly changed your tune now that you are the one handicapped with that stiff leg," she sniffed disgustedly. "And don't tell me when to leave, damn you. I'll go when I'm good and ready and I certainly do not need your permission!"

Devlin hitched his thumb toward the sunlight. "There's the door. Of course, I don't need to tell you since you can see it as plainly as I can and probably could for the whole damned month. Good-bye, Moriah. It has been quite an experience knowing you. I won't expect you to be here when I wake up."

When he eased onto his side and closed his eyes, Moriah stared at him for a long moment. She ought to leave him to fend for himself, the cranky lout! But she couldn't, not knowing when Makado and Chanos would be back. But one thing was for certain, Devlin's foul disposition negated any affection he had once claimed to feel for her. Now that his pity for her had dissipated, he was anxious to have her out of his life. He had never really loved her at all. Sure enough, he had felt sorry for her because she was blind and had nowhere to turn.

Heaving a frustrated sigh, Moriah rose to her feet and ambled toward the mouth of the cavern, wondering if this wouldn't be a good time for a bath. The vipers had abandoned the spring and the wounded lion was roaring in his den. But Moriah didn't get very far when Devlin's wordless scowl halted her in midstep.

"Damnit, Riah, don't you dare leave me when I don't have the strength to chase after you!" he growled at her.

Moriah flinched when his thundering voice echoed around the cave. Pivoting, she peered down into his glistening golden eyes. "I thought you said you didn't care what I did."

"That's what I said because that's what you *think* I *think,*" he muttered as he rolled to his side. "I'm fed up with saying what you expect to hear instead of what I really feel. Blast it, woman, I love you, blind or no. I don't care if you have somewhere else to go or if you don't. I didn't want you to take the gold and leave because I didn't want you to have any other choices."

Devlin threw up one arm in a gesture of futility. "What do I have to do to convince you that I care? I love you so much that when I close my eyes and imagine life without you I dread what I see. There have been no other women because I can't look at another female without comparing her to you, without seeing your face overshadowing hers."

A rueful smile hovered on Moriah's lips. "Even if I believed you, there are still obstacles between us. Your sister despises me and I have somehow managed to make another enemy in Tucson. The night I fled the ranch and bunked in the blacksmith barn, someone tried to push me to my death from the hay loft."

Devlin's dark brow shot up to an incredulous angle at the disturbing news. "Who was it?"

Her shoulder lifted in a shrug. "I was still blind and couldn't identify him."

"Well, Jessica is no longer one of your concerns," Devlin assured her. "All that really matters is how you feel about me and how I feel about you and I've already expressed my sentiments—straight from my heart."

Moriah frowned dubiously. The last time she had seen Jessica she had been in a full-blown snit. "Outside influence is still an important consideration," she contended. "I cannot imagine what you could have said to Jessica to convince her I wasn't after the security you could provide. She hates me and she probably always will."

"The fact is my kid sister has decided she idolizes

you and despises her brothers," Devlin informed her.

"What?" Moriah ambled over to sink down cross-legged beside him.

He nodded in confirmation. "After I tried to explain my feelings for you, that led to another explanation. Rett and I have procrastinated in giving Jess a lecture on the facts of life." Devlin expelled a heavy sigh. "Things went from bad to worse. All we managed to do was confuse her. When we tried to explain how it was between men and women, Jess wound up with a distorted view of men and courtship. Since Rett and I happen to be of the male persuasion Jess refuses to forgive us for the damnable sin of being born into that despicable gender. All we were trying to do was warn her away from adventurers who wanted her money and physical favors. I think that little chat should have come from another woman. Jess vowed to search for you. She planned to run away with you and avoid men forevermore . . . her brothers especially."

An amused smile pursed Moriah's lips. She could well imagine how awkward that conversation between brothers and sister had been.

"You've got to come back with me, if only to straighten out Jess," Devlin murmured as he reached up to trace Moriah's petal-soft lips. "As for me, I'll even settle for your pity if that's all you have to offer. I'm getting damned desperate."

He sadly shook his head as he stared into Moriah's enchanting face. "You haven't given yourself credit, love. You have every confidence in your ability to manage by your own devices. But you are doubtful that a man could honestly love you. For over a month you have refused to accept my love for what it is. You have spun your sticky theories like a spider and I'm tired of having my affection for you reduced to analytical equations that you have boiled down to lust and pity. It's a helluva lot more than that and I resent the fact that you think I'm so shallow!"

His hand twisted around her tangled gold tresses like a rope, tugging her toward him. "Look into my eyes and tell me this isn't love staring you in the face, the kind of love that is meant to last forever."

Moriah looked into those amber pools and her heart melted like snow on a roaring campfire. Now that she had regained her sight, she could see what she had been too blind and cynical to notice. Love was staring back at her in the tender expression that captured his rugged features. Love was glowing in those golden-brown eyes that were rimmed with long black lashes.

Devlin smiled in satisfaction. He could read her thoughts once again. She had finally realized that he truly cared for her. "The last two weeks without you have been pure and simple hell. I could barely concentrate on my confrontation with Burkhart without your memory burning holes in my mind. I need you, Riah. Please stay with me. Without you my life is incomplete. I never understood all the emotions love encompassed until I found you."

The love she had harbored for the magnificent man who matched these rugged mountains came flooding out. When he murmured his affection and his lips whispered over hers, Moriah's heart swelled with so much pleasure she feared it would burst. She gave herself up to the floodtide of desire that his explosive kiss evoked.

If Devlin's wounded leg inconvenienced him in the least he certainly didn't show it. He molded her against his hard contours and his caresses migrated beneath her flannel shirt to make stimulating contact with her satiny flesh. A soft sigh escaped her lips when he peeled the garment away to worship every inch of her exposed flesh. His hands and lips were everywhere at once, doing impossible things to her body and her self-control.

When she was in Devlin's powerful arms, no obstacle seemed unconquerable. All she knew was that she loved him—heart, body, and soul—and he returned her affection. It had been forever since she had lain in his arms and surrendered to the maelstrom of sensations that only his masterful kisses and caresses evoked. She never wanted to leave him again.

"I love you, Moriah," Devlin whispered raggedly. "I'm wild in love with you."

The magical glitter in his golden eyes assured her that he meant every word he said. The exquisite tenderness of his touch conveyed his affection. The genuine emotion in his voice erased any lingering doubts. Moriah let go of all her fears and reservations. If Devlin loved her they would find a way to overcome the obstacles. He was the luxury of life, her legendary treasure, the happiness that had always eluded her.

"I couldn't have left you, even if I'd tried," Moriah whispered against his sensual lips. "You're all I'll ever need. You're my one and only love . . ."

Her softly uttered confession ignited his passions. Weak and injured though he was, his love for her gave him strength. Rediscovering every luscious inch of her body was like a healing balm that soothed his throbbing leg. Sharing Moriah's tantalizing kisses breathed new life back into him.

Like a stirring lion, Devlin roused, consumed by the pleasure he derived from caressing her. His hands and lips coasted over her shoulder, leaving wildfires burning in their wake. He didn't merely caress her, he cherished her as if she were a priceless gift that had been bestowed on him. He breathed love words on her silky skin, showering her with all the affection he had kept bottled up inside him for two tormenting weeks. At long last Moriah believed in him and accepted his love and he wanted to shout his joy to the mountains.

A tremulous sigh escaped Moriah's lips as Devlin taught her the secret intimacies of passion embroidered with everlasting love. He had always been a marvelous lover, but he was teaching her things about passion that she never believed possible. She felt his arousing words upon her skin, felt the flow of skillful caresses that left her burning to the very core of her being. Her body was his to do with what he would. She was clay in the hands of a master craftsman. His caresses and kisses molded her to fit his loving hands—hands and lips that left not one inch of her flesh untouched.

Helplessly, Moriah arched toward him, wanting all of him, wanting to feel that warm flame flickering inside her, wanting to be one with him. As his bold caresses stole her breath away, her lashes fluttered up to see his golden eyes twinkling down at her. Devlin twisted, favoring his injured leg, and propped himself against the stone wall. His rakish smile set her heart into a flurry of rapid palpitations. His grin broadened as he drew her down on top of him and settled her exactly upon him.

"This time, sweet witch, you set the cadence of love. I'm yours—body, heart, and soul. Do with me what you will . . ."

A shudder of pleasure ricocheted through her as he clasped her to him and then lifted both hands to cup her face. As his sinewy body arched toward hers, he slanted his lips across hers. His possessive kiss and the feel of his muscular body moving intimately beneath hers drove her wild with excitement. Moriah lost touch with reality as passion raced through her like a raging river dragging her into the rapidly flowing channel. Suddenly her body was moving on its own accord and the fervent crescendo built like swells upon a storm-tossed sea. Dizzying sensations swirled around her as Devlin's greedy hands caressed, instructed, and pleasured.

Moriah clutched him to her as the dark, sensual world of passion exploded like an erupting volcano. Ecstasy drenched her as she met Devlin's demanding thrusts, exulting in the fervent sensations that spilled over her. Indescribable rapture flooded over her and she pressed a breathless kiss to his muscular shoulder as they shuddered together in sweet release. She whispered her love for him over and over again, until there was no question about her feelings for him.

After a long moment, Devlin tunneled his fingers through the golden strands that trailed over her arm. Languidly, he tipped her head back to grace her with a roguish smile. A hot blush stained her cheeks, conscious of their intimate position, half leaning, half sitting against the wall. Fearing she was aggravating his mending wound by sitting upon him the way she was, Moriah tried to ease down beside him, but Devlin's hands slid down her ribs, holding her in place.

"Don't move, love," he rasped, and then broke into another wry smile. "This is the only position that eases the pain in my leg."

Moriah eyed him suspiciously as she combed her hands through his ruffled raven hair. "I think you are taking advantage of your injury," she teased playfully. "You're looking for my sympathy."

His thick brows lifted suggestively. "If you think

all I want from you is your sympathy, minx, you're a fool."

"I do wish you would stop calling me that," Moriah insisted. Her blue eyes flared as they slid down his muscular chest, adoring everything she saw. "Just what do you want from me, if not my sympathy?"

"I was hoping you would ask me that." Devlin kissed her wildly, and then leaned far enough away to stare into her face. "I want all your love, now and forevermore, Moriah."

His voice was ragged with desire. He had but to peer into her lovely face and he went hot all over. The feel of her silky body sitting familiarly upon his left him to burn with a need that only this blue-eyed angel could fully arouse and completely satisfy. At least temporarily, Devlin amended as his caresses mapped each well-sculptured curve and swell. This blond-haired temptress was his addiction. He could never seem to get enough of her. She was in his blood, his heart, and his mind.

"Are you sure you're ready for this?" Moriah whispered against his sensual lips. "After all, you're just recovering from a bout with fever."

"You're my fever and my cure," Devlin assured her huskily. He pressed her closer and bent his head to flick at the rose-tipped peaks of her breasts. "Don't ever stop loving me, Riah. Nothing is more important than winning and keeping your love."

When his hungry kiss stole her breath away, Moriah surrendered all over again. His love lifted her from one wondrous plateau to another until she was soaring like the eagle of sunlight that glided in eternal flight. And it was much later when Moriah and Devlin returned from their intimate journey across the wide horizon to nestle in each other's arms—content and secure in a love so fierce and wild that nothing could sever the bond between them.

On the ridge above the Valley of the Eagle, Chanos and Makado stared speculatively at the entrance of the cave.

"I think we should check on White Shadow," Makado declared.

"I think he has all the healing potion he needs," Chanos insisted with a sly grin. "He has the Angel of the Wind to watch over him."

A disgruntled frown furrowed Makado's dark brows. "I may call him my friend, but I still envy his prestige with the tribal leaders."

Chanos burst into a snicker. "But you envy him far more now, just as I do," he countered with his usual candor. When Makado puffed up, Chanos chuckled again. "I have long felt the lure of the goddess with sky-blue eyes. But she belongs in White Shadow's world, not ours. It is as it should be, even if I would prefer it otherwise myself."

Makado hated knowing the medicine man was right. But there was something utterly irresistible about the feisty blonde he had chased over hill and dale. Her enchanting memory called to him, luring him, even when he knew her heart belonged to White Shadow.

Resolutely, Makado wandered away, but his thoughts kept circling back to those tantalizing moments he had spent with the sassy young woman who had dared to challenge the Apache domain. A fleeting thought skipped across his mind, putting a mischievous smile on his lips. The Angel of the Wind had not seen the last of him, he vowed as he and Chanos trekked along the rim of Eagle Canyon. He knew exactly where to find her in the days to come. And he knew how he could lure her back to the mountains with him. Knowing that eased the sting of leaving Moriah behind for the moment. But one day soon he would make her realize that he could offer her everything she wanted . . .

Part V

Chapter 28

It had been a long, tedious journey over rough terrain on a tender leg. Devlin was exhausted, and yet he was determined to press on. He was anxious to reach the ranch and ease his aching muscles in a warm bath. He had donned his serape and breeches before he and Moriah descended from the mountains to trek through the valley to his ranch. But weary though he was, Devlin was content. Having Moriah by his side after they had resolved their differences had done that for him. Now he was eager to settle into his new life, and, more important, to settle into his bed with this blue-eyed enchantress nestled in his arms.

"Home," Devlin murmured as he paused by the corral to tug Moriah into his arms. "With you . . ." His lips feathered over hers in the slightest breath of a kiss.

Moriah looped her arms over his broad shoulders and lifted her chin for another stirring kiss. Although she still had reservations about her encounter with Jessica, Moriah was as anxious to begin their new life together as Devlin was.

"Mmmm . . . I've had visions of sinking into my

feather bed. But tired as I am, it isn't only sleep that I have in mind," he rasped as he pulled her full-length against him, letting her feel his desire for her.

They might have stood there like that for a few more minutes if the front door of the ranch house hadn't opened to reveal Barrett's silhouette amid the flood of lanternlight. Resigning himself to the fact that he would have to save the kissing and caressing until later, Devlin clasped Moriah's hand, gave it a loving squeeze, and propelled her toward the door.

Devlin had only set foot in the front door and murmured a greeting to Rett when Jessica appeared out of nowhere. Before Devlin could catch his breath, Jessica chewed him up one side and down the other for the degrading way he had treated Moriah.

Barrett simply stood aside and grinned, thankful Devlin had finally returned to receive his share of the tongue-lashings. Since the moment Barrett returned from the military proceedings in Santa Fe, Jessica hadn't let up on him. Devlin's name was now free of the charges against him, but his name was still mud in Jessica's book. She rolled out the heavy artillery the moment he limped inside and she blasted away at him, uncaring that he was weak from injury and weary from a long journey.

"Moriah is not staying in the guest suite that adjoins your room!" Jessica declared as she pushed her way in front of Moriah like a protective shield. "She is going to stay with me. And come morning, we are both going to take up residence at the hotel. If you wish to see either of us, you can request an audience there!"

An amused grin pursed Moriah's lips as she studied Jessica's rigid stance and the defiant thrust of her chin. My, what a switch it was to have this fifteen-year-old spitfire defending her instead of condemning her. She had been certain Devlin had exaggerated the situation when he explained the about-face in Jess's attitude. From all indication, Devlin hadn't exaggerated one iota.

"This really isn't necessary, Jessica," Moriah interjected while Jessica inhaled an angry breath and prepared to read her elder brother another paragraph of the riot act. "I have regained my sight and I see now that all I want is Devlin's love. I'm not planning on running away again."

Jessica wheeled about, her jaw gaping. "After the shameless way he has treated you?" she chirped incredulously, her dark eyes wide as silver dollars. "His behavior was beneath reproach! You of all people know what despicable creatures men are. All they want from women is what they can get away with. Before Devlin became a fugitive, he was never between women. He had more lady loves than you could shake a stick at and they flocked after him constantly. Why, it was appalling the way he—"

"Good God, Jess," Devlin snorted, cutting her off before she voiced another damaging remark that would cause conflict between him and Moriah. The little firebrand had said too much already! "I'll have you know that I have never had as many . . . er . . . tête-à-têtes as gossips credit me with having. In the past year and a half there have been none at all. Criminey, girl, you make me sound like a—"

"A womanizer? A lusty libertine?" Jessica sniffed disdainfully. "That's exactly what you are and so is that other miserable excuse for a brother." She glared at Barrett.

Devlin also glared at Barrett who was thoroughly enjoying not being on the firing line for a change. "I thought you were going to straighten her out while I was gone," he grumbled sourly.

"This is an improvement," Rett snickered at Devlin's scowl and Jessica's condemning glower. "You should have seen her before I left for Santa Fe. You are no longer a wanted man, by the way, except by our dear little sister. I doubt you will ever be granted forgiveness for being born a man. She hasn't forgiven me, either."

Moriah clutched Jessica's arm and steered the fuming brunette toward the parlor. "Before you verbally crucify both your brothers, I think we should have a little chat."

Flinging Rett and Dev a parting glare, Jessica allowed Moriah to shepherd her into the parlor.

"Sit down, Jess," Moriah requested as she eased the door shut behind her. "We need to talk."

Jessica held up her hand in a deterring gesture. "Before you say anything, I want to apologize for the horrendous way I treated you," she blurted out in a rush. "I'm deeply sorry and ashamed of my behavior. If I had known what you had been through, I would never have spoken so disrespectfully to you. Indeed, you were to be praised and my brothers scorned. But, taking women for granted as men do, Dev didn't bother with details and I was left with the wrong impression."

Moriah ambled across the room to survey Jessica's animated features. The high-spirited brunette had already begun to show the signs of maturing that drew men's eyes like magnets. With her olive complexion, dark curly hair, and glistening black eyes, Jessica was destined to have more than her fair share of men hovering around her. And in so many ways, Jessica reminded Moriah of herself—fiercely determined, cynical, hot-tempered, and teeming with a pride that was easily offended. Moriah would have liked to spare this sassy sprite a few of the unpleasant encounters she had endured to make her voyage to womanhood a little smoother. She wished there had been someone around to help her through those difficult years.

"You know, Jess, it isn't easy being a woman in a man's world," Moriah said with a sigh. "And you are bound to confront your share of trouble because you are such a vivacious, extraordinarily lovely young lady."

"I'm not half as pretty as you are," Jessica scoffed. "I saw the way all the men at the Haverns' party were ogling you, even if you didn't. They all *lusted* after you."

"Beauty can be both a blessing and a curse," Moriah replied as she sank down on the sofa beside Jessica. "It seems that men have a natural affinity to females. The more independent, spirited, and attractive they are, the greater the challenge, I'm sorry to say."

"Well, I'm not about to become a man's conquest," Jessica declared with perfect assurance. "I'm going to become a man-hating spinster."

"So was I until I met a unique man who forced me to reevaluate my low opinion of men." A faint smile bordered her lips as she met Jessica's belligerent stare. "The danger of speaking in generalities is that you sometimes confront impossible exceptions. Your brothers are two exceptions to the rule."

"Those philanderers?" Jessica sniffed in contradiction. "Hardly!"

"Perhaps once in a lifetime, and sometimes not even that often, a special man comes along to leave a woman questioning her cynical philosophy. When I met Devlin, I stubbornly told myself he was just like the endless rabble of men who wanted to take without giving, one of those annoying men who looked upon women in a disparaging light, using and discarding them when it met their whim. But I was wrong about him. Devlin learned to read my moods and became attentive to my needs. He began to see me as his equal instead of his challenge."

Jessica stopped being defensive and settled back against the couch to absorb Moriah's words.

"I had no one to guide me during my adolescence. I knew nothing of trust and honest affection, only of men's animal desires and their betrayal. I refused to let my heart rule my head, refused to succumb to empty words of flattery that were meant to crumble my defenses. I preferred distant respect to relationships that left me doing all the giving while men did all the taking."

Moriah squirmed uneasily on the sofa. She was unaccustomed to this kind of chat. All she had was firsthand experience and a woman's point of view to lead her through the delicate discussion. She didn't want it to end in disaster like the time Dev and Rett attempted to explain the facts of life to their sister.

"Your ability to judge character will be sorely tested in the upcoming years, Jessica. And if you should find a man who is willing to defend you simply because of his respect and affection for you, a man who is responsible and generous of heart, you will have to ask yourself if your stubborn pride is as important as your love for him."

"But how am I to know for certain if a man wants me for myself or for the wealth he can acquire in the bargain?" Jessica sighed. "How can I trust what I'm not sure I understand?"

"Love has nothing to do with thinking," Moriah informed her gently. "It has to do with feeling. When this special man's memory steals across your mind and his image constantly distracts you, you will know there is something unique about him. You have to look deeper than his appearance and ask yourself what it is about him that lures you, that preoccupies you. It won't be easy, I'm sad to say. I was too much the cynic to believe that love existed. I only hope it won't take you quite so long to recognize the man who can make you happy, the one with whom you yearn to share your life. He may arrive when you least expect him, and as your brother once told me, 'Always expect the unexpected.'"

"And if I decide I'm in love, shall I give in to whatever it is that lures a woman to a man?" Jessica questioned point-blank.

"Yes, immediately after you marry him," Moriah qualified, and nervously waited for the inevitable questions.

"Why? You and Devlin didn't." It was not meant to be an insult, only a direct question. "And if you truly love him, why did you leave him, even when I said those horrible things to you? Why didn't you stay and fight for him?"

Moriah carefully formulated her thoughts and stepped out on thin ice. "Devlin and I found ourselves alone in the mountains. Alone by yourselves is a dangerous thing when feelings are running high. There was nothing normal about our courtship. We were together day in and day out instead of seeing each other once or twice a week for a few select hours under the watchful eyes of chaperones. We faced storms, attacks of wild creatures, and dozens of pitfalls that left us bound together to confront unexpected dangers. Unfortunately, there was no home into which I could closet myself, no parents or guardians to ensure that our relationship didn't get out of hand. I had gone to the mountains to avoid all contact with civilization and I discovered the one man who tempted me as no other man before him had."

Moriah didn't want to defend her actions, only to explain that she had asked for trouble by venturing out on her own. "When Devlin brought me here, I knew how I felt about him and I stopped pretending I didn't love him. But I still wasn't sure how he really felt about me. I was convinced that he blamed himself for the accident that left me blind and that he felt sorry for me because I had nowhere to go. I was too proud to settle for his pity and so I left, vowing it was best for both of us."

Now for the toughest part, Moriah reminded herself. "We shouldn't have become so involved, but circumstances played too great a role in our relationship. Sometimes the need to express affection overshadows logic. And sometimes the time seems right, especially when there doesn't seem to be a future. A woman must have confidence in herself to analyze her feelings and the situation. She must learn when to let logic rule her head and when to allow her heart to show her the way. I made mistakes that I hope you will be able to avoid."

Moriah's velvet lashes fluttered up to stare into Jessica's bewitching features. This rambunctious young woman was going to have all sorts of decisions to make the next few years! Moriah predicted.

"I wish I had all the right answers for every situation, Jessica. But I do know that you only torment yourself when you run from what you feel for the special man who comes into your life. Running doesn't solve the problem. I stand as proof of that."

She patted Jessica's hand and graced her with a consoling smile. "Your brothers care deeply for you, and they have tried to teach you right from wrong.

And when the time comes, you will have to ask yourself what is best for you. But if you give in to passion for passion's sake when you aren't certain if you are truly in love, it will only bring disappointment. Never give your body away if your heart cannot be part of the bargain."

A wry smile pursed Moriah's lips as she met Jessica's unblinking stare. "I think, if the truth be known, men are just as confused about this magnetic attraction to us as we are. Oh, they like to think they have women figured out, but they don't. They are more daring with physical affection, but they are as unsure of themselves and as afraid of getting hurt as women are. Sometimes they allow what is below their belts to control their actions instead of what is between their ears. It isn't difficult to be popular with men, but a woman is the one who pays, either by soiling her reputation or bearing a child she must raise while she is too much the child herself. You must have respect for yourself and remain in control of situations."

A faint blush crept to Moriah's cheeks. "It seems to me that men are like smoldering coals and it takes very little to ignite a fire in them—a glance, a touch, a kiss. But women are a bit more reserved with men. When your amorous suitor tries to take more than he *needs* and allows himself to be overwhelmed by what he *wants*, you are the one who must call a halt to the encounter. *No* is not a familiar word in a man's vocabulary when desire rears its head."

"This sounds awfully complicated," Jessica grumbled. "I think it would be easier to simply take a wide berth around men."

Moriah's gaze drifted toward the closed door. "I shared your sentiments until Devlin came along, but your brother's very presence fills my life to overflowing. He taught me to believe not only in men but in lasting happiness."

She grinned and gave Jessica's hand a fond squeeze. "That is not to say we live in perfect harmony. We have our share of disagreements because I'm stubborn and quick-tempered and he is headstrong. But we all have to bend a little occasionally if we want to hold on to the important things in our lives. And I would be grateful if you would consent to being my maid of honor at our wedding the day after tomorrow." She rearranged a renegade strand of hair that dangled on Jessica's temple. "I can't leave him, you see. I had the chance when he was wounded after his confrontation with Burkhart, but it was love that kept me beside him because he needed me and I needed him."

"You love him, faults and all?" Jessica quizzed her.

"Very much, and he has agreed to do the same, in spite of all my failing graces," Moriah declared without hesitation.

Jessica sighed heavily and shook her head. "I'm still not sure what loving is all about and if I'll know when I'm in love."

"You will learn to trust your instincts and intuition," Moriah comforted her. "And your first test is to take a deep look at your brothers who think the world of you. If you can see past their failing graces to admire their endearing traits, you will have taken the first step toward understanding men as well as any woman will ever understand them. What you respect about your brothers may well be what you long to find in the man who awaits you in your future. Dev and Rett have warmth, depth, concern, and they love you for what you are, even while you are scorning them for being men. Through the good and bad times, the anger and joy, they have cared for you. If you need them they will always be there for you. Isn't that what all love is really about, Jessica? Caring, sharing, and learning to be attentive of another's needs as well as your own?"

Jessica thought it over for a moment and then burst into an impish grin. "I'm going to like having you around, Moriah. And I suppose my brothers aren't such bad sorts after all. They have tolerated my childish tantrums and tirades without booting me out of the house."

"When you open your arms to them and dazzle them with that radiant smile, you're going to realize just how much they do love you," Moriah predicted. "Why don't you go make amends. Devlin has been concerned that the talk he and Rett had with you ruined you for life."

Getting up from the sofa, Jessica inhaled a deep breath. "There is just one more thing I want to know before I make peace with Dev and Rett."

"What is it?" Moriah questioned.

"You have cleared up several of my misconceptions, but what I really wanted to know was what is it like to sleep with a man. I should hate to blunder in, ignorant of what to expect."

Moriah's face blossomed with color. "It is . . . extremely satisfying . . . if you're sleeping with the right man. At least your brother has assured me of that—and I suppose he should know since you have insisted that he has been around quite a lot in his thirty years." Her face turned a deeper shade of red when Jessica looked as if she was about to ask for specific details. "When things simmer down around here and the wedding has been planned, you and I will discuss that matter in detail."

That seemed to satisfy Jessica, much to Moriah's

relief. Criminey, Moriah was going to have to sort out her thoughts before she had their next little "chat" with Jessica.

Jessica aimed herself toward the door. As she opened it, two anxious faces riveted on her. As Moriah suggested, Jessica blessed her brothers with a dazzling smile and opened her arms to them. She hadn't taken even one step forward before they rushed her, scooping her off the floor to hug her from both sides at once.

While Jessica murmured her apologies and returned the affectionate embraces, Moriah propped herself against the doorjamb and watched the touching scene with a contented sigh. Glistening golden eyes lifted over Jessica's head to toss her a smile that was a mixture of curiosity and relief.

Devlin didn't know what Moriah had said to calm Jessica down and change her cynical attitude, but he couldn't wait to find out. After pressing one last kiss to Jess's forehead, Devlin limped over to slip his arm around Moriah's trim waist. Bidding his brother and sister an absent good night, Devlin accompanied Moriah up the steps to his room—to his bed to be more specific. It would be the first time any woman had slept with him in his room. He was thankful that there was at least one first for him! Had he known Moriah awaited him in his future, he would have wanted her to be the first woman he had ever touched! Too bad he had been so impatient to find out what went on between men and women. Good God, he hoped Jessica wouldn't be that curious! If she were, the next few years would wear him out worrying about her.

"Well?" Devlin inquired as he opened the door to the master bedroom.

"Well what?" Moriah questioned his question.

"What magic potion did you feed Jess to reverse her low opinion of men?" he wanted to know.

Moriah closed the door and sashayed over to slide her arms over Devlin's massive shoulders. "I thought you said you had something more arousing in mind than conversation when we returned to the ranch."

The warm draft of kisses that whispered over his cheek and throat subdued the demons of curiosity that danced in his head. "I did say that, didn't I?" Devlin growled seductively. "You can tell me all about your conversation with Jess tomorrow, but tonight you and I are going to—"

Devlin had no opportunity to explain what he had in mind. The door burst open and banged against the wall, shattering the romantic spell and the magical moment.

"Oh no you don't!" Jessica announced. She grabbed Moriah's hand and tugged her out of Devlin's arms. "Perhaps this romance of yours proceeded in an unconventional manner, but there are going to be a few proper things about this short engagement and wedding." Her free arm swept the room. "This bridal suite will be properly prepared for the bride and groom and you will be sleeping in different rooms until after the ceremony."

Jessica's unrelenting gaze fastened on her scowling elder brother while Barrett stood in the hall, chuckling to himself. "You will not be allowed to see Moriah on the day of the wedding until you speak the vows. It's a jinx, you know, and I, for one, do not wish any more bad luck on my future sister-in-law. Until the wedding, Moriah will stay in my room with me and you will adjourn to the guest room. Moriah and I will begin preparing the bridal suite first thing in the morning."

Devlin rolled his eyes and opened his mouth to

complain about the sleeping arrangements in general and Jessica's domineering attitude in particular. Before he could voice one comment, Barrett was beside him, jabbing him with an elbow.

"Give into Jess on this," Barrett insisted in a confidential tone. "We just got her over hating us. Let's don't push our luck so soon after the truce. A couple of days won't kill you, Dev. As Jess said, there should be *something* proper about this courtship."

Devlin stared at the stubborn tilt of Jessica's chin and noted the determined glimmer in her dark eyes. "Very well," he said with a compromising sigh. "I suppose there should be a few proprieties observed. I certainly wouldn't want to set another bad example for you."

Jessica nodded in agreement. "You will sleep in the guest room until your wedding day," she repeated, pointing a tapered finger toward the adjoining door.

Devlin muttered under his breath as Jessica whisked Moriah away. Still grumbling, he scooped up his necessities and limped into the guest room where Moriah had slept during her last visit. After calling to the servants to fetch his bathwater, Devlin plunked down on the empty bed and silently cursed the fact that he didn't have his own private home. He would have to build one, he decided. He couldn't have Jessica spouting demands and Barrett peeking at his wife forever . . .

"Glad to see you're being such a good sport about this," Barrett snickered as he moseyed into the guest room. "This will be a breeze compared to the hell I've been through the past three weeks with Jess."

"Compared to the hell *I've* dealt with the past three months, I'm sure it will be," Devlin grumbled. "It took me forever to convince Moriah that I loved her.

And if anything goes wrong the next two days, I'll—"

"Nothing will go wrong," Barrett declared with great conviction.

Devlin flung him a ridiculing glance. "Yeah, and you're the one who also said Moriah would be here waiting for me when I got back. So much for your empty promises!"

"Well, I tried to find her!" Barrett protested indignantly. "And it would be nice if you thanked me for traipsing to Santa Fe to present your defense to the military court. Thomas Havern and I prepared one helluva case. And since Burkhart didn't show up to contest the countercharges against him—"

"I wonder why he didn't?" Devlin smirked, indicating his wounded leg.

Barrett stared at his brother and decided Devlin had gotten the worst end of the deal all the way around. "Where is Burkhart?" he questioned curiously.

"As deep in hell as a buzzard could fly in a fortnight," Devlin declared. "And he tried to take me with him. If I hadn't dived to the ground he would have. And after all that, I came home to find my kid sister ordering me around and hauling Riah away from me as if I have been quarantined!"

Barrett decided to leave Devlin to soak and sulk since that seemed to be his want. It was obvious that he had only begrudgingly consented to Jess's demand for conventional behavior before the wedding—he didn't like it one damned bit.

"Sleep well," Barrett teased on his way out the door.

Devlin grumbled something Barrett didn't dare ask him to repeat.

After his bath, Devlin lay abed brooding. His sweet dreams had been shattered by Jessica's interference.

He supposed it was best to observe propriety, but, blast it, winning Moriah's affection and her trust had taken forever. If anything went wrong in the next forty-eight hours, if Jessica or Barrett did anything to undermine Moriah's affection for him, he was going to strangle both of them! Damn, maybe he and Moriah should have stayed in the mountains, thought Devlin. Heaving a frustrated sigh, he closed his eyes and allowed his dreams to offer him what reality and his relatives had stolen from him.

While Devlin was drifting off to sleep, Moriah was listening to Jess plan the wedding. Jessica had appointed herself the head of the grand affair and insisted on accompanying Moriah into town the following morning to select her gown, issue invitations, and purchase supplies for the refreshments.

Moriah didn't even try to digest every sentence while Jessica was rattling on about the wedding. Her thoughts centered around the man in the guest room.

When Jessica finally stopped talking and fell asleep, Moriah sighed wearily. Only two days, she consoled herself. Then she could cuddle in Devlin's brawny arms and look forward to a bright future. Two days wasn't an eternity, after all. *No,* her pining heart agreed, *but it seems like forever when you can't be with the man who put the sunshine in your days and the starlight in your nights.* But as Jessica had proclaimed, there should be *something* conventional about this romance between Devlin and Moriah. For Jessica's sake, Moriah reminded herself as she willed her eyes to close without Devlin's rugged handsome image materializing in the darkness. No such luck. Golden eyes twinkled down at her, making her wish she were elsewhere doing something far more tantalizing than sleeping.

Had Moriah known that there was still more

trouble to come, she would have concentrated her efforts on eluding it instead of dreaming of snuggling into Devlin's arms. But she didn't know the Thatchers were in Tucson, only that Devlin was in the guest room and Moriah was forbidden to join him until after their wedding.

Chapter 29

Ruby Thatcher very nearly suffered heart seizure when she spied Moriah ambling down the street toward the shop. It didn't take her long to realize that whatever had caused Moriah's blindness had corrected itself. Moriah and that pretty little chit Jessica Granger were nodding greetings to each individual they passed on the street and Jessica wasn't leading Moriah around by the hand.

With her heart racing, Ruby zipped through the shop, mumbling orders for Dorita to tend any customers who came in. Plastered against the wall of the office, with the door slightly ajar, Ruby tensely waited to see if Moriah and Jessica entered. Of all the miserable luck, they did.

Ruby strained her ears, listening to Dorita voice her pleasure in finding that Moriah had regained her vision. Ruby, however, cursed that fact, for it would increase the risk of disposing of Moriah once and for all.

While Jessica babbled about the upcoming wedding the following afternoon and the relief that came in having Devlin exonerated, Ruby gnashed her teeth. Something had to be done and quickly. Once

Moriah was married into the influential Granger family, it could prove impossible to abduct her with a husband watching over her. Ruby's mind teemed with sinister plots.

After listening to Jessica invite Dorita and the entire town to the ceremony that was to be held at the ranch the following day, Ruby scuttled out the back door and made a beeline toward the blacksmith's barn. She pulled up short when she spied Barrett Granger and a huge mountain of a man who she presumed to be Barrett's brother Devlin, Moriah's intended husband. Yes, indeed, she and Vance were going to have to devise their scheme to dispose of Moriah posthaste! The last thing Ruby wanted was to tangle with the Granger brothers who looked as if they could constitute a two-man army.

As the two men strode along the boardwalk, Ruby mashed her back against the rough-hewn wall of the stable and held her breath, hoping she wouldn't be noticed.

"Our first stop should be the sheriff's office," Barrett announced. "I want to ensure that Sheriff Cummings rips those wanted posters to shreds and sends out an all-points bulletin. We don't need any money-hungry bounty hunters showing up to gun you down before the wedding."

"Maybe I could divert their attention to Jess," Dev grumbled resentfully. "I swear that girl is taking this propriety business a few steps too far. She won't even allow me one private word with Moriah until after the ceremony. Hell, I'm surprised she even permitted me to ride into town in the same wagon as Moriah!"

Barrett grinned broadly. "Jess hadn't intended for us to share the same mode of transportation, but I talked her out of that notion before you came downstairs this morning."

Devlin rolled his eyes skyward and muttered to himself about his meddling sister. "Our second stop is going to be Havern's office," he insisted. "I want him to get in touch with that lawyer friend of his in California. Although Moriah hasn't mentioned it lately, I want to hire a detective to track down the Thatchers."

Ruby's face bleached snowy white under layers of powder and paint when she heard that distressing news.

"I want those two guardians of hers to pay dearly for what they did," Devlin growled. "Moriah deserves her inheritance money and her revenge. I damned well plan to see that she has both. Once we're married, I don't want any ghosts from her past or mine haunting us."

While the Grangers strolled down the boardwalk and Moriah and Jessica selected Moriah's wedding gown, Ruby staggered through the back door of the stable and half collapsed against the wall.

Upon seeing his wife who was turning a shade of ghastly white, Vance lumbered toward her. "What are you doin' here, honey?" he asked.

Ruby wanted to choke the big oaf, but she didn't have the strength left after what she had seen and heard. If not for Vance's two bungling attempts to dispose of Moriah, Ruby wouldn't be suffering this anguish! Curse the man!

"Moriah is back. She is going to marry Devlin Granger. She can see again and we've got to get rid of her tonight," Ruby gushed like an erupting geyser.

Vance turned a chalky white color to match his wife's. "I think we should pack up and get the hell out of here while we still can," Vance croaked after the unsettling news sunk in.

"We will do no such thing," Ruby railed, breasts heaving. "I overheard Moriah's fiancé talking. Neither of them know we're here." Her frantic gaze fastened on Vance who was already shaking his head negatively before she even unfolded her scheme. "We are going to sneak to the ranch and abduct Moriah. I will be there with you to make certain you don't botch it up this time."

"I ain't gonna do it and you can't make me," Vance said stubbornly. "We're leavin' town."

"Oh no, we're not!" Ruby hooted. "All our money is invested in our store and the house. We won't get very far on what we've saved the past two months. We most certainly couldn't start over without starving to death first."

"I still ain't gonna do it."

"The third time will be the charm," Ruby declared with great conviction. "Moriah's curse will be lifted from our heads and no one will be the wiser. We'll drug her and then carry her away. Everyone will think she came down with the reluctant-bride jitters and ran away before her wedding."

"No," Vance repeated sternly.

Ruby's head tilted in defiance. "Then you leave me no choice but to march over to the sheriff's office and tell him that you tried to kill Moriah twice. I will insist that I couldn't stop you and that you swore you would beat me if I tried to intervene."

"That's a damned lie, Ruby," Vance scowled at her. "This was all your idea."

"You see! Moriah is still doing it, even when she isn't here," Ruby hissed bitterly. "She always tried to come between us, always tried to persuade you to kick me out. She always despised me." Her eyes sparked with irritation. "You old fool, don't you know she would have shoved us out in the cold if she'd had the chance? At this very moment Devlin is on his way to hire a detective to track us down and have us arrested for attempted murder. She means to have her revenge on us. If we don't strike first, Moriah will have us locked away. Once we dispose of her, we can sell the house and store and go somewhere where Devlin Granger won't think to search for us. It's us or her, Vance," Ruby said grimly.

Vance didn't like it. He surely didn't. But Ruby had always been better at getting them out of their dilemmas and making the decisions. He supposed she was right about that sassy little hellion. Once Moriah married into money, she would begin an extensive search for her stepparents.

"Oh, all right," he muttered begrudgingly. "We'll do what you say. But we're sellin' the store and movin' as soon as possible. We'll go to Fort Worth where nobody knows us."

"And we'll take on assumed names," Ruby interjected.

"Yeah, that, too, I s'pose," Vance sighed.

Pleased with her solution, Ruby drew herself up to her full stature and whizzed out of the stable. "I'll have all the details worked out by the time you come home for supper. You bring some horses. And this time there aren't going to be any mistakes because I'm planning this abduction, right down to every last detail."

Vance tugged off his work gloves and slammed them into the straw. Damnit, he wasn't going to have any peace and quiet until Moriah was dead and gone. Ruby had been hell to live with the past few weeks, fretting over Moriah. But Ruby was right, he reckoned. Moriah would track them down and turn them in if they didn't act quickly.

Wrestling with that unnerving thought, Vance scooped up his gloves and went back to work. It was a long and trying afternoon for him as he tried to stay out of view of the street, just in case Moriah and the Grangers happened by. It would probably be an even longer night, Vance supposed. After they abducted Moriah and disposed of her, Ruby would probably have him sweeping away the hoofprints to ensure that no one detected their coming and going.

Vance inhaled a deep breath. Damn, the things a man had to do to keep his woman happy. Sometimes he wondered if it was worth it.

Moriah very nearly melted under Devlin's heated gaze at the supper table. Jessica had positioned Moriah as far away as possible from Devlin at each meal—and everywhere else for that matter. It seemed Jessica had taken it upon herself to right every wrong in this unusual courtship between her brother and Moriah. She had appointed herself chaperone and forced them to abide by the standards Dev and Rett had set for her the past few years. Moriah might have even found the situation as amusing as Rett did if she hadn't been left aching for Devlin's loving touch, or at least a steamy kiss now and then. As it was, her eyes and her thoughts were centered on the broad, muscular man whose intimate glances devastated her.

For Jessica's sake she would observe this celibacy, Moriah told herself for the umpteenth time. They had to provide a good example. And if it meant keeping their distance for forty-eight hours, then they would. Moriah didn't like it, but she consented to it. She wanted to give Jessica the chance to see that a man and woman could curtail their lusts, as Jessica insisted upon calling the sparks that flew between men and women, for the sake of propriety. But if Devlin didn't stop ravishing her with his amber eyes, Moriah swore she would reduce herself to a puddle of frustrated desire. Criminey, the hours were creeping along at a snail's pace!

"When I informed Regina Havern of the wedding, she volunteered to arrange for the refreshments and send her cook and servants to assist us," Jessica announced between the main course and dessert. "Regina also promised to pick up Moriah's wedding gown after Dorita finishes with the alterations," she told Devlin. "The whole town has been invited to the ceremony and I took the liberty of asking several of your friends out this evening to celebrate the last few hours of your bachelorhood."

Dark eyes twinkled at her scowling brother, who would have preferred a hasty exchange of nuptial vows and a quick hop in bed to appease his lusts. "However, there will not be a scantily garbed harlot popping out of an oversize wedding cake to entice you and your friends," she razzed Devlin, just to hear him mumble to himself under his breath. He didn't disappoint her.

"While you men reminisce about your days of sowing wild oats, Moriah and I will be upstairs putting the finishing touches on the bridal suite—adding a flair of femininity to your utterly masculine bedroom. So don't think you'll be allowed any private moments with your bride-to-be tonight or anytime tomorrow. We will observe all the proper traditions that go hand in hand with matrimony."

"Good God, girl, what have you been studying to be at school?" Devlin snorted explosively. "A prison warden?"

Jessica shrugged off the insult. "You and Rett have

always harped on the fact that I should accept responsibility and carry it out." She blessed both brothers with an impish smile. "Propriety, you always proclaimed, was of utmost importance in relationships between men and women, even if you set examples of how *not* to behave." The barb struck like a well-aimed arrow. "No one in the community will know this courtship started out on the wrong foot or that you didn't follow the socially acceptable procedures in your dealings with your fiancée."

"As always, Jessica, you are getting a little carried away." Devlin gave a volcanic snort that indicated his displeasure with the situation.

Jessica emitted a contradictory sniff. "The pot is calling the kettle black. You are the one who got carried away, Dev. You put the cart before the horse, not I!"

"When I have more time, remind me to strangle you for throwing my words in my face," Devlin grumbled. "I can't wait until you get married. We will be following this rigid process to . . . THE LETTER!"

"That won't happen for quite some time," Jessica declared with firm conviction. "At least not until after Moriah gives me that little talk she promised, the one about the specifics of lovemaking."

Moriah choked on the morsel of ham she had just swallowed. Her face bloomed scarlet red.

"And anyway," Jessica rattled on. "Moriah says I have to shop around to determine what I want in a man. My Prince Charming will have to possess several qualities that my two brothers are lacking. Restraint for one, and discrepancy for another. From what I gather, it may take some time and effort to locate a fine, upstanding man. And even then, I'll have to train him to fit my expectations."

Perfectly serious, Jessica glanced at Moriah who was choking to catch her breath. "Do you think I should overlook the fact that my perfect man is as experienced with women as my two brothers are? Do you suppose there is even such a thing as a male virgin after he reaches the age of eighteen?" Her inquisitive gaze swung back to Dev and Rett. "How old were the two of you when you seduced your first woman?"

Devlin and Barrett strangled on their scalloped potatoes.

"We don't talk about such things at the dinner table," Devlin chirped, and then glared at Moriah. "What in the hell did you tell this girl anyway?"

"Things she needed to know about being a woman so she can deal with men," Moriah replied with an elfin grin and a suggestive wink that melted Devlin. "I thought it wise to discuss, in detail, that which you and Rett merely scratched on the surface. Jessica was more confused than enlightened."

"They were terribly vague," Jessica proclaimed, picking up her knife to whittle at her ham. She sliced her brothers with an ornery grin. "Moriah knows a great deal more about men than they know about themselves. But those are a woman's secrets to keep to herself."

Devlin blotted his lips with a napkin and elevated a thick brow. But Moriah, who looked positively angelic, simply smiled back at him. She was determined not to divulge what she had said to Jess.

"And now if you will excuse us, gentlemen, Moriah and I have to redecorate the master bedroom for tomorrow." Jessica bounded from her chair with her usual energy. "Devlin, you will not be permitted to have any contact with Moriah until the ceremony. That is the custom and we will strictly adhere to it. If you have anything you wish to say to your fiancée, now is the time."

Devlin stared at Moriah, stone-cold sober. "I would greatly appreciate it if you would stuff a gag in my kid sister's mouth," Devlin replied. "I'm trying to be a good sport about all this, but I'm not sure I can tolerate having her boss me around for the next twenty-four hours."

"Be that as it may, we are following the rules," Jessica sniffed as she gestured for Moriah to finish her meal and accompany her upstairs.

When Jessica and Moriah swept out of the room, Barrett slumped back in his chair. "What do you suppose Moriah told Jessica about us men that we don't know about ourselves?" he pondered aloud.

"Damned if I know," Devlin scowled as he stabbed at his peas. "But I suppose this is better than having Jess hate us . . . though not a lot. She's letting the authority we granted her go straight to her head. And by the way, I intend to begin construction on our new home next week. You will be in charge of screening Jess's suitors and overseeing her courtships. I'll have a wife to manage. That will be a full-time job, considering my wife."

"Thanks a heap," Barrett muttered. "I think I'll build my own house. Now that Jess is learning what it's like to rule the roost, there will be no living with her."

"Maybe we should ship her off to boarding school in the East," Devlin said thoughtfully, and then gave his raven head a dismissive shake. "No, that wouldn't work. She might drag home some tenderfoot who didn't know beans about how to handle a rambunctious gal like her. I guess we're stuck with ensuring that she finds a man who can handle her."

"There won't be a man anywhere on the earth who can handle her now that she is your future wife's protegée. They're both so high-strung that I'm not sure anyone can ride herd over them," Barrett grunted.

Devlin draped an arm over the back of the chair and smiled to himself. "Ah, but there are ways to handle feisty women, little brother."

Barrett scoffed at Devlin's confident smile. "Since when did you figure women out? It doesn't seem to me that you are in control of Moriah and I seriously doubt you will ever be."

"I've learned not to take females for granted since I happened on the Angel of the Wind," Devlin murmured, a faraway look in his eyes. "Handling high-spirited women is simple really. You just have to love them, every minute of every day of your life."

"It sounds like too much trouble to me," Barrett declared.

"More challenge than trouble." Devlin's gaze lingered on the enchanting image of blue eyes and blond hair that materialized above him. "When you fall in love, it makes all the difference. I love Moriah so much it scares me sometimes. Every time I came close to losing her it nearly killed me."

A cryptic smile curved Devlin's lips. "She does have her gentler moods. When we were staying in the cave in Eagle Canyon she challenged me to set a new record in—" Devlin clamped his mouth shut so quickly he nearly bit off his tongue.

Barrett swore he saw a blush pass across Devlin's bronzed features before his usually self-composed brother regained control of his wayward thoughts. Barrett grinned, knowing full well what his brother had refused to say.

"Just what is the record?" he kidded him unmercifully. "I might want to try to break it . . . or at least match it."

Saved by the rap at the door and the chatter of voices on the porch! "Shall we go celebrate my upcoming wedding?" Devlin got up from the chair, purposely avoiding Barrett's mocking smile. "It sounds as if the party Jess arranged for us has already begun."

Barrett peered at his brother and shook his head in amazement. He never expected to see his brawny brother so consumed by tender emotion that he was willing to sacrifice his freedom and settle down with one woman. But, giving the matter careful consideration, Barrett supposed he himself would consent to having his wings clipped if he could find himself a woman like Moriah. Barrett just hoped there was another Moriah Laverty on the continent. He wouldn't mind giving up his rough and rowdy ways for a prize like that golden-haired beauty his brother had latched on to first.

Granger Ranch was crawling with male guests. They were as thick as swarms of mosquitoes, and the liquor was flowing freely. Friends and acquaintances who Devlin had been forced to avoid for eighteen months turned up to celebrate his return to society and his upcoming wedding.

Twice, Moriah, with Jess one step behind her, had sneaked downstairs to spy on the menfolk who were making fools of themselves and guzzling whiskey like thirsty camels. Someone had designed an oversize crown and plunked it onto Devlin's head. Joke gifts were strewn around the parlor and office.

Besotted men were draped over every piece of furniture; some were sprawled under it, too inebriated to notice where they were.

Biting back an amused grin, Moriah herded Jess back upstairs when the topic of conversation became boasts of male prowess. Moriah decided Jessica didn't need that sort of education and Moriah wasn't sure she did, either.

After Moriah and Jess put the finishing touches of lace tablecloths and vases of flowers in the master bedroom, Moriah insisted they call it a night. It was well after midnight and the party downstairs had finally begun to wind down. Now there were only occasional outbursts of loud hooting and drunken laughter, compared to the constant racket that clamored through the house the previous two hours.

"Do men always kiss and tell?" Jess questioned, mulling over the remarks she had overheard.

Moriah grinned impishly. "It sounded to me as if they were conducting a liar's contest. He who voiced the biggest lie received another glass of whiskey. But yes, I suppose some men are prone to brag about their exploits and conquests with women."

"They remind me of a pen of roosters, each one trying to outcrow the others," Jessica smirked as she slid onto her side of the bed. "And I would never want to have my name bandied about like that!"

"I should hope not," Moriah chortled. "Better to be the quiet smile on a man's lips than the boast on his tongue."

"Then you are saying the easier it is for a man to get what he wants, the louder he brags?" Jessica frowned, puzzled. "I would have thought it would be the other way around."

"That, my dear dear Jessica—" Moriah declared as

she fluffed her pillow and eased her head upon it, "—is another of the hopeless inconsistences of men. They seem to cherish what is difficult to acquire and boast about what is easily obtained as it pertains to women. When a lady gives in without a fight she not only loses her virtues but her respect and her reputation as well. And men are by far the worst gossips, no matter what you have heard to the contrary. They nurture and prune 'the grapevine' and embellish tales to bolster their pride."

Jessica expelled a heavy sigh and closed her eyes. "I think perhaps that adage about a woman being 'woe to man' is all wrong. Woman, it seems, was put on earth not to bring woe to man, but rather to say *whoa* to man. They are like runaway stallions that need a woman's firm grasp on their reins."

Moriah pried one eye open to glance at Jessica's shadowed features. "I couldn't have put it better myself, Jess. You are catching on quickly."

"Only because you are here," Jessica clarified with an affectionate smile that enhanced her bewitching features. "Before, Dev and Rett talked in circles. But now I'm finally getting some straight answers. My brothers kept putting me off and insisting we would discuss the 'sensitive' topic another day. And when they finally did broach the subject—"

"Cut their own throats, did they?" Moriah queried with a snicker.

"Beheaded themselves was nearer the mark," Jessica giggled.

"Good night, Jessica."

There was a noticeable pause.

"I really like you, Moriah. Devlin was right. You truly are something special."

With a contented smile, Moriah drifted off to sleep.

For the first time in a decade she had a place to call home and a friend to call her own.

With the soot Ruby had insisted on smearing on their faces, the Thatchers crept up the trellis to the balcony. They had been forced to hide in the shrubs for hours, waiting for the noise to die down and the guests—those who could still walk—to make their journey back to town from Granger Ranch.

Once they reached the balcony, Ruby tiptoed to each door to squint into the darkened rooms. Locating Moriah proved to be more difficult than she anticipated, but she was determined of purpose. Her life was in jeopardy and she wasn't leaving without Moriah.

Utilizing the moonlight to scan the quiet chambers, Ruby surveyed the master bedroom that was overflowing with flowers and decorated with white satin streamers. The bridal suite, she presumed. She paused beside another door to view the feminine decor and canopy bed. Jessica Granger's room, she decided before moving silently along the terrace.

"We'll never find her without wakin' everybody up," Vance whispered.

"Hush up," Ruby hissed over her shoulder. "I know exactly what I'm doing . . ." Her voice trailed off as she peered into the next glass door to examine the modestly furnished room. "This has to be it. This looks like a guest room."

Ruby fished into her pocket to retrieve the chloroform she had swiped from the physician's office that afternoon. "If you follow my instructions, this will be a simple matter," she assured her skeptical husband. "When Moriah is unconscious, all we have to do is pick her up and tote her to the river. The curse will be lifted and we can get on with our lives."

In grim resignation, Vance took the cloth that Ruby had saturated with anesthetic and eased open the door. When the hinges creaked, Vance reversed direction. Muttering under her breath, Ruby gouged him in the belly and gestured toward the bed. Like two shadows hovering in the night, the Thatchers inched across the room, squinting at the bed that was enveloped in darkness. The drapes on the window just behind the bed had been drawn, making it difficult to identify the sleeping form beneath the heap of quilts. A pillow covered Moriah's head, concealing her features.

With a nod, Ruby indicated that Vance was to snatch away the pillow and hurriedly cover Moriah's face with the saturated cloth before she awakened to find herself under assault. Vance did as he was ordered. He swiftly covered Moriah's face with the oversize cloth and waited for the chloroform to take effect.

Only it wasn't Moriah who lay sleeping in the guest room, of course. It was the besotted Devlin Granger who'd had a tad too much to drink. Ruby's miscalculations had landed them in the wrong room. By the time they realized their mistake it was way too late!

The instant Devlin felt the cloth draped over his face, he sucked in a startled breath. The pungent odor jolted his senses. Drunk though he was, he clawed at the cloth, realizing that someone kept it clamped over his nose. With a roar, he swung a heavy arm, catching Vance on the head. Vance stumbled, knocking Ruby flat on her back. Her startled yelp echoed around the room, bringing Devlin fully awake and aware of imminent danger.

Like a rousing lion, he vaulted off the bed, yanking the sheet around his hips. Although his reflexes weren't as keen as usual due to his bout with the bottle, he was still a challenging opponent, who far exceeded Vance's clumsy capabilities.

The sight of the shadowed forms floundering on the floor like two overturned beetles caused a furious growl to erupt from Devlin's lips. With jaw clenched and body taut, he reached down to yank up the closest body to him. Ruby let out a howl that could have raised the dead when she found herself dangling in midair with a fist of steel knotted in the collar of her jacket.

The yelps and growls that clamored through the guest room brought Moriah straight out of bed. Instinctively, she bounded to her feet, certain Devlin was in some sort of trouble. Her body tense, she started toward the door.

"You can't go in there!" Jessica gasped, clutching at the hem of Moriah's nightgown. "It's after midnight and you'll be jinxed if you see your groom!"

"I have every intention of finding out if I still have a groom," Moriah countered, worming free. She didn't waste time explaining to Jess that this was one of those situations, like so many in her unconventional relationship with Devlin, when tradition and propriety had to be put aside. She and Devlin had been coming to each other's rescue for so long that it was second nature when one heard a shout of alarm.

Before Jessica could launch another protest, Moriah shot across the room and darted down the hall.

* * *

A pained grunt erupted from Devlin's lips when Vance rolled to his feet and charged like an angered bull. Devlin dropped the squawking bundle the instant before he was slammed back against the bed with Vance atop him. A doubled fist plowed into Devlin's jaw, causing him to erupt in a furious snarl.

The fight was on! Vance was doubled fists and desperation. While Vance tried to hold Devlin down, which took considerable doing, big and strong as he was, Ruby snatched up the chloroform cloth and tried to cuff it around his nose.

Again the offensive smell caused Devlin to jerk away, and he took both Ruby and Vance with him to the floor. All three bodies landed with a thud and Ruby squealed like a stuck pig when she wound up on the bottom of the pile. She had hoped to subdue the growling giant with chloroform and make good their escape since they had attempted to kidnap the wrong person. But subduing Devlin Granger was no small task. He refused to hold still!

Rising to the challenge, Vance slammed his fist into Devlin's eye, but all he succeeded in doing was infuriating his opponent. With another snarl, Devlin retaliated with a beefy fist that sent Vance's head snapping backward. Tangled appendages and squished bodies strained against one another as Devlin struggled to gain the advantageous position. While Devlin landed another staggering blow to Vance's jaw, Ruby vaulted to her feet and scuttled toward the terrace door.

It was at that moment that Moriah, garbed in her nightgown, entered the room. In the batting of an eyelash, she streaked across the room and, with a flying leap, she hooked her arms around the cloaked intruder while Devlin pounded Vance into the floor.

Another squawk flew from Ruby's lips when Moriah shoved her facedown on the carpet. Repeatedly, Moriah lifted the assailant's head and slammed it against the floor.

While Devlin and Moriah engaged in battle, Barrett stumbled into the room, drunk as a man could get. From beneath droopy eyelids, he fumbled to light the lantern.

Seconds later, Jessica burst inside, screeching for her brother to douse the lantern before Devlin and Moriah saw each other on their wedding day and put a curse on themselves.

It was mayhem. Devlin and Moriah were battling their unidentified enemies, Jessica was ranting about breaking tradition, and Barrett was weaving about on hollow legs that sloshed with too much whiskey. Before Jessica could douse the lantern herself, Devlin peered down at the unfamiliar face that was bruised and swollen from punishing blows.

"Who in the hell are these people?" Devlin growled in question.

Moriah rose from her straddled position to shove Ruby to her back. A shocked gasp burst from her lips when she recognized the face under the smeared soot.

"What are *you* doing here?" Moriah croaked in astonishment.

"You and your bright ideas," Vance muttered out the side of his mouth that wasn't puffed up to twice its normal size. "You cursed me for bunglin' my attempts. But you aren't so damned smart, either! I told you we should have packed up and left town!"

Devlin still didn't know what the devil was going on. When he tried to glance at Moriah, hoping she could shed some light on his confusion, Jessica leaped in front of him like a mountain goat, blocking his view.

"Don't you dare look at her. It's bad luck," Jessica insisted.

Moriah did something she had always wanted to do and had never had the chance for fear of Vance thrashing her. She doubled her fist and delivered a blow to Ruby's smudged cheek. Moriah felt ever so much better, having retaliated for the years of anguish and frustration Ruby had put her through.

When Ruby wailed like a banshee and sputtered in vile curses, Moriah grabbed the chloroform cloth and mashed it into her stepmother's outraged face. "Devlin, I have the displeasure of introducing you to my stepparents—Ruby and Vance Thatcher. I don't have the slightest idea what they are doing here, but it looks as if they came to dispose of me and wound up assaulting you instead."

Furiously, he clenched his fist, reared back, and slammed his knuckles into Vance's jaw. The blow packed enough of a wallop to fell a grizzly bear. With a dull groan, Vance collapsed to the floor like a limp mop.

"Jess, hand me the chloroform cloth," Devlin demanded.

"I will if you promise not to look at your bride," she bargained.

"Good God, we've got a crisis here. Enough is enough!" Devlin exploded.

"I still want your promise," Jess insisted, tilting a stubborn chin.

"All right, damnit, just get the rag or I'll get up and get it myself." He glowered at his persnickety sister. "The second face I smother in chloroform is going to be yours!" Devlin snapped his head around to locate his brother. "Barrett, fetch me some rope."

Barrett fetched nothing. He had barely managed to

stumble down the hall and light the lantern before he wilted on the end of the bed and succumbed to the swirling darkness.

When Jessica handed Devlin the saturated cloth, he dropped it over Vance's battered features. "You get the rope, Jess. Your brother is no help at all."

"Are you going to look at Moriah while I'm gone and invite a jinx?" she wanted to know, still shielding Moriah from Devlin's view.

Devlin emitted another venomous growl. "If you would like to live to see your sixteenth birthday, get that rope, MOVE IT!"

Rarely had Devlin employed such a thundering voice or displayed such a murderous frown. Jessica suddenly realized just how threatening Devlin could be when he was furious. High-spirited though Jessica was, she found herself instinctively cowering from the snarling lion.

When Jessica dashed out the door to tend her errand, Moriah rose to her feet and allowed her betraying eyes to wander over the sheet that barely concealed Devlin's powerful physique. She didn't care if she broke tradition. Her all-consuming gaze flooded over Devlin, making it more than obvious that she liked what she saw, that she loved him more than life itself. Since the Thatchers were drugged on their own chloroform and Barrett had collapsed in a drunken heap, Moriah sashayed across the room and sank down in front of Devlin.

"If you won't tell Jess, I promise not to, either," she murmured as her hands coasted over the whipcord muscles of his arms to draw lazy circles on his rock-hard chest. It seemed like months since she had been allowed to touch this dynamic man!

All the frustration drained from Devlin's body as he crushed Moriah to his chest and devoured her lips.

"I do feel sorry for you," he whispered and then dropped another kiss to her sweet mouth. "I can't imagine life with these two blundering idiots. It's a wonder you escaped with your sanity."

"Winning your love made it all worthwhile," Moriah assured him as she nibbled at his puffy lip. "And tomorrow night, I intend to prove how happy you make me."

Before Moriah could offer him another tantalizing kiss to sustain him until their wedding night, the clatter of footsteps heralded Jessica's arrival. Devlin and Moriah retreated and faced the opposite corners of the room, refusing to glance in each other's direction. But Jessica didn't detect the conspiratorial smiles that played on their lips.

Once Moriah and Devlin had tied the Thatchers in intricate knots, Jessica was sent to rouse the vaqueros who were appointed to haul the intruders to the sheriff's office. Jessica did as she was told, but not before she escorted Moriah back to the bedroom where she was to spend the night. Grumbling at Jessica's strict adherence to custom, Devlin ambled to Barrett's room to catch a few hours' sleep while his brother dangled on the edge of the bed, oblivious to the world.

One more day, Devlin consoled himself. And when the ceremony was over, no one was keeping him from Moriah's bed. In a way, he was thankful the Thatchers had blundered into the wrong room. It saved him the trouble of tracking them down. At least they hadn't managed to abduct Moriah, he thought in relief. It always scared another ten years off his life when Moriah courted catastrophe. Now, maybe he and Moriah could look forward to a normal life. After all, Devlin couldn't think of a single solitary thing that could possibly go wrong that hadn't already.

Chapter 30

Again the Granger's home was flooded with guests. Well-wishers had come to view the wedding ceremony and stayed to indulge in the drinks and feast that had been prepared for them. Laughter rang through the air and musicians provided accompaniment for the well-fed guests who danced on the lawn.

By nine o'clock that evening Devlin had had enough of socializing. He still had not been allowed one moment of privacy with Moriah.

Nursing a bruised jaw and a slight hangover, Devlin had ridden into town that morning to learn what he could about the Thatchers' surprise attack the previous night. After pressing charges against the Thatchers and having them sign their shop and home over to Moriah, Devlin had hurried back to the ranch to bathe and change for the wedding.

Barrett had been no help whatsoever. He had imbibed so much whiskey that he couldn't drag himself off the bed until afternoon, and even then he swore some prankster had implanted a bass drum in his head to torment him.

After what had been a long, hectic day, Devlin kindly thanked his guests for coming and bluntly declared it was time for them to leave. He didn't give a whit that he received a few snickers from his friends or that Jessica scolded him for his rudeness. His sister could refer to him as a lusty rake until she was blue in the face. Devlin didn't care, so long as he got Moriah all to himself.

Announcing that he didn't want to see his brother or sister or anyone else except Moriah until the following morning—if even then—Devlin scooped up his bride in his arms and carried her upstairs and across the threshold of his bedroom.

"I thought Devlin was rude in shooing our guests away," Jessica muttered to Barrett who had plunked limply into a chair and slapped a cold cloth over his throbbing head. "Every last one of them knew why Dev was so eager for them to leave. You would have thought he could have restrained his lust for a few more hours!"

Barrett raised one corner of the soggy cloth to peer at his sister with one bloodshot eye. "Kindly be quiet. You're giving me a worse headache than I already have. And if you use that word again, I swear I'll strangle you, hangover and all!" Barrett groaned when he accidentally raised his voice to a pitch that sent a stabbing pain plowing through his skull.

Clamping her mouth shut, Jessica ambled onto the porch to think about the men who had fluttered around her during the course of the afternoon. All the while she was being courted by one suitor after another, she kept recalling Moriah's words about searching for endearing qualities in men. Although there were a half dozen men who had piqued her feminine curiosity, she couldn't name one who stirred her physically, intellectually, and emotionally.

This was going to be an exhaustive search for her

Prince Charming, she thought dispiritedly. Her gaze lifted to the faint light in the master bedroom and watched it vanish while she was staring in its direction. A wry smile pursed her lips, wondering when Moriah would get around to informing her about the details of wedding nights. Having an inquiring mind, Jessica was anxious to know exactly what went on between a man and a woman. She wondered if she would ever fall as hopelessly in love as Moriah and Devlin seemed to be.

My time will come, Jessica assured herself before she strode back inside to badger Barrett in his pathetic state of duress. But it would probably take her a while to find the right man, Jessica cautioned herself. There weren't too many men like her brothers running loose. They both possessed numerous wonderful qualities that endeared them to women. But somewhere out there in that big wide world, Jessica knew, her knight in shining armor awaited her.

"Alone at last!" Devlin sighed in relief.

"It's been a long forty-eight hours, trying to keep my hands off you," Moriah agreed as Devlin set her to her feet.

Moriah pushed the black velvet jacket from Devlin's shoulders and loosed the buttons of his shirt to rake her fingers over the dark matting of hair on his chest. Devlin's soft moan encouraged her to continue her bold caresses. She peeled away the garments that hampered her from admiring this magnificent man who had stolen her heart and inflamed her soul.

When Moriah plied him with fiery kisses and adventurous caresses, Devlin could barely remember his name. A groan of unholy torment burst free when her petal-soft lips drifted over each male nipple and whispered over his belly. Wildfire sizzled through his blood, and Devlin didn't recall if they were lying on his feather bed or a pile of rocks. His body was ablaze with hungry passion—that same mindless desire that consumed him each time he took Moriah in his arms and set sail across the star-spangled sky. Loving her had become as natural to him as breathing. Wanting her had become as essential as his need for nourishment. She made all his tomorrows glow with promise.

"I love you," Moriah whispered as Devlin braced himself above her. Her slender arms trailed up his chest to cup his face. "Come, let me show you how much. And those other women in your life who Jessica ranted about . . . ?" Moriah grinned mischievously when Devlin tensed warily. "They're probably wishing they were me tonight."

"All of them put together don't mean half as much to me as you do," he assured her, his voice thick with desire and genuine emotion. "You're all I want and need, Riah. Believe it. It's true."

And to prove that he meant what he said, he came to her, taking tender possession. He conveyed his love in a language that required no words. He absorbed her strength and filled her world with such blissful pleasure that Moriah swore she couldn't survive it. One soul-shattering sensation after another riveted her. Living fire avalanched through her blood, burning her from inside out. And just when she thought she would turn into smoldering ashes, Devlin's hoarsely whispered words of everlasting love lifted her to the pinnacle of ecstasy and kept her there, leaving her dangling in time and space.

For what must have been forever, Moriah clung to

Devlin, swamped and buffeted by such overwhelming sensations that she feared she would lose all touch with sanity. When his muscled body strained against hers, seeking ultimate depths of intimacy, she held on for dear life . . .

Much later, the lingering rapture ebbed and Moriah lay content and satisfied in his arms.

"This is how it is going to be . . . always," Devlin vowed as he cuddled her supple body to his. "I want to give you children who will grow up, basking in the warmth of my love for you. I want to give you everything you have been deprived of. And in return, all I ask is your love." He pressed an adoring kiss to her heart-shaped lips. "For me, that will be more than enough."

When Devlin drifted off to sleep, Moriah smiled dreamily to herself. The past two weeks had been hectic and exhausting ones for Devlin. He had not fully recovered from his injury and she hadn't allowed him to rest as much as she should have each time they had paused for the night during their trek to Arizona. The incident with the Thatchers hadn't helped much, either. That, compounded with the arrangements for the wedding and reception, had sapped most of Devlin's strength. And although she yearned to wake him and demonstrate her love that seemed to overflow with each thought of this captivating man, she . . .

A fleeting shadow snaked across Moriah's line of vision. She glanced sideways to see an unidentified form disappear from sight. Moriah knew her step-parents were behind bars, but there was definitely someone prowling around the terrace! Moriah decided to investigate.

Cautiously, she eased from bed, wondering if Jessica was taking a midnight stroll on the balcony or if they had another unwelcome visitor who meant to do them harm. Hurriedly, she grabbed her robe and crept toward the terrace door.

When Moriah stepped outside, she caught sight of the silhouette that lingered on the balcony. Sensing her presence, Makado pivoted. His probing gaze wandered over her barely concealed figure, envying the intimacy she had known with Devlin.

"Makado?" Moriah blinked in bewilderment. "What are you doing here?"

He opened the heavy pouch that hung on his hip, fished into it, and then opened his palm. "I brought this for you," he whispered, watching the stones glisten in the moonlight. "Apache gold."

His gaze lifted to roam possessively over Moriah's captivating figure and glorious mane of blond hair. "You can have all of it, as well as all we can carry away from Eagle Canyon . . . if you will come away with me. The gold will buy you all that will make you happy and we will live in the mountains together . . . away from the white-eyes who have caused you so much trouble."

Moriah walked toward him. Her fingertips skimmed the nuggets Makado held out to her. "All the gold in the Old Man's tears cannot buy my love, Makado," she murmured gently. Her eyes darted back to the darkened room. "My heart belongs to him and it always will."

Makado heaved a frustrated sigh. He had been so certain he could lure this stunning beauty away with the treasure that white men lusted after. Apparently not. It seemed White Shadow's hold on Moriah was stronger than mere greed and the acquisition of wealth.

The Apache warrior jerked to attention when a tall, broad silhouette appeared beside the door. When

Devlin emerged from the concealing shadows, wearing a smile instead of an angry frown, Makado shrugged awkwardly.

"I wanted her, just as Chanos did," he admitted unrepentantly. "You cannot blame me for that, White Shadow."

There had been a time when Devlin had feared another man would take Moriah away from him. But no longer. Moriah had thoroughly convinced him that her love for him was as fierce and lasting as his love for her.

In truth, he pitied Makado. There weren't all that many Moriahs in this world and the Apache warrior would probably never truly get over wanting her. That was the way Makado was. He held grudges forever and harbored emotions that took the longest time to fade into dimly remembered memories.

"No, my friend, I cannot blame you," Devlin calmly agreed. He gestured his raven head toward the nuggets of gold that were clasped in the Apache's hand. "Leave your gift for Moriah so she will remember her adventures in the valley where only a few privileged white-eyes are allowed to tread. In return, I will bring wagonloads of clothes, food, and supplies to the Dragoon Mountains."

A sympathetic smile pursed Devlin's lips as his loving gaze strayed to the sylphlike beauty whose golden head was surrounded by an aureole of moonlight. "I cannot give you what you want most, Makado, but I can give you what you need, what your people need to endure the coming winter."

"I would prefer not to like you quite so much, White Shadow," Makado grunted, half seriously, half in jest. His dark eyes shifted to Moriah's enchanting features and he lifted his hand to smooth the tangled golden tresses over her shoulder. "Come back with him to the mountains one day, Sunflower." He dropped a gentle kiss to her lips to prove to her that he could be as tender as the man she had married. "If I cannot have your heart, I would at least like to see you now and again."

Moriah nodded and smiled warmly at the Apache brave who had changed dramatically since her first enconter with him. He, like she, had become less cynical and more trusting. Devlin, on the other hand, was as he had always been—as constant as the mountains. Moriah loved that about Devlin and she longed for stability in her life. She needed to know he would be there each time she reached out to him. What they shared was more than physical pleasure. It was a mental and emotional bond as well, one that time and their many trials and tribulations had never managed to sever.

Makado broke into a wry smile. "If he does not treat you well, you know where to find me," he reminded her. "And I will let you have all the gold and me as well."

As Makado draped a leg over the railing and vanished from sight, Devlin swaggered over to hook his arm around Moriah, drawing her suggestively against him.

"I intend to meet Makado's challenge," he murmured, his lips whispering over hers. "And I think you had it all wrong, Sunflower," he added, calling her by the nickname Makado had given her. "It seems there are many *men* hereabout who are wishing they were *me* tonight."

Moriah tilted her head to slide him a provocative smile. "I need only one lover . . . if he thinks he is man enough to keep me satisfied," she teased him saucily. "And if he can't, I know where to locate one who will try to replace him."

One thick brow climbed to a lofty angle. "Are you challenging me, too, minx?"

"It certainly sounds like it, doesn't it?" Moriah replied, raising the pouch of gold that Makado had given her. "And if things turn out as well as I anticipate, this sack of gold is yours and I'll have everything I'll ever need to keep me satisfied."

Devlin's chuckle wafted through the night air as he followed Moriah inside. He was mesmerized by the graceful sway of her hips and aroused by her alluring invitation. Tired as he was, he would never be too tired to take Moriah in his arms and share the splendor that, except for a few lucky ones, didn't always come around even once in a lifetime.

As it turned out, Devlin was awarded the pouch of gold and Moriah acquired all she desired in life—a most incredible man to match the rugged mountains into which she had fled. They had created the legends of White Shadow and the Angel of the Wind who stood constant vigil over the Valley of the Eagle, protecting its riches of Apache gold. But more important, Moriah and Devlin had discovered that special brand of love so fierce and wild that it would endure beyond eternity.